KU-635-901

For C. F.

In loving memory.
You were so sure that you didn't even wait
for the finale.

'A deliberate, seemingly unprovoked episode of homicidal or incredibly destructive behaviour (towards others), where the act of violence in question endangers, injures or even kills a number of people.'

The definition of 'amok' according to the World Health Organization (WHO)

'Fate gives us the hand, and we play the cards.'

Arthur Schopenhauer

SEBASTIAN FITZEK

AMOK

translated from the German by
Jamie Lee Searle

An Aries Book

First published in Germany as *Amokspiel* in 2007 by Droemer Knaur

First published in the UK in 2021 by Head of Zeus Ltd
This paperback edition first published in the UK in 2022 by Head of Zeus Ltd
part of Bloomsbury Publishing Plc

Amokspiel copyright © 2007 Verlagsgruppe Droemer Knaur
GmbH & Co. KG, Munich, Germany

Translation © 2021 Jamie Lee Searle

The moral right of Sebastian Fitzek to be identified as the author
and Jamie Lee Searle as the translator of this work has been asserted in
accordance with the Copyright, Designs and Patents Act of 1988.

All rights reserved. No part of this publication may be
reproduced, stored in a retrieval system, or transmitted in any form
or by any means, electronic, mechanical, photocopying, recording,
or otherwise, without the prior permission of both the copyright
owner and the above publisher of this book.

This is a work of fiction. All characters, organizations,
and events portrayed in this novel are either products of
the author's imagination or are used fictitiously.

9 7 5 3 1 2 4 6 8

A catalogue record for this book is available from
the British Library.

ISBN (PB): 9781838934576
ISBN (E): 9781838934583

Typeset by Divaddict Publishing Solutions Ltd

Printed and bound in Great Britain by
CPI Group (UK) Ltd, Croydon CR0 4YY

Head of Zeus Ltd
5–8 Hardwick Street
London EC1R 4RG

WWW.HEADOFZEUS.COM

Prologue

The phone call that would destroy his life forever came at exactly 6:47 p.m. During the investigations that followed, everyone was amazed that he had retained the exact time in his memory. The police, his incompetent lawyer and the two men from the German Federal Intelligence Service who had initially introduced themselves as journalists and then planted the cocaine in the boot of his car: all of them wondered why he was able to remember the time so precisely. It was such a minor detail compared to everything that followed. The answer was very simple. Just after picking up the phone, he had glanced at the rhythmically blinking digital clock on his answerphone. It was something he always did when he wanted to concentrate. His eyes searched for something to fixate on. A speck of dirt on the windowpane, a crease on the tablecloth, or the needle of a clock hand. An anchor to hold on to. As if this could moor his mind safely like a ship in a harbour, bringing it into a restful state which would enable him to think more clearly. Long before any of this had happened, whenever his patients had confronted him with complicated psychological problems, his eyes had always rested upon an incidental pattern in the grain of the heavy wooden door of his private practice. Depending on how the light was falling through the stained-glass windows into the tranquil consultation room, it had reminded him either of a constellation, a child's face, or an indecent nude drawing.

When he picked up the telephone receiver at exactly 6:47 and 52 seconds, the very last thing on his mind was a potential catastrophe. As a result, it took him a few seconds to absorb the information. His gaze wandered restlessly across the lower floor of his two-storey apartment in Berlin's Gendarmenmarkt. Everything was perfect. Luisa, his Romanian housekeeper, had done a great job. Just last week he had been thinking that his second apartment in Berlin's new centre was merely a waste of money he had been conned into by a cunning investment banker. But now he was happy that the estate agents hadn't yet managed to rent this luxury piece of real estate for him. It meant he could surprise Leoni here today with a four-course dinner, which they would enjoy on the roof terrace with a view over the illuminated concert hall. And then he would ask her the question which, so far at least, she had forbidden him from asking.

'Hello?'

He walked with the telephone receiver against his ear into the spacious kitchen, which had been delivered and installed only yesterday. As had almost all the furniture and home furnishings. His main residence was in the Berlin suburbs, a small villa with a lake view near the Glienicke Bridge to Potsdam. The wealth which enabled him to lead this lifestyle was based on a spectacularly successful therapy case which, remarkably, had come along even before he began his studies. With his empathetic words, he had prevented a despairing schoolmate from committing suicide after she failed the school-leaving exams. Her father, a businessman, had expressed his gratitude with a small equity stake in his then almost-worthless software firm. Just a few months later, the stock had shot up to dizzying heights overnight.

'Hello?' he said again. He was just about to get the champagne from the fridge, but now he stopped and tried to concentrate on the words being spoken at the other end of the line. His efforts were in vain, however. The background noise was so loud that he could only make out broken syllables.

'Sweetheart, is that you?'

'... I'm... sor...'

'What are you saying? Where are you?'

He walked swiftly back over to the telephone's docking station, which was in the living room on a small table, directly in front of the large panoramic window looking out over the theatre.

'Can you hear me better now?'

It would make no difference, of course. His telephone had equally good reception all over the house. He could even get into the lift with it, travel down the seven floors to street level and order a coffee from the hotel lobby of the Hilton opposite without any problems whatsoever with the reception. The difficulty he was having right now was most certainly due to Leoni's phone, not his.

'... today... never again...'

The other words were drowned out by sibilant, staccato sounds, similar to those of an old analogue modem connecting to the internet. Then they stopped so abruptly that, for a moment, he thought the line had gone dead. He lowered the receiver from his ear and looked at the green, shimmering display.

Active!

He yanked it back up to his ear. Just in time to hear one single, clear word before the cacophony of wind and static interference set in again. One word from which he could be unequivocally sure that it really was Leoni who was trying to speak with him. That she was trying to tell him something was wrong. And that they were not tears of joy she was crying as she forced out the four letters which would haunt him every single day for the next eight months: 'Dead'.

Dead? He tried to make sense of the whole thing by asking her whether she was trying to tell him that the mobile connection was about to die. At the same time, a feeling spread out within him that he otherwise knew only from when he drove into unfamiliar neighbourhoods. The feeling that made him instinctively lock the driver's door at a traffic light when a pedestrian was approaching his Saab.

Surely not the baby?

It was only a month ago that he had found the empty packaging of the pregnancy test kit in the bin. She hadn't said anything to him. Just like usual. Leoni Gregor was, as he lovingly described her to others, 'quiet' and 'secretive'. Less well-meaning people would have called her 'cagey' or even just 'weird'.

From the outside looking in, he and Leoni looked like one of the couples in those pictures which were placed in photo frames as an incentive for the customer to buy. Caption: 'Newlywed Happiness.' She, the gentle beauty with dark curly locks and a complexion the shade of cane sugar, alongside the youthful man in his mid-thirties with the slightly-too-formal haircut, whose playful eyes betrayed a spark of disbelief at having such an beautiful woman by his side. Aesthetically speaking, they were in perfect harmony. But in terms of character, they were worlds apart.

While he had practically revealed his entire life story on their very first date, Leoni had barely divulged even the most basic of details. Only that she hadn't been living in Berlin long, that she had grown up in South Africa, and that her family had been killed in a chemical factory fire there. Aside from that, to him her past seemed like a tattered diary with loose pages. Some of them had been hastily filled with scribbled writing, but here and there large sections were missing. And whenever he tried to talk about it – about the missing photos from her childhood, the absence of a best friend or the barely visible scar on her left cheekbone – Leoni either immediately changed the subject or just gently shook her head. Even though this set off alarm bells in his head, he knew that none of this secretiveness would prevent him from making Leoni his wife.

'What are you trying to tell me, sweetheart?' He switched the receiver to his other ear. 'Leoni, I can't hear you properly. What are you sorry about? What will be "never again"?'

And who or what is dead?

This was the question he didn't dare to ask, even though he wasn't sure whether she could hear him at the other end of the line anyway. He made a decision.

'Listen, sweetheart. The line is so bad – if you're able to hear me – then please hang up. I'll call you back right away. Maybe it will be…'

'No, don't! DON'T!'

All at once, the connection was crystal clear.

'Oh, finally...' he laughed in relief for a moment, then stopped abruptly. 'You sound strange. Are you crying?'

'Yes. I've been crying, but that's not important. Just listen to me now. Please.'

'Has something happened?'

'Yes. But you can't believe them!'

'What?'

'Don't believe what they tell you. Okay? No matter what it is. You have to...'

Once again, the rest of her sentence was swallowed by crackling interference. A second later, he gave a start and whipped round to stare at the front door.

'Leoni? Is that you?'

He was speaking both into the receiver and towards the door, where there had just been a loud and firm knock. Now he was silently hoping that his girlfriend would be standing there on the other side of it, and that the bad reception had been due to her being in the elevator. That was sure to be it. That would make sense. '*I'm sorry*, sweetheart, I'm late. Rush hour, I'm *never* taking that route *again*. I'm *dead* tired.'

But what am I not supposed to believe? Why is she crying? And why would she be knocking the door?

Earlier today, he had sent a spare key by courier to the tax office where she was working as a secretarial temp. Together with a note telling her to open today's *Frankfurter Allgemeine* to page thirty-two. On it was an advert which he had commissioned with a sketch showing the route to his apartment.

But even if she had forgotten the key, how could she – or

anyone for that matter – have gotten upstairs without the porter first notifying him from the reception?

He opened the door, and his question remained unanswered. Instead, it was joined by another, for the man standing before him was a complete stranger. A man who, judging by his physical appearance, didn't seem to be a frequenter of the gym. His belly bloated his white cotton shirt out so far that it was impossible to tell whether he was wearing a belt, or whether his threadbare flannel trousers were held up solely by rolls of fat.

'Please excuse the disturbance,' said the man, touching the thumb and middle finger of his left hand to both temples self-consciously, as if he were about to suffer a migraine attack.

Afterwards, he was no longer able to remember whether the stranger had introduced himself or shown a badge. But just these opening words alone sounded so routine that he immediately understood: This man was forcing his way into his world for professional reasons, as a policeman. And that wasn't good. It wasn't good at all.

'I'm very sorry, but…'

Oh, God. My mother? My brother? Please don't let it be my nephew. He went through all the possible victims in his mind.

'Are you acquainted with a Leoni Gregor?'

The detective rubbed his stubby fingers through his thick, bushy eyebrows, which stood out in stark contrast to his almost-bald head.

'Yes.'

He was too confused to take notice of the fear growing inside him. What did all this have to do with his girlfriend?

He looked at the telephone, the display of which assured him that the connection was still live. For some reason, it felt as though the receiver had become heavier over the last few seconds.

'I came as quickly as possible, so that you didn't have to find out on the evening news.'

'Find out what?'

'Your partner... well, she had a serious car accident an hour ago.'

'Excuse me?' An intense sensation of relief flooded through his body, and only now did he realise how afraid he had been. Much like someone must feel if they received a call from the doctor and were told that there had been a mistake. Everything was fine. The lab had mixed up the HIV test tubes.

'Is this supposed to be a joke?' he asked, half laughing. The policeman looked at him uncomprehendingly.

He lifted the receiver to his ear. 'Sweetheart, there's someone here who wants to speak to you,' he said. But before he could hand the receiver over to the policeman, he stopped again. Something wasn't right. Something was different.

'Sweetheart?'

No answer. The static hiss was suddenly just as loud as it had been at the beginning of the telephone conversation.

'Hello? Honey?' He turned around, put the index finger of his free hand in his left ear and paced quickly across his living room towards the window.

'The reception's better here,' he said to the policeman, who had hesitantly followed him into the apartment.

But this proved to be a mistake again. It was quite the opposite. Now he couldn't hear a thing. No breathing. No meaningless syllables. No scraps of sentences. Not even crackling any more. Nothing.

And for the first time, he realised that silence can inflict pain in a way that even the loudest of noises cannot.

'I'm very, very sorry.' The policeman's hand lay heavy on his shoulder. In the reflection of the panoramic window, he saw that the man was just a few centimetres away from him. Presumably he had experience of these situations. Of people collapsing when they received this kind of news. And that's why he was standing so close, so that he could catch him. In case he fell. But it wouldn't come to that.

Not today.

Not with him.

'Listen,' he said, turning around. 'I'm expecting Leoni for dinner in ten minutes. I was just talking to her on the phone moments before you knocked on the door. In fact I'm still on the phone to her now and...'

Even as he spoke this last sentence, he was aware of how it must sound. Shock: that would be his own diagnosis if someone were to ask him as an impartial psychologist. But today he wasn't impartial. Today he had been involuntarily cast in the lead role. The look in the inspector's eyes eventually robbed him of his last strength, his ability to speak.

Don't believe what they tell you...

'I regret to inform you that your partner, Leoni Gregor, came off the road in her vehicle an hour ago, on her way to see you. She crashed into a traffic light and a house wall. We don't know the specific details yet, but it seems that the car immediately caught fire. I'm sorry. There was nothing the doctors could do. She died at the scene.'

★ ★ ★

Later, as the sedative slowly lost its effect, a memory battled its way into his consciousness. Of a former patient who had once left her pram outside the door of a pharmacy. She had just wanted to quickly pick up a tube of superglue for the loose heel of her high-heeled shoes. Because it was cold, she had tucked up her five-month-old baby David tightly before she entered the shop. When she came out again three minutes later, the pram was still in front of the window where she had left it. But it was empty. David had vanished, and was never found again.

During his therapy sessions with the emotionally broken mother, he had often wondered what he would have felt. If it had been him pulling back the blanket in the pram, beneath which everything was so strangely still.

He had always assumed that he would never feel that woman's pain. But from today onwards, he knew better.

PART I

Eight months later
Today

In our play,
We reveal what kind of people we are.

Ovid

1

Salty. The barrel of the gun in her mouth tasted surprisingly salty.

Strange, she thought. Until now, I never would have dreamed of putting my duty weapon in my mouth. Not even as a joke.

After the thing with Sara had happened, she had often thought about breaking into a run during a mission and exposing her cover. On one occasion she had marched over to a frenzied attacker without a bulletproof vest or any protection whatsoever. But never before had she put her revolver between her lips and sucked at it like a baby as she was now, her right index finger trembling on the trigger.

So today was a first. Right here and now, in her filthy open-plan kitchen on Katzbachstrasse, in the Berlin neighbourhood of Kreuzberg. She had spent the entire morning covering the floor with old newspapers, as though she was planning to redecorate. But in truth, it was because she knew only too well the mess a bullet can unleash when it shatters a skull and scatters bone, blood and pieces of brain across a fourteen-square-metre room. Probably they would even send someone she knew to do the forensics. Tom Brauner, perhaps, or Martin Maria

Hellwig, who she had been at police school with years ago. Anyway, it didn't matter who it was. Ira didn't have the energy left to worry about the walls now. Besides, she had run out of newspaper pages, and she didn't have any plastic sheeting. So now she was sitting astride the wobbly wooden stool with her back to the sink. The laminated wall unit and metal sink could be easily sluiced with a hose after the forensic investigation. And there wouldn't be much to investigate anyway. All her colleagues would know why she was putting an end to things. The case was clear-cut. After what had happened to her, no one would seriously contemplate the possibility that this was a crime. This was why she hadn't even bothered to write a note. She didn't know anyone who would have wanted to read it anyway. The only person she still loved knew better than all the rest, and had made that crystal clear last year. Through her silence. Since the tragedy, her youngest daughter hadn't wanted to see her, speak to her, or hear from her. Katharina ignored Ira's phone calls, returned her letters, and would probably cross over to the other side of the road if she saw her mother approaching.

And I can't blame her, thought Ira. Not after what I did.

She opened her eyes and looked around. As the kitchen and living area were open plan, she could see the entire lounge from where she was sitting. If the warm rays of spring sunshine hadn't been falling on the streaky windowpanes in such an unspeakably cheerful manner, she would even have been able to catch a glimpse of the balcony and Viktoriapark beyond it. Hitler, thought Ira Samin suddenly, as her eyes rested on the small bookcase in the lounge area. During her training with the Hamburg police, she had written her thesis about the dictator. 'Psychological manipulation of the masses'.

If that maniac did one thing right, she thought, then it was killing himself in the bunker. He shot himself in the mouth, too. But through fear of doing something wrong and ending up in the Allies' hands as a cripple, he had also bitten into a potassium cyanide capsule moments before the fatal shot.

Maybe I should do the same thing? Ira hesitated. It was not the hesitation of a suicidal individual sending out a cry of help. Quite the opposite. Ira wanted to be absolutely sure she succeeded. And there was an adequate supply of poisonous capsules at hand in the freezer compartment of her fridge, after all. Digoxin, highly concentrated. She had found the stash next to the bath during the most important mission of her life, and had never handed it in to the evidence room. For good reason.

On the other hand, thought Ira – shoving the barrel so far into her mouth that it almost stimulated her choke reflex, then holding it completely centred – how high is the possibility that I'll only shatter my jaw and fire the bullet past the main arteries and through irrelevant parts of my brain?

Small. Very small. But not completely impossible!

Ten days ago, a Hells Angel had been shot in the head at a traffic light in the Tiergarten. The man was due to be released from hospital next month.

But the probability that something like that would repeat itself was...

Bang!

Ira jumped so much at the sudden noise that she scraped

the weapon against her gum, making it bleed. Damn it! She pulled the barrel back out of her mouth.

It was just before half past eight, and she had forgotten the idiotic radio alarm clock that went off loudly at this time every day. Right now, some young woman was crying her eyes out about having lost one of those dumb radio competitions. Ira laid her gun on the kitchen table and trudged lethargically into her darkened bedroom, from where the commotion was forcing its way out to the kitchen:

'… we selected you at random from the phone book, and you would now be in possession of €50,000 if you had answered with the Dosh Ditty, Marina.'

'But I did – I said "I listen to 101 Point 5, now gimme the dough".'

'Too late, though. Unfortunately you said your name first. You need to say the Dosh Ditty as soon as you pick up, so that's why…'

Ira pulled the plug out of the wall in irritation. If she was going to kill herself, then preferably not to the hysterical shrieks of some distraught office temp who had just lost the jackpot.

Ira sat down on her unmade bed and stared at the open wardrobe, which resembled a washing machine with clothes stuffed into it haphazardly. At some point she had decided to stop replacing the broken clothes hangers.

She had never been good at organisation. Not where her own life was concerned. And certainly not when it came to her own death. When she had woken up this morning, on the tiled bathroom floor next to the toilet bowl, she had known that the time had come. That she couldn't keep going any longer. That she didn't want to. And yet it was less about the way she had woken up than the dream which had been haunting her for the past year. The one in which she was always walking up the same stairs. On every step, there was a handwritten note. Except for the last. Why not?

Realising that she had been holding her breath while she was thinking, Ira breathed out heavily. Now that the screeching radio had been silenced, the other sounds in the apartment seemed twice as loud. The gurgling hum of the fridge could be heard even here in the bedroom. For a moment, it sounded as though the ageing device was choking on its own coolant.

If that isn't a sign, then what is?

Ira stood up.

Fine then. Then it'll have to be the tablets after all.

But she didn't want to wash them down with the cheap vodka from the petrol station. The last drink of her life should be something she knocked back for the taste, not for its effect. A Cola Light. Preferably the new lemon-infused one.

Yes. That would be a good last meal. A Cola Light Lemon and an overdose of digoxin for dessert.

She went into the hallway, reached for her door key and glanced at the large wall mirror, on the top left of which the lamination was peeling off the glass.

You look awful, she thought. Decrepit. Like a bedraggled allergy sufferer whose eyes are red and swollen from hay fever.

But what did it matter anyway? She wasn't trying to win some beauty contest. Not today. Not on her final day.

She took her battered black leather jacket down from the hook, the one she used to love wearing with tight-fitting jeans. If someone were to look at her closely, they would be able to see that despite the huge, dark rings under her eyes, she could once have posed for the police pin-up calendar. Back then, in another life. When her fingernails were still filed and her high cheekbones still accentuated with a dust of blusher. Today, she concealed her feet in canvas sneakers and her slim legs in loose pale-green cargo pants. She hadn't been to the hairdresser in months, but her long, black hair wasn't showing one single grey strand, and her even teeth were snow white despite the countless cups of black coffee she imbibed daily. Her career as a criminal psychologist, in which she had acted as negotiator on some of the most dangerous missions of the SEK, Germany's special forces unit, had brought with it only minor externally visible impact. Her one scar was barely visible, ten centimetres beneath her belly button. Caesarean section. She had her daughter Sara to thank for that. Her firstborn.

Maybe it also helped that Ira had never smoked, therefore enabling her to keep her wrinkle-free skin. Or maybe not, because she had fallen victim to another addiction instead. Alcohol.

But I'm done with it now, she thought sarcastically. My sponsor would be proud of me. As of this moment, I wont have another sip, and I'll stand by my word. Because the only thing I'm going to drink from now on will be Cola Light. Maybe even the lemon one, if Hakan has it in stock.

She let the door click into the lock behind her, and breathed in the typical smell of cleaning products, street dust and kitchen aromas that waft through old Berlin apartment buildings. Almost as intense as the mix of dirt, cigarette smoke and lubricating oil that rises from the steps leading down into U-Bahn stations.

I'll miss that, thought Ira. It's not much, but I'll miss the smells.

She wasn't afraid. Not of death. But perhaps of the fact that it might not be over, even afterwards. The fear that the pain might not stop, that the image of her dead daughter would haunt her even after her last heartbeat.

The image of Sara.

Ira ignored her overflowing aluminium letterbox in the hallway and stepped out into the warm spring sunshine with a shiver. She pulled out her purse, removed the last of her change and threw the purse into an open skip at the edge of the street. Along with her ID, her driving licence, credit cards and the registration certificate for her old Alfa. In just a few minutes' time, she would no longer need any of it.

2

'Welcome to your tour of Berlin's most successful radio station: 101 Point 5.'

The petite volunteer tugged nervously at a crease on her denim skirt, blew a blond strand of hair from her forehead and smiled at the group of visitors who were looking up at her expectantly from five steps below. Her shy smile revealed a small gap between her upper incisors.

'I'm Kitty, the lowest member of the food chain here at the station,' she quipped, appropriately for her figure-hugging T-shirt with the caption 'World's Most Successful Failure'. She went on to explain what the radio listeners' club members would experience over the next twenty minutes. '... and as the crowning glory of the tour, you'll meet Markus Timber and the morning team in person in the studio. At twenty-two years of age, Markus isn't just the youngest presenter in the city, but ever since he first went on air with 101 Point 5 a year and a half ago, also the most successful.'

Jan May shifted his weight on his aluminium crutches and leant over to his Aldi shopping bag on the floor, in which he had stowed the folded-up body bags and spare ammunition. As he did so, he studied the enthusiastic faces of the group members with contempt. A childlike woman next to him with brightly painted talon-like fingernails was wearing a cheap department-store suit which was surely one of the best pieces in her wardrobe. Her boyfriend had gotten equally dolled up for the tour and was wearing jeans with ironed creases, accompanied with new trainers. *Chav chic*, thought Jan snidely.

Next to the couple stood a greasy accountant type with a horseshoe-shaped ring of hair and a bloated belly, who for the last five minutes had been talking with a red-haired woman. Her stomach was equally rounded, but most certainly for a different reason. Now the pregnant woman was talking on the phone, a little aside from the group, behind a cardboard cut-out depicting the idiotically grinning star radio presenter in life-size format.

She's about seven months gone, estimated Jan. *Probably even more. Good*, he thought. *Everything's in excellent order. Everything...*

His neck muscles tensed as the electronic door suddenly opened behind him.

'Ah, here comes our latecomer,' said Kitty, greeting the burly delivery man with a smile. He nodded at the volunteer grumpily, as if she was responsible for him being late.

Fuck. Jan debated feverishly how he could have made a mistake. The man in the brown uniform wasn't on the list of winning listener club members. He had either come directly from work or was planning to do the tour before his early shift. Jan ran his tongue nervously across his fake teeth, which distorted both his face and his voice completely. Then he reminded himself of the basic rule they had repeated again and again during their preparations: 'Something unexpected always happens.' Sometimes even in the first few minutes. *Fuck.* It wasn't just the fact that he didn't have any information on the guy, but also that the bearded UPS delivery man with the carelessly gelled-back hair looked like trouble. Either his shirt had shrunk in the wash, or he had grown too big for it by lifting weights in the gym. Jan briefly contemplated calling the whole thing off. But then he dismissed the thought. The preparations had been too intense. *No!* There was no way back now, even if the fifth victim hadn't been factored in.

Jan wiped his hands on the stained sweatshirt with the sewn-in fake beer belly. He had been sweating ever since he'd put on the clothes ten minutes ago in the elevator.

'... and you're Martin Kubichek?' he heard Kitty read his alias from the visitor list. Clearly everyone here was required to introduce themselves before they could start the tour.

'Yes, and you should really check your disabled facilities before you invite people,' he spat as a response, hobbling towards the steps. 'How am I supposed to get up these cursed steps?'

'Oh!' Kitty's gap-toothed smile became even more self-conscious. 'You're right. We didn't know that you, erm...'

Nor do you know that I have two kilos of plastic explosives strapped to my person, he added silently.

The UPS driver gave him a contemptuous look, but stepped aside as Jan limped awkwardly past him. The couple and the office worker acted as though his abusive outburst was excused by his disability.

Wonderful, thought Jan. *Put on a cheap tracksuit*

and some crappy wig, then act like a lunatic – and you immediately get everything you want. Even access to the most successful radio station in Berlin.

The visitors followed him slowly up the narrow steps.

At the front of the group, Kitty headed towards the editing rooms and studios.

'No, my darling. But I promised I'd ask him, didn't I? Yes, I love you very much too…'

Straggling behind, the red-haired pregnant woman hurried to catch up the group, apologising as she put her phone back in her trouser pocket.

'That was Anton,' she explained. 'My son.' She opened her purse and showed the group a well-thumbed photo of the four-year-old toddler. Jan had rarely seen such a happy-looking boy, despite his evident mental illness.

'Too little oxygen. The umbilical cord almost strangled him,' she explained, managing to smile and sigh simultaneously. Without her needing to say a word, everyone knew how afraid the heavily pregnant woman must be of this birth trauma repeating itself. 'Anton's father left us in the delivery room,' she said, her lower lip trembling a little. 'Anyway, now he's missing out on the best thing that ever happened to him.'

'He certainly is,' agreed Kitty, handing the photo back. Her eyes were shining, and she looked as though she had just finished reading some wonderful book.

'My little darling was actually supposed to come with me today, but he had another attack last night.' The mother-to-be shrugged, suggesting that this was a frequent occurrence for Anton. 'I wanted to stay with him of course, but I couldn't. "Mama," he said to me, "you have to go for me and ask Markus Timber what kind of car he drives,"' she said, imitating a child's sweet voice.

Everyone laughed, moved, and even Jan had to make sure not to slip out of character.

'We'll find out for him very soon,' promised Kitty. She brushed away an eyelash from the corner of her eye, then led the group a few metres further on into the large editing room. Jan May was relieved to see that the floor plan corresponded to the one which the dismissed security guard had sketched for him in exchange for a quarter gram and a syringe.

The entire radio station was located on the nineteenth floor of the Berlin Media Center, an ultra-modern glass high-rise in Potsdamer Platz with a breathtaking panoramic view of Berlin. To create the editorial space, all the internal walls had been removed and replaced with cream-toned room dividers and a vast number of monthly rotating rental plants, giving the place a trendy loft atmosphere. The white and grey solid-wood floorboards and the subtle scent of cinnamon blended in with the air conditioning system gave the private channel a respectable ambience. Perhaps that was intended as a distraction from the rather shrill programming, pondered Jan, letting his gaze wander over to the right-hand corner of the floor. It was occupied by the 'Aquarium', the immense glass triangle which contained the two broadcasting studios and the newsroom.

'What are those guys over there doing?' asked the overweight accountant type with the horseshoe haircut as he pointed at a group of three editors near the studios. They were standing around a desk, at which a fourth man was sitting, his lower arm tattooed with a yellow-and-red flame design.

'Are they playing battleships?' he quipped.

So Mr Pen-Pusher clearly fancies himself as the group clown, noted Jan. Kitty smiled politely.

'Those are the show's writers. Our chief editor is writing a segment that has to be ready in just a few minutes' time.'

'*That* man there is the chief editor?' asked the couple, almost in chorus. As she spoke, the young woman unashamedly pointed her long fingernail at the man, who Jan knew had been nicknamed 'Diesel' by his colleagues on account of his pyromaniac tendencies.

'Yes. Don't be fooled by his appearance. He may seem somewhat eccentric,' said Kitty, 'but he's known as one of the most genius brains in the industry and has been working in radio since he was sixteen years old.'

'Aha.' A brief, disbelieving murmur went through the group, then they set off on into motion again.

I've never worked in the radio industry, but on my very first day I'm about to attract the same audience numbers as a World Cup final TV broadcast, thought Jan, falling behind the group a little to release the safety catch of his gun.

3

The dog's severed head lay in a dark red, almost black, pool of blood, about half a metre away from the refrigerator counter. Ira didn't have time to look around the small convenience store for the other remains of the dead pit bull. The two men pointing their guns at each other and screaming in an incomprehensible language were taking up her full attention. For a moment, she wished she had taken the warning of the yob at the door seriously.

'Hey, sweetheart, are you insane?' the guy had called to her as she pushed her way past him into the shop. 'They'll blow your brains out!'

'Fine by me' had been her only response as she left the teenager standing there in confusion. Two seconds later, she found herself in the middle of a set piece: a conflict that may as well have come straight from the mobile mission commando textbook which had been pressed into her hand on the first day of training. The bible of crime scene negotiation psychology. Two rival immigrants were moments away from shooting each other's heads off. The man with the hate-contorted face and gun in his hand was familiar to her. He was the Turkish shop owner, Hakan. The other man looked like the cliché of a Russian thug.

Brawny body, a thickset face with a beaten-flat nose, eyes which were too far apart and a fighting weight of at least 150 kilos. He was wearing flip-flops, jogging bottoms and a stained muscle vest which only sparsely covered his abundant body hair. The most notable thing about him, however, was the machete in his left hand, and the pistol in his right. For sure he was on the payroll of Marius Schuwalow, the leader of Berlin's Eastern European organised crime ring.

Ira leant against the glass-doored fridge containing the soft drinks and asked herself why she had left her gun at home on the kitchen table. But then she realised that it didn't matter today anyway.

Back to the handbook, she thought. *De-escalation chapter, Section 2: Crisis Intervention.* While the two men continued to yell at one another without taking any notice of Ira, she went through the checklist in her mind.

Under normal circumstances, she should have spent the next thirty minutes assessing the situation and closing off the crime scene. The aim of this measure would be to prevent the stationary emergency becoming a mobile one, for example with the Russian running amok through Viktoriapark, firing his gun.

Normal? Ha! Under normal circumstances, she wouldn't even be standing here. A direct confrontation such as this, eye to eye and at close proximity, without having built up even a hint of trust with the escalation parties beforehand, was a suicide mission. And she didn't even know what any of this was about. The two men were yelling at each other simultaneously in different languages; she would have needed the best interpreter the *Landeskriminalamt* had to offer. And Ira would be instantly swapped for a male negotiation leader. For even though she had graduated from her psychology studies and subsequent police training with honours, here, at this moment, she might as well use her diploma and certificates to wipe the floor. Neither the Turk nor the Russian would listen to a woman. Their religion probably forbade them from doing so. And their motives for being here.

In this neighbourhood it was usually about some matter of macho pride, and it certainly didn't look like a protection racket. Otherwise the Ukrainian wouldn't have come alone, and Hakan would already be lying face down in the refrigerated display counter full of feta, riddled with bullets. As Ira heard the Russian cock the trigger of his double-action revolver and drop the machete so that he had both hands at his disposal to fire, she glanced through the window looking out onto the street. *Bingo. There's the motive.* Parked outside was a white BMW with a lowered chassis, chrome-plated rims and a minor blemish. Its front-right headlamp was shattered, and the bumper was hanging off at half-mast. Ira made note of the crime scene puzzle pieces on an imaginary flip chart.

Turk. Russian. Machete. Damaged Pimpmobile. Dead dog. Clearly Hakan had crashed into the Russian's car, and now the latter was here to put things straight 'his way', by chopping off Hakan's attack dog's head by way of greeting.

The situation is hopeless, thought Ira. The only good thing was this: Should the shoot-out suddenly kick off, there was no other customer at close range besides her. And there was no doubt that it would come to an exchange of bullets. After all, this was about damage of at least €800.

The only question was who would fire the first shot. And how long it would take for a stray bullet to hit her.

Right. Clearly no one here would be backing down. That wouldn't be an advisable move for either of the two men. The first one to lower his weapon would have a nine-millimetre cartridge in his head. And dishonour to go along with it. Because if he himself hadn't fired a shot, everyone at his funeral would think him a coward.

But at the same time, neither wanted to lose his honour and be the first to scatter bullets all over the place. That was the only reason why they hadn't long since launched a bloodbath, apart from the dead pit bull on the tiled floor, of course.

Ira nodded concurringly as she observed a further escalation action from the Russian, who took a step towards the display counter and stamped angrily on the dog's head as hard as his flip-flops would allow. Hakan, almost out of his mind with rage, screamed so loudly that Ira's eardrums popped.

Another ten seconds perhaps. Twenty at most, she thought. *Shit.* Ira hated suicide negotiations. She specialised in hostage situations and kidnapping. But she did know this: the best option with those who had grown weary of life was to distract their attention. Away from their own death. Towards something less important. Something banal. Something where there wasn't as much at stake if it went wrong.

Of course, thought Ira, opening the fridge door.

A distraction.

'Hey,' she called, with her back to the two duelling men. 'Hey!' she bellowed, more loudly now, when neither of them seemed to take notice of her.

'I want a cola!' she shouted, then turned around. Now she had succeeded. Without lowering their weapons, the two men looked over at her. Their expressions revealed a mix of disbelief and pure hate. She could almost hear what they were thinking.

What does this crazy bitch want?

Ira smiled.

'A Cola Light. Preferably a Cola Light Lemon.'

Breathless silence. Just for a moment. Then the first shot was fired.

4

Kitty hurried into Studio A and almost stumbled over Markus Timber, who was sitting cross-legged on the floor and leafing lethargically through some men's magazine. 'Pay attention to where you're going, for God's sake!' he snapped, awkwardly getting to his feet. 'How much time left, Flummi?' he asked his lanky producer grumpily.

Benjamin Flummer looked up from the mixing desk at the studio monitor, where the digital display told him how much time there was left of the Madonna song currently playing.

'Another forty seconds.'

'Okay.' Timber ran his long fingers through his light-blond hair.

'So what are we doing next?'

As always, he had no idea about the programme schedule, and blindly trusted his producer to tell him about the next highlight of his own show.

'It's 7:28 a.m. The first Cash Call has just been broadcast. We can play one more song, then we have a little something to tug at the heartstrings. Three-year-old Felix only has four weeks to live unless he can find a bone marrow donor.'

Timber grimaced in disgust while Flummi continued,

undeterred: 'You'll be appealing to the listeners to have their blood types tested in order to find out whether they could be potential donors. We've arranged everything: there are stretchers ready and waiting in the large conference room, and from midday onwards there will be three doctors to take a half-litre of blood from everyone that comes in to donate.'

'Hmm.' Timber grunted reluctantly. 'Are we at least going to have the little brat on the phone crying his eyes out with gratitude?'

'The boy is *three* and has *cancer*. You'll be speaking to the mother,' answered Flummi curtly, checking with the pre-fade listen button to see whether the first spot had been correctly placed by the computerised advertising program.

'Is she hot?' Timber asked now, throwing the magazine into the bin.

'Who?'

'The mother!'

'No.'

'Then Felix is a dead man.' Timber straightened up and grinned at his own tasteless joke.

'What's your problem?' he snarled at Kitty, seeing that she was still standing in front of him. 'A bone marrow donation? Saving lives? This was probably your trite idea, wasn't it?'

Kitty had to struggle not to lose her composure. 'No.'

'So why are you in here using up the studio's valuable oxygen?'

'It's about the group,' she said finally.

'The what?'

'I forgot to tell you that there's a tour group today.'

'Who?' Timber looked at her as though she had lost her mind.

'The listeners' club members?' She said the answer like a question, as though she herself was no longer sure who was currently in the neighbouring studio waiting to be let into the most holy one. Normally it would have been Kitty's job to inform Timber about this event the day before. As she hadn't done so, in a matter of seconds he would be on display to his most loyal fans unshaven and in ripped jeans. In his short time with the station, he had kicked off about far less than that, and this time she probably wouldn't even be able to save herself with the thing he had hired her for in the first place: her cleavage.

'When are they coming?' asked Timber, thunderstruck.

'Now!'

As soon as that asocial guy on crutches finally comes back from the toilet. At least there was one good thing about the fact that he was now holding up the other visitors.

The presenter glanced past Kitty through the tinted, soundproofed glass window that separated Studio A from the service area that lay beyond it. A group of four listeners were in the process of applauding something the news chief had just said to them.

'In about three minutes.'

'Get my autograph cards right away!' he ordered, jerking his head towards a side door next to the unit with the archived CDs.

At least there's still a small scrap of professionalism left in him, thought Kitty gratefully as she ran off. It wouldn't have surprised her if he had become verbally abusive right in front of his guests. Kitty flung open the small door to the 'experience area'. This was the ironic nickname given by the presenters to the small, windowless room where they could eat, smoke and freshen up. Its inventory consisted solely of a kitchen counter and a wobbly table. The area was only accessible via Studio A, and also led to a technical room and the emergency fire exit. The last was a masterpiece of architectonic misplanning. If there were to be an emergency, it would be like running straight into a trap. Behind the door, an aluminium spiral staircase wound its way around the outer wall, down half a floor to a green-covered roof overhang, and that was where it ended. In nothingness. Somewhere between the eighteenth and nineteenth floor.

Kitty looked around. Timber had put his black designer rucksack next to the sink between an ashtray and a half-full coffee cup. She rummaged around in it feverishly, trying to find the damn autograph cards. At the very moment when she pulled out a small pile displaying Timber's retouched face in high-gloss, she froze in shock.

'Welcome!'

She turned around and looked through a glass pane in the 'experience area' door into Studio A, where Timber was stretching out his hand in greeting. *Oh, please no!* Kubichek must be back from the toilet, and the news chief must have already guided the group into the studio, against what had been agreed. Timber would go mad, that much was sure. Another reason for him to have it in for her.

'How nice that you could join us!'

The star DJ's voice echoed dully through the closed door. It had fallen shut behind Kitty as she had come into the room. And as it could only be opened from the outside, Kitty would now have to wait until all the listeners had squeezed their way past the door and found a place at the 'bar'.

The 'bar' stretched out around the large mixing desk like a horseshoe, and in front of it were the bar stools, intended for studio guests. Kitty went back over to the door and peered intently into the studio. By now, almost all the visitors were on their seats. All except one.

What was taking that idiot so long? she wondered. *Why doesn't he come in with the others? Ah, there he was. Finally.*

He came hobbling in. But why was he closing the heavy studio door behind him? You could hardly breathe in the small studio as it was.

Oh God. Kitty held her hand in front of her mouth, an involuntary reflex. *What's he going to do?*

Ten seconds later, she saw it. And then she began to scream.

5

Jan had just one chance of using the moment of surprise to his advantage during this critical phase: He had to injure someone as quickly and as spectacularly as possible. He needed to engineer something with intense impact. Something shocking that would immediately paralyse an innocent bystander. And so he held out his hand in greeting to Timber, but before the presenter could grasp it, Jan pulled his away again, raised the aluminium grip of his crutch and smashed it down into the DJ's nose with brute force.

The stream of blood that gushed out of Timber's face onto the mixing desk in front of him, along with his subsequent horrified cry, achieved the desired effect. No one in the room did a thing. Exactly as he had expected. Jan could see from the presenter's face how his brain was trying in vain to process what was happening. Flummi had been expecting a harmless meet-and-greet consisting of superficial small talk. The sight of the presenter whimpering and holding his face in both hands just didn't fit in with these expectations. And this was exactly the kind of confusion Jan had been counting on. It gave him time. At least one and a half seconds.

With a karate chop motion, he shattered the small glass panel of the emergency box on the wall and activated the alarm. Instantaneously, a shrill siren drowned out the final chords of U2's latest hit. At the same time, a heavy metal shutter tumbled down the outside of the large window, concealing the chaos within Studio A from the outside world.

'What on earth…?' As expected, the UPS driver was the first to find his voice again. He was perched at the end of the bar, the furthest away from Jan. Between them sat the pregnant woman, the young couple and the overweight, wisecracking pen-pusher.

Jan tore his wig off with his left hand, then pulled his pistol out of the pocket of his jogging bottoms with the other.

'Oh, God. Please…' Amid the deafening racket, he could only guess at what the pregnant woman was trying to say to him. But she didn't manage to complete her sentence. She froze as he aimed the pistol at Timber's blood-smeared face, glancing briefly at the studio clock as he did so. 7:31 a.m.

He had ten minutes, seven hostages and three doors. One led to Studio B. One to the news area. The third, directly behind him, into a small kitchen area. The junkie security guard hadn't told him about that one, but if he remembered the building's floor plan correctly, it wasn't possible that it led to an exit. So he would deal with that one later. For now, he had to prevent his seven hostages from leaving the studio through one of the other two doors. The building security team would already be on their way, summoned by the alarm, and would be taking up their positions outside in less than sixty seconds. But that didn't worry him in the slightest. This was why he had come in last and manipulated the key code lock on the studio door. In terms of security, the electronic lock was an absolute joke. If the wrong numerical code was typed in three times consecutively, no one could gain access to the studio area any more. The door was automatically locked, and a timer ensured that they would have to wait ten minutes before trying again.

As if by way of confirmation, the guards began to rattle on the door handle from the outside. They couldn't see into the studio because of the lowered shutters, so the poorly trained security team now had no idea what they should do next. They weren't prepared for this kind of situation.

Then, at the very moment when Jan was congratulating himself on the fact that everything was running to plan, things suddenly things got out of control.

He had guessed it: the UPS driver! Later, he admonished himself severely for not having considered the possibility that he wasn't the only one in Berlin with a weapon on his person. If someone needed to ring the doorbells of complete strangers on a daily basis, of course that person would value the reassurance that a pistol can bring. In the brief moment when Jan had turned his back on his hostages for the first time to go behind the bar and in front of the mixing desk, the delivery man had pulled out his duty weapon.

So you want to play the hero, huh? thought Jan, feeling irritated that he would have to sacrifice a hostage so early in the proceedings.

'Lower your weapon!' called the delivery man, just like he had heard it done on TV crime series, but Jan refused to be deterred. Instead, he dragged the groaning Timber in front of him.

'You're making a big mistake,' said Jan, holding his Beretta against Timber's temple. 'But luckily you still have time to correct it.'

The driver began to sweat. He wiped the right side of his forehead with the sleeve of his brown uniform.

Another seven minutes. Maybe six, if the guards outside were quick and knew anything about their job.

Fine then. Jan saw the panic in the delivery man's nervous, pale-green eyes, and felt sure that he wouldn't shoot. At this early stage, however, he couldn't take any big risks. But just as he was about to push Timber away in order to give himself enough room for a sure shot, he saw the central mains switch on the mixing desk and had a much better idea. He put Timber back in a stranglehold and pulled him half a metre backwards to the wall, the pistol still pressed against his head.

'Don't come any closer!' screamed the driver in agitation. But Jan just smiled wearily.

'Okay, okay. I'll stay where I am.'

And then he seized the element of surprise once more. Simply by flicking off the large switch behind him on the wall. The lights went out. Before the hostages' eyes had a chance to adjust to the sudden gloom, Jan used his free left hand to turn off the mixing desk and all the flat-screen monitors. Now the studio had been plunged into almost total darkness. Only the red light of two emergency LED lights still flickered, like glow-worms in the darkness.

As expected, the hostages froze, paralysed once again. The UPS driver couldn't see his opponent any more, so he was unsure what to do next.

'You goddamn bastard, what the hell?' he cursed.

'Stay calm,' Jan ordered into the darkness. 'What's your name?'

'Manfred, but that's none of your fucking business.'

'Your voice is shaking, Manfred. You're scared,' Jan established.

'I'll blow your fucking head off. Where are you?'

For a brief moment, the artificial darkness was partly illuminated by a tiny yellow lighter flame. After that, the red-glowing tip of a cigarette could be seen hovering in mid-air.

'Here. But I'd advise you not to shoot in my direction.'

'Why the hell not?'

'Because you'll probably only hit my upper body.'

'And what would be the problem with that?'

'Nothing at all. Apart from the fact that you would disturb the plastic explosives I have strapped around my stomach.'

'Oh, my God,' groaned the office worker and the pregnant woman simultaneously. Jan hoped that the other hostages wouldn't free themselves from their shock in the next few seconds. One rebel he could probably handle. But not a whole group of them.

'You're lying!'

'Do you think? If I were in your position I wouldn't bet on it.'

'Shit!'

'You said it. Now throw your weapon to me over the mixing desk. And be quick about it. If I still see that gun in your hand when the light goes on again in five seconds, I'm firing a bullet straight into the head of our star DJ here. Is that clear?'

The driver didn't answer, and for a moment the only thing to be heard was the whirring of the air conditioning unit.

'Right then, here we go.' Jan clapped Timber on the shoulder. 'Count backwards from five!' he commanded.

After a short sniff and a dull groan, Timber began the macabre countdown in a nasal and unusually shaky voice: 'Five, four, three, two, one.'

Then there was a loud bang. When the light went on again, the rest of the hostages saw something they would never forget.

The delivery driver was slumped unconscious across the bar. Markus Timber, completely soaked in his own blood from his smashed nose, was grappling fearfully with his producer, into whose mouth Jan had put his cigarette. Right before calmly walking around the bar to knock Manfred out from behind.

Jan noted with satisfaction the looks of horror on his victim's faces. Now that he had immobilised the only alpha in the room and still retained all of his hostages, everything was going to plan for him again. He ordered Flummi and Timber to hand over their keys, then locked the door to the news area. Then he secured Studio B, snapping the key in the lock once he had done so.

'What do you want from us?' Timber asked him nervously. Jan didn't answer, instead motioning him with a wave of the gun towards a stool behind the bar. Flummi, on the other hand, was instructed to stay with Jan. Now that they knew he was a walking bomb, no one would dare lift a hand against him, so he could have the scrawny beanpole alongside him without any danger. Besides, he needed someone who knew his way around the equipment. He ordered the show's producer to perform all the necessary steps so that they could go back on the air.

'Who are you?' Timber asked another question, this time from the other side of the mixing desk. Just like before, he didn't receive an answer.

Registering with satisfaction that the monitors and mixing desk were working again, Jan pulled the microphone towards him. Then he pressed the red signal switch in front of him on the touchscreen keypad, just like he had practiced again and again on the mock-up at home. It was time. Things were about to kick off.

'Who in God's name are you?' asked Timber again, and this time the whole city could hear him. 101 Point 5 was back on air.

'Who am I?' said Jan, responding at last as he pointed the pistol at Timber. Then his voice became businesslike and serious. He spoke directly into the microphone:

'Good morning, Berlin. It's 7.35 a.m. And you're listening to your biggest nightmare.'

6

Ira was sitting cross-legged on the grey patterned tiles of the minimarket floor, and had now been staring into the barrel of the Russian's gun for over twenty minutes. His first bullet had missed her by several metres and ripped a coin-sized hole in the Perspex window of the fridge. Since then, he had been aiming it at her chest, while Hakan, in turn, had his gun pointed at the muscleman's head.

'Leave her alone!' he commanded, to which the Russian responded with an incomprehensible volley of words. The situation had become completely hopeless. As far as Ira could make out from the incessant gibberish coming from the Russian, he would now be willing to accept the money from Hakan's cash register as compensation for his rage. Otherwise the second shot would meet its target.

And so he made a move to take the money.

The first cartridge smashed through his shoulder blade, while the second projectile shattered his kneecap and meniscus. The Russian let his weapon fall, collapsing in front of the counter. Only when he hit the floor, and realised how unnaturally his leg had bent, did he begin to scream. Clearly his brain, much like Ira's, had needed some time to process the change in circumstances.

'Put your weapon down and your hands up!' yelled a voice from the entrance of Hakan's shop. Ira stood up and turned, a little dazed, towards the heavily built SEK officer who was filling the entire shop door in his full mission gear.

'What on earth are you doing here?' she asked in surprise.

She had recognised him from the way he pushed up the visor of his titanium-lined helmet with the back of his hand. His alert gaze studied her, revealing an unusual mix of decisiveness and melancholy.

'I could ask you the same thing, sweetheart.'

Oliver Götz still had his machine gun aimed at Hakan, who had followed his instructions without any objections and was currently raising his hands to the ceiling. With his left hand, the officer fished two plastic handcuffs from his chest pocket and threw them to Ira.

'You know what to do.'

First she collected up the weapons on the floor and passed them to Götz. Then she bound Hakan's and then the Russian's hands behind their backs, making the latter cry out in pain.

'Where are the others?' Ira looked through the window, but couldn't see anyone else. Normally the Berlin SEK worked in a team, just like any other special operations unit. On a mission like this, at least seven men would usually be sent in. But Götz was standing there alone before her. To top it all off, she didn't have the faintest idea how the SEK could have gotten to the scene of the crime so quickly.

'I'm alone,' answered Götz, and she couldn't help but smile. Those were the words he had always uttered on the phone when he had wanted her to spend the night with him. Or the rest of her life, if he could have had his way. Sometimes she wondered whether things might have turned out differently if she had allowed herself to have more than just a fling. But then she had found Sara, and all her thoughts of a happy future had died along with her daughter.

'Alone?' cried Ira. 'You go out *alone* in full riot gear and with your gun in tow? To the grocery store?'

She moved slowly towards the chief commissioner, five years her senior, with whom she had gotten through most of her Berlin missions. *And a fair few nights, too.*

'Why? Did you want to fetch some milk?'

'No,' he answered briefly. 'You.'

'Me?'

'Yes. You have a mission. The rest of the crew is waiting in the park. I just happened to walk past here because I was on my way to pick you up from your place.'

They both walked outside, and Ira saw for the first time what a crowd they had provoked. Half the neighbourhood was standing there staring at her as she exchanged words with the heavily armed man. From afar, she could hear the sirens of the approaching ambulance.

'I don't work for you any more,' she said to Götz.

'I know.'

'Well then, look for someone else.'

'Don't you even want to hear what's going on?'

'No,' she answered, without looking at him. 'I don't care. I have more important things to do today.' *Like poisoning myself. And for that I still need a Cola Light Lemon.* But she kept that thought to herself.

'I thought you'd say something like that,' replied Götz.

'I see. So then why did you come?'

'Because I'm going to convince you.'

'Now I'm intrigued. Exactly how do you intend to do that?'

'Like this!' he answered with a smile, before tripping her with lightning speed, throwing her down to the floor and putting on a pair of handcuffs with such breathtaking speed that two of the onlooking teenagers applauded.

'Steuer authorised me to do anything necessary in order to get the crisis under control.'

'I hate you, Götz,' grunted Ira. As he pulled her upright, she noticed that a few of the onlookers were taking pictures on their camera phones. By now the ambulance had arrived, and a contingent of squad cars was hurtling down the road.

'And I don't give a damn what Steuer says! You know what I think of that reactionary fascist pig.'

'Yes. Except, unfortunately, the "fascist pig" is tactical mission leader today.'

Oh, thought Ira, as she reluctantly let Götz pull her along with him across the street. It must be something big if Andreas Steuer, the leading police director, was personally pulling the strings on the mission. Something very big indeed.

'Where are we going?' she asked.

'As I said, to the park.'

'Don't be ridiculous. You left the police car in the park? Wasn't there anywhere more obvious?'

'Who said anything about a car?' Götz was rushing Ira along even quicker. 'Where we need to go it's already too late for a car.'

'Aha.'

While Ira was still wondering where they might be going, the SEK official activated his in-helmet microphone, pressing the talk button on his armoured chest.

Then he gave the order to start the helicopter at once.

7

Viktoriapark moved further and further away below her amid the droning, leaving the gaping passers-by in a cloud of foliage, earth and stirred-up litter. Once it became clear to Ira that Götz didn't have any intentions of taking the handcuffs off her, she stared with boredom into the narrow cabin of the brand-new helicopter. As well as her, Götz and the pilot, there were four SEK officials on board. All of who were, just like their team leader, in full battle gear.

'Where are we flying to?' she shouted, breaking the silence. The helicopter had turned and was flying in a southerly direction.

'To Postdamer Platz. The MCB building.'

Götz's voice sounded a little tinny, but despite the background noise over the helmet headphones it was clear enough to make out.

'How many?' Ira could guess they had come for her because of her specialism: hostage situations.

'We don't know yet,' answered Götz, pulling off his gloves in order to free a piece of chewing gum from its aluminium paper. 'But maybe you can find out from the boss himself.' He signalled to the pilot, and Ira grimaced

48

when, after a brief crackle, an all-too-familiar, rasping voice became audible.

'Is she on board?' Andreas Steuer came straight to the point without any word of greeting.

'Yes, she's listening,' said Götz in response to the man who was in charge of the Berlin SEK units, and therefore over 180 officers.

'Good. Here's the situation report: About thirty-three minutes ago, an unknown man took a group of visitors hostage in the studio of the 101 Point 5 radio station, along with the presenter of the morning programme. He's threatening his victims with an as-yet-unidentified gun, and claims to be rigged up with plastic explosives which he is allegedly carrying around his stomach.'

'What does he want?' asked Ira.

'So far, he hasn't said anything about that. The technical team have already established an initial overview of the situation. The scene of the crime is not visible. The studio is in the east wing of the nineteenth floor, and is completely sealed off by shutters.'

'So right now you're groping around in complete darkness,' commented Ira.

'There are currently fifty-four people working on the mission,' continued Steuer, ignoring her snarky interjection, 'and I've personally taken over the leadership. Chief Commissioner Götz is in charge of the operative command of the special forces at the station. All measures to cordon off the surrounding streets and divert traffic have already been taken. The whole square has been blocked off. Two sniper teams of seven men each are positioned in the offices of the high-rise buildings opposite. And special operation Cash Call has already begun criminal investigation measures.'

'Cash Call?' asked Ira. 'What kind of stupid name is that?'

'Maybe you should refrain from making unqualified observations and instead listen to this recording we have from 7:35 a.m. this morning.'

There was another crackle on the line, then the radio recording began in astonishingly clear digital quality. While the hostage taker was mid-sentence.

'... you're listening to your biggest nightmare. I am interrupting this radio programme for an important announcement. I have just taken Markus Timber and some other individuals hostage within this radio studio. And for once, this isn't one of the jokes of the oh-so-hilarious 101 Point 5 morning team. This is deadly serious. Markus, could you please come to the microphone and confirm what I'm saying?'

There was a short pause, then Timber's voice could be heard. His familiar tone sounded different. Unsure. Fearful. And nasal.

'Yes, it's true. He's threatening me... I mean, us, with a gun. And he has explosives on his...'

'Thank you, that will do for now,' said the hostage taker, curtly interrupting the famous DJ. He had clearly grabbed the microphone back, and was now continuing with his announcement. Paradoxically, his voice sounded pleasant, almost friendly. Albeit not anyway near as practiced as Timber's.

'Don't worry. Those of you listening in front of your radios don't need to be afraid. The fact that I've taken a few people hostage won't stop you getting the same asinine mix of bad music, lame gags and irrelevant news you're used to from this moronic radio station. And there will even be a competition. That's the kind of thing you guys like, right?'

The stranger let this question hang for a moment, then clapped his hands.

'Right then. That's why I'm promising you the following: I'm going to continue to play Cash Call with you. That's a guarantee. I'm going to phone someone in Berlin. And if it's you, and you answer my call with the right slogan – then there's something to win. You know how it works. And it will be just like usual, except that today we're going to play Cash Call with two minor modifications to the rules.'

The hostage taker laughed for a moment, as though he were a small child getting excited about a game. Then his voice became quieter as he spoke away from the microphone to another person, someone who it seemed was standing next to him.

'Hey, you. What's your name?'

'They call me Flummi,' a young man answered hesitantly.

'Okay, Flummi. If I understand correctly, you're the show's producer. Which means you know your way around the mixing desk and all this computer stuff. Is that right?'

'Yes.'

'Do you have a drum roll somewhere? Like in the circus when the elephant comes in? Okay, then I want to hear it when I give you the signal in a moment. Right…'

The hostage taker began to speak to all the listeners again. His voice now took on a penetrating presence, as though he was sitting directly next to Ira in the helicopter.

'Here is rule change number one: I'll continue to call

someone at random from the Berlin telephone book. But there's no €50,000 to be won. Instead, there's something much more valuable. But more on that in a moment. Because first you need to understand the second rule change. That's the most important.'

A drum roll set in, and the hostage taker now began to speak in the tones of a fairground announcer:

'Rule change number two, ladies and gentlemen. The Dosh Ditty has changed. From now onwards, it will be: "I listen to 101 Point 5, now set a hostage free!"'

The drum roll stopped abruptly.

'To sum it all up one more time: It's now 7:36 a.m. As of now, I'm going to play Cash Call every hour, according to my rules. The first will be at 8:35 a.m., when a telephone will ring somewhere in Berlin. Maybe it will be in your house. Or your office. And if you pick up and answer with the new slogan, then I'll let one of the hostages here go home. Sounds fair, doesn't it?'

During the last few words, Ira registered a change in the hostage taker's tone. She could guess what was coming next.

'But if I don't hear the correct slogan, then that will be a shame. Because that will mean someone has lost this round.'

Oh God. Ira closed her eyes.

'Which means the following, ladies and gentlemen: if the person I call says their name after they pick up, or "hello", or anything other than "I listen to 101 Point 5, now set a hostage free", then someone here in the studio is going to get shot.'

8

There was a brief crackle in the built-in helmet speakers, then Ira opened her eyes as Steuer began to speak again. 'So that's the recording. It's now 8:06 a.m. That means we have less than thirty minutes until the first round of the game. We have to work on the assumption that this guy means business. The negotiation team led by Simon von Herzberg have already taken up their position at the station...'

'At the station?' Ira interrupted the SEK boss. 'Since when have we negotiated right in the danger zone?'

Normally, a fully equipped stationary control centre in Tempelhof was used for crises like these. In some exceptional cases, they drove a mobile mission vehicle directly in front of the building. But they never set foot onto the scene of the crime.

'For once, the MCB high-rise is perfectly suited as a mission control centre. The sixth floor isn't yet occupied, so we can practice the attack even while the negotiations are ongoing,' explained Steuer impatiently.

'Come on, I'm sure it can't be that perfect,' said Ira.

'Why not?' asked Steuer, and she noticed the background echo for the first time. He must be in an empty room or a large storage space.

'Because you wouldn't fetch me if you already had a decent negotiation leader. Simon von Herzberg is an inexperienced windbag. So now you expect me to leave my breakfast uneaten at home, so that you don't make a laughing stock of yourself when some newbie from the *Bundeskriminalamt* messes up the whole job.'

'You're wrong,' snapped Steuer. 'Herzberg is far from being our problem. Unlike you, he's not just a psychologist, but also an official member of our task force.'

There it was again. The same old reproach. The pre-conception that it was easier to teach a good policeman how to negotiate than it was to teach a bad psychologist how to be a policeman. The fact that Ira was both, psychologist and policewoman, was something that Steuer refused to recognise. Her basic training in Hamburg with the Mobile Task Force, the only task force in Germany that admitted women, was worthless in his eyes, because afterwards she had chosen to work as an on-scene criminal psychologist only on selected cases, in order to spend the rest of her time teaching applied psychology at the police academy. Due to her spectacular successes, including the Zehlendorf hostage drama, Steuer tolerated her at the crime scene now and again, if only so that no one could later accuse him of not having done everything in his power.

'Herzberg is an experienced man. And just to make this clear once and for all, Frau Samin, I consider you to be a washed-up alcoholic with a dysfunctional family life, whose best days are long gone. It's only a question of time until you bring your personal problems to work with you and become a much greater danger for the lives of others than any crazed psychopath you're trying to negotiate with.'

'Yeah, yeah, I love you too,' responded Ira, thinking once more of her Cola Light Lemon. 'So then why am I about to land on the roof of the MCB building rather than being at home in my kitchen by the stove, which in your opinion is where I belong?'

'Why are you asking me? Do you seriously think this was my idea?' Steuer sounded amused. 'If Götz hadn't been so insistent, there's no way I would waste my time with you.'

Ira threw a questioning glance at Götz, who turned away from her with a shrug of his shoulders.

'If it were down to me,' Steuer piped up again, 'and it *is* down to me, then you will be replaced as quickly as possible with someone more competent. Until then, you'll take Herzberg's place, because for some reason the psychopath is refusing to speak with him.'

That makes him instantly more likeable, thought Ira, but she kept it to herself.

'And there's a further complication due to the fact that he only wants to negotiate over the radio. Publicly. He wants everyone to listen in,'

Steuer sighed heavily.

'And if we take him off the air, he says he'll shoot someone *immediately*.'

9

The door flew open while Diesel was sitting behind his desk, pouring half a litre of charcoal lighter fluid into the wastepaper bin.

'What are you still doing here?' shouted the little man, who had clearly not expected anyone to still be in this section of the building.

The MCB building had been completely evacuated twenty minutes ago. Diesel knew very well that the question from the well-dressed fop with the metal-rimmed glasses was only meant rhetorically. But he still gave an answer.

'What am I doing? Well, what does it look like? I'm burning the show.'

'You're burning what?'

A bright darting flame shot out of the zinc-coated bin about a metre and a half towards the ceiling, momentarily stunning Simon von Herzberg into silence.

'Dammit!'

'Hey, hey hey!' Diesel interrupted the man. 'No swearing in my sodding office, for fuck's sake!'

Then he laughed loudly, because the weedy official at the door clearly didn't know what to direct his bewilderment at first. The fact that he was standing in a room that resembled a toy shop more than an office. Or the fact that the lunatic opposite him surely couldn't be the person who, according to the sign on the door, was supposed to inhabit this space. Namely, the chief editor of the radio channel 101 Point 5.

'Put your hands up and stand up slowly!' bellowed Herzberg, nodding to the two officials behind him who had already pulled out their guns.

'Ho, ho, take it easy,' replied Diesel. Instead of following the negotiation leader's order, he stayed seated and slowly began to pull his grey sweatshirt over his head.

'It's gotten damn hot here all of a sudden, don't you think?' his voice emerged muffled through the material, interspersed with laughter. He continued to tug at the garment. But clearly Diesel was suddenly having problems in getting the sweatshirt over his platinum blond-dyed hair.

'Dammit. I've gotten it tangled up in my nose piercing...'

Herzberg turned around to his colleagues, in truth just to make sure they were seeing the same thing as him. Because by now Diesel had stood up and was stumbling across the room.

'Can you help me, please... otherwise... shit.'

Diesel crashed with full force against a slot machine, the type that would usually only be found in run-down train station bars, and certainly not in the office of a department leader. But as the boss of the craziest radio show in Germany, Diesel had been allowed certain freedoms in his contract. As long as the listening figures were high, he could make his office into an adult Disneyland if he wanted to. It was a work environment which allegedly inspired his creativity. And people even forgave him his pyromaniac tendencies, which had both inspired his nickname and resulted in the smoke detector being removed from his office.

While the two criminal police officers covered him, Herzberg took two steps into the room, his gun cocked.

'Where am I?' screamed Diesel, almost in a panic now, ramming his head into a punch bag which was hanging from the ceiling. Now his arms, too, had become hopelessly entangled in his sweater. He almost fell flat on his face, and the fall was only broken by the *Star Wars* pinball machine which stood in the middle of the room. He was now draped across it stomach down.

'Get up!' yelled Herzberg, his weapon still aimed. 'Nice and slow.'

'Okay.' Diesel obeyed the order, his voice muffled as though he were speaking through a cushion. 'I don't think I can breathe.'

Herzberg took a step towards the chief editor and patted him down with his free hand for weapons.

'Keep your hands up. Don't turn around!'

By now, more policemen had gathered in front of the office, and they were all watching the ludicrous scene through the glass window with open mouths.

'Okay.' Having established that Diesel was unarmed, Herzberg was reassured.

'So how can I be of assistance?' It was clear from Herzberg's voice that he was starting to feel more in control again. As a psychologically trained negotiation leader from the *Bundeskriminalamt*, he had adequate experience of crisis intervention. But this particular one here certainly wouldn't have been in his training manual.

'My nose ring is stuck somewhere in the zip.'

'Okay, I understand. But that's no prob-lem…'

Herzberg screamed the last word like a teenager plunging into the depths on a rollercoaster. As he did, he jumped backwards in panic. All of a sudden, Diesel had whipped around and abruptly torn the shirt from his head.

'Boo!'

Herzberg's shriek ended as abruptly as it had begun, and now his mood changed from pure fear to pure horror. Diesel had somehow managed to put on some comedy glasses beneath his sweater, and at the press of a button, two bloody eyeballs tumbled out. They rolled across the floor and came to a halt right by Herzberg's feet.

'April Fool!' Diesel burst out laughing and registered with amusement that the policemen in front of his office were struggling to contain their grins.

'Are you insane? I… I could have killed you,' panted Herzberg once he could think clearly again. 'You, you… you're disrupting a sensitive mission and behaving irresponsibly,' he continued. 'I'm outraged.'

'Nice to meet you. I'm Clemens Wagner,' grinned the chief editor, winning another smirk from the policemen as he gave himself the pseudonym of the Red Army Faction terrorist. 'But I let my enemies call me Diesel.'

'Lovely, er, Mr Wagner. Then I assume that, along with Markus Timber, you're the highest-ranking employee here at the channel this morning?'

'Yes.'

'So why are you behaving like a child? Why, instead of leaving the building like all the others, are you torching your… er' – Herzberg looked at him with contempt – 'torching your office?'

'Oh, is that why you're so pissed at me?' Diesel looked over at the wastepaper bin, from which a gentle cloud of smoke was still rising up. 'It's just one of my old habits.'

'An old habit?'

'Yes. If a show wasn't so good, I print out all the scripts and burn them. It's a ritual of mine.'

Now that Diesel was no longer wearing his sweatshirt, the licking flames tattooed on his lower arm were plain to see.

'And this morning's show was particularly bad, don't you think?'

'I have no idea. Nor do I have any more time to waste. An officer will accompany you at once to the reception camp we've set up in the Sony Center.'

Herzberg nodded his head towards the exit, but Diesel didn't make any move to go.

'That's nice, but I'm not going.'

'What's that supposed to mean?'

'Exactly what I said. I'm staying here.'

Diesel went over to a life-size Barbie doll and pressed her right breast. Her lips immediately opened, and the on-air programme could be heard from her mouth. There was currently an advertisement running on 101 Point 5.

'The hostage taker wants everything to carry on as normal,' explained Diesel. 'That means: news twice an hour, weather and traffic every fifteen minutes, and lots of music and happy stuff in between.'

'Yes, I'm familiar with your content.'

'Good for you. But perhaps you're not familiar with how much work goes into a programme like this. It doesn't just run all by itself. And as I'm the chief editor of the show here, you're going to have to put up with my presence whether you like it or not. Otherwise that lunatic in the studio is not going to get what he wants. And I imagine that wouldn't be in your interest.'

'He's right, you know.'

All heads turned towards the door, from where the deep voice had resounded out. Diesel registered with amusement that Herzberg was clearly greatly in awe of the two-metre giant who was wheezing his way into his office. In any case, he immediately straightened his posture. 'What's going on here?'

'Everything's fine, Commander. I left the mission control station downstairs in order to get a quick overview of the situation, and then we suddenly noticed smoke in the corridor. I investigated the situation and discovered the, er' – Herzberg shot Diesel a contemptuous look – 'the chief editor. Clemens Wagner.'

'I know who he is,' said Steuer dourly. 'We just checked him out; he's clean. And he's right. He can stay here and take care of the programme functions.'

'Yes, sir,' nodded Herzberg, looking as though he had just swallowed a hot potato in one gulp. Diesel grinned triumphantly.

'And we're also moving your negotiation centre from the sixth floor to up here.'

'Here?'

'Yes. The closer you are to the studio the better. After all, you don't just need to negotiate, but also distract the maniac so that Götz's team has a better chance of attack. This office is ideally located. It's far enough away from the studio but still has a full view of the scene. And you'll also be undisturbed up here, whereas on the sixth floor we're in the process of constructing a mock-up of the entire station complex in order to run through the attack.'

'I see,' murmured Herzberg, clearly not overly enthused about spending the next few hours within range of a possible explosion.

'Of course,' he added a little louder, when Steuer laid his right hand questioningly behind his ear.

'Great. So let's get a move on. We only have another twelve minutes until the first deadline. And I need to introduce an old acquaintance to you.'

Diesel watched with amazement as the fleshy giant stormed out of the office with surprising speed and returned a few moments later with a moody-looking, black-haired woman in tow, whose hands were in handcuffs.

'Gentlemen, please give a warm welcome to Ira Samin.'

10

He debated who he would take. The first round would be the most difficult, that much was sure. If one assumed that around 330,000 people were listening to the programme right at this moment, then there were over three million more Berliners who knew absolutely nothing about the fact that he had stormed into the studio, taken hostages and changed the rules of the Cash Call. No question about it. The first round was impossible to win. And that's why there were no volunteers when he asked for them.

'Steady on, don't all rush to volunteer at once,' called Jan May, letting his gaze wander over the group by the studio bar. First he looked at Timber, whose nose had finally stopped bleeding, then the couple, Cindy and Maik, clinging to one another fearfully. Then the wisecracker Theodor, who was clearly under shock and had left his sense of humour in another world. The UPS hero Manfred had now regained consciousness and was leaning against the grey-material-clad studio wall. Right next to him was the pregnant redhead, who had revealed herself to be Sandra, a nurse. Jan had allowed her to tend to Timber with bandages and Manfred with aspirin from the studio's first aid box.

'We have about three minutes to go, ladies and gentlemen,' he said continuing with his monologue. 'As you can hear, Queen has just begun "We are the Champions". And as soon as this song… sorry' – Jan turned to Flummi, who was taking care of the music schedule in an astonishingly calm manner – 'what do you call a song like that?'

'A mega-hit,' answered Timber in Flummi's place. Because of his broken nose, he sounded as though he were suffering from a heavy cold.

'Thank you. As soon as this mega-hit by Queen comes to an end, I'll ask Flummi to give me an outside line. And then we'll play the first round of Cash Call with the new rules.'

Jan lifted his left hand, which he had balled into a fist, and counted off every point on his list on his fingers.

'So, I have a producer, I have a telephone, and I have an outside line. I have the rules. All that's missing is the human wager. Who should I set free if the correct slogan is said at the other end?'

No one dared to make eye contact with him. Everyone knew that it wasn't just about being set free. Only Sandra lifted her head briefly, and Jan could see the burning hatred in her pale eyes. Unlike Theodor, who was in a state of shock and shaking his head, Sandra seemed to be a brave woman, the only one with the guts to stare danger in the face. Jan was surprised at how much could be read from a single glance. But then he pulled his concentration back to the next step, and began his perfidiously thought-out selection process.

'Yeah, yeah, I know. You all want to be the first. So given that you can't decide between yourselves, I guess I'll have to make the choice myself.'

'Oh, my God...' Cindy let out a sob and buried her face in her husband's chest.

'Please...' Jan lifted both hands in a placating gesture. He was still holding the weapon, angled slightly, in his right hand. 'Don't celebrate too soon. It's not time yet. I won't make my decision until *after* the first round is played.'

The two women in the studio closed their eyes. All the others tried not to show any reaction, which only made them look more nervous.

'So let's recap one more time,' said Jan, louder again now. 'I'm about to call a telephone number somewhere in Berlin. Then we'll all wait with bated breath to see if the person answers with the slogan, which is...?'

Jan pointed the pistol at Maik, who went pale and began to stutter: 'I... I... listen to... er... 101... Point... er... Five. N... now...'

'... now set a hostage free. Correct,' completed Jan at double-speed. 'And immediately after that I'll choose the person whom I'm going to release, or – if the person I call should happen to say the slogan incorrectly – the person whom...' He left the remainder of his sentence unfinished, but it was all the more threatening as it lingered on in the room.

Jan glanced at the clock out of the corner of his eye and compared the remaining time with the display on the computer. Another minute and thirty seconds. Queen was just beginning the last refrain.

'Manfred?' He glanced at him briefly, reaching for the first volume of the telephone book which he had discovered on the shelf next to the CD cabinet.

'Yes?'

'I'm dying of thirst. There's a kitchen out back, right?'

'Yes.' Timber nodded.

'Could you please put on a big jug of coffee for us all while I'm making the call here? It could be a long show. After all, we haven't even played the first round yet.'

As he spoke, Jan let the thin pages of the telephone book glide past his finger like a flipbook, then looked questioningly in Timber's direction.

'*Round* – I'm sure you have an expression for that in radio jargon. Don't you?'

'Pay-off.' This time it was Flummi who answered.

'Pay-off,' repeated Jan, opening the thick tome as he spoke and thwacking his hand down on the right-hand side. 'Ha!' Everyone in the studio jumped.

'We're starting the pay-off in sixty seconds with a randomly selected number from the Berlin telephone book, letter H. Let's find out who the lucky person is.'

11

When Ira stepped over to the nineteenth-floor window of the provisional negotiation headquarters, she could see that the traffic jam was already stretching back to Bulowstrasse in the West and to the city hall, the Rotes Rathaus, in the East. At this moment, sixty-seven police officials were busy cordoning off an area the size of around seventy football fields to all traffic and pedestrians. No one was allowed to enter the danger zone around the MCB building. It was now shortly before half past eight. In less than forty minutes the shops would be opening in the arcades of Potsdamer Platz's 'glass palace', and 70,000 Berliners would be setting off, just like every other day, to do their shopping. They wouldn't reach their destination today. Nor would the countless people who were trying to get to their workplaces in the centre of the city, including high-ranking government officials and politicians who were expected at a Federal Council meeting or in parliament. Never had the term 'exclusion zone' been as applicable as today.

'How about if you finally make a start with the work instead of just admiring the view?'

Ira turned around to face Steuer, who was standing in the doorway observing the activities of his subordinates.

Herzberg had dismantled the punch bag and pushed the pinball machine aside so that there was enough room in Diesel's office for the essential hardware: a mobile computer unit including the surveillance equipment as well as the large standard mission carry case and two flip charts. Right now, he was in the process of attaching the recording device to the telephone unit. He was being helped by an assistant with snow-white hair. Ira had never worked with him before, and presumed he was the minute taker.

'Who's the third man?' she asked. It was an unwritten rule that every negotiation team worked as a three. One spoke, one took notes and the third maintained an objective view and took over the negotiations once the negotiator was exhausted. Conversations with kidnappers and hostage takers could draw out for hours, sometimes even days. The psychological strain was too much for one officer alone.

'*You* are,' answered Herzberg. 'The hostage taker has refused to have any further contact with our negotiation team.'

Ira's pulse quickened suddenly, as though she had just stepped off a treadmill, and for this reason she didn't comment on Herzberg's words. This first weakness in her circulatory system was a clear sign that she shouldn't be here, not unless someone fixed her a drink very soon.

Herzberg picked up the telephone receiver from where he was sitting at the mobile mission computer and swivelled around to face Ira in his chair. 'I can't get through. He's not answering the studio telephone any more.'

'Dammit,' grumbled Steuer, pulling a cigarette from its box.

'Hey, there's no smoking in here!' barked Diesel in jest,

and Ira couldn't help but smile. The smell from the burned paper in his wastepaper bin still hung in the air.

'Try again, Herzberg. Frau Samin has to speak with him before the first deadline.'

'No chance,' said Ira calmly but firmly. 'Under no circumstances will I be leading a negotiation. Not today. Completely aside from the fact that...' she stopped, clearing her throat in order to suppress a coughing fit.

'The fact that what?' Steuer asked.

... that you'll soon be witnessing the live show of me going cold turkey if we keep talking for much longer, was what she wanted to say in response. But instead, she provoked him: 'Completely aside from the fact that there's no way negotiating can achieve anything in this case.'

Steuer's eyes glinted. He hadn't seen that one coming.

'No negotiations? You're saying that we should storm? I never thought I'd see the day, Frau Samin.'

'Nonsense. Although I'm sure that's what you'd like to do.'

Ira knew exactly what Steuer thought of psychological negotiations with serious criminals. In his opinion, they were pointless, and negotiation leaders like Ira were namby-pamby softies who didn't have the guts to solve a crisis with armed force. The idea of reaching out even his little finger to a criminal sickened him. Let alone the idea of bringing them pizza or cigarettes, even if he managed to free a hostage in exchange by doing so.

'Okay then, we have another five minutes to the first Cash Call. You don't want to negotiate. You don't want to storm. So what's your plan, if I may ask?'

'You don't know?' asked Ira with feigned surprise. Then

she looked up at the ceiling and rolled her eyes. 'Ah yes, I forgot that in your role all you know about crime scenes is from the perspective of your desk. Okay, so I'll give you a little clue: What we have here is a classic textbook situation. Even he could solve it.' Ira nodded in Herzberg's direction. 'All we have to do is this: Nothing. We just wait.'

'Nothing?' asked Diesel, who had been following the conversation from the other corner of the room. 'Normally I'd do that happily. The whole day long. But on this occasion it sounds like a stupid idea, particularly for the hostages, don't you think?'

'Yes, unfortunately that's true. The people in the studio are going to die. All of them.'

Ira lifted both hands to brush a strand of hair off her forehead. Clearly Steuer had no intention of unlocking her handcuffs until she began a conversation with the hostage taker.

'It is of course a great shame, and I know sounds harsh. But a negotiation like this is almost never about the lives of the hostages.'

'So what is it about then?' Even Steuer was completely dumbstruck now.

'The lives of thousands of others.'

'Thousands of others? Are you kidding me? How on earth is the maniac in the studio supposed to endanger them? Rubbish!' cursed Steuer. Herzberg turned around to him once more.

'Still no answer.'

'Keep trying,' barked Steuer gruffly, before looking back at Ira.

'We have two sniper teams in position, and Götz is

leading an elite group that has extensive experience in crisis situations.'

'How nice for you. But none of that is any use if the hostage taker demands a helicopter and flies it into a skyscraper. Or into the fully packed Olympiastadion tonight. He has six people under his control right now...'

'Seven,' corrected Steuer. 'Two employees, five visitors.'

'Okay. But it doesn't actually make much difference. What I'm saying is that at least we have a stable situation right now. The studio is sealed off; there's no way out. The building has been evacuated. So the number of victims is manageable. And given that he wants to shoot his hostages one by one, we can even roughly predict how long the drama will last. All we need to do is prevent the stable situation from turning into a mobile one, like that time in Gladbeck. If you give the order to storm, Steuer, it would be the stupidest decision you could make. All you would do is risk increasing the number of victims.'

'So then why don't you want to negotiate?' asked Herzberg. He had stood up and was tapping his index finger on his watch, which was much too big for his scrawny wrist. 'We only have another three minutes, for heaven's sake, and you're standing around here chatting.'

'And what should I be doing as far as you're concerned, Einstein? After all, you couldn't even get the hostage taker back on the phone for me. And besides...'

Ira watched with irritation as an officer from special operation Cash Call came in from the corridor and whispered something into Steuer's ear, presumably some findings from the investigation.

'... and besides, we don't even have any leverage to

negotiate *with*,' Ira continued after a brief pause. 'You can't suggest a deal, because there's nothing you can offer him in return. He already has the thing he wanted most.'

'And what might that be?' asked Steuer, his head still leant over close to the police officer.

'Attention. Publicity. A media frenzy. We're not dealing with a sociopath here; it's too well planned for that. And it's clearly not a politically motivated attack, otherwise he would have made his demands by now. Unfortunately, our hostage taker is a very intelligent man who wants to be in the spotlight at all costs.'

'So he will kill them?' asked Diesel.

'Yes. In order to get even more attention. Unfortunately. And at the moment, there's nothing we can do to stop him.'

'Yes there is,' said Steuer, taking a step towards Ira and pressing the small key to her handcuffs into her left hand.

'We'll just divert the calls from the studio.'

So that was it. Ira lost control of her facial muscles. That was what the official had just been whispering into Steuer's ear.

A call diversion!

'You can continue to stand around her talking bullshit if you like, Frau Samin, but I have a mission to lead. Good day to you.'

With those words, Steuer kicked his foot angrily against Diesel's metal wastepaper bin and marched out of the room.

Ira hesitated for a moment, then hurried after him.

12

She finally caught up with him by the open elevator doors. 'You're planning to manipulate the outgoing calls from the studio?'

Ira climbed into the lift with Steuer, simultaneously attempting to free herself from the handcuffs with the miniscule key. He didn't respond.

'Is that really what you're planning?'

The mission leader turned his head and looked down at Ira with a tired smile.

'Why? Are you upset because you didn't think of it yourself?'

The elevator set into motion gently, almost imperceptibly, and Ira finally succeeded in freeing one hand from the metal grasp of the handcuffs.

'The officials in the call centre have been well briefed on how to answer the phone if the worst comes to the worst. They know the slogan.'

'Surely you can't be serious?' Ira stared into the police director's bloated face. Countless fatty snacks and unnecessary workplace nibbles had left their mark.

'I'm utterly serious. Unfortunately, though, the studio equipment is very complicated. The technicians can't yet guarantee that all outgoing calls can be diverted. They need to do another test run first.'

'This would be a huge mistake,' protested Ira, but Steuer was ignoring her again. The elevator had reached the sixth floor and opened its doors to the mission control area. Steuer's diversion centre. Upstairs, on the nineteenth floor, the negotiation team had just an average-size room. Down here, Steuer had occupied an entire floor of the MCB building for his mission. A market research team had been planning to open its district office here next month. The floor was ninety per cent ready, and looked like an exhibition hall the day before the show opening. Removal boxes, shrink-wrapped office furniture and huge rolls of carpet lay among the future telephone work stations of the open-plan office. From here, badly trained part-time employees would be calling randomly selected people and asking them their opinion on the popularity of the government. The telephones and computers that had been delivered were already functioning. At some of the desks, officials were sitting, talking on the phones.

'So, Ira, make your decision. Either you take the elevator back upstairs and start work, or you say goodbye here and now. But you're not going to hold me up from *my* work one minute more.'

As Steuer hurried off to the control room, Ira stood there stunned in the elevator. It was impossible to deny that the SEK boss had achieved a lot in a short time. In the right-hand corner of the space, all the room dividers had been torn back down, making way for a faithful reproduction of the studio complex on the nineteenth floor. So far, there was just a plasterboard wall. The glass panes were still missing.

But one was in the process of being carried through the room by two men.

Ira shook herself free from her dazed state and stepped into the open-plan office. On the floor, white stickers marked the spots where the carpet-laying firm were supposed to position a runner with the company's emblem the following week. Ira followed them and saw that the path led her to the manager's office in the left-hand corner of the space. The heavy wooden door stood open, so Ira was able to see Götz and Steuer both staring at a monitor, which sat enthroned on an obscenely large, oval curved desk. Steuer was sitting on a black leather chair. Götz was standing behind him, leaning over his shoulder.

'Can we switch to observation camera twelve from here?' Steuer was asking as Ira entered the room. Both of them looked up at her. While Götz gave her an encouraging nod, Steuer's gaze contained unconcealed contempt. But if he wanted to say something, he swallowed it down, presumably to save time. On the desk next to the computer stood a portable box radio with a digital time display. 8:34 a.m. Just thirty-three seconds to go until the first round.

Götz leant over Steuer's shoulder and typed something into the mobile computer unit. An image of the main entrance to the radio station was building up on the plasma screen. Ira was able to follow everything with razor-sharp definition on a second monitor, which was positioned on the side of the desk closest to her. Presumably for one of Steuer's assistants. The screen showed the reception desk on the nineteenth floor, which had a metal ladder in front of it. Alongside it stood a lanky policeman who was in the process of taking off his uniform.

'Everything is just as you ordered,' explains Götz, and Steuer nodded. 'Luckily Onassis is so thin that he fits through the shaft of the air conditioning unit.'

Onassis wasn't the man's real name, of course: SEK officials tended to work anonymously and with code names.

'He'll get through there without any problems. As you can see, he's just about to set off now.'

'But it's at least fifty metres to the studio,' groaned Steuer, looking at the digital display on the radio. 'We only have a few seconds.'

'Even if he doesn't manage it before the first call, he can still shoot before the object gets his hands on one of the hostages.'

'And that would be an even bigger mistake,' said Ira, but no one, neither Götz nor Steuer, paid any attention to her. They continued to stare at the monitor, on which the now almost naked police officer was climbing up the rungs of the ladder, armed with a nine-millimetre pistol.

Diverting the calls! A sniper in the air conditioning shaft! thought Ira. *Didn't they realise the catastrophe they were heading towards?*

13

Manfred Stuck guessed that he hadn't been sent to the experience area in order to make coffee. And for that reason, he didn't waste any time pouring water into the five-litre chrome machine or looking for the coffee filters. He opened the small fire door at the top end of the room and rejoiced when he saw that it led out into the open air. But the relief didn't last long, for he soon saw that he was in a trap. Nineteen floors, ninety metres high over Potsdamer Strasse. The green terrace led into nothing. If he walked out onto it, he would be fair game just half a floor below. *Shit!*

Manfred's head began to pound as hard as it had right after the blow the maniac in the studio had dealt him.

Why couldn't I just control myself? Of course he'll want to get rid of me first now.

He walked back into the break room. There was another door next to the kitchen counter. Locked. Manfred rattled the plastic handle. Nothing. Regardless of what lay behind it, this route was blocked off to him too.

He flung open the wall cupboard above the sink in the hope of finding a key here. But he knew that it was hopeless. Why would someone go to the effort of locking a door, only to leave the key somewhere so readily accessible? They might as well just leave it open.

Nonetheless, he leant down and opened the white laminate doors directly under the sink. Then promptly crashed his head against the edge of the worktop in shock.

'Holy...'

'Sshh!' A petite blonde woman was cowering beneath the sink next to the bin, pressing her index finger against her lips.

'Who in God's name are you?' whispered Manfred. As he looked around nervously at the studio door, a new wave of pain sloshed inside his head from one side of his skull to the other. The hostage taker was still leaning over the mixing table while Flummi explained the telephone unit to him. Clearly no one had noticed him or the young woman.

'I'm Kitty. I work here, remember?'

'Good. You have to help me. How can I get out of here?'

'You can't. The only way out is back through the studio.'

'And what about that door there?'

'That leads to the technical room. And only Timber has the key. But it's just another dead end.'

Manfred looked to the right once more, through the narrow glass panel in the door to the studio. The hostage taker had picked up the phone and was beginning to dial a number. It was happening.

'Please,' whispered Manfred. Sheer panic was etched all over his face now. 'Is there nothing at all you can do to help me?'

'What's that?'

'What?'

'At the back of your jeans.'

Because the UPS man had knelt down, his brown uniform shirt had rucked up over his wide behind.

'Is that a mobile phone?'

Manfred reached for the leather case on his belt loop.

'This thing? Good God, no. It's just our damn company walkie-talkie. What do you want with that?'

He ripped it out of the case and pressed it into Kitty's hand.

'What are you planning to do, call for help or something? Why do you think he didn't search us for mobile phones, for heaven's sake? Because the whole world is already listening to us on this goddamn radio station anyway!'

14

> *I have him directly in sight.*

Ira stared at the screen in disbelief. The image flickered slightly whenever the sniper moved. But there was no doubt that he was very close to the target. He had pushed his way through the dusty shaft of the air conditioning unit to Studio A quicker than anticipated. His knees were bleeding and the palms of his hands deeply grazed, but the effort hadn't been in vain. He was now lying next to the ventilator outlet directly above the studio mixing desk. The remote-controlled microfibre endoscopy camera on the sniper's helmet supplied a close-up view of the back of the hostage taker's head. Unfortunately, it wasn't possible from this perspective to see all the other people who were in the room. For this, the officer would need to lift up the ventilation plate. The narrow slit between the metal rotor blades of the ceiling fan offered just enough space to bring the mouth of the Heckler & Koch gun into position.

There was a brief signal tone, then the top right-hand corner of the screen in front of Götz, Steuer and Ira was filled with a new message. The policeman was working with a mini text computer; a radio connection would be too loud.

> *Awaiting further instructions.*

'He's ready,' said Götz.

'Good,' answered Steuer.

'No, it's not good!' objected Ira vehemently. 'You cannot shoot, not under any circumstances!'

'Keep quiet!' Steuer stood up from his chair and put his hand on Götz's shoulder. 'He's your man.'

Götz sat down and pulled the wireless keyboard towards him.

His fingers flew over the keys.

'Activate your weapon.'

The answer came promptly: >*Activated.*

'You can't shoot,' repeated Ira.

'What is the object doing?'

> *He's dialling.*

'What number?'

The resolution over the mobile camera was too bad to read the sequence of numbers off the telephone computer in the studio.

> *Begins with 788.*

That's Kreuzberg. My neighbourhood, thought Ira, but she said nothing. Ever since it had become possible to take your telephone number with you when you moved house, it was no longer possible to reliably pinpoint a caller's location by the first few digits.

'Wait,' Götz typed into the keyboard, before turning around to Ira with the question: 'Why can't we shoot?'

'Don't waste your time listening to that old lush,' protested Steuer, picking up the paper cup of coffee which an unshaven assistant with a unibrow and Prinz Valiant haircut had just placed on the table for him. The man sat down silently in front of the monitor across from Götz and the police director.

'Because you don't know what will happen if you fire at him,' Ira continued. 'He's carrying enough explosives on his body to blow away this entire high-rise.'

'So he says. But even if he is, he won't even have time to break wind when we blow his brains out, let alone pull an ignition cord.'

Now it was Ira's turn to ignore Steuer's torrent of words. She turned the radio up so she could hear the programme better.

The hostage taker was just dialling the final digit. The ringing tone sounded out and filled the entire office.

Once.

Ira looked at Götz and shook her head.

'Don't shoot,' she mouthed silently.

Twice.

Steuer put down his coffee cup and stared at the screen. The sniper didn't move a single millimetre. The camera viewfinder clung to the back of the hostage taker's head as though it were nailed into place.

Three times.

Ira took a deep, loud breath and held it.

Four times.

In the middle of the fifth ring, the phone was picked up.

15

Sonya Hannemann was twenty-four years old, a loyal listener of 101 Point 5, and sound asleep. At 8.29 a.m., while she was dreaming of a life in an art nouveau villa on Hertha Lake, four radio channels were already broadcasting the live programme of her favourite station in an attempt to make the population aware of the deadly game. At 8:32 a.m., Sonya activated the home movie projector of the subterranean swimming pool in her dream villa. As she swum her lengths in the Olympic-sized pool, the local TV channel was interrupting its repeat showing of a diet cookery programme for a special news report. Every five minutes, viewers were being informed of how they needed to answer the telephone in order to prevent disaster. By this time, the home page of 101 Point 5 online had already crashed due to overload. Tens of thousands of users were attempting to click on the studio webcam, which the hostage taker had actually deactivated just a few minutes after the hijacking.

At 8:34 a.m., Sonya swam two lengths, then retired to her villa's adjoining spa area. At this time, numerous electronic advertisement banners at Alexanderplatz and around Kranzler Eck were asking Berliners to turn on their radios at once. To frequency 101.5 MHz.

At 8:35 a.m. – just as Sonya was standing naked before her tennis coach while he opened the door to the Finnish steam sauna for her – the telephone on her nightstand rang. After it had rung four times, she finally picked it up. A little hesitantly. Irritated. And a little confused. She had just been lying in the muscular arms of a testosterone miracle, and the mundane ring of the telephone had destroyed her wonderful dream about the luxury life of a millionaire's wife. It catapulted her back into the harsh reality of a worn-out waitress who had gone to sleep in her subsidised Kreuzberg flat after a stressful night shift. Just three hours ago. When the world was still in order.

16

'Hello?' Under normal circumstances, the sleepy female voice would have sounded quite sultry. But for the people in Studio A of 101 Point 5, it had all the eroticism of a machine gun.

'Who am I speaking to, please?'

'Sonya Hannemann, why? Who is this?'

Jan pulled the microphone a little closer to him.

'This is 101 Point 5, and we're playing Cash Call.'

At the other end of the line, Jan heard a brief rustling noise, then a muffled curse.

'Sorry, I was asleep. Have I won something?'

'No. Unfortunately you didn't answer with the correct slogan.'

'But...' Sonya sounded wide awake all of a sudden. 'I listen to you every morning. You're Markus Timber, right?'

'No. But he's sitting opposite me.'

'I, erm... I listen to 101 Point 5, now gimme the dough,' cried Sonya hastily, her voice tripping over almost every word. 'I know the slogan. I'm also registered in the winner's club for the €50,000, so please...'

'No.' Jan shook his head.

'But I had a nightshift,' she cursed. 'I've barely slept, and I need the money.'

'No, Sonya. It's not about money today. We've changed the rules.'

The woman at the other end paused. 'What do you mean?' It was plain to hear that she was fighting back a yawn.

'The correct slogan should have been: 'I listen to 101 Point 5, now set a hostage free!'

'A hostage?'

'Yes.'

'And what then?'

'Then I would have set a hostage free.'

'Just a minute, who is this again?' The young woman now sounded as confused as she had at the beginning of the conversation.

'101 Point 5. Unfortunately I can't give you my name, but you're live on a special programme. For the last hour, I've been holding several people here hostage in the studio.'

'Is this a joke?'

'No.'

'And... what happens now?'

'Now, unfortunately, I need to hang up and shoot someone.'

17

Ira was frustrated because no one had wanted to listen to her warnings. But she knew she would soon feel a lot worse if her fears were realised. Because she knew that there was no way someone who had familiarised themselves with the interval function of the electronic lock on the studio door would ever have overlooked the ventilation shafts.

> *Target is moving. Order?*

The cursor was still blinking behind Onassis's last text message. After the first Cash Call had failed – as predicted – everyone was now expecting the worst. Especially as the hostage taker had stood up and was now moving slowly forwards with the gun in his hand.

Götz tapped his index finger on the outer left-hand side of the screen and turned around to Steuer.

'What's that door there, next to the shelving unit?'

'It leads to the experience area,' answered the assistant by Steuer's side.

'To the what?' Götz turned around.

'The studio kitchen.'

'Dammit. He's probably already isolated the first hostage in there, the one he wants to shoot first.'

Götz looked back at the monitor and frantically hacked the next sentence into the computer.

'Target is about to leave the room. Shoot as soon as he starts to leave your field of vision.'

'Okay, that's enough, you idiots,' shouted Ira. 'You can blow yourselves up for all I care, but if I'm going to die then preferably not in your company.' She had just reached the door of Steuer's office when Götz called out.

'Hey, hey, hey…!' he called. 'Something's happening.'

'What is it? Is he out of shooting range?' Steuer asked.

'No. The hostage taker already had the doorknob in his hand. But… see for yourself…' Ira stopped in the doorway and turned around. And then felt breathless with shock. On the monitor facing her, the hostage taker was suddenly looking upwards. To the ventilation shaft in the studio ceiling. He was looking directly into the sniper's camera. And then he began to speak with them.

'Sound,' bellowed Götz, and the assistant with the Prince Valiant haircut turned the radio up to full volume. The microphones in the studio were still on air, so they could hear the hostage taker's voice over the radio too:

'… but just in case you're confusing me with a target, you should know this: you can't stop me by force. The explosives I have under this stylish sweatshirt are connected to a device that measures the heart rate on my carotid artery. If my pulse were to stop for longer than eight seconds, the entire charge will be immediately detonated. I'm not sure, but I think the shock wave would even blow out the panoramic window in the Beisheim Center opposite. Certainly no one here will survive. So think carefully about whether you want to prevent me from going into this kitchen. Because you would only have eight seconds to defuse the explosives.'

The man smiled briefly, then moved slowly backwards towards the door of the experience area.

'Oh, and another thing,' he said, with a cynical grin. 'If that sniper up there doesn't throw down his weapon by the time I count to three, I will immediately shoot two hostages.'

'That's a bluff,' said Steuer, but no one paid any attention to him.

> *Order?*

The message from the sniper announced itself once more with the usual signal tone. From where Ira was standing, she only had a limited view of the screen transmitting the events in the studio. But it was enough to grasp that everything had gone completely out of control. She had gone through a number of missions with Götz by now, but seldom had he been this nervous. His fingers drummed wildly half a centimetre above the keyboard, without making any contact with the keys.

'One!' the hostage taker began to count.

Götz was clearly still not sure what order to give his man in the ventilation shaft. And Steuer was of no help. No mission leader here nor there. When it came down to it, he didn't want to bear the responsibility for a final, fatal shot.

'Two!'

The ceiling loudspeaker transmitted the hostage taker's voice loud and clear over the radio.

'Don't shoot. Drop the weapon!' called Ira one last time.

'He's bluffing,' said Steuer stubbornly, looking around the room. But neither his unshaven assistant nor Götz nor Ira were able to tear their gazes away from the screen, on which the hostage taker had paused in the threshold of the kitchen door. The man tapped his index and ring finger against his carotid artery.

> *Ordr?*

For the first time, the sniper had mistyped amid the chaos. Götz wiped the sweat from his brow, hesitated one last time.

'Three!'

Then Götz wrote the decisive four words: 'ABORT.' And then: 'Drop your weapon.'

Ira sighed with relief as, after a brief moment, the pistol clattered down onto the studio floor. Steuer was the only one to curse loudly.

The sniper was quick-witted enough to re-adjust the camera before his retreat. But now there was nothing be seen on the screen any more. The space by the doorframe was empty. The target had disappeared into the darkness of the adjoining room. And Ira knew precisely what Jan May had taken with him: the sniper's loaded gun. Now the hostage taker had one more weapon. And he was on his way into the studio's kitchen to use it.

Ira left the mission control office. If she remembered correctly, she would pass a soft drink machine in the foyer on her way out.

18

Kitty was cowering next to the dirty rubbish bin beneath the sink, and could only make out the trouser legs of the two men through the slats in the cupboard door. On the right, the UPS driver in his brown uniform. On the left, the hostage taker, who was now barely recognisable. His false teeth, the matted wig and even his beer belly had disappeared, and Kitty was almost annoyed by this. Because the unfriendly outsider from before would have been a much better fit for these criminal acts than the hostage taker's real, almost likeable face. The psychopath with the close-shorn brown hair looked like some friendly bachelor that you let go ahead of you at the supermarket checkout because he only has one purchase. Someone who, at first glance, seems a little too thin, a little too tall and a little too pale to be considered handsome. But Kitty was familiar with this type of man: the more time you spend with them, the more attractive they become. She watched with horror as Jan let something he had just taken out of an Aldi bag drop to the floor. When she realised what it was, she had to bite the back of her hand to stop herself from screaming out loud.

Body bags.

'I'm sorry,' said the hostage taker, and Kitty noticed that his voice sounded much more hesitant in real life than over the radio, which of course was turned on here in the kitchen too. Just as it was all over the station.

'Wait!' pleaded the UPS driver, his voice breaking.

'Don't worry. It won't hurt.'

'Please.' The heavy-built man was trembling all over, and from his voice Kitty could tell that he was crying.

'I'm very sorry. But don't worry.'

'I don't want to die.'

'You won't.'

'I won't?'

'No.'

Kitty couldn't believe her ears. But it seemed that he was telling the truth. Instead of shooting the man, the hostage taker walked over to the sink and filled a glass with water.

'Here, take this.'

'What is it?'

'A headache tablet. I'm sorry I hit you so hard earlier.'

The hostage taker's voice suddenly sounded completely different. No longer cynical, but almost friendly instead. Kitty felt confused. What was going on here?

'Why are you doing this?' asked the UPS man.

'It's a long story. I'd love to tell you more, but I can't leave the others in the studio waiting any longer.'

The hostage taker stepped closer to the UPS man. He was a head taller, so he had to lean down slightly. Kitty held her breath. But her heart was hammering so loudly that she couldn't hear what he whispered in his ear.

The bang which tore through the silence a few moments later was so deafening that she jumped in shock and banged her head against the worktop panel. She feared that she had betrayed her hiding place, but the horrified screams from the studio had drowned out any sounds that Kitty caused beneath the sink.

She wasn't sure if she was still screaming when the UPS delivery man stumbled. Then fell down and died right in front of her eyes.

19

Dazed fear. Ira couldn't find the words to describe that feeling when you are wrenched out of a deep sleep at night by an unfamiliar noise in your darkened apartment. Your pulse tears at your veins, your heart pounds like a malfunctioning ship's engine, and all your other senses try to shake your night-blinded eyes awake. Dazed fear.

When the shot rang out and was transmitted throughout Berlin and Brandenburg over the radio, Ira experienced a similar sensation. Except that it was magnified thousands of times.

A hostage was dead. The perpetrator had meant what he said. And the fact that Ira had predicted it made the certainty no less painful. On the contrary.

Ira put her twenty-cent coins into the vending machine in the radio station foyer and suppressed the self-accusations. She had assessed the situation correctly. It was not negotiable. Certainly not by an alcoholic who had already decided that her life was over.

'Hey!'

She suppressed the impulse to turn around towards Götz, and instead continued to feed in the coins. She hadn't been

94

mistaken; there was a drinks machine in the foyer, just a few metres away from the guarded exit. The heavily armed policemen were there to prevent people from entering the cordoned-off area, so she wouldn't have any problem getting out.

'What are you doing here?' asked Götz.

'What does it look like?' she answered, a sarcastic undertone in her voice.

'I'd say it looks like you're running away.'

She felt his hand on her upper arm and was irritated by the fact that her body was still so sensitive to his touch. After all this time.

'Listen, if I need a bad psychologist then I'll just call myself.' She threw in the last coin.

'You're not bad. You know that. Just because...'

'Because what? Just because I couldn't keep my own daughter from committing suicide, that doesn't say anything about my abilities as a psychologist? Sure...' Ira laughed contemptuously. 'Maybe I should write a guidebook on it.'

She pressed the button for Cola Light Lemon, and the half-litre glass bottle rattled down into the delivery shaft.

'I have an even better idea. How about this: You pull yourself together at long last and stop this goddamn self-pity party.'

'And then what?' she snapped. 'What do I do then?'

'Your goddamn job!' he shouted. Two policemen at the entrance looked over at them. Götz lowered his voice.

'There are seven hostages sitting inside there, and one of them in particular really needs your help.'

'What's that supposed to mean?'

'Well, what do you think it means?' he said, imitating her tone.

Ira leant over to take the bottle out of the tray, but Götz immediately took it from her hands again.

'Do you think I don't realise what you're planning to do?'

'So now you're a psychic too, huh?'

'You're not alone in this world, for fuck's sake. Sara is dead. Okay. You didn't give our relationship a chance after that. Fine. You distanced yourself from everyone that was close to you, and most of all from yourself. Also fine. But maybe right now you should at least think about your other daughter.'

'Katharina will be just fine without my help.' Ira reached angrily for the bottle and tore it from Götz's strong grip.

'I wouldn't be so sure about that if I were you.'

'Oh, she will, trust me. She hasn't wanted to talk to me for a year now. She blames me for Sara's death.'

And she's not far from the truth.

'That's all very possible,' said Götz. 'But now things have changed a little. I'm in contact with her.'

'Since when?'

'Since twenty minutes ago.'

'She called you?'

'Not me. A short while ago an emergency call came through to the UPS headquarters. The hostage who was shot used to work there. And a radio station employee somehow got hold of the man's walkie-talkie.'

'Who?'

'Your daughter!'

Ira dropped the heavy glass bottle. It cracked around the

neck on impact, and the brown liquid immediately began to foam out onto the stone floor.

'But… but, that's not possible…'

'Yes it is. Why do you think I wanted to have you here at all costs? First it was just a suspicion. Katharina has been working on the listener phone lines for a month now. But when we went through the employee lists, we established that she was missing. It seems she's hidden herself under the sink in the studio kitchen.'

'You're lying.'

'Why would I be?'

'Because she's studying law.'

'She jacked it in.'

'But why… why are you only telling me this now?'

'Because I wasn't sure until the walkie-talkie call. She's registered in the employee files under her father's surname, and she only uses her nickname: Kitty. I haven't told Steuer anything about this yet. He can't find out that you're personally affected by the situation until he absolutely has to. He's already against your involvement as it is.'

'You're an asshole,' Ira snarled at him, wiping a tear from her cheek with the back of her hand. 'A goddamn fucking asshole.'

'And you're the only one who can save your daughter.'

He pulled her into his arms and held her close to him. There was a time, in another era, when this empathetic gesture would have been able to make her feel safe and secure. But today all she felt was the fearful certainty that her daughter was lost.

It's hopeless, thought Ira. *Katharina's fate is in the hands of an out-of-control psychopath and a suicidal alcoholic.*

As she stood there crying in Götz's arms, a bitter realisation unfurled deep within her: her daughter had more chance of winning a round of Cash Call this morning than Ira had of successfully leading this hopeless negotiation.

PART II

It's the part of my work that has always seemed the most interesting to me. Having direct conversations with people who live in worlds that we can never gain access to.

Thomas Müller, *Bestie Mensch*

You can discover more about a person in an hour of play than in a year of conversation.

Plato

PART II

1

'Hmmm.'

In the weak hope of fending off the panic attack that was threatening to take over her entire body, Ira inhaled deeply, right down to her belly.

Katharina – Kitty – Katharina – Kitty! Her youngest daughter's forename and nickname shrilled in alternation in her head while the last images of the surveillance video played before her on the computer monitor. She had returned to Diesel's office only a few minutes ago, but Igor, the technician, had already given her direct access to the central server.

'Hmmm,' sighed Ira again, stopping the recording so that the hostage taker, limping along on crutches, froze in midmovement on the landing of the nineteenth floor. She was evaluating the images for the third time already, and yet again she hadn't managed to focus her attention on them.

Ira felt waves of emotion convulsing her body. First rage, then despair, and finally a feeling that she hadn't felt in a long time: fear. Reinhold Messner had once said, after a near-death experience while climbing Mount Everest, that the actual process of dying was the easiest. That the hard part comes before that. While you still have hope.

But in theory, once you have decided you are going to die, everything was really easy.

Ira had said her goodbyes this morning, and hadn't felt any more fear since then. Until now. Fortunately the others in the room, Herzberg and Igor, were oblivious to her panicked state. But deep inside she was like a scared little girl, cowering in the furthest corner of the room through fear of being beaten, hiding from the screams of abuse: 'You're a wreck! A washed-up alcoholic. YOU CAN'T DO IT!'

Ira agreed with her inner voice. Just a few hours ago, she had been about to cross a line from which there was no going back. Now she was moments away from speaking to a potential mass murderer who was holding her only surviving daughter hostage. Katharina. Or Kitty, as she was now calling herself. *It seemed that she hadn't just rejected her mother, but her name too*, thought Ira. *Oh, God! I'm so deeply involved that, legally speaking, there's no way I should take this case on.*

'Do we have a camera in the elevators too?' she asked, mainly just to contribute some intelligent thought.

'No.' Herzberg came to stand next to her and shook his head. 'And the perpetrator has discovered the endoscopy camera that Onassis left up there in the ceiling, and he's put it out of action with a spray can.'

'Well, that was bound to happen.' Ira closed the video window on her computer and opened a Word document, which she titled 'Hostage Taker'. The routine hand movements made it a little easier for her to suppress the surging waves of panic. She opened two further documents and headed them with 'Hostages' and 'Me'.

'Then let's go through everything we know about the perpetrator,' she said a few seconds later, once she was done. All three documents were now aligned alongside one another on the monitor.

'Not very much, unfortunately.' Herzberg shrugged.

'Okay, how about…' Ira stood up, picked up a permanent marker and stepped over to the flip chart, which stood directly in front of the window overlooking Potsdamer Strasse. She tried to remember what had stuck in her mind from the appraisal of the video recordings.

'He's between thirty and thirty-five years old, slim, around a metre eighty-five in height, in good physical shape. He's German, well-educated, an academic. Presumably he graduated in a humanities subject, or medicine.'

As she spoke, she noted the most important facts on the chart, and found herself wondering how much longer she would be able to read her own handwriting for today. Her hands were already perspiring a little. And they would soon start to shake if she continued to neglect her blood alcohol level.

'Okay,' grunted Herzberg, standing up. 'We have his physical description from the video. We're currently running this image through the police database.' He took an A5 colour printout from the scanner and stuck it up on the flip chart. 'But how do you know what he does for a living?'

'Well, first there's the way he talks,' answered Ira mechanically. 'It's noticeably elaborate. The perpetrator uses loanwords, and his sentences consist of more than six words. He uses colloquial speech, dialect and swear words consciously in order to provide a contrast to his otherwise carefully selected vocabulary. He expresses himself eloquently, and his profession probably involves having to speak with people frequently. His voice is trained, and has an agreeable tone. He knows that people enjoy listening to him. And whether it's through his career or in his private life, he has close connections to theatrical performers.'

'How could you possibly know *that*?'

'I'll show you.' Ira pressed the permanent marker into Herzberg's hand, then went back to the desk and opened the file with the surveillance video again.

When she found the right point, she tapped her index finger against the monitor.

'Wig, false teeth, jogging bottoms, beer belly, crutches. The man is perfectly disguised. And do you see how he walks?'

She moved the mouse, and the last few images of the video showed the hostage taker as he slowly shuffled across to the flight of stairs.

'He's acting wonderfully. Not too over-the-top, as an inexperienced amateur might perhaps imitate a man with a disability. Do you see how carefully he positions his bad leg? Either he's an actor himself, or a make-up artist, or – much more probably – he has contacts in the scene, and someone gave him lessons.'

'Don't you think that's a little far-fetched?' Herzberg looked at her sceptically.

'Don't forget the act itself. The hijacking was carried out in an almost military fashion. And the Cash Call idea suggests a perpetrator with above-average creativity.'

'Wonderful. Is there anything else you've deduced from the video?'

'A great deal. But I don't want to waste our valuable time

here with pointless chatter. So I'll just summarise the most important detail in one sentence: He knows someone here at the station.'

Herzberg opened his mouth, but was so stunned that his words came out with a little time delay.

'And how did you figure that out?'

'Think about it. Why did he disguise himself? Why go to the effort?'

'So that he isn't recognised.'

'Okay. But by whom?'

'You mean…?'

'Exactly. The surveillance cameras prove that he only changed in the elevator. So the person who he didn't want to recognise him is unlikely to be someone in the reception. It has to be someone here at the station. Right?'

'Interesting,' Herzberg admitted. 'But why didn't he disguise himself before he even entered the MCB building? Why do it in the elevator, where he had to rush? He could just have gotten ready in his own time at home.'

'Those are the first sensible questions you've asked all morning. And there's one simple answer to all of them: Because our man isn't just creative, but an excellent planner too. Look at this.'

With three mouse clicks, Ira rewound the surveillance video and restarted it at the images recorded at 7 a.m. that morning.

'All the studio guests, with the exception of the UPS driver, arrived in the studio before the hostage taker. And almost all of them had to present their bags for inspection.' Ira turned around to Herzberg, checking to see whether he was paying attention to her words.

'Our friend, on the other hand, arrived at 7:24 a.m. with a briefcase, looking like a typical lawyer. He was waved through without any questions. Clearly he wanted to look serious. He knew that if he showed up in his disguise, he would run the risk of an over-zealous guard frisking him and ruining his plan. He didn't want to take that risk.'

'For some reason this doesn't sound like good news,' said Herzberg, sitting back down in the seat opposite Ira.

'It's not. Because it doesn't just tell us about the perpetrator, but also about what's still to come: The hostage taker is intelligent, creative, and leaves nothing to chance – as we've known since the interlude in the ventilation shaft, if not before. There is a method to everything he does. Even the way in which he executes the hostages. And that's probably the most striking detail about him. Because the fact that he kills systematically is very unusual, as we know.'

Herzberg nodded silently, and Ira was grateful that she didn't need to further explain these basic rules to him. To hostage takers, victims were the best forms of insurance. As long as the hostages were still alive, they were like pawns protecting them from attack, a way of buying their way to freedom. For that reason, contrary to the popular opinion perpetrated by TV crime series, it was very rare for hostage situations to have fatal consequences. For the perpetrator, a dead hostage was useless.

'We can't allow ourselves to get distracted from the game,' Ira continued. 'At first glance it might seem like the act of a lunatic, but it's too well planned for that. This could be a politically motivated attack. That would explain the choice of a radio station, as terrorists often use public media for their aims. But that's contradicted by the fact that he didn't immediately state his demands. Release of prisoners, exchange of hostages, retreat from war zones; usually extremists say right away what they want, and set an ultimatum. Whichever way we look at it, there's only one thing we know for sure!'

'And what's that?'

'He will continue to kill for as long as it takes for him to achieve his goal. Whatever that might be.'

'So that means you're right?' For the first time, fear became visible amid the uncertainty in Herzberg's furrowed expression. Ira briefly reflected that there must be some women who were impressed by his usually pompous manner. But she certainly wasn't one of them. 'There's nothing we can do?' he asked.

The telephone rang. It was in its docking station between Ira and Herzberg's computer monitors. Igor had redirected the main studio number to it.

'Yes, there is,' said Ira, putting her hand on the receiver. 'We have to find out more about this man. And about what he's doing.'

She pointed at the Word document she had created with the title 'Hostage Taker'.

The phone rang a second time. It had a clear tone, almost like a mobile phone or a cheap alarm clock.

'We know that he wants attention. But why? Why today? Why here at the station?' The telephone rang a third time. 'We need to find out his motive.'

Ira let it ring one more time. Then she picked up.

2

'Hello, this is Ira Samin, your negotiator for today. Who am I speaking to, please?'

'Good, very good.'

Ira had turned on the loudspeaker, which meant that everyone in the office could hear the hostage taker's sonorous voice. But she still held the cordless telephone receiver against her ear regardless, to be able to hear the man's words more clearly. Even with the slight hybrid distortion, his baritone still sounded inappropriately likeable.

'Have you already outlined my profile to Herzberg?'

She looked up and through the glass office walls over to the studio complex. As the fire safety shutters to Studio A were still down, she couldn't make out what was going on just a few metres away inside it.

And in the adjoining room. Beneath the sink.

From where she was sitting, all she could see was the first row of news and service desks. Normally at least two people would be sitting there at this hour, taking turns to read the news, present the weather report or establish a connection with the traffic helicopter. Now the entire section was abandoned.

'Yes, we were just talking about you,' said Ira, grimacing

as a grating whistle started up out of nowhere, steadily increasing in volume.

Diesel, who had been just about to make himself comfortable on the garish yellow seat cushion in the opposite corner of the office, jumped up and turned down the ceiling loudspeaker using the button next to the door. Then he pressed the life-size blonde doll's breast, which turned off the radio.

'Rookie mistake,' he mumbled, shaking his head in amusement at the feedback.

'We're on air,' continued the hostage taker. 'Everyone can hear us. So please turn your radio down, Ira. Or better yet, turn it off right now so we don't have any more disturbance.'

'Have done.'

'Thank you. Now we can get started.'

'Do you want to tell me your name, so I know how to address you?'

'This isn't about me, Ira. But it's nice that you're keeping to the guidebook. Good old-school procedure: tell the hostage taker your name, but not your rank, so that he doesn't demand to speak to your superior. And then ask him his own name, in order to establish a personal connection as quickly as possible.'

'You seem to know my line of work very well. Okay then, so what should I call you?'

'Again: that's irrelevant.'

'But I'll have to call you something if we intend to keep talking.'

'Fine then. How about Jan?'

Ira typed the forename into the word document headed 'Hostage Taker'.

'Okay, Jan, I'd like to help you, but you're not going to make it easy for me if you shoot a hostage every single hour.'

'Interesting, you said "hostage". It's normally advisable not to do that, isn't it? Wouldn't it be safer to distract my attention from the people around me and involve me in a less dangerous conversation instead?'

'Normally, yes,' confirmed Ira. It was true; the word 'hostage' was indeed one of the forbidden words during a negotiation, along with 'no', 'give up', 'punishment', 'crime' and 'kill'. But by her estimation, this was a different case. She briefly contemplated whether she should speak openly with Jan about her strategies, then decided it was worth the risk. Jan had clearly read everything there was to read on negotiation theories. If she wanted to win his trust, then she could only do it with absolute honesty. 'We both know you're playing a game here. That's why I'm mentioning the hostages. Because by doing so, I humanise them.'

'So that they seem less like toys to me?' The man laughed briefly, his tone revealing genuine amusement. 'Nicely put, Ira. I'm glad they exchanged that windbag Herzberg for you. You seem to know your stuff.'

'Thank you, Jan.'

She saw with relief that Götz, who had just come into the office, was giving her an encouraging look. Clearly he approved of her unconventional approach. Unlike Herzberg, who looked like someone had just slapped him in the face.

'So, it seems you're the boss in the studio now?' asked Ira, in the hope that she would find out something about any possible accomplices from his answer.

She was astounded when Jan gave her a clear response, without beating around the bush: 'Let's not waste our time with irrelevant details. I work alone. No accomplices. And in order to answer your next question right away: Yes, we're all fine. The remaining seven, at least. Including me.'

'Seven hostages = six living/one dead,' wrote Ira in the document entitled 'hostages', adding a mental question mark. The information corresponded with the documents Götz had given her: the personnel rota for the morning show and the guest list for the station tour. Alongside Timber and his producer Flummi, the hostages also included a pregnant woman, a young couple and a middle-aged administration worker. The seventh hostage, the UPS driver, was already dead. Ira offered up her thanks to a higher being that Kitty wasn't yet included in Jan's list, that she was obviously still cowering undiscovered beneath the sink.

'Listen, Jan, we'd like to remove Manfred Stuck from the studio.'

'Why? He's dead.'

'We could bring you something you need in exchange. Food, medication? How is Sandra Marwinski doing?'

'Our mother-to-be has everything she needs,' answered Jan. 'And no, thank you. We all had a good breakfast this morning. We don't need anything.'

'So what exactly is it that you want?' she asked directly, in the hope of getting a clear statement.

'Don't you know, Ira?'

'No. I wouldn't presume to judge you or read your mind. I don't know you, but I'd like to get to know you better.'

'That's good. That's very good...' The hostage taker

laughed out loud, then continued: 'I thought it was an unwritten rule for negotiation leaders never to lie to the perpetrator?'

'Yes, it is.' Ira had even given a presentation on the topic once. The negotiation during a hostage situation was a lot like a relationship. Both can only be successful if there is a foundation of trust. And nothing destroys trust more fundamentally than the hostage taker uncovering a lie from the negotiator.

'We've only been talking for two minutes, and I've already caught you telling a lie,' Jan continued.

'How do you mean?'

'That the last thing you really want to do this morning is have a conversation with me. Unless I tell you something about your daughter Sara. Is that right?'

Ira looked at the storage container beneath Diesel's desk and wondered if there was anything to drink inside it.

In an attempt to concentrate her thoughts, she fixed her gaze on the light-blue mouse pad next to her computer.

'How do you know Sara?' she asked eventually, her tone steady.

'I don't. I just Googled your name while we've been talking. "Daughter of criminal psychologist drowns in bathtub." A year ago, Sara's *accident* was worthy of a whole six lines in the *Berliner Zeitung*.'

From the way he emphasised 'accident', she could hear that he knew. The story about an epileptic fit had been a lie, of course, to save Sara from the autopsy that suicide victims are normally subjected to. Ira hadn't been able to bear the thought of some unknown pathologist cutting Sara open and weighing every one of her organs. Back then, Götz had needed to use all the contacts he had in order to cover up the real cause of death in the files.

'So you know what it's like to suddenly lose a loved one forever.'

To Ira, Jan's words sounded genuine. *But he's an actor*, she reminded herself.

'Yes.' Ira tensed up. On the one hand it was good for her to quickly establish a personal line of communication with the hostage taker. But on the other, this was about her dead daughter. The reason why she had wanted to put an end to it all today. *The reason why I still want to put an end to it all!* And now she was talking about her deepest emotional wounds to an unpredictable psychopath, and one who unknowingly had her daughter Kitty under his control.

'Again: what do you want?' she asked abruptly, forcing herself to concentrate. When the answer came, it was one she hadn't reckoned with.

'Please open the following webpage: http://leoni1X2dD. net.'

Without putting down the phone, Ira reached for the mouse, and the screensaver disappeared from the monitor. Then she opened the internet search engine, and just a few seconds later the browser began to search for the website.

The image of an attractive young woman appeared. She had dark brown-black eyes, the same tone as her thick, curly hair. A brief glance at the picture was enough to stir a mix of envy and melancholy in Ira. She had looked like that once, and it wasn't so long ago. Although she had to admit that she herself had never looked quite that perfect.

With the exception of a small scar above her cheekbone,

this woman had an almost flawless face with gentle Eurasian features, elegantly arched brows and full lips, behind which beautifully straight teeth were sure to be concealed. But they couldn't be seen in the photo, for the woman was staring solemnly into the camera without smiling. And yet she didn't exude that unapproachable coldness common in attractive women who are aware of their beauty. She seemed serious, but at the same time vulnerable. Strong, but in need of support. A combination that most men find irresistible, for it stirs both the protective instinct and the romantic in them. Ira was unable to estimate her body measurements. The picture was cropped just beneath her slender neck, which was framed by a white silk blouse with a sweeping neckline.

'Who is she?' asked Ira.

'Leoni Gregor!'

'That's a beautiful name.'

'And a beautiful woman.'

'Yes, you're right. Who is she?'

'My fiancée. Find Leoni.'

'Okay. We'll look for her. But to do that I'll need to know more about her. What information can you give me?'

'She's the woman I'm going to marry. Leoni Gregor. Eight months ago today she was kidnapped. I'd like to know where she is.'

Ira saw with satisfaction that Herzberg was noting down all the important details. The conversation would be digitally recorded, but she didn't want to rely on that. Especially as she probably wouldn't have time to listen to the audio files again.

'Kidnapped? What exactly happened?'

'That's exactly what I'd like to find out from you. That's why I'm here.'

Ira looked up and flinched in shock. Steuer was standing directly in front of her. She hadn't even noticed that Götz had left the room and that the mission leader had taken his place. Now he was staring down at her with an enraged expression. He was also waving his fat index finger around in the air threateningly and making a clear gesture with the other hand.

Hang up.

What was his problem?

She shook her head angrily and pulled her concentration back to the negotiation.

'Okay, Jan. I'll see what I can do. But I'm going to need time.'

'No problem. You have all the time in the world. In the meantime, I'll continue to present my new radio show. So don't worry, I won't get bored.'

'Then you're going to suspend the next Cash Call?' asked Ira hopefully.

'Why on earth would I do that? The next round will start in forty-five minutes.'

'Jan, I can't help you this way.'

'Yes you can, by finding Leoni. And until then I'll keep playing. Round after round. Hour after hour. As long as it takes until I finally see my fiancée again.'

'Please, Jan. It won't work like this. Either we agree on a compromise, or...'

'Or what?'

'Or I'll hang up and go home.'

'You won't do that.'

'Give me one reason why I shouldn't.' Ira was slowly becoming enraged. She shouldn't be here. She felt helpless because of Kitty. And even more so because her daughter wasn't the only thing constantly on her mind. The thought of taking a sip of alcohol was almost as constant.

'Fine!' she blurted out. 'Then off you go, Jan. Play round after round, shoot all your hostages one by one. Your audience is big enough already, so you don't need me as an onlooker too. Either we make a deal now, or you can negotiate with Herzberg again. Because one thing's for sure: If you don't give me some elbow room, then sooner or later I'll be pulled off the negotiation. No politician can afford to have the entire nation listen to public executions. And the mission leader is a very good politician, if you get what I mean.'

An uneasy silence hung in the air. Not realising that she was holding her breath, Ira tried to imagine the hostage taker's face. Was he debating feverishly? Weighing up his options calmly? Or was he grinning mockingly at her laughable stammers?'

'Fine,' he said, finally interrupting her thoughts. 'I'll give you a period of grace. The next Cash Call won't be played until 10:35. Use the time wisely.'

'Thanks, but that won't...'

Ira gave a start as her sentence was interrupted by Phil Collins singing 'In the Air Tonight'. The conversation had come to an end. The perpetrator had started the next song. The show was going on.

3

'Report to me downstairs in the control centre. Right now!' barked Steuer at the very same moment Ira hung up the phone. He was leaning forwards with both hands on her desk, and Ira noticed that the stench of his breath had gotten even worse. Currywurst with onions.

'What's your problem, you great big…' she exploded.

'Go ahead, say it,' he challenged her. 'Just give me a reason!'

She swallowed down the bitter retort, but not her rage. 'What is this? Why are you bursting in here in the middle of my negotiation, distracting me during the first contact initiation… and now you expect me to waste valuable time by running along after you for a meeting? You heard it yourself; I only have one round's respite. He'll be starting the next Cash Call in 100 minutes.'

'Yes. Thanks to your amateur display just now.'

'Amateur?'

'You heard me.' Steuer was almost yelling, but then lowered his voice down to the volume which an angry father might use on his drunken son who had stayed out too late. 'The perpetrator knows every one of your negotiation tricks.

And you're even giving him extra tutoring, for God's sake! Do you realise that all the radio stations across Berlin and Brandenburg are transmitting the 101 Point 5 programme live to warn people to answer the phone with the correct slogan?'

'Good.'

'No, it's not good. You're making a laughing stock of the entire SEK. You're letting yourself be made a fool of. I don't know what on earth possessed me to let Götz talk me into this. I already felt sick to my stomach when he dragged you here this morning, but I had no idea it would be this bad. I gave you a second chance after the failure with the sniper, and you went and flushed it straight down the can! One thing's for sure: You've failed, Ira. All you've managed to do is postpone the inevitable by an hour. That man is going to see this through, regardless of how long you ramble on with him. Because he knows he's a goner. The maniac has already killed one hostage. He's already broken the dam, the decisive threshold to the fatal act has already been crossed. What do you plan to do now? You can't offer him open prison any more. Or probation. He'll be banged up for life, and he knows it.'

Ira counted slowly to ten before she responded to his verbal torrent. This was less for the purpose of calming herself down, and more to give herself time to think. *What's going on here? What's Steuer up to?* Fine, so he has to make it clear from the start that he doesn't want her here. When she headed off towards the exit earlier, he congratulated her snidely on her wise decision. But then Götz had talked her into carrying on. Steuer had been irritated by her sudden change of mind, of course, but ultimately he had let her take up contact with the hostage taker. Probably just so that he could later say he had tried everything possible. But now he was losing his composure again after the very first negotiation conversation. *Why? What happened?* Ira's thoughts were on a rollercoaster. It seemed to her that his criticism of her tactics was just a pretence. Did it have something to do with the fact that Jan had mentioned her dead daughter? Did Steuer already know about Kitty? Götz had expressly promised her that he wouldn't tell anyone about that.

But maybe it had already leaked out? No. If it had, Steuer would have torn her to pieces. None of this makes any sense.

'You're overlooking one thing,' said Ira, once she had counted to eight. 'I was wrong earlier. There is a way to stop him. The negotiation was successful after the very first minute.'

'Nonsense,' snorted Steuer.

'It was. At first I thought he just wanted attention. But that's not true. I was wrong. The man has a motive, and now we know what it is. Leoni. He's looking for his girlfriend. It's really simple: We just need to find this woman and bring her to him.'

Ira nodded at the monitor, where Leoni's photo was still displayed. Herzberg had already made a printout and pinned it next to the picture of Jan on the flip chart.

'Well, that might be a bit difficult, my dear,' said Steuer sarcastically, wiping the sweat from his brow with his bare hand.

'Why?'

'Because that woman has been dead for eight months.'

Ira felt the wind being knocked out of her, and her lips formed a silent 'Oh!'

'Now do you see why there's nothing you can do to fix this? You're negotiating with a psychopathic mass murderer. He lives in a different world to you, Ira, and he speaks a different language.'

Ira pressed her furry tongue against the back of her teeth, as if that were the only way to prise her mouth open.

'So what are you going to do?' she asked.

'What I do best. Solve things by storming.'

As if he had needed onomatopoeic back-up to his words, an undecipherable volley of words hissed out of Steuer's walkie-talkie.

'Yes?'

'… it's best you… take a look,' Ira heard the broken sentences of some know-it-all special operation officer. Then, clearer this time: 'I think we've found something.'

'What is it?'

Steuer waited impatiently for the answer, asked a quick follow-up question, then strode out of the negotiation centre. Ira stayed there alone. A feeling of loneliness overwhelmed her, and it took her a while to realise what she had really heard:

'There's an anomaly here.'

'An anomaly?'

'Yes, with the employee list.'

4

'What's going on here?'

Every word spat out by the chief prosecutor in his Reinickendorf office was imbued with a mixture of contempt and disbelief.

'Sorry?' The Croatian housekeeper, who had come running, cast her gaze nervously over the vintage furnishings, which only irritated Johannes Faust even more. *Stupid cow*. Of course she would act as though there were nothing wrong.

'Who's been in my study?'

Faust looked down at her. In contrast to his tall, gaunt figure, Maria looked like a garden gnome with an apron and a mop.

'Did I not expressly forbid you from coming in here alone?' he asked threateningly. Faust knit his grey eyebrows so tightly together that his usually taut, bony forehead became completely covered with wrinkles. Maria was only permitted to clean in here while he was present, and so far she had always strictly obeyed his instructions. Just like she did the cleaning plan which he had compiled for her, the contents of which had to be completed fastidiously and in the prescribed order. First wipe the floorboards (with a damp, not wet, cloth!), then empty the paper bin, then dust the walls, ceiling and bureau.

'Who's been in here? Come on, out with it!' commanded Faust again. His voice had now taken on that strict tone that usually only defendants in court rooms needed to fear. As he spoke, he held his head in such a way that his rimless glasses threatened to slip right off his nose.

'*She* was here,' the housekeeper admitted finally. 'She said she was allowed.'

'She *who*?'

'The young woman.'

Of course. Only Regina could be that impertinent. Faust went over to the built-in wall shelving and shook his head. He hated disorder. Now of all times, while he was preparing for what might be the biggest case of his career, not one single file was on his desk. And now this too! He always took such painstaking care to make sure that all his legal reference books were tidy, ordered on the shelves by edition and – this was the most important thing – with their spines flush with one another. His ex-wife had had the nerve to move the brown *NJW band 1989 I* three centimetres backwards. Because she knew that this would send him into a rage. And because she wanted him to know that she had been here. Unannounced.

'What did she want?'

'She didn't say. She waited for a while, and when you didn't come she left again.'

'Hmm.' The parquet flooring creaked under his cleated soles as Faust took two big steps over to his desk. He pulled open the top, copper-hinged drawer and checked to make sure that the wad of money was still in the small strongbox.

Not that the loss would have affected him financially. After all, following recent events he had more than enough money. But it was the principle of the matter. Last time she had found the cash he had been keeping in the house for a rainy day, and had made off with the €5,000. 'As a little compensation for our marriage,' she had scribbled on a sheet of his own stationery. Bitch! As if the monthly payments weren't more than enough for the few happy hours he had managed to scrounge from her in fourteen years.

'Should I stay?' As Maria shyly directed her question to him, his mobile began to ring.

At first he felt confused. Then sick to his stomach.

Until now, Faust had only needed to use this mobile telephone once. And then only as a test run, when they were explaining the functions to him. Faust hated modern communication technology and avoided everything that even remotely resembled the internet, email or wireless telephones. But right now he needed to be contactable at all times. He had even gotten himself a laptop. Too much was at stake right now, so close to the trial. With an impatient gesture, Faust shooed away his housekeeper, who closed the double doors behind her with visible relief. Then he laboriously opened the mobile and prepared himself for the worst. His contact had promised to use this number only in an emergency.

'We have a problem!'

'The hostage taking?'

'Not directly.'

'What then?'

'The hostage taker's demand. He wants *her*.'

Faust stood rooted to the spot in the middle of his office.

Her!

Her name didn't need to be uttered; he knew immediately who was meant.

Leoni!

And it was also clear what this meant for him.

'How is that possible?'

'I can't tell you more than that right now.'

Of course. The line wasn't secure. Faust reminded himself to keep a clear head and not to act carelessly. Despite the fact that naked fear was wrapping itself around his body like a wet towel.

'When can we talk undisturbed?'

'I'll think of something. First you need to figure out the situation from your end. We'll talk in twenty minutes' time.'

'Twenty minutes,' repeated Faust. He cleared his throat hoarsely and hung up without saying goodbye. Looking over at the bookshelves, he found himself wishing that the askew volume had remained his biggest problem this morning.

Twenty minutes, he thought. *Twenty minutes? Maybe by then it will already be too late. Maybe by then I'll already be dead.*

5

Ira leant exhaustedly against the wall in Diesel's office, which now looked almost like a proper negotiation centre and no longer like the playroom of a barking-mad eccentric. After Igor and Herzberg had been assigned to the mission leadership, Götz had come in and covered the windows with copies of the site floor plan, including information on the location of all important technical cables.

'Has he found out about Kitty?' she asked him as he tacked up the last plan. Diesel was out fetching himself a coffee, so they were undisturbed for a moment.

'Who?'

'Steuer. His men found something on the employee list.'

'I know. But that's not a problem, it's intentional. I palmed him off with an outdated list before. So it's no wonder that they ran into difficulties doing the inventory.' He looked at her with concern. 'Besides, you should be worrying about yourself instead.'

'Why, what's wrong with me?'

'You need to get a grip of yourself. Don't keep attacking Steuer in front of everyone like that.'

'Why not, what do I have to lose?'

'Your daughter,' he reminded her. 'Steuer is a hothead.

I had to use all my powers of persuasion to convince him to let you negotiate. You know what he's like. Just because he's wearing a suit and doesn't carry a gun doesn't make him any less dangerous. Quite the opposite, in fact. I don't know why, but he wants to storm in there no matter what. So don't give him any reason to break off the negotiations prematurely. Because if he sends me and my guys in, there's nothing I can do about it.' He looked her deep in the eyes. She had to avert her gaze, as if just his intense, clear-blue gaze alone could inflame her pupils.

'There will be nothing else I can do to help you and Kitty if it comes to that,' he added, pressing a red scrapbook into her hand. 'Here.'

'What's this?'

'Everything that the researchers were able to gather together on Leoni Gregor in such a short space of time.'

Ira opened the folder and saw a collection of newspaper article printouts. She scanned the headlines: 'Severe accident with fatal consequences.' 'Young woman dies at the scene.' 'Car fuel tank explodes due to workshop error. Insurance has to pay.'

She leafed through to the penultimate page. An A3 sheet. On the left-hand side was what had probably been the last ever photograph of Leoni. A completely charred body on an aluminium table with a drain tube. On the right-hand side was a fax copy. It had clearly been made from a thin carbon copy, and was hard to decipher. But it was easily recognisable nonetheless as the autopsy report.

Leoni Gregor, 26, female, German, 1.72 m; 56 kg. Cause of death: Cervical fracture with basal skull fracture and cerebral compression resulting from a car accident. Burns post mortem.

'She was a secretary in a large, respected law firm here in Potsdamer Platz,' Götz continued. 'Steuer's right. That madman wants us to arrange a meeting with a ghost.'

'How did the accident happen?' Ira asked.

'The workshop dropped the ball. The nuts weren't screwed on correctly when the summer tyres were put on. They held out for six months, then the bolts came loose, and two wheels came off at the same time. In her initial shock, Leoni must have confused the accelerator with the brake, and ended up racing at high speed towards a traffic light then colliding head-on with the wall of a house. There was a chain reaction. Her car burst into flames.'

Götz took the folder from her hand and pulled out a photo she had flicked past.

'Ouch.' Ira grimaced as though she had just swallowed some bitter cough mixture.

The BMW looked as though it had collided with a fuel tanker. The charred bodywork had been compressed both from the side and the top, almost all the window panes were missing or shattered, and the boot and bonnet curved upwards into the sky like an outstretched tongue.

Ira reached up to her neck and tried to loosen the tension in her shoulders by gently circling her head. But she didn't hold out any great hope. Her steadily intensifying headache wasn't triggered by anything orthopaedic. If she wanted to carry on, she would have to find something to drink as soon as possible.

'What information do we have on Jan?'

'An investigation team is looking into Leoni Gregor's

social connections right now. But we only have a forename to go on, and I very much doubt that it's his real one.'

'And what do we know about the hostages?'

'What is there to know? It's just a randomly selected group. They won the studio tour in a sweepstake. We're currently locating their next of kin.'

'Good.' She paused, then asked the question that had been on the tip of her tongue the whole time. The one she had swallowed down again and again through fear.

'Is there any news on Katharina?'

Now Götz paused briefly and took a deep breath before he answered.

'No, Kitty hasn't been in touch.' He lifted his right hand, which was clad in a black glove, and for a moment he looked like a fielder in an American baseball game. 'But that's a good sign,' he assured her.

'Not necessarily. I have to talk to her.'

'I can't allow that.' Götz shook his head vigorously.

'What do I need to do to be allowed to speak to her?'

Götz pulled off the heavy glove, and was just about to brush a strand of hair out of Ira's face when the telephone rang. He flinched and pulled his hand back.

'Speak to Jan first.'

6

Why is it taking so long?

The hostage taker drummed the fingers of his left hand impatiently on the edge of the studio mixing desk. They left behind clear imprints on the black foam cladding.

He cleared his throat. After the fourth ring, Ira finally picked up. He didn't wait for her to offer any hackneyed words of greeting.

'Have you found anything out yet?'

'Yes, I just received the autopsy report.'

'Leoni's? Then you're just wasting the precious time I so generously gave you.'

Jan glanced over at the large TV which hung from the studio ceiling on a sturdy support arm. This was normally where the presenters followed the latest news on the teletext. Now he was speedily flicking through the fifty-seven channels with the remote control, noting with satisfaction that he was the main topic on almost all the channels.

'What do you mean by that?' asked Ira.

'Like I said: I'll only stop when you bring Leoni to me. Here. Alive. In the studio.'

He paused on the twenty-four hour news channel.

A looped report was explaining to the population

how they needed to answer the phone. There was also an announcement of a press conference in which the Minister for Internal Affairs would be giving an overview of the hostage situation.

Good. Very good.

'As soon as I hold Leoni in my arms, alive and well, this whole nightmare will be over,' he continued.

'I know,' says Ira, her voice sounding slightly resigned. 'But I'm not yet sure how I'm supposed to achieve that, Jan. According to the documents I'm currently holding in my hands, your fiancée died in a car accident. On the nineteenth of September. At 5:55 p.m.'

'Yes, yes. I know the report. I saw it myself. I even have a copy at home. But it's nonsense. Complete bullshit.'

'Why?'

'Because Leoni is still alive!'

'What makes you so sure?'

Jan scratched himself on the back of his neck with the gun. 'Well, I'll leave out for the time being all the madness that has occurred just in the last half hour since I mentioned Leoni on the radio, Ira. You can't even begin to imagine what's going on here.'

He glanced at the thirty-three wine-red LED lights of the telephone unit next to the studio mixing desk. They were blinking rhythmically in unison. Based upon the show producer's disbelieving expression, even an experienced radio professional like Flummi had never experienced such a sustained display of pyrotechnics.

'All the lines are busy. Incessantly. Can you believe that, Ira? All over the city – no, what am I saying? – all over the *country*, by now, there are people wanting to speak to me. And every other one allegedly has information about Leoni's whereabouts.'

Jan looked back up at the television. To the side of the newsreader, there was now a photograph of his fiancée. Then the shot changed, and an image of the MCB building filled the studio's slightly dusty TV screen. Either they were archive images, or the high-rise was being filmed right at this moment from a helicopter.

'A forty-four-year-old woman from Tübingen was convinced that she picked up Leoni as a hitchhiker yesterday,' Jan continued. 'And an elderly man from Kladow wanted money to bring her to me. Someone even offered me naked photos.'

'You've really summoned the spirits now.'

'No I haven't!' Jan contradicted her vehemently. 'It's not my fault. It didn't have to go this far. Someone out there is lying to me. Someone with a lot of influence and power. And either I draw them out into the open, or a lot of people are going to die today.'

'If I'm honest, I don't understand,' said Ira. She sounded genuinely confused.

'Okay, Ira.' Jan looked at the big studio clock. 'We have about another forty minutes until the next round. But we won't need that long. I'm going to tell you a story. My story.'

7

Where is Diesel?

Ira mouthed the words silently as she put on the telephone headset; she wanted to be able to walk around the room as she talked. Herzberg merely shrugged his shoulders before continuing to type on his computer. Igor just gave her a questioning glance. Both of them had come back into the negotiation centre only a few moments ago, after Steuer had given them God-knows-what kind of instructions, and the chief editor still hadn't come back from his trip to get coffee.

'I always knew that I was privileged, Ira. My whole life, the sun was always shining on me,' she heard Jan say, and there was a hint of regret in his voice. 'I had everything you could wish for: a respectable job, financial security and a beautiful woman. But one day, completely out of the blue, it was torn away from me. My girlfriend was abducted, and once I began to investigate her disappearance, from that moment on my life shattered into a pile of worthless shards.'

'Just a moment! Why do you believe that someone abducted Leoni?' probed Ira.

'Not *someone*. The state.'

'That sounds a little...'

'Unbelievable? I know. But only the state has the power to do what was done to me.'

'And what was that?'

'Let me pose a counter-question: Apart from love, what constitutes a human being? What do you need in order to exist? In order to breathe? To push back the warm blanket in the morning and step into the cold world?'

My children, was the first thought that shot into Ira's mind. But he had already excluded *love*.

'What could you really not do without? What could someone not take away from you, because without it you would just be a shadow?'

'I don't know,' hesitated Ira. 'Maybe my music.'

As soon as she spoke, she wished she could take back her answer. In truth, she wasn't even sure why she had said it in the first place. Once, in another life, she had made a lot of music. Played the drums. She had taken lessons for years, then spent even longer keeping numerous bands together with her dedication. She was almost embarrassed that she had forgotten the time when they used to perform in Berlin's backstreet bars, how wonderful it had been. And even more so that it had taken the prompting of a homicidal hostage taker to remind her of it.

'Music is a good answer,' said Jan. 'Some say sex. Others say sport. And with me it was my work. I was a psychologist. And I was really good, too. I had my own practice and didn't have to worry about money. But that's not the most important thing. Do you know the difference between a job and a profession? For me, practicing psychology wasn't a job, but a profession. More than that, it was a calling. Without my work, I can't exist. And they took it from me.'

'Who are *they*? And how did *they* do that?'

'Well, when I first started to ask questions, everyone was friendly and patient. The man from the district office showed me the death certificate. The police showed me the autopsy photo. But when I asked to see Leoni's body, they said it wasn't possible. Then I wanted access to the investigation files regarding the alleged accident. After all, the car did explode.'

'*Explode?*' Ira thought back to the newspaper photos that Götz had just shown her.

'Yes. It's a little unusual for two wheels to suddenly fall off at the same time. But that was just the catalyst for the short circuit in the alternator. The cable caught fire. Caused by a faulty replacement part, which I allegedly installed myself. Me! And yet I can barely measure the oil. I would never voluntarily mess around with an alternator. But that's very convenient, don't you think?'

'In what way?'

'Well, the manufacturer is off the hook, because it wasn't their mistake. And I can't make a complaint because the workshop's insurance paid for all the damages. But wait, it gets even better.'

As she listened, Ira wrote a reminder on a yellow Post-it note and stuck it to the file containing the autopsy report.

Where are the investigation files?

'I wanted to see the car. Of course it had already been scrapped. Can you imagine? The tank explodes, my girlfriend burns to death, but there's no lawsuit for involuntary manslaughter? Instead, €125,000 lands in my account from the insurance company. And another €100,000 from the manufacturer. Without any legal proceedings or verdict. Even though the official claim was that I was responsible.'

'That sounds hard to believe.'

'Wait, it gets even better. I wanted to go public with the case, and wrote to every TV, newspaper and radio editorial I knew. Even here at 101 Point 5. But no one answered. Instead, I received a visit from two men who I presume were from the Federal Intelligence Service. They told me in no uncertain terms what would happen to me if I didn't immediately stop my investigations.'

'But you didn't stop?'

'No. And the two gentlemen in the black suits kept their word. First drugs were found in the boot of my car during a routine speed check. Then the chamber withdrew my licence without a hearing. And that took away the only thing I still had left along with my grief over Leoni. My profession.'

'Listen...'

Ira reached gratefully for the paper cup that Herzberg was handing her and took a sip. Either he had seen her dry lips and the thin veil of sweat on her forehead, or he had noticed that her voice was becoming croaky. Maybe there was an attentive gentleman hiding in there beneath his baby-like face after all.

'That all sounds terrible, Jan. Almost unbelievable. I can't even begin to imagine what you have had to go through in the last weeks. Everything you have told me is, without a doubt, unjust, cynical and cruel. It may well be proof of the despotism of our state, in which some people have more rights than others. But it is *not* proof that Leoni is still alive.'

She took another sip. The water was cold. But not as cold as Jan's last words before he broke the connection again.

'I think we're wasting our time, Ira. Instead of talking, we should do what we're actually here to do. You find Leoni. And I'll play Cash Call.'

8

The air inside the small radio studio was stuffy. The soundproofed cabin wasn't equipped for the prolonged presence of so many people, and the six hostages were producing a mix of fear-induced sweat, adrenaline and bodily heat that was being sucked from the room far too slowly by the air ventilation system. Even though Jan had long since taken off the fake wig and extricated himself from the majority of his disguise, he was still sweating in his tracksuit and had to keep wiping his forehead. But that could also be down to the fact that the anti-anxiety tablets he had taken on his way to the station were slowly losing their effect. The recommended dose was once every four hours. He hadn't expected this to last any longer than that. *Not beyond the death of the first hostage.* But the third hour was already beginning, and the second Cash Call was imminent. Ira was proving herself to be cooperative and non-judgemental. But quite clearly no one out there was providing her with the relevant information. He would have to step up the pressure. And that meant: Something had gone wrong!

Jan was just about to get a glass of water from the next room when Sandra, the pregnant redhead with the disabled

He looked her up and down, then jerked his head towards the studio kitchen.

'There's a sink in there. I can't offer you any more than that.'

'And how is that supposed to work? I'm not a contortionist, you know,' she said, but walked towards the kitchen all the same. Ever since he had eliminated the UPS driver, she was the only one of the hostages who still dared to speak to him. Timber and the accountant were staring nervously at the floor, the couple from Marzahn were gripping onto one another, and Flummi was stoically lining one music file up after the next. Jan was allowing him to consult with Timber for this. Normally all the music was scheduled by a computer programme, but for Timber's morning show there was no playlist. The star presenter was the only one at the station who was still allowed to hand-pick his songs. A privilege which he was granted as long as the listening figures delivered.

'I guess you overlooked that in your plan, didn't you?' hissed the nurse. 'Hostages need to go to the toilet now and again, you know.'

Jan was surprised. It was as though no one wanted to stand out, for fear of becoming one of the first choices for the next round. Everyone was trying to make themselves as invisible as possible. Everyone except Sandra.

'What's wrong?' she whispered to Jan as she pushed past him into the kitchen. 'Why is it taking so long?'

He looked at her with irritation and, almost by reflex, laid a finger on his lips.

'Don't worry. Everything's under control,' he whispered back, pushing her into the neighbouring room.

'And bring me a glass of water, please,' he called as the door closed behind her.

When he turned back towards the mixing desk, Jan registered out of the corner of his eye that the accountant had also slipped out of his role for a brief moment. He was sitting just two steps away at the studio bar and looked as though his body couldn't make up its mind between a brief fainting spell or a complete nervous breakdown. But then his shaking stopped abruptly. His breathing became calm, and he looked at the big studio clock on the opposite wall. Just another thirty minutes to the next round.

Theodor Wildenau turned his head back in Jan's direction, whose body tensed up as though he had just stepped beneath an unexpectedly cold shower. Jan felt afraid. Intensely afraid that the man would say something. Now. Far too soon!

But the accountant remained calm. He shook his almost-bald head in a barely perceptible manner. Looked downwards at the floor. Then, a moment later, he began to tremble again.

Jan looked around the studio. He breathed out in relief. None of the others had noticed a thing.

9

One floor below, Diesel stood there in the 101 Point 5 accounts department, singing cheerfully as he cut a hole in the document safe with a blowtorch.

He could have asked for permission, of course. Probably the managing director of the station would even have hurried over in person with the appropriate keys. But only probably. He could check his suspicion much more safely and quickly with the flame cutter. And besides, Diesel had been wanting to test this thing out for ages. From the minute he had found it in the warehouse two weeks ago, he had been longing for a good opportunity to arise. And here it was.

'Sandy...' he sang off-key to the melody of the Stones classic 'Angie'. 'Saaandieee... is your file heeeeeeeere?'

By the time he reached the third chorus, he had completed the uneven circle around the lock. Diesel was almost disappointed at the unspectacular ease with which the door opened after that. But it wasn't like there was hoards of money stored in the cupboard-sized safe, after all; it was just the listener index. The fact that it was locked away at all was only down to the strict regulations of the data protection act. No one had ever wanted to steal it. Until today.

Diesel grimaced as he saw the fifty grey files with their carefully labelled backs turned to him. For him they were the ultimate physical manifestation of mindless boredom. How could anyone earn a living by hole-punching and filing paper? What was wrong with these people? He wouldn't last twenty seconds here as an admin worker.

Diesel pulled from his back trouser pocket the list with the names of the listener club members who had won the studio tour today:

Martin Kubichek
Sandra Marwinski
Cindy and Maik Petereit
Manfred Stuck
Theodor Wildenau

There were two 'K' files, and three with the letter 'M'. Diesel grabbed the first of each. A few moments later, he had already confirmed his suspicion. He quickly found what he was looking for in 'P', too. Only 'S' interfered with his good mood. He couldn't find the name 'Stuck' anywhere in the index. 101 Point 5 Berlin, unlike the other stations in the city, had made a late start in building up a listeners' club, so they only had around 70,000 registered members in their database. This was why the entire index could be housed in one single cabinet safe. But despite this, at first Diesel wasn't able to locate the UPS driver in any of the four folders covering the letter 'S'. Eventually he noticed that two sheets of paper were stuck together. His joy over this discovery immediately vanished again when he read the A4 sheet on which the club member's relevant personal information was provided. It included everything from their place of residence to their age, telephone number, music preferences, birthdate, email address and the date their membership in the competition club had began.

Damn it! thought Diesel as he checked Manfred Stuck's details. *Everything normal. Was I wrong after all?*

The fourth name, Theodor Wildenau, was another match. Only the UPS employee, Stuck, didn't fit the pattern.

Diesel leant back against the welded-open document cabinet and pulled a crumpled packet of chewing gum from his back trouser pocket. He had given up smoking four months ago, and chewed spicy cinnamon gum to help with the cravings.

Think! Think, damn it!

When the hostage taker had mentioned the name of his girlfriend for the first time, Diesel had remembered a conversation he had had months ago down in Potsdamer Platz. His conversation partner had been a guy who looked as though he had been wearing the same clothes for a week. The man had been poking around in his latte macchiato with a fork the whole time, but hadn't drunk a single sip during their conversation, instead telling a completely insane story. About a woman called Leoni.

But what had his name been?

Diesel was just following a spontaneous moment of intuition and reaching once more for the folder with the letter 'M' when someone cleared their throat behind him. He jumped so violently that he swallowed his chewing hum. Without knowing what was lying in wait, he turned slowly around to the door. Then he tried to capture the gaze of one of the men who had their machine guns aimed at him. He didn't succeed. All three SEK officials were wearing riot helmets with screened panels.

'Do you have a death wish or something?' asked the leader of the troop, taking a step towards him. His voice sounded familiar to Diesel. 'You're supposed to be keeping the programme running upstairs. What are you doing down here?'

'I had a suspicion.'

'What are you talking about?'

'M.' Diesel gestured with his head towards the filing cabinet.

'M what?' asked Götz. At his discreet signal, one of the two other SEK men stepped to Diesel's side and grabbed the file with the corresponding letter.

'M for May. I checked the name of the hostages, and I found something.'

Götz looked at him distrustfully. 'I'm listening.'

'Ira said, didn't she, that the hostage taker would know someone here in the station? That it was the reason why he disguised himself?'

'And?' Götz leant forward impatiently.

'I think that someone is me.'

10

The thin cardboard file smelt of Götz's aftershave. For a fraction of a second, Ira asked herself whether that was why she was keeping the autopsy report in her hands as she spoke with the 'Radio Killer' again. This was the name the private TV channels had already given the hostage taker. All of them had interrupted their normal programming for the special report. On a twenty-four hour news channel, the slogan 'Radio Killer Runs Amok' was displayed in large letters on the screen. The hostage slogan was on constant loop at the bottom of the screen: 'Please answer your telephone at all times with: "I listen to 101 Point 5, now set a hostage free." At intervals, a photo of Leoni was being displayed too.

'Do you think your fiancée would have wanted all this?' Ira opened the autopsy report and smoothed down the crumpled corner of the first page.

'*Would want*.'

'Sorry?'

'You said "would have wanted",' explained Jan. 'But it should be: "Do you think Leoni *would want* all of this?" Because she's not dead. So please don't speak of her in the past tense.'

Ira nodded, made a note on the error list, then said: 'Sorry. So, do you think she's in agreement with what's happening here?'

Silence. The pause was a heartbeat too long, and Ira could almost picture Jan there in the studio, thinking. As if, until this moment, it hadn't even occurred to him.

'No,' he said finally. 'I don't think so.'

'So how will she react when all this is over?'

'As long as she reacts full stop, that's all that matters to me. Because that would mean I finally find out what happened to her.'

Ira flicked one page further, and pulled out the photo of the crashed car.

'Let me speak openly with you, Jan. My fear is that you won't get Leoni back either way. Either she won't be able to come to you at all, because you're mistaken...'

'I'm not mistaken.'

'... or she won't *want* to come back to you, because she hates you for what you've done here today. You can't get what you want, so why don't you put a stop to things before it gets even worse? Before even more people die?'

As she spoke, Ira zoned out all her surroundings. The negotiation centre in Diesel's office, Herzberg at his mobile computer unit. Igor, who was checking for the hundredth time whether the telephone call was being recorded onto the hard drive. She suppressed her ever-increasing thirst, to quench which she would need something much stronger than the coffee in the paper cup in front of her, which was slowly going cold. She even suppressed the burning thoughts of Kitty and the terror her daughter was sure to be going through right now. Instead, she concentrated on the one person everything depended on today. Life and death. Future and past. She closed her eyes and visualised Jan's face, which so far she only knew from the security camera. With and without the wig. Eventually, she asked again:

'Why don't you stop?'

There was a crackle at the other end of the line. Then Jan coughed before he answered. 'Let me pose you a counter-question: You lost a child, am I right?'

That has nothing to do with you, Ira screamed inside.

'Yes,' she whispered.

'But in the press it also says that you're a mother to two daughters? What's the other one's name?'

'Katharina.' Ira opened her eyes, and for a moment her surroundings resembled an overexposed film. Then she adjusted to the sudden brightness. *Had he discovered Kitty?*

'Good. Now, please do me a favour and imagine you're on a cruise with Katharina.'

'Okay.'

'The ship encounters difficulties and sinks. Katharina is thrashing around in front of you in the waves. You can save her very easily; you just need to stretch out your arm and pull your daughter onto the raft you're sitting on. Would you do that?'

'Of course.'

'Good. So Katharina is saved. And now you see another girl alongside Katharina. It's Sara.'

'Oh, God,' groaned Ira. Her right hand was cramping around the autopsy report.

'Imagine that fate is giving you a chance to turn back time. You can save your daughter. But you can't pull both children onto the raft. There isn't enough space and it would sink. Would you push Katharina off and pull Sara up?'

'No!'

'Would you let Sara die instead?'

'No, of course not,' gasped Ira. 'What's this about?'

'I'm sorry, I don't mean to torment you, Ira. I'm just answering your question. About why I have to do this today, even if Leoni will hate me for it. Sometimes we all have to do things that we don't want to do. Things that hurt others. And which push away the very people we're doing something good for. Just think of the raft. I'm sure Katharina would hate you for it later if you didn't save Sara. Because the price of Katharina's survival would be her knowing that she it was only possible at the cost of her sister.'

Pain suddenly shot through Ira's hand, while at the same time she felt as though Jan was stabbing her in the eye with a needle, pumping his evil thoughts directly into her brain with a syringe.

One did survive, and hates her mother. You have no idea how close to the truth you are, thought Ira, only now noticing the fleck of blood on the autopsy report summary. She had given herself a paper cut. Right in the fold of skin between her thumb and index finger.

'Do you understand, Ira? I don't have a choice. I have to see this through. Regardless of what Leoni thinks.'

'But what makes you so sure that she's still alive? Do you have any proof?'

Ira put the injured ball of her hand into her mouth like a slice of lemon just before knocking back a shot of tequila. The blood tasted pleasantly metallic and reminded her of the gun in her kitchen this morning.

'Yes. Lots. I have lots of proof.'

'Like what?'

'She called me.'

'When?'

'An hour afterwards.'

'After what?' Ira fired off her questions at lightning speed, trying to ensure the conversation didn't falter.

'After her supposed accident. I had just set the table out on the terrace. We were planning to have dinner. It was supposed to be a special day.'

'But she didn't come?'

'No. Everything was ready. The food, the champagne. The ring. Like in a movie, you see? And then she called.'

'What did she say?'

'It was hard to make out what she was saying because the connection kept cutting out. But it was definitely Leoni. Suddenly there was a knock at the door. I opened it, and a policeman told me that my girlfriend had died. Now you tell me: How is that possible? How could I have been speaking to her if her car had allegedly already gone up in flames?'

'How do you know that it wasn't a recording when you were on the phone?'

'Who would want to play such a gruesome prank on me? And besides, that's impossible. She responded to my questions.'

'What did you ask her?'

'I asked whether she was crying, what was wrong.'

Strange, thought *Ira. Either Jan is completely insane, or it wasn't a recording. Presumably the first.*

'How did the conversation continue?'

'Well, of course I wanted to know what happened. From what she had said so far I had understood only one word: "Dead".'

'Dead?'

'Yes. But she didn't say it again. Instead, she said that I wasn't to believe them.'

'What did she mean by that?'

'No idea. "Don't believe what they tell you," those were her last words. After that, I never heard anything from her again. One second later, this policeman tries to tell me that Leoni had already been dead for an hour.'

'But you didn't believe it?'

'I know what you're thinking. That I was traumatised. That I sought refuge in an imaginary world *after* I received the news of her death. But it wasn't like that.'

'What makes you so sure?' asked Ira.

'Everything. The autopsy report, for example.'

Ira stared at the open folder. The fleck of blood on the side had taken on the shape of a fingerprint.

'What about it?'

'It's faked. Look under "Specific Observations".'

Ira opened the folder and flicked through to the section he was talking about. 'There's nothing there.'

'That's the proof.'

'Why?'

'Do you know what I found a week after the funeral, in a jacket that Leoni had left hanging in my cupboard? A small package with a note.'

'What did it say?'

'*Not to be opened before your birthday*.' It was a present. I didn't wait, of course. I ripped it open, and a little test tube rolled out.'

'You mean, she was...'

'Pregnant,' completed Jan. 'Exactly. And if a blood test can figure that out, how on earth could the pathologist have missed it?'

11

Ira sat on the toilet seat cover and pressed the last tablet out of the foil blister pack.

Hopefully I can get at least one of them down me, she thought, laying the blue pill on her tongue. Luckily she had found the anti-anxiety tablets in one of the numerous pockets of her cargo trousers. Directly after her last conversation with Jan, she had gone to the bathroom to throw up. But apart from bile, nothing had come out of her. Not even the nausea she was carrying around inside her, the cause of which she was unable to pinpoint. Was it because of the dead UPS driver? Because of the madman in the studio, rummaging around in her past? Or because of Kitty, with whom she still hadn't been able to make contact?

Ira swallowed, and wouldn't have been surprised if her larynx had creaked like a rusty bike chain. The tablet didn't go down.

For God's sake! She stretched her right hand out in front of her and tried to keep it steady. But in vain. She might as well sit here and wait for Jan to give up of his own accord.

She needed a drink, or at the very least to get this pill down her. Otherwise there was no way she would survive the next telephone conversation with the psychopath. Let alone get her daughter out of there.

Ira laid her head on the handle of the toilet door and started to laugh. Softly at first, then louder and louder. The situation was so ludicrous. Of all the things that had already happened today, it was a sedative tablet on her tongue that was making her lose her composure. Ira was almost roaring now, and kicking her feet wildly against the door at the same time. Her whole body was shaking, and she didn't even notice that her laughter had long since turned into a hysterical shriek. Suddenly she heard someone calling her name, loud and clear. In a pause, while she gasped for breath because she had choked on her own spit.

'Hello? Ira? Are you in here?'

'What are you doing in the women's toilets?' she coughed, checking with her tongue to see if the tablet was finally gone. Negative.

'Steuer sent me,' Götz called into the bathroom. 'He's looking for you.'

'What does he want?'

'He has to take you to an important meeting.'

'With who?' She sniffed.

'He didn't say.'

'Is he completely out of his mind? I need to talk with Jan again soon. The next round is imminent.'

Ira took the hopelessly soggy tablet from her mouth and listened in confusion as the tap was turned on outside. She flushed, so as not to have to offer Götz any explanation, then opened the door.

'I need to...' She stopped. 'What's that?'

Götz was holding a glass of water out to her.

'It's for whatever you need to swallow so you don't have a complete breakdown. Do it. And then hurry. Steuer's already waiting in the stairwell.'

'What's he doing there?' After all the coughing, Ira's voice sounded as though she was heavy with cold.

'Waiting to take you to your meeting. On the roof.'

12

While Ira hurried up the grey-green concrete steps in the MCB building stairwell, her leather jacket began to vibrate. For a moment she feared it might be Jan, but the number on the display wasn't the one from the studio.

'It's me. Don't say anything.'

Diesel.

'I have to give you some information I discovered in the listener index. But keep it to yourself. Götz and I don't trust the Big Mac you're heading off with now.'

Ira couldn't help but laugh at the fitting description of Steuer. She had just met him on the twenty-forth floor and was now a few steps behind him.

'The hostage taker is called May. Jan May. With a y.'

Ira panted. Firstly because she was out of breath. And secondly because she wanted to discreetly prompt Diesel to continue.

'I could say that I hacked the police database or that I have psychic powers. But the truth, as always, is much more simple. I decided to check the listener index. To check the hostages' details, in truth. Unfortunately your friend Götz caught me in the act. At first he wanted to hang, draw and quarter me, but then I showed him what I found. Brace yourself for this: Our perpetrator is registered. In the station database. I entered him into the system myself, last year. May wrote me an email shortly before Christmas. I didn't remember at first, but when Jan first mentioned the name of his bride-to-be, it came back to me.'

Ira panted again. Louder this time.

'After I replied, May called me, and we met in a café. He wanted to talk me into broadcasting a missing person's announcement for Leoni. Timber was against it, because…'

'Can't you go any faster?' asked Ira sarcastically, hiding the mobile behind her back for a moment as Steuer turned around and gave her the finger. But Diesel had caught on and began to summarise the facts more swiftly.

'Okay, about May himself: He's thirty-seven years old, from a middle class background, born and raised here in Berlin and a psychology graduate of the Freie University. He fast-tracked, and was the best in his year. Then came his post-doctorate, and his employment at the Charité Hospital. By the end of his twenties, he already had his own practice on the Ku'damm. He's unmarried, has no children, and has been completely beside himself with grief for the last eight months. He has criminal charges against him that cost him his licence. He shagg– erm, sexually harassed a former patient. It seems there was some issue with cocaine, too. Not all of that was in our index, of course, but I searched our news database on him. And he's not just a run-of-the-mill therapist, but a serious professional. He wrote his thesis on psychological treatment methods. He knows all the tricks.'

'Damn it,' panted Ira, and Steuer nodded in front of her, assuming her comment referred to the remaining steps they still needed to conquer.

'There's something else you should know, wherever you are right now.'

'What?' whispered Ira. Just a few more steps, and then she would be at the top and need to hang up the phone.

'Something doesn't quite add up with the hostages.'

'I can't keep going,' wheezed Ira, thinking of Kitty. Steuer waved his hand behind him dismissively, but Diesel had understood again.

'Okay, I'll tell you later. Götz asked me to help him and…'

Unable to listen any more, Ira pressed the button to end the call. They had arrived at the top, and her head was as full as the autobahn on a Friday afternoon. Not even the strong, fresh wind that met her on the roof helped to clear it. Countless thoughts shot into her mind, each of them tumbling over the last: Why had there been no reference to Leoni's pregnancy in the autopsy report? What was the thing about the hostages? Why was Götz, who normally preferred to work alone, asking a civilian for help, of all people? Why did Steuer want to speak with her on the roof?

And what in God's name was the other tall man doing up here, the one who was currently shaking the mission leader's hand – and whom she recognised from the television?

13

'Thank you for coming,' said Faust, and Ira hesitated a second before grasping the elderly chief state prosecutor's bony hand. They were standing, sheltering as much as they could from the wind, behind a little aluminium shack on which a sign warned of the danger of high voltage. It was clearly part of the forest of communication technology behind it, which included three satellite dishes and an antenna the size of a mobile phone mast.

'My name is...'

'... Dr Johannes Faust, I know. You're the leader of the department responsible for fighting organised crime,' completed Ira. Then she looked at Steuer, who was about to light up a cigarette.

'What's all this about? What's going on?'

Faust looked her slowly up and down, puckering his narrow lips into a rehearsed interview grin.

'First of all, Frau Samin, I would like to apologise for Herr Steuer's behaviour towards you.'

Ira looked distrustfully into Faust's eyes. She didn't know much about the man, but what she had heard didn't suggest he was in the habit of apologising to complete strangers.

'I'm sure it's no secret to you that Herr Steuer doesn't want to have you in the team. But I would like to assure you that this is not personal. His prejudice is purely related to professional matters.'

'Oh, come on!'

'It's true. He doesn't consider you to be fit to perform your duties since your eldest daughter passed and you subsequently became – how shall we put it? – indisposed.'

'I don't see how my work is any of your business. Let alone my family.'

'It is, unfortunately. And believe me, I wish I could steer clear of your personal affairs. But now the hostage taker has brought your dead daughter into the game. Legally speaking, and you know this yourself, that means you can't lead the negotiation one minute longer.'

'Well, God knows I didn't ask to be leading it in the first place.'

'I know. Even though I'm not God.' The only one to laugh at the state prosecutor's tired joke was Steuer, who had overheard despite being a few paces away from them.

'But allow me to ask you one question, Frau Samin. Are you sweating yet?'

'Excuse me?'

'Yes, I think you're already perspiring. I felt it when you gave me your hand just now. How long has it been since your last drink?'

'I don't have to stand here and listen to this.'

'I think you do. And I fear that you may already have begun to shake too. Your sensitivity threshold will sink lower and lower, until eventually you leave your desk in a quiet moment to search for alcohol in the station kitchen.

Because otherwise the gauge will have dropped too low. Am I right?'

Ira felt the firm grip of his hand on her left shoulder, making it impossible for her to turn away from him and leave. Which she had just been planning to do.

'Stay here.' Faust's voice became icy, and his grin died away as quickly as a burning match in a draught of air. 'Okay. Now listen up: Even though I know everything about you – like the fact that you found your daughter Sara dead in the bathtub a year ago, something for which your other daughter blames you, or the fact that you've been ordering two pizzas every night since then just as an alibi for the two bottles of Lambrusco – even though I know very well that you have contemplated following your daughter on several occasions, and that there's probably already a sharpened razor on the edge of your bathtub... even though I know all this, I have still gone to the effort of flying here by helicopter, just to personally convince you of how important your participation in today's mission is to me. Do you understand?'

'No,' answered Ira honestly. 'I don't understand a word of all this. If I'm supposed to be so important, then that idiot over there should just let me do my job!'

'That idiot over there,' Faust nodded in Steuer's direction, who was taking a deep drag of his cigarette, 'is doing his job wonderfully by not wanting to have you on board, by putting obstacles in your way. Because let's be honest: You are a wreck, Ira Samin, and anyone can see that without needing to read your personal file. A brief glance at your pupils is enough.'

He had said it. Faust had cracked the whip of truth right

in her face by calling her a nervous wreck, and now she was standing 114 metres above Potsdamer Platz, surprised at how little it had hurt. Perhaps because it was the truth, and even the worst truth is easier to bear than the most compassionate lie.

'*I* am the only one here,' continued the state prosecutor, 'who wants you to go back downstairs at once and continue the negotiations.'

Ira raised her eyebrows. 'Why did you really come here?'

Her gaze alternated back and forth between Faust and Steuer. She shivered. She was starting to feel cold, and didn't know if it was down to the weather or the company.

'I want to be completely honest with you,' said Faust, his tone resembling an announcement from a bad-tempered bus driver. 'I see little chance that you will be able to convince the hostage taker to give up. Or that you will get another postponement. But you have to give it your best regardless, because we need every second we can get. Steuer's elite team is currently testing a paralysing shot.'

'You're planning to sedate him?'

'Exactly. It's our only hope,' interjected Steuer. He ground his cigarette out and smoothed down his dishevelled hair.

'We've found a way to approach the studio from below, and we're currently testing an all-or-nothing shot through the floor panels in the studio mock-up on the sixth floor. As we're now assuming that Jan May is cabled up to a heart rate monitor, we have to paralyse him with the first shot in such a way that he won't be able to move a finger to trigger the explosives. But he can't die, either, otherwise everything will blow up around us if his pulse stops.'

'And I'm supposed to play the telephone Samaritan long

enough for the mobile mission command to be done with the test run?'

'Exactly. You're the only one he talks to. If we pull you out now, we run the risk of a knee-jerk reaction. So stall him. Convince him that Leoni is dead. Talk about your daughter, for all I care. It doesn't matter how, just play for time. But for heaven's sake don't get dragged into his delusions by wasting your time searching for a phantom. Forget the autopsy file. Leoni was *not* pregnant. Do you understand? That's just another of his hallucinations. Don't offer him any more support with his crazed conspiracy theories. Leoni is dead. Is that clear?'

'Why does the fact that you're emphasising this so much give me an uneasy feeling?' asked Ira.

Faust took a linen handkerchief out of his coat pocket and dabbed at his cheeks in an affected manner. Ira wondered whether he secretly wore lipstick at home. The state prosecutor forced a smile, but it didn't extend to his eyes. Ira knew that the difference between an honest smile and the vacant facial expression of an artificial grin lay in the gaze. Faust may have been smiling, but the eyes behind his glasses were ice cold. And that could only mean one thing – that everything he was about to say was a lie:

'Leoni is dead, you have to believe me on that one. And yes – I know what you're thinking. That something here is very suspicious. I would think that too. Any halfway intelligent person who gets summoned to the roof of a high-rise and then left with unanswered questions would think the same. I repeat: There is obviously a reason why I, as state prosecutor, am involved in this. But for reasons of state security, I can't tell you why. As much as I would like to, I simply can't tell you the plain truth. But what I can tell you is this: You'll be endangering the lives of countless people if you sow even the hint of doubt about Leoni Gregor's death in the public eye. You can't even begin to imagine who is out there listening to you! So?'

'So, what?'

'Will you promise me that you'll help us? Can I rely on you?'

In the middle of his sentence, Ira's leather jacket began to vibrate again. She pulled out her mobile, happy to not have to answer Faust's question right away. But the pleasure didn't last long. It was the studio; Igor had redirected the call. Jan May wanted to speak with her.

14

The car radio in Diesel's old Porsche Targa only worked when it was raining. The antenna had been stolen the previous week, right in front of the betting shop where he put money on the Hertha match every Saturday. Now, on his way to the airport, he had to follow the conversation between Ira and Jan with occasional interruptions. Luckily the weather report was predicting rain showers for later, and a lone dark cloud was already appearing over the autobahn to Schönefeld. For some reason, the reception just happened to be better in bad weather. It was almost as though, in brilliant sunshine, the old receiver was relieved of its duties by some workplace law about the temperature reaching a certain level on the thermometer.

'Let's speak openly. I know your daughter didn't have an accident. She wasn't epileptic; she took her own life. Why?' Diesel wondered why Jan May kept bringing up this sensitive subject. As if he were the negotiator and needed to distract Ira from something. But even more than this, Diesel wondered why Ira was even responding to this psychological torment. He had realised by now that she needed to build up a personal relationship with the perpetrator. But surely not at the cost of her own emotional wellbeing?

The only greater puzzle than this for Diesel was why *he* was asking himself these questions. Something in Ira's sad gaze must have appealed to his protective instinct, and he secretly admitted to himself that he would liked to have met this courageous woman under different circumstances.

'To be honest, I don't know why Sara did it.' Ira's answer, which was simultaneously a confession, resounded out huskily from the bad radio speaker. 'In the last few months before' – Ira paused for a millisecond – 'before her death, I hardly had any contact with her. She had some problems. But I wasn't the person she chose to speak to.'

'That was her sister Katharina, right?'

'Yes, sometimes. So who was *Leoni's* best friend?' asked Ira, in an attempt to change the subject. 'What about her family?'

'She's an orphan. Her parents died of a hairspray overdose.'

'Excuse me?'

'It was in South Africa. Leoni's parents worked together as chemists in the industrial production of "Wackmo", a medium-sized public holding company that also produced consumer goods, like hairspray. There was an explosion in the factory, and forty-four employees lost their lives. Six were burned to such an extent that they could no longer be identified. Including Leoni's parents. She was four at the time. Her mother's sisters took her back to Europe with them. She grew up in Italy, studied in Paris, and has only been living in Berlin for a short while.'

'So that means she didn't have any close friends here, besides you?'

'Yes, correct. And how about Sara?' asked Jan, taking

the lead again. Diesel started to feel as though the duo on the radio had an unspoken agreement about the rules of their conversation. *Do ut des*. Like in 'truth or dare', one of them has to confess intimate details before they are allowed to pose a further question. Except that this wasn't a party game, but deadly serious.

'I'm assuming that Sara was born and grew up in Berlin?'

'Yes.'

'Did she have a steady boyfriend?'

'*One?*'

Diesel was surprised. The way Ira emphasised the word didn't sound like a mother who was proud that her pretty daughter had scores of men running after her.

'So she had lots of admirers?'

'No. You couldn't put it like that.'

'So what then?'

'Well. Sara didn't want to be "admired". She didn't have a conventional mindset when it came to love and sexuality.'

'So she was promiscuous?'

'Yes.'

Diesel approached the autobahn exit and wondered how much further Ira would go with millions of people listening in. Why was she exposing all of this? Why the compulsive truth-telling? Ira answered Diesel's silent questions with her next words.

'Look, I could tell you something now, Jan, and to be honest I don't feel entirely comfortable talking about it. But according to what I know about you so far, I'm pretty sure that you've already found the tasteless article about my daughter on the internet anyway.'

'You mean the one about the sex clubs?'

'That's the one.'

'And? Is it true?'

'Is it true that one of your patients reported *you* for sexual assault, Jan?' Turning the dagger back around again. Diesel was almost ashamed to admit it, but he felt a hint of pride that she was using information he had supplied her with.

'Yes. Allegedly I drugged and raped her. But that's not true. I never touched her.'

'Just like you didn't do anything to Manfred Stuck?' asked Ira spitefully, and Diesel sensed that she was close to crossing the line. He contemplated pulling over onto the hard shoulder, and knew that numerous other listeners in their cars must be debating the same thing right now. As perverse as the conversation was, their interaction was morbidly fascinating.

'That's another matter,' answered Jan. 'I've never laid a finger on any of my patients. But that was all part of the plan.'

'What kind of plan? Whose plan?'

'The government's. The state's. How should I know? They wanted to finish me off. I already told you how they systematically destroyed my life. First they took Leoni away. Then my licence. And finally my pride. That's why we're here, Ira. That's why I had to take the hostages.'

'And kill?'

'There's always a reason,' answered Jan quietly, and every listener knew that he was referring to both the execution in the studio and Ira's daughter suicide.

An electronic alarm signal sounded out, like the ring of a

cheap travel clock, and Diesel looked with confusion at his dashboard until he realised it was coming from the radio.

'It's time, Ira. The next round.'

'Jan...' Ira tried to interject, but the hostage taker didn't let her speak.

'Save yourself the trouble. You had your postponement. You didn't use it very wisely.'

'You're right. I haven't made much progress yet. But I can't speak to you and research at the same time. I'm receiving my information only in fragments. Give me a little more time.'

'No.'

'But why can't we just keep talking for now? Skip the next round. We'll talk about how your life got destroyed. And about Sara. Let's find an answer together. About why all this is happening. About what was done to you. And Sara. And me. Okay? Just don't hang up. We shouldn't stop talking yet; it's going so well, don't you think?'

No, no, no, thought Diesel. *That won't help, you sound too desperate.*

He shook his head vigorously as he tapped the palm of his hand nervously against the wooden steering wheel.

'Can I trust you?' asked Jan May after a long pause. Diesel turned the volume up even louder, even though he was having no problems hearing the conversation.

'Why are you asking that? I've been open and honest with you so far. I'm not responsible for the fact that they sent a sniper down through the ventilation shaft.'

'Yes, I know.'

'Then skip the next round. Let's keep talking.'

'I'd like to.'

'Okay, then…'

'But first I need to test something.'

'What do you mean? What do you want to test?'

'You'll find out in a moment.'

He hung up.

15

'What does he mean by "test"? Is there something going on in mission control that I don't know about?'

Ira was talking to Götz on her personal mobile so the other line remained free for Jan. Even though it was very unlikely that he would be calling in the next few minutes. In a few seconds' time, the next Cash Call round would be taking up all of his attention.

'I'm not doing anything at all,' answered Götz. His voice sounded as though he was talking through a handkerchief. Muffled and a little nasal. 'The team hasn't made that much progress yet. We don't know how to eliminate the noise factor when we come through the floor.'

'Good.' She pressed the elevator button with the downward-facing arrow, but then decided to take the stairs after all so that she wouldn't lose mobile connection. Ira felt slightly relieved that the paralysing shot wasn't yet going to be deployed. She feared it would be a failure. If she was going to take her own life today, then she didn't want to have her other daughter on her conscience too.

'I have to speak to Katharina. At once.'

'That's not a good idea, Ira.'

'None of this is a good idea, so stop fobbing me off with that crap,' she said, heading up the stairs taking two at a time. 'I know exactly what Diesel found out about the hostages, and what you didn't want to tell me. They're in on it, right? They're not victims, but accomplices.'

'We don't know for sure yet. But yes, it's possible that Jan has an accomplice in there.'

'Or several. Which means that Katharina is in even greater danger. Is that why you didn't tell me?' Ira took the long pause to be an agreement.

'You son of a bitch! You trust the station's chief editor, a complete stranger, more than me. Have you forgotten how many missions we've had together?' *And how often we climbed into bed with one another?* she almost added. 'You know nothing about him and yet you've made him your right-hand man. What on earth has gotten into you?'

'I can't discuss it.'

'Excuse me? What's that supposed to mean? And where have you sent him, anyway?'

'I really *cannot* discuss it right now,' repeated Götz. This time, his rage was blatantly audible in his hissed whispers. Ira's rubber soles squeaked on the grey concrete steps.

'Fine. I'll be with you in just a moment. You owe me an explanation. Until then, make the connection. I want contact with Katharina.'

'And what if *she* doesn't want it?'

Ira paused on the stairwell of the eighth floor and panted heavily into the receiver. Her lack of condition wasn't just down to not having worked out for the last year. It didn't bear thinking about how she would feel if she had to run up the stairs one more time.

'Has she said that?'

'Listen, Ira. I understand how you feel. But there's nothing you can do for your daughter right now,' said Götz, evading her question. 'And besides, it's not the appropriate time for a conversation. The next Cash Call will be starting any second now.'

'That's the *best* time,' she argued, coughing. Her mouth was so dry it felt like she had scrubbed it with blotting paper. 'Jan will be distracted by the round. I have to speak with her at once and warn her. And perhaps Kitty can give us some information I can use for the negotiation. Maybe she's seen something that we couldn't hear out here.'

She flung the door to the main corridor of the sixth floor open. A policeman in front of the emergency exit jumped in surprise as Ira stormed in out of the stairwell. She headed towards the mission central, but didn't even make it four steps along before crashing into Götz. He challenged her like an American football player, twisting her arm and pushing her into the little room in front of which he had been waiting for her.

'Have you completely lost your mind?' she screamed at him as the door slammed shut behind them. He turned on the light.

Ira stared at him angrily. The room was one of those windowless ones which were becoming increasingly common in modern office complexes, the kind which would prompt any sensible person to ask themselves what the architect had been thinking to include something like this in their blueprint. Too small to be a store room and too big for a box room, it was full of useless junk that no one would miss if it were thrown away. Götz leant against the grey plastic door, ensuring that Ira had no chance of getting past him.

'What the hell are you…?'

He held a finger up to his lips, silencing her. She watched in amazement as he took a small radio device from the inside pocket of his leather jacket, which he was wearing over his bulletproof vest. He turned it up to full volume, and 'Don't Speak' by No Doubt echoed glaringly off the bare concrete walls.

Götz pulled Ira's body close to him, and for a moment she genuinely thought he wanted to exploit the situation for a quick fumble.

'We have to be careful,' he whispered in her ear. 'Someone is playing against us.'

'Who?' she whispered back. From one second to the next, her rage at Götz had transformed into a feeling she had last felt before her exams. An adrenaline-fuelled mix of fear, thirst for adventure, and nausea. Except that, back then, it had been much weaker.

'I have no idea,' answered Götz. His lips were almost touching her earlobe. 'Someone close to us. A mole. Maybe even Steuer himself.'

'But why would he do that? What makes you think that?'

'I'm getting practically no useful information from him. The file on Jan, for example. Steuer said there wasn't one. And yet Diesel found out that he had been accused of sexual assault and drug possession. Now Steuer is telling me that it's irrelevant. He keeps pushing for us to storm at any cost. I think he's trying to cover something up.'

'What about the hostages? Diesel called me just before my meeting with Faust. I know they're not victims.'

'Yes, that's right.' Götz blinked as though he had something in his eye. 'Diesel is right, I think. He checked the listener database. Four of the five shouldn't even have won the station tour in the first place.'

'Why not?'

'Because these studio visits are in high demand and only given to long-standing listeners. Most of the hostages only registered recently. I requested a check on this and sent Diesel away from the station.'

'Why?'

'He's too smart. He's already found out too much. It's only a matter of time before he discovers that Kitty is still in the studio, and if he runs to Steuer with that, you'll be pulled off the mission. So I've given him something to do to keep him busy. In the meantime, my guys are checking the backgrounds of Jan and the other hostages.'

'And?'

'I'm still waiting to hear back. I'm being fobbed off on this too. Something stinks. And it's not just Steuer's breath.'

Ira nodded her head carefully, as though she had a migraine and couldn't move too quickly. Gwen Stefani was just launching into the final chorus, and the song was slowly being faded out.

'It's about to start,' said Götz. 'The Cash Call.'

'Then get me Katharina on the line at once.'

She stared at him stubbornly. He shook his head and stretched one hand behind his back. 'Stop playing games,' said Ira more loudly. 'I want to speak to my daughter.'

She listened in surprise as, after a brief station jingle, another song began to play. She had heard a dialling tone sound and assumed it was the next round. Jan had gone well

173

over the scheduled time. But now she was hearing a country pop song by Shania Twain, the title of which she couldn't remember. Had he changed his mind? Was Jan skipping this round too? It didn't matter. Whatever was going on in the studio right now, it gave her time. Time for her daughter.

'Get me Katharina on the walkie-talkie right now, you stubborn piece of shit, or...'

As she searched for a suitable threat, Götz opened the belt bag behind his back and pulled out the walkie-talkie.

'Be careful what you say.' He handed it to her. His large thumb was pressed firmly on the speak button. 'Go ahead, she can hear you.'

16

'What do you want?'

Ira couldn't help it. She had been so determined to hold it all back. But now tears shot into her eyes. Never had she been so happy to hear such a blatantly hostile voice.

'Are you okay?' She asked the question every mother automatically asks when speaking to her child again for the first time in ages. Except that on this occasion Katharina wasn't forcing herself into an obligatory Christmas phone call, but instead was huddled beneath a sink, just a few hundred metres away as the crow flies, and in mortal danger.

'Why are you telling those disgusting stories, Mama?'

For a moment, Ira was confused, then she closed her eyes as it suddenly hit her. *Sara! Of course!* Kitty had heard it all over the radio.

'Is it not enough that you weren't able to help Sara? Do you really have to drag her through the mud on public radio as some kind of sex slut now too?'

You wouldn't know, Ira wanted to answer. *You weren't the one who followed her. To the cinemas. To the parking lots. And nor do you have any idea why I need to speak to*

Jan about it. Because that's the only chance I have of getting closer to him. And of saving you.

'We don't have time for that now,' she answered, surprised at how toneless were the words crossing her lips. 'Please don't talk too much. Turn the walkie-talkie down as low as possible. And only speak when the music is on, and only when I ask you something.'

'Sure. So that you don't have to listen to my accusations. Because you can't handle the truth.'

Ira swallowed. 'No. Because you need to save the battery. And because you can't risk being discovered.'

Instead of an answer, there was an atmospheric crackle. Katharina had pressed the talk button only briefly, but in Ira's ears it sounded like a contemptuous snort.

'Listen to me now. I need your help to get all of you out of there.'

'You want to save us? You didn't even manage to save Sara. And she didn't have some lunatic threatening her. She even called you beforehand.' Katharina may have been whispering, but she might as well have bellowed the words into a microphone. Every one of them clashed against Ira's eardrum like a razor blade.

But she's right, thought Ira.

The first time her mobile phone had rung that day, she had been near Wolfsburg. But the reception in the train had been so bad that Ira had to call back several times. Not the greatest of conditions for a negotiation in which she was trying to prevent her own daughter from committing suicide.

You won't take any pills, will you, sweetheart? she had asked.

No, Mama had been Sara's answer. A lie.

'Please,' said Ira now, trying once more to get through to Kitty. 'I need you to briefly put out of your mind how much you hate me, and answer just one question.'

Silence at the other end.

Shania Twain was singing, and for some reason the stupid title came back into Ira's mind, now, of all times: 'Come on Over'.

Götz glanced at his diving watch, but Ira didn't need the subtle hint. She knew the time pressure she was under.

'Where's the UPS driver's body?' she asked.

The silence was interrupted by a crackle. Followed by another pause. Then Katharina finally answered.

'In the small CER.'

'That's the central equipment room,' explained Götz in a whisper as he saw Ira's confused frown. 'The studio has a door leading to the kitchen. The kitchen leads out onto a terrace and a cubbyhole where some of the programming equipment is kept. Modems, devices to improve the sound quality, an emergency generator.'

'Can you see the body?' Ira had to ask the question twice, because on the first attempt she forgot to press the speech button.

'No, but I saw the hostage taker finish him off.'

Katharina's voice had taken on a different tone now. Or maybe that was just the wishful thinking of a mother who would rather hear an emotion such as fear than pure hatred towards her.

'He put him in a body bag and...'

Suddenly there was a clatter, then the connection went dead.

'What's happening?' cried Ira, louder then intended, staring pleadingly at Götz. He lifted his hands in an calming gesture.

'Goddamnit, what's going on in there…?' Ira was almost yelling now. She felt like a motorcyclist who had raced too quickly into a bend and realised too late that she should have put a helmet on. She was losing control, and the realisation was practically strangling her. After two seconds, which felt like an eternity, a renewed crackle finally brought relief.

'It's starting again,' whispered Katharina, so quietly that neither Ira nor Götz could understand her. But it didn't matter now anyway. Ira had heard it on the radio herself. Shania Twain had made way for the characteristic dial tone of a digital telephone.

17

While Jan dialled the first digits of the number he had selected for the next round of his perverse version of Russian roulette, Kitty set the walkie-talkie to silent and crept as quietly as possible out of her hiding place. The cupboard door with the yellowed plastic slats squeaked a little, but that would be swallowed by the thick door to the studio, which she crept past on tiptoes. Kitty felt agitated by the conversation she had just had with her mother. It would have been better if she hadn't even spoken to her. Or just told the truth!

She realised with horror that the glass door to the studio was steaming up, because she was standing too close to it. She edged backwards so that her breath couldn't betray her presence.

As the misty veil on the windowpane slowly dissipated, she prayed that Jan wouldn't choose this precise second to look over at the kitchen door. Daring a quick glance, she was reassured. The hostage taker was standing in front of the telephone unit, his head bowed over it. He pressed the last digit, and for a short while nothing happened. It was as though he had dialled an international number.

But then the switchboard computer finally seemed

to spring into life. The switch point found the correct connection. A plaintive tooting started up.

The truth. What if you never speak to her again and never told her the truth about Sara?

Kitty suppressed the thought and counted the ringing tones.

One.

Two.

She pictured someone somewhere reaching hesitantly for the phone. Maybe a man. In his car? Or at the office, his colleagues standing around his desk. Or maybe the call was reaching a housewife. She was sitting at home in the living room, while her husband reminded her once more of the correct slogan.

What if someone picks up and says the wrong thing? Who has he chosen to be his next victim?

Kitty tried to concentrate, but didn't know what she should concentrate on, so instead she let her thoughts have free rein again.

What if it works this time? Who would he set free? The pregnant woman? What happens if an answering machine picks up? Would that mean a death sentence for a hostage? And why didn't I tell Mama the truth?

Her tempest of thoughts died with the fifth ring. As the phone was picked up. And the first word was spoken at the other end.

18

Ira and Götz stood in front of the studio mock-up in the open-plan office of the mission control centre, barely daring to breathe. They were both wearing headphones over which they could follow the conversation. For some reason, all the loudspeakers across the entire floor were turned off. *Dial – ring – pick up.* Until just a few hours ago, the banal sound of a telephone ringing had been one of the innocuous background noises of modern day-to-day life. Now it had lost its innocence and become a nightmarish harbinger of death. To add to this, listening via the headphones gave it an even stronger, almost tangible intensity, which increased boundlessly until the phone was finally picked up.

'I, er, I listen to 101 Point 5, and now set a hostage free.'

Relief. Limitless relief.

As the jubilation broke out in the mission control centre, an unfamiliar sensation of happiness streamed through Ira's body. The last time she had felt something comparable, something so alive, was after the birth of her daughters. She wanted to bottle the emotion. The grin on Götz's face, the fists pumped into the air by the officials in the open-plan office, her own tears of joy – she wanted to capture it with an internal camera in her memory for all eternity.

But a mere four words from the hostage taker brought her crashing back down to reality.

'That was a test.'

Ira's smile died. Her hope collapsed like a pyramid of tin cans after someone had pulled out the wrong one.

A test!

Now she knew what Jan had meant before. Why he had asked her if he could trust her. And now she also knew why the loudspeakers were turned off. Why they were all wearing headphones.

Feedback!

She turned slowly 120 degrees in a clockwise direction. Her gaze searched the rows of desks, some of which were still shrouded in their protective plastic wrapping. But numerous unknown faces were sitting at them regardless, headsets on.

'Dammit, Götz! What did you do to the calls?'

The team leader, who had been just about to embrace a colleague, flinched as though he had trapped a nerve.

'I… I don't know. I'm not…'

Ira ran off without waiting to hear the rest of his answer. Towards Steuer's office. As she rushed past one of the desks, she saw something out of the corner of her eye which confirmed her worst fear. An input screen on the monitor. All the officials sat here were waiting for phone calls.

The door was open, and Ira could already see Steuer's grinning face even from afar.

'Are you responsible for having that call redirected?' she shouted towards him.

Dammit! Please say it's not true. Ira's thoughts were racing just as fast as she was.

'What are you getting so worked up about?' laughed Steuer as she practically flew into his office. 'I already told you I was going to.'

'You stupid idiot!' she yelled, noting with surprise the husky tone of her voice. As the tears in her eyes blurred the brazen grin on Steuer's face into a cruel mask, she realised she was crying again. She repeated the insult, but it didn't seem to bother Steuer. On the contrary, it only intensified his deeply contented expression.

'Thank you for having said that so openly in front of witnesses. Now it will be unlikely to stop at a simple disciplinary complaint...'

He was silenced by the first shot.

The second robbed him of his mocking smile and replaced it with an expression of complete bewilderment.

Ira's hands flew up to her face.

Steuer reached with trembling fingers for the remote control and turned on the radio at his desk.

'That was a test,' repeated Jan in a stern tone. 'And you didn't pass.'

19

This was insane. Jan closed his hand as tightly as he could around the Glock he had taken from the UPS man just a few hours ago and hammered the artificial grip down on the studio mixing desk.

Insane!

The pistol felt far too light. It hardly weighed a thing. A few weeks ago he would have thought it were a dummy. A toy gun with which one could easily march through airport security without the metal detector giving even a lethargic peep. Today, three weeks after the crash course in guns that the junkie guard had given him during one of his more lucid moments, he knew better. The weapon wasn't heavy, but that didn't make it any less deadly.

'What's wrong with you?'

Jan lifted his head and couldn't help it. He couldn't help but laugh at Markus Timber's question, which in the face of the situation they were all in right now, was far beyond absurd.

What's wrong with me? Nothing? Just a minor tantrum. It happens to me sometimes; I get a bit nervous during a hostage situation and start to shoot a few people. Sorry. A silly habit of mine.

'I mean, what was wrong with the answer?' asked the star presenter, clarifying his question. With his blood-encrusted nose, he looked like some crazy person who had rubbed a cloth stained with strawberry jam over their face to pass the time. His nostrils were stuffed with two saturated bungs made of rolled-up tissues, and they were waggling precariously with every word he spoke.

'The answer was okay. The person wasn't.'

Jan tapped Flummi on the shoulder, who understood the signal to start playing a new song. Since the two gunshots, the producer hadn't moved a millimetre, staring at a point on the computer screen as if he were in a trance. Because of this, he was the only person in the room who didn't know who Jan had just shot.

'What's that supposed to mean?' asked Timber as the distinctive drums from 'Running Up That Hill' introduced Kate Bush's greatest hit.

'Since when has that been part of the rules?' You said you would set a hostage free if someone answered with the correct slogan. And that's exactly what happened.'

'Yes.' Somehow, Jan managed to give his positive answer a negative tone.

'And?' The presenter stared at him expectantly, and once again Jan couldn't help but smile. He knew that no one in the studio would understand his amusement, that they would think him a cynical asshole. But the sight of Timber so agitated, his swollen nose now much more of a match for his plump face, was simply too comical. Or maybe it wasn't, and he really was losing his mind. Maybe he should take another one of the pills after all, the ones he had tucked away in the pocket of his jogging bottoms for an emergency.

This was the only part of his disguise he was still wearing. He assumed that by now his photo would be projected onto the wall of the SEK mission control centre in life-size format, and that at this very second dozens of officials were turning his villa in Potsdam upside down. A disguise was no longer necessary.

'What was wrong with this Cash Call?' Timber demanded to know.

He slowly emphasised each word in precise rhythm with the flickering red LED light of the studio telephone.

Ira!

Jan briefly contemplated ignoring her. But then he signalled to Flummi, who turned the music down and switched to On Air.

20

Ira was just about to open the door to the staircase when, after the twenty-first ring, Jan finally picked up.

'How many are injured?' She came straight to the point.

'Well, how many times did you hear me shoot?' he answered drily.

'Twice. So there are two victims? Does someone need help?'

'Yes. I do! I need someone to help me find Leoni!'

Ira was initially taking two steps at once, but took it down a gear when she realised she wouldn't be able to keep up the exertion for the next thirteen floors.

'I know. I'm working on it. But first I need to know who you shot.'

'Well, maybe I'll tell you if you explain to me what kind of scam you just pulled.'

She briefly contemplated making up an excuse, but then decided on the truth. 'The calls from the studio were redirected.'

'To where?'

'To a call centre. To an appropriately instructed official, who of course picked up with the correct slogan.'

'Aha. And how do you think I found out?'

Ira felt as though her breathing was double the speed of her own pace as she ascended the stairs. She had to struggle not to pant as she answered him.

'You phoned yourself. On your own mobile phone.'

It should have been blocked! Under no circumstances should someone have been allowed to pick up. Steuer was such an idiot. How could he overlook the possibility of this happening?

'Correct. How did you crack the €500,000 question, Ira? Did you phone a friend?'

'I understand that you're angry. I know you think I lied to you. But I had nothing to do with it. The lines were manipulated without my knowledge.'

'Fine, so let's assume for a moment that I believe you. Why should I waste any more time with you? It seems you don't have any influence at all out there. I mean, you're not even being briefed about the mission tactics.'

'You were going to tell me who you shot,' she persisted, ignoring his reproaches. She needed information.

'No one.' A brief pause. Then he added: 'Not yet.'

'Good.' Ira stopped. She held tightly onto the handrail and leant over as though she was about to throw up on the grey concrete steps.

'Very good.'

But her relief over the good news didn't last long.

'I'll soon be making up for it though,' hissed Jan. 'Right now, in fact. And I've already decided. This time I won't be restricting myself to just one victim.'

Of course not, you piece of shit. You want to punish me. With the pregnant woman.

Ira's breathing still hadn't slowed down. But she carried

on regardless. Two blue numbers at head height on the bleak concrete wall informed her that she had only reached the twelfth floor.

'I understand,' lied Ira. 'But Sandra Marwinski is a mother-to-be. She and her baby have nothing to do with the situation you are in right now.'

'Ha!'

Ira jumped as though Jan had spat through the telephone into her face.

'Give it a rest. Do you really think that by using the words *mother* and *baby* you can appeal to my moral compass? I have nothing more to lose, Ira.'

Nor do I, she thought, before nearly tripping up. The laces of her canvas sneakers had come loose, and she stumbled over her own feet like a gangly schoolgirl.

'As I already said: any further negotiation with you is a waste of time.'

Thirteenth floor. The numbers were painted carelessly on the landing walls, as though the interior architect hadn't been able to imagine that someone would venture out of the luxurious interior of the MCB complex into this depressing staircase. Ira attempted a weak counter-attack.

'If you hang up now, you will lose the only person out here who has done nothing to hurt you.'

'But that's exactly the problem, Ira. You've done *nothing*. Like back then, with Sara. Am I right?'

From a professional point of view, it should have been clear to her that he was angry and wanted to hurt her. But at this moment in time, Ira was unable to look at things from a professional point of view. She was agitated too, and it was better for her to say nothing so that her aggressive emotions didn't stir themselves up even further.

'Is this the only reason we're talking, Ira? Because *you* want to overcome your trauma? Because you couldn't prevent the catastrophe with your daughter back then? Are you trying to make up for it here today? Yes, I think that's it.' Jan laughed. Ira's anger gauge climbed back up again. 'There's only one reason you're negotiating with me. To you, I'm just some pill to numb your own pain.'

Even though he was only grazing the truth, somewhere between the fourteenth and fifteenth floor his words hit Ira like a ricocheting bullet. Now she couldn't hold it back any more. Instead of staying rooted to the spot, she began to take two steps at once again. She didn't care what her body was telling her. The rage drove her on. And if she broke down hyperventilating on the nineteenth floor, what did it matter? She intentionally ignored everything she had learnt about psychologically restrained negotiation techniques and spoke in plain terms: 'That's nonsense, Jan, and you know it. None of the mistakes made today are my fault. I'm not responsible for the call diversion. But do you know what? I don't care what you think. If you don't want to talk to me any more, then fine, I'll get you another negotiator. I'm sure Herzberg is bored and in need of something to do. But you should remember one thing: Right now I'm the only person standing between you and a combat troop who are just waiting to put a bullet through your head the second you make one single mistake. And that will happen, sooner or later. Probably sooner. As soon as you run out of hostages.'

She wheezed out the last few words, no longer able to suppress the coughing fit.

She only stopped panting once she was by the elevator of the nineteenth floor. Her lungs were burning, her thigh muscles numb with exertion. But the thing that hurt the most, yet again, were Jan's words: 'You said you hadn't made any mistakes *today*. But how about on the twelfth of April?'

Ira trudged exhaustedly to the reception of the radio station, towards the mission control centre. Everything was spinning around her.

'Why should I tell you that, of all people?' she asked eventually. *Why are you so intent on talking about the twelfth of April? What does my daughter's death have to do with any of this?*

'Why should I trust you again, of all people?' came the counter-question.

'Okay' – Ira passed two uniformed officials at the station entrance, taking no notice of them – 'then let's make a deal. I'll tell you what my daughter did to herself, and you leave Sandra Marwinski in peace.'

'Bad trade. You need someone to talk about Sara with anyway. What do I get from this?'

'One more hostage. I'm not asking you to keep to your own rules and set someone free. We'll simply overlook this round. That way we'll win time for the search for Leoni, and you'll have one hostage in reserve.'

Ira had arrived back in Diesel's office. The negotiation centre was abandoned.

'I see.'

'Do we have a deal?'

'No, not yet. First let's talk about Sara. Then I'll decide whether I still trust you.'

Ira looked out of the window down to Potsdamer Strasse, which was cordoned off. On the green strip of grass in the middle, there was a glass display cabinet with three rotating placards. One was an advertisement for cigarettes. Even from up here, the boldly printed warning was easy to make out: *Smoking Kills.*

'Ira?'

Even if she hadn't been so worn out and tired. Even if, at this moment, she had possessed the energy to do so. She couldn't. She just didn't want to talk about it. Not about the night when she had secretly read Sara's diary, to try to understand her eldest daughter at least to some small extent. The men. The violence. Sara's desires.

'Are you still there?' asked Jan mercilessly.

No. She didn't want to talk about it.

But it looked like she didn't have any other choice.

21

The only thing about him that said 'pilot' was his name. Hawk had rolls of fat around his belly, a David Copperfield neck (in other words, it had been conjured away), and a little ponytail resembling a shaving brush at the nape of his neck, tied together with a rubber band.

'What are you doing out here in the sticks?' he laughed. That was a kind of tic of his. Hawk was always laughing. Usually for no reason. Diesel suspected that he had flown his traffic report helicopter with an oxygen shortage too many times. Or maybe he was just crazy. Right now, they were sitting in Hawk's office at Schönefeld Airport; the pilot behind an unbelievably messy desk, and Diesel on a metal folding chair which was about as comfortable as a shopping trolley.

'I hate to admit it, but I need your help.'

In fact, Götz had instructed him to visit the driver of the ambulance who had been first on the scene at the accident that day. But in Waldfriede Hospital, where the paramedic now worked, no one had wanted to tell him anything. He hadn't even been permitted to see Herr Waschinsky, Warwinsky or Wanninsky, or whatever the name was of the man who had signed the accident report in his illegible handwriting.

'I'm not flying any cocaine over the border for you, if that's what you want!' Hawk laughed, searching for something on his desk. He knocked over a coffee cup in the process. 'Dammit. That was your drink, sweetheart!' He laughed even louder.

Diesel wondered whether it had really been that intelligent of him to ignore Götz's instructions and take it upon himself to drive to the airport. But if there was anyone who could help, then it was this lunatic in front of him now.

'Is this about your new radio game? It's without a doubt the most insane thing I've heard on your shit station in a long time. How many has he bumped off now?' Even though Hawk had been doing the aerial traffic report almost every morning for over seven years, he still didn't want to identify himself with 101 Point 5. He never said 'our' station, but always 'your'.

'Did you fly on the nineteenth of September?' Diesel came straight to the point.

'Yes.'

'I mean last year.'

'Yes.'

'Don't you need to check your calendar or ask your secretary or something?'

'Why?' Hawk looked at Diesel as though he had a bogey hanging out of his nose. 'The nineteenth of September is my birthday. I always fly on my birthday.'

Good. Excellent, in fact.

Diesel pulled a crumpled piece of paper from the inside

pocket of his battered leather jacket. He laid it on the desk, with the blank side facing upwards, and smoothed it flat.

'Do you have a card of an accident in Schöneberg on that day?'

Hawk grinned broadly, exposing teeth which were in astonishingly good condition compared to the rest of his appearance.

'A *birthday* card?' Hawk laughed heartily at his own joke.

Diesel nodded.

'Card' was Hawk's favourite word. He and a handful of other sickos collected photos of accidents: an upended lorry on the city circular, a burned-out Golf after a multiple pile-up or a cyclist under the tram. The sicker the better. Most of the photos were taken by the paramedics at the scene of the accident. All of whom were Hawk's pals, and only able to get to the scene so quickly because he, as a pilot, was the first to see the accidents from above in his Cessna. As an expression of their gratitude, he usually received a copy of the photo as a trophy. Hawk made them into trading cards, which he stuck into an album like other people would transfer pictures of football players. Sometimes he swapped them with other traffic reporters from all over Germany. He wasn't the only person on the radio openly acting out his fetishes.

'Wasn't that the day that idiot stretched his head out of the side window because his windscreen wipers weren't working and he couldn't see in the rain?'

Hawk spun his chair around 180 degrees and stared at a metal shelving unit. With his back turned, he couldn't see Diesel shaking his head. The 'idiot' in question had crashed his head into an oncoming side mirror at sixty miles an hour.

Hawk hummed 'I'm Singin' in the Rain' as he pulled out one ring binder after another.

'I knew it.' He turned back around, holding an A6 school notebook in his broad hands. He opened it in the middle. Diesel stared, nauseated, at the 'card' in question. A paramedic was pressing his hands in vain against a blood-soaked ribcage. The man in the photo was already dead.

'That's not the one I mean. I'm looking for a black BMW.' Diesel briefly explained the nature of the accident to him, based upon the information he had found in Leoni's autopsy report.

Hawk looked at him briefly, then clapped his paw down on the desk with a laugh.

'You're so sick, Diesel, do you know that?' He carried on laughing, and Diesel had no choice but to agree with him. The whole situation was simply too grotesque. In front of him sat a clearly disturbed pilot with a penchant for morbid close-ups, and *he* was calling Diesel sick.

'A collision? With a traffic light? A write-off? Burned-out? With a fatality?'

Diesel nodded in response to every question, but Hawk had already turned back around to his shelves. One file after the other was pulled out, opened and furiously shoved back in.

'Nope,' Hawk finally shook his head.

'Are you sure?'

'If it happened in my city and on my roads, I would know about it.'

'It was in the paper.'

'It's also in the paper that every other woman wants to have sex with a stranger, but none of them have ever asked me.'

'So what do you say to *this*?'

Diesel turned over the paper from his jacket and pushed it towards him. It was a colour copy he had made earlier from the accident photo in the file.

'Cool, how much do you want for it?'

'It's not a card, Hawk. I want to know what you can tell me about this accident.'

'No idea.' The traffic pilot was staring entranced at the paper in his hands. Presumably he was already sticking it into a new album in his mind.

'I don't know anything about it. Honestly. But I could check it out if you want.'

Now it was Diesel's turn to laugh. Sure. 'Check it out' meant he would brag about it to his friends. But fine, let him go ahead and email it to them. It was worth a try.

'But there's one thing I can tell you right now.'

'What?'

'It was definitely not on the nineteenth of September. And certainly not at this location.'

'What makes you so sure?'

'Come with me. I'll show you…'

With these words he stood up, and Diesel watched as he walked towards the exit. Towards the airfield.

22

Ira was firmly convinced of one simple truth: The more a person is able to suppress, the happier they are. Her unhappiness had begun when the signs became too obvious with her daughter and Ira's suppression mechanism had failed.

'She was fourteen. And I walked in on her having sex.'

Ira spoke in a whisper, even though she was alone in the negotiation centre. That was a double paradox, because at this moment around nineteen million people could hear her, regardless of where she retreated to. Almost every major radio station in Germany was broadcasting the 101 Point 5 programme on its own frequency. The homepages of numerous internet platforms were demanding the correct slogan from their readers. Even the German-language radio on the island of Mallorca was keeping the sunbathing holidaymakers informed. Ira ignored the uncomfortable thought that every word exchanged between her and Jan would soon be disseminated by a number of foreign media outlets too.

'Okay. Perhaps fourteen is a little premature. But isn't that the average age in big cities for first-time sex?'

'For a threesome?'

His response to Ira's curt interjection was a short grunt, the kind that men utter when they're standing over an open car bonnet and don't want to admit they haven't the faintest idea what the problem is.

'I always considered myself to be open-minded,' continued Ira. 'I prided myself on my uncomplicated approach to life. After all, my parents raised me in a very liberal and open way. My first boyfriend was allowed to stay the night from the first day on. I even talked to my mother about problems reaching orgasm.' She changed the tone of her voice, speaking more quickly with every word. 'Don't get me wrong, I wasn't from some hippy family where the father answers the door naked, with a joint in his mouth, and lets in complete strangers. No. It was just… casual, and not in the sleazy sense that the word gets used in lonely hearts columns. When I went through my experimental phase at the age of seventeen, for example, I didn't have any problems in bringing a girlfriend home to stay the night. I swore to myself back then that I would do exactly the same if I had children. And when Sara reached puberty, I felt mentally prepared for everything. The pill, maybe coming out as a lesbian, or an older boyfriend. I thought I could cope with anything.'

'But you were wrong?'

'Yes.' *More wrong than I had ever been before.*

Ira contemplated how much she really had to reveal in order to win back Jan's trust. Sara's constantly changing sex partners. 'Toys' that definitely didn't belong below a teenager's bed. Sara's open confession over breakfast that she could only reach orgasm if pain was being inflicted on her at the same time.

If she left out the details, he would notice that she was fobbing him off.

Or, even worse, he wouldn't be able to understand her. And for some reason she had become painfully aware of how much she wanted to be understood by someone.

The best option is to tell him about the most significant moment, she thought. *The moment I became drastically aware of just how irretrievably Sara had slipped away from me.*

'Do you know the big parking lot on the Teufelsberg?'

'Yes. I went there now and again with Leoni. We sometimes parked the car there when we went walking in Grunewald. It's a really beautiful place.'

'During the day, perhaps. But don't go there after eleven at night.'

Ira closed her eyes, and the pictures in her memory slowly drew into focus, taking on their horrifying contours like photographic film in a developing bath.

The cars in the dark. Far too many for this late hour. Her own headlamps illuminating them as she steered the van into the uneven parking lot. Dark figures behind the steering wheels. The flare of cigarette lighters. And slightly to the side, a small gathering of people. Around a station wagon. With the boot open. And against it...

'I've read about these meeting places,' admitted Jan. 'I even went once, to convince myself that they weren't an urban myth. There are a lot of them in Berlin, actually. Most are by the lakes, like in Tegel, and on the Teufelsberg as you said. And at some of the rest stops on the autobahn. There's even a website where you can find out the latest meeting points in exchange for a fee. The rules of play and rituals there are always the same: You park your car. When someone comes, you spark up your lighter in the dark. Sooner or later, someone will get in. The sex is hard, fast and silent. No names. No parting words. Although to be honest I thought that only…'

'What? That only men go?' Ira laughed self-consciously. 'I thought that too. Until I followed my seventeen-year-old daughter there. Maybe it actually was a gay meeting point. It's possible. But if they were all homosexuals, then at least ten of them made an exception that night. Probably even more than that; I couldn't count the hands. There were so many that I could only recognise my daughter by the knee-high leather boots on her skinny legs.' Repulsed, Ira spat the last few words into the telephone. 'They were jutting out of the car boot like snapped-off toothpicks. The rest of her body was submerged, like a light bulb beneath a horde of horny midges.'

'What did you do?' Jan asked, after a short pause in which neither of them said a word.

'Nothing. At first I wanted to get out of the car. But then I got scared.'

'Of the men?'

'No. Of Sara. As long as I stayed sitting in the car and didn't see her face, I could convince myself that…' She left a long pause again. Eventually, Jan finished her sentence for her.

'… that she wasn't enjoying it.'

Ira nodded as though in a trance. He had seen through her. Not for the first time, she realised how good he must have been at his job, before he had turned to criminality after the trauma. No mother wants to watch her daughter being devoured like a cheap piece of meat by a pack of hungry dogs. And voluntarily? Out of autonomous desire? To Ira, it was unimaginable. She had fled the parking lot that night. Only once she arrived back home had she noticed the dent on her mudguard. She had been so in shock that she hadn't even noticed bumping into another vehicle on the way out. The physical damage hadn't bothered her, especially as there was no way the horny newcomer would have risked attracting the attention of the police. But the internal injuries were hard to bear. She was devastated. All her knowledge about the human psyche failed when it came to applying it to her own daughter. There was no textbook she could open, no expert she could consult. In her despair, Ira even briefly contemplated whether she should call her ex. But given everything she knew about him, she couldn't be sure that he himself wasn't in a dark parking lot somewhere, sparking up a lighter. After all, he had left her for an underage girl back then, when she was pregnant with Kitty.

'Did you talk to Sara about it?'

'Yes. But much too late.'

'What did she say?'

'Not much. I went about it the wrong way. I asked the wrong questions.'

Just like in our last telephone conversation, thought Ira.

'*You won't take any tablets, will you?*'

'*No, Mama!*'

'What questions do you mean?'

'Well, naturally I was searching for a reason for her behaviour. As a mother, I wanted a logical explanation. My suspicion was sexual assault. I went through everyone that it could have been. But she denied it all. She even smiled and said: 'No, Mama, I *wasn't* raped. But yes, it's true. There is someone who did something to me. You know them. Very well, even.'

'Who?'

'I don't know. And that's precisely what's driving me so insane.' *So insane that all I want is a Cola Light Lemon, so I can finally swallow the capsules in my freezer cabinet. But before that I need to rescue my only remaining daughter, even if she doesn't want my help.*

'She even said I would find out.'

'What were her exact words?'

For a moment, Ira was surprised by the question. But ultimately she saw no reason not to tell him.

'Well, I think Sara said something like: "Don't worry, Mama. Soon you'll know who did this to me. And then everything will be fine."' Ira swallowed hard. 'But it was never fine. Everything just got worse and worse. I never found out, do you see?'

For a while, they were both silent.

The moment didn't last long, but it was enough for Ira to realise how close she was to collapsing. Her hands were shaking, and the film of sweat on her forehead was condensing into pearl-sized drops.

'The people we love most are the greatest puzzle to us,' declared the hostage taker, in the same moment that Ira was wondering whether Götz would bring her something to drink soon. *A proper drink.*

She was so confused by the sudden despair in Jan's voice that she did something she hadn't done for fifteen minutes now. She opened her eyes.

'We're not talking about my daughter any more, are we?'

'No,' confirmed Jan softly, and then she knew it.

She had had to pay a high price. But she had done it.

Jan wouldn't be shooting any hostages in this round.

'You're right,' he confirmed again. This time a little louder. 'Now we're talking about Leoni.'

23

The negotiation centre was still deserted. Herzberg and the technician had appeared briefly, but Ira had shooed them out again with furious hand movements. It didn't matter how many people were listening to her on the air – she still had to be alone in the room while she was on the phone. It had always been that way. She couldn't stand it when someone was in the room. It was a tic that didn't exactly make her work as a negotiator any easier. On missions, she had needed to get used to the presence of a team whether she liked it or not. But privately, she always closed the door behind her as soon as she took a phone call. And this was definitely a private conversation. The most intimate one she had ever had.

Ira's gaze rested on the container beneath Diesel's desk. She walked across the room, continuing to listen to Jan on the hands-free device.

'At least a part of everyone who means something to us in life will always remain a mystery, Ira.' His voice sounded thoughtful, introspective. Like a scholar talking to himself in order to find the solution to a problem. 'If you understand what I am about to tell you, you'll be able to find Leoni more quickly. And maybe it will even solve the final puzzle that your daughter gave you.'

Ira refrained from making any comment, not wanting to interrupt his flow of words. Besides that, she was a little distracted. There was an open bottle of single malt between a boxing glove and a trophy for 'Miss Wet T-Shirt' in the drawer she had just pulled open.

Maybe that's why I'm happy no one else is here, Ira reflected. *Because I knew what Diesel would have in his desk for me.*

'Let's take marriage as an example,' Jan continued. 'During my sessions, I experienced the same thing time and time again: The most fulfilling partnerships were those which had an element of secrecy to their love. Nothing makes us more lethargic than a story we already know the ending to. And nothing binds a couple together like a big question mark. What is my partner really thinking? Will he be faithful to me forever? Do I share everything with him, or are there feelings that he hides from me? If we're honest, we never really want to get to know our great loves. It's their secrets that stop them from becoming boring to us...' He cleared his throat. 'That's why I thought Leoni and I would work so well.'

Ira was so occupied trying to open the bottle that she almost missed that last, decisive sentence.

'So what was Leoni's secret?'

'I never found out. I think that's why we're here today, don't you think?' He gave a forced laugh. 'Not that I didn't try. Shortly before she disappeared, I followed Leoni once. Just like you with your daughter and the parking lot, I crept along behind my girlfriend through the streets of Berlin.

She dropped by my practice one lunchtime and wanted to go out to eat with me. That was unusual in itself, because Leoni never normally makes spontaneous decisions. Don't get me wrong, she's not boring or uptight. She once filled the bedroom of my Potsdam house with foam, just because she wanted to see what it felt like to make love in the clouds. She was extraordinary and surprising, but only so long as we didn't leave our own four walls. Something about being in public made her afraid. Very afraid. When we made plans, she always wanted to know precisely where we were meeting and what route we would take. Every time we went out in the car she would keep looking nervously in the rear-view mirror.'

'But that day she just turned up in your practice and wanted to go to lunch?' asked Ira.

'Yes. And I felt so bad about it. Because that was the only place that *I* couldn't be spontaneous. I was waiting for the mother of a thirteen-year-old patient, to tell her that her daughter's problem unfortunately wasn't just of a psychological nature. The young girl had Aids.'

'My God,' groaned Ira. In her mind's eye, Sara's face lit up like an overexposed photograph.

'To cut a long story short – just a couple of minutes after Leoni left, the mother called and postponed the appointment. So I ran after Leoni and was just about to catch up with her on the Ku'damm, when' – he hesitated briefly – 'when I noticed the others.'

'Who?'

'The people following her.'

Ira stared at the bronze screw cap of the whisky bottle in front of her on the desk. Two things were now clear to her:

her shaking hands would spill some of the meagre contents as soon as she raised the bottle to her lips. And Jan was about to tell her something that would make her doubt about Leoni's death even stronger.

24

'The disguise was perfect, really. Who would suspect a young woman with a small child in one hand and a dog in the other of following someone?'

'Then why did you?'

'I didn't, at first. Initially I was just confused about the route Leoni was taking. She had never let me accompany her home. She always said she was embarrassed by her one-bedroom flat in Charlottenburg, because I had a villa in Potsdam. Even though I assured her again and again that this didn't matter to me, she always made me drop her off by the district court after our initial dates. Later, she practically moved in with me anyway, and hardly ever stayed the night at her place any more.'

'So you never saw Leoni's apartment?'

'Not to this day. But I knew roughly where it was, so when I saw Leoni walking towards Lietzenburger Strasse that day, at first I thought she must have had some errands to run there. But then she suddenly crossed over to the other side of the street, and went into a fashion store for plus-size women, which was absurd considering her figure. I watched, keeping my distance, as she left the shop again a few minutes later through a side entrance. Only to cross over to the other side of the street again. And then again. Then she started acting really strangely, and began to run. That's when I noticed.'

'What?'

'The woman just left the dog and child standing there and ran after Leoni, talking into her mobile as she went. I was rooted to the spot in shock, and then a station wagon pulled up at the side of the street. A man got out, and in less than ten seconds he had rounded up the child and dog into the vehicle.'

'What did you do?'

'I hesitated at first. Of course I wanted to know what was going on. I had already lost sight of Leoni and her pursuer in the lunchtime crowds. But I knew a shortcut towards Stuttgarter Platz. I hoped that Leoni was heading to her apartment, and that sooner or later our paths would cross.'

'Which they did.'

'Yes. It was pure chance. By then I had given up searching and sat down in a café on the good side of Stuttgarter Platz.' Ira smiled a little. The "Stutti" was a Berlin phenomenon. A mere few hundred metres separated a family-friendly neighbourhood of pre-war buildings, delightful street cafes and playgrounds from seedy brothels and lap dancing clubs.' My lunch break was long over, and my next patient had already been waiting for a while. So I called her. And what happened next almost gave me a heart attack!'

'What?'

'Right in front of me, a red-haired woman with her back to me, a complete stranger, answered her phone. Only then did I register that a phone had rung right by me in the café, at the very next table. I hung up at once. The stranger looked at the display and seemed to recognise my number. Something about it made her very nervous. She quickly put some money on the table and left the café without turning around even once. And that's when I realised, of course.'

'What?' asked Ira again, breathless with suspense.

'That she was wearing a wig. That's why I hadn't recognised her when I came in. Leoni must have overlooked me too. So I started to follow her again. But it didn't last long this time. Just a few hundred metres away, she turned into Friedbergstrasse and hurried across to a residential building.'

'Where she lived?'

'Yes. I'll never forget the look in her eyes when she opened the door to me. How can you describe an expression that contains love, surprise and pure fear all at once?'

Ira knew that Jan wasn't expecting an answer, so she posed the next question: 'What did she say?'

'Nothing, at first. I was just glad she wasn't angry. After all, I had broken my promise of never visiting her at home. So I was happy that she didn't slam the door in my face. Instead, she invited me in. But before I could say a word, she pulled me close to her, hugged me and whispered: 'Please don't ask. I'll tell you everything, someday. But not here. Not now.'

'And that was enough for you?' *After all, you wanted to marry the woman*, Ira added in her thoughts.

'Of course not. But she had promised me. She was going to tell me everything at some point. And didn't I already say that it's the secrets, more than anything else, which bind us together?'

'You also said I would hear something that would make the search for Leoni easier.'

'Before I went back to my practice, I washed my hands in the bathroom. Leoni hadn't been expecting visitors, remember. So she hadn't had the opportunity to put out a fresh hand towel, nor to take her spare mobile phone from the charging dock over the sink.'

'You checked her messages?'

'Isn't that a national sport nowadays? Yes, I read her texts like a jealous husband hunting for messages from a lover.'

'And?'

'Nothing.'

'What do you mean, nothing?'

'The mobile phone was full of information. But nothing I could read. I didn't understand a word. The texts were all written in the Cyrillic alphabet.'

'What's that supposed to mean?'

'That if it really was Leoni's mobile, Ira, then the woman you're looking for is Russian.'

25

It was ringing for the third time already. Here, alongside the station lockers at Ostbahnhof, it echoed twice as loud as normal. Faust looked at the display of his mobile as though the device had some contagious disease. *The number!* he thought, nervously feeling the pulse in his neck. It was throbbing visibly. In addition, an enlarged lymph node between his chin and neck felt sore, as though he had a bad cold coming on.

How did they manage to get this number? And so quickly?

The last time the state prosecutor had felt this afraid was when he had been summoned back into the consultation room of the oncological practice after a routine cancer check.

How could the plan have gotten this out of control? And so close to the end?

The mailbox signalled the arrival of a new voice message, and Faust felt incredibly tempted to throw the phone at the tiled station wall. He didn't have the strength to listen to it right now. If the message was even half as bad as he expected it to be, today he would need to use the contents of his locker for the first time.

It's probably even worse than the diagnosis my doctor

gave me back then, thought Faust. *And he gave me fifteen months to live.*

He waited until a group of rowdy youths had passed by. Only once there was no one else in sight did he open the slightly stiff locker. Usually the lockers were emptied by the station staff every seventy-two hours. But not number 729. The third locker from the left in the top row was a secret locker belonging to the police, intended for transferring money to confidential informants and the like. For the last year, however, Faust had been using it solely for his own purposes. Thanks to his stature, it was at an easily accessible eye level. The state prosecutor sighed with relief once he had pushed the 'Out of Order' sign aside, turned the key and opened the door. As expected, everything was in its place. And why wouldn't it be? He had changed the lock. No one else knew what was stored in here. So who would take out the money and the IDs? Of course, on a day like today, anything was possible. So to be on the safe side, he stuffed the entire contents of the locker into the canvas bag he had brought along with him. Including the handgun.

Faust left the locker door open and hurried over to the toilets. After he had made sure he was alone, he checked the cleaning rota next to the door. *Good!* The cleaning crew had just been through and wouldn't be back for at least two hours. Faust tore the plan out of its metal frame and wrote 'Out of Order!' in large letters on the back. He took a roll of sticky tape from his bag and ripped off a strip with his teeth, then used it to fasten the makeshift sign to the door. He opened the door and slipped into the room. As a further precaution, he then locked himself in from the inside with a square section key that he was carrying on a key chain.

The initial preparations had been made; he was alone and standing in front of a mirror. Now he just needed to get undressed. He laid his starched white shirt, along with the vest he had been wearing beneath it, on the counter next to the washbasin. Then he took the first bundle of notes from the bag, ripped off another piece of tape and fastened it to his side, just above the groin, on his gaunt body. As he was about to do the same with the second bundle, his phone rang again. A glance at the display reassured him. This caller posed no danger.

'Dammit, Steuer. What's going on there?' he snapped in greeting.

'Jan May. He knows where Leoni is from.'

'I heard that too. Loud and clear. On the radio!'

Faust reached for the third bundle of cash. He would have to hurry if he wanted to conceal the entire contents of the bag in this way. But that was the only way. Under no circumstances did he want his chauffeur to see him leaving the station with this conspicuous bag. And who knows? Maybe he wouldn't even go back to his limousine. Maybe he would get on a train right away. It depended entirely on what message the caller from before had left.

'I still don't think we need to worry yet,' the SEK boss reassured him. 'I've put all the investigations on ice. My people are either not searching at all, or are going in the wrong direction. So far there are no facts, just suspicion and suppositions.'

'Don't treat me like I'm senile,' barked Faust. 'That maniac in the studio is sowing the seeds of doubt. And that's the beginning of the end. I'm not just talking about the trial, Steuer.'

'Yes. I realise that. But still—'

'I don't understand how this could have happened! I mean, I thought I made it crystal clear to that lush of a negotiator: No conversations about Leoni!'

Faust surveyed his gaunt upper body and suddenly felt a wave of intense pressure. What had he gotten himself into? Now he was standing here, half naked, emaciated from the disease, hiding himself away in a stinking station toilet like a drug addict. In the midst of making preparations to flee. Just because Steuer was cocking everything up over there. The sight of his ridiculous form only made him more angry. Faust went into a rage, no longer keeping to his otherwise eloquent manner of speaking:

'As far as I'm concerned, Ira Samin can work the whole city into a sexual frenzy with her stories about her whore of a daughter. Even if the slut did it in a dog kennel under a full moon, I don't give a shit! She can shout it from the rooftops for all I care. But every word about Leoni Gregor is one too many, Steuer. And you know why!'

'Yes.'

'Right. So what are you planning to do now?'

'I think we'll be ready in an hour.'

'We don't have that much time. You have to storm in sooner.'

'I... I...' Steuer paused. Then he sighed heavily. 'I'll see what I can do. I just don't want to go in until we've tested the attack properly. Another mistake like the last one and I'll be done with either way.'

Faust jumped at the sound of someone rattling the door

handle from outside. He moved faster with the last bundles. It was lucky that not much body surface was needed for three quarters of a million euros.

'Right then,' he said as the intruder finally withdrew to find another toilet. 'It's your choice, Steuer. Either Ira or Jan. Pick one.' He pulled his vest back on. 'It doesn't matter who, and it doesn't matter how. But silence him.'

26

The test run had gone well, but Götz still had a bad feeling. A dry run in which you weren't under real fire was one thing. Breaking through the floor panelling from below, throwing a stun grenade into a studio full of hostages and shattering the spine of an armed murderer with one single shot, well... that was a completely different matter. And the rubber bullet could not be allowed to kill Jan, or to miss him entirely. It had to paralyse him. Otherwise, either the absence of a pulse or the hostage taker himself would turn the situation into a complete catastrophe. And then there was the noise problem. So far they hadn't yet figured out how to cover the sound of the drilling. After all, to enter from the eighteenth floor below, they would have to first mill through half a metre of reinforced concrete and then through the wooden base on which the whole studio was built. And that just wasn't possible without making a hell of a racket.

Götz was standing before Steuer's office in the mission control centre, with the aim of discussing this very problem, when his mobile phone vibrated.

'I'm busy right now, Diesel.'

'Don't hang up... Oh, Gohhhd, I have to throw up...'

'Excuse me?' Now Götz was doubly confused. One, because Diesel sounded very strange. Ill, for some reason. And also because he could hear propellers in the background.

'Where are you?'

'In a Cessna, 700 metres over Berlin. But that's irrelevant. Much more important is... Oh, my Gohhhd!'

In the background, Götz heard a crazy laugh and someone shouting 'Looping!' Then he could have sworn that Diesel really was throwing up.

'I'm back,' he wheezed a few seconds later.

'Okay, what's going on?' asked Götz in irritation. He could see Steuer on the telephone at his desk, a deadly serious expression on his face, and would much rather have known what was occupying the mission leader right now. But perhaps, contrary to his expectations, Diesel really had discovered something.

'I can guarantee that Leoni definitely did not have a car accident on the nineteenth of September. Nor was it in the BMW in the photo from the file.'

'How do you know that? Did you speak to the paramedic?'

'No, I didn't.'

'I figured as much, because it certainly doesn't sound like it,' Götz retorted in irritation. Clearly no one around here did what they were asked to.

'Do you still remember the picture of the car?' Diesel asked.

'Just a moment.'

Götz went over to a vacant desk and used his password to open the file with the investigation material. He noted with surprise how little new information had been deposited here in the last few hours. What had the Steuer's men been doing the whole time?

'I'm just pulling it up now.'

'Good. Look at the edge of the street. Right at the front of the picture. What do you see?'

'Parked cars?'

'Correct. And that's the proof.'

'Of what?'

'That the picture is faked. The nineteenth of September was a Wednesday. Just like today. I'm flying over the street now, and Hawk is adamant that it's built up there every Wednesday. I can see it right now.'

'Who's Hawk? And what's built up?'

'Hawk is the pilot of the 101 Point 5 traffic helicopter. And I'm talking about the market stalls. Wednesday is market day, and whoever made the picture overlooked that detail. It's a mistake, do you see? The cars can't have been parked there at that time. The photo must have been made from archive images that were photoshopped together.'

27

Four minutes late. Under Steuer's furious gaze, Ira hurried with Götz into the conference room for the hastily arranged emergency meeting between the mission leaders.

This was unbelievable! What Götz had told her of Diesel's discoveries was impossible to take in.

'We're all in a rush today, so let's make a start right away, gentlemen.'

She registered tiredly that Steuer had just consciously ignored her in his address. Ira was the only woman in the darkened conference room. Along with her and Götz, there was also Steuer's unshaven assistant, the decommissioned negotiation leader, Herzberg, and two further officials at the long frosted-glass table. At the head of it stood the mission leader, as though he was the committee chairman of a large international corporation.

'I want to briefly bring you up to speed on the latest investigation results. After that, you will be informed on the next logical steps.'

Steuer pressed a button on a small remote control, which looked like a miniature cigarette lighter in his hairy paw. A gently humming projector mounted just below the ceiling cast a poster-sized profile photo onto the wall. Jan May.

It was probably an official publicity photograph from the psychologist's better days.

'From the beginning, our investigations have been focused on two aspects: the hostage taker and the hostages. The investigative team has done a great job here.' He nodded at the two officials, who Ira was now meeting for the first time. They were sitting closest to Steuer, right at the end of the table. The projector reflecting off the wall covered their expressionless faces with an interplay of red and blue light. As a result, they reminded Ira a little of cartoon characters. She mentally nicknamed the men Tom and Jerry.

'And what about Leoni?' she asked. 'Didn't you research in that direction too?'

'Listen,' Steuer rolled his eyes, irritated by this interruption to his explanations, 'I thought that had already been clarified to you from the very highest of authorities. Perhaps *you*, due to your situation, want to cling on to the hope of life after death…'

Tom and Jerry smiled hesitantly.

'… but *we* haven't wasted our valuable time chasing a ghost.'

The researchers nodded vigorously and grinned more broadly. Ira re-named them Asshole and Scumbag.

'So then why…' Ira persisted, but then was silenced by Götz's hand on her knee. He was right. Steuer wouldn't give a damn what Diesel had found out about the staged accident. She waved her hand dismissively when the mission leader raised his eyebrows questioningly.

'Excellent, so if there aren't any more interjections from Frau Samin, I can finally continue.'

Götz left his hand on her knee a little longer than

necessary, then gave it a gentle squeeze and discreetly withdrew his hand.

Steuer pressed on the remote control again. The photo of Jan became smaller and moved to the top left, making room for seven further images.

'These are the hostages. This one' – Steuer pointed with an infrared pen at the courier Manfred Stuck – 'was the first victim. Apart from the station employees, he was probably the only *genuine* hostage out of the tour group.' He emphasised these last words with a poignant expression.

'What about the others?' asked Götz.

'It seems likely that they're all in cahoots.'

Steuer began a list of points, using a finger for each one.

'All of them are unemployed. But they all share the same profession: acting. They all know each other from the Scheinbar, a meeting place for amateur artists in Kreuzberg. And this is the most suspicious detail: they all registered for the 101 Point 5's listener's club just a few weeks ago. This one here' – Steuer pointed at the picture of a plump man with a thinning head of hair – 'is Theodor Wildenau. He makes a living as a computer repairman. We presume that he manipulated the database so that they could all take part in the station tour on the same day.'

'What does this mean for our work?' asked Herzberg, visibly astonished.

'It means that what we're dealing with here is a bluff. A fake. An enactment. Jan May and the hostages are working together.'

'That's what you *presume*?' asked Ira loudly. It was more a statement than a question.

'Yes. And we have good reason to: All the hostages

have had previous contact with the hostage taker, at least indirectly. The owner of Scheinbar was one of Jan May's long-term patients. There's a further connection when you take a look at May's bank accounts. Three weeks ago, he closed a number of savings accounts and withdrew €200,000 in cash. Four hostages. That would be €50,000 each.'

'Just a moment. Do the four have previous criminal records?' Götz was the first to speak up.

'Nothing to speak of.' The projector light flickered ghost-like over Steuer's pudgy face as he walked up and down in front of the conference table.

'The couple were once caught at a Workers' Day demo with stones in their hands. The pregnant woman has a penchant for smoking pot while driving. But there are nothing more than warnings.'

Ira groaned. *He can't be serious?*

'Hang on,' she interrupted him. 'Are you seriously trying to tell us that four previously inconspicuous Berliners have suddenly become serious offenders just because Jan May offered them €50,000?'

Steuer nodded.

'My theory is as follows: May is cuckoo, but not homicidal. He convinces a naïve and debt-ridden amateur dramatics troupe to help him. They believe his story that Leoni is still alive. As our work-shy friends aren't that fond of the state themselves, they accept Jan's conspiracy theory. Or maybe they just want the money. Either way. When he promises them that there won't be any violence and lays €50,000 each on the table, everything is set to go. They play the role of their lives and pretend to be hostages.'

'And how does the dead UPS driver fit into the picture?' Herzberg spoke up again.

'Not at all. But that in itself is further proof of our presumptions being correct. Because the computer analysis showed that Manfred Stuck wasn't originally intended to take part in this station tour. He was invited at the last minute, and only by mistake. Stuck was supposed to receive cinema tickets, but a temp mixed up the forms and sent out the wrong prize.'

Ira knew exactly what was happening right now in Steuer's bureaucrat brain. He wasn't just speaking to the team, but to himself too. With every word, he was becoming more and more convinced by the theories he had patched together only minutes before at his desk.

'Presumably Jan went into a panic when he saw the stranger. He didn't keep to his agreement. He had to eliminate the one man who could blow the whole thing open. Stuck's colleagues at UPS, by the way, reported that he was a hothead and a gun fanatic. The man was a threat to the perpetrator's plan from the first minute on.'

'But that would mean Jan really is a danger,' Ira interjected. 'So we can't underestimate him or the threat he poses.'

Steuer waved his hand contemptuously, looking at Ira like she was a fly that had just fallen into his coffee.

'But there is another plausible alternative. An even more probable one: Stuck isn't dead after all. What we heard on the radio may just have been an enactment. There are no witnesses to the death.'

Yes there are, thought Ira. *My daughter.*

'What evidence is there for this theory?' Herzberg asked.

'We checked Jan's emails from the last few months. He has been buying dummy weapons and explosives online on Spanish militaria sites. Including a tranquiliser gun. It's entirely possible that he's the best actor of them all. There's a reason why he led Stuck out of the studio and into the adjoining room.'

'Objection!' exclaimed Götz, standing up. Ira was almost shocked when she saw the look on his face. Götz's entire body was tensed. She had never seen him this angry.

'With all due respect – these are just speculations, not facts. What if there is no relationship between the hostages? What if pure chance happened to lead them into the wrong studio at the wrong time? Like Stuck. People say that everyone in the world is connected with every other person by six degrees of separation at most. So in this city it's perfectly normal, in a room with seven people, for four of them to have friends in common. One of my friends plays poker with the drug king of Berlin. Does that make me an accomplice in organised crime?'

Steuer tried to say something, but Götz wouldn't even let him get a word in.

'Despite the current state of evidence, we have to continue to classify Jan as highly dangerous. I won't send my men in without briefing them that the maniac is cabled up like a condemned building just before demolition.'

'And I won't argue with you on that,' countered Steuer. 'Caution is certainly advisable. But I believe Jan May to be a harmless nut. I reckon he's holding the DJ and his producer in check with a water gun.'

'You're forgetting Stuck's weapon. And the pistol that Onassis had to throw down when the mission in the ventilator shaft went wrong. I'm sorry, but I don't share your point of view.'

'I've noticed. But that doesn't change my decision.'

'And what might that be?'

'We're going in. In fifteen minutes.'

28

Götz hurried after Ira, who had stormed out of the conference room.

'Ira, wait!'

He could imagine what she was thinking as she rushed towards the elevators. Stuck was dead, and she knew that first hand. But she couldn't tell anyone about the eyewitness. If it came out that Ira was concealing the existence of an eighth hostage, especially one who happened to be her daughter, Steuer might even have her arrested. The inner conflict must be tearing her apart. Should she do her job and distract Jan while the SEK storm in? Or should she prevent it from happening by laying her cards on the table? But if she did that, there would be nothing more she could do to help Kitty. Either way, she was putting her daughter's life at risk.

'Where are you running to?' Götz had almost caught up with her.

'Come with me!' she answered, without turning around to him. He caught up with her and touched her softly on the neck. She stopped abruptly, as though he had pressed an invisible stop button. He knew this spot. He had touched her there so often back then, stroked her there, kissed her there. But never under such extreme circumstances.

'I'm so sorry, Ira,' he said. 'Steuer's making a mistake. I guess he's under pressure from above. But I have no idea how I can change his mind now. Especially with such little time. I should have briefed my team by now.'

She turned around to him. Beneath her dark eyes lay even darker rings, which in a bizarre way harmonised with her flushed cheeks.

'Then go. But leave the walkie-talkie with me.' She pointed at the bulging side pocket in his camouflage trousers, containing the UPS walkie-talkie.

'What are you going to do?'

Ira pulled her T-shirt from her cargo pants and used it to wipe the sweat from her forehead. Even though it was a completely inappropriate thought given the situation, Götz found himself wishing he could touch her belly button.

'I have to speak to her,' she said eventually. 'With Kitty.'

'What is that supposed to achieve?'

'She's the only one who can help us make the right decision now.'

29

'What is it now?'

Kitty's voice cracked a little, because she hadn't spoken a word in a while and now needed to whisper. It was in keeping with how the rest of her body felt. Due to the uncomfortable position she was hunched in beneath the sink, all her muscles had welded together into one big cramped knot. And she was thirsty. Her head was pounding, and she felt like she did shortly before coming down with a heavy cold. Even the battery light of her walkie-talkie was flickering feverishly. It wouldn't be much longer until it conked out entirely.

'You have to help me, sweetheart.' Her mother was speaking as quietly as her.

The warmth of her words touched Kitty in a way she was completely unfamiliar with. Like a comforting massage. She didn't want to admit it, even to herself, but it relieved some of the pressure weighing down on her to know that there was someone out there who loved her, someone who was worried about her and wanted to get her out of here. Even if it was the very person she had wanted to break contact with forever.

'How?'

'If I understood you correctly earlier, the hostage taker took the body into the technical room.'

'Yes. Into the CER.'

'Can you get in there?'

'I don't know. I don't have a key.'

'Can you try it without putting yourself in danger?'

Kitty opened the slatted cupboard door a crack and looked out cautiously.

'Possibly. If he's on the phone in the studio, then I'm safe.'

'Good. Then I'll distract him. I hate to ask you to do this, sweetheart, but if you have the opportunity to get into the CER safely, then please do it.'

'Why?'

She knew it was possible. Jan hadn't locked the technical room again after the first execution.

'I need you to check for us whether the UPS driver is really dead.'

'But I saw very clearly that he shot him.'

'Yes, and I believe you. But sometimes things are different from how they appear at first glance.'

'The man didn't move after that, Mama. He put him in a *body bag*. There are another three of them lying around in here!'

'Which makes it all the more important for you to be careful.'

30

Diesel raced down Kantstrasse towards the courthouse. If he got caught speeding now, he would get three points on his licence. He could cope with that if it came to it. Although admittedly he would have to fork out an extra fine for speaking on the phone without a hands-free set.

But what did it matter?

Before he reached the pale-blue house in Friedbergstrasse, there was something else he wanted to tell Götz.

'Why aren't you back at the station by now?' snapped the team leader in place of a greeting as he answered his phone. In the background, Diesel could hear the industrious activity in the mission control centre.

'Why the attitude, sweetheart, are we married or something?' he replied in a honeyed tone.

'Very funny. Listen to me. The tip about the weekly market was golden. But I hope this is just as important. All hell is breaking loose right now.'

'It's about the music on the radio. I realised something.'

'That you're always playing the same old shit?'

'Yes, exactly.'

'Is this supposed to be a joke?'

'No. You're right, normally we repeat the same titles

again and again. But today's different. Have you paid attention to the songs from the last hour?'

'No. I have more pressing things to do.'

'I'm sure you do. But do an air check of the last hour.'

'An air what?'

'Check the recording.'

Diesel had reached Friedbergstrasse. As always, there were no parking spots in the dead-end street. So he double-parked his Targa next to a skip and jumped out.

'You'll see that the songs played over the last few hours are ones that we would normally never play.'

'Why not?'

'Because they failed our tests at the station. They're too bad. Or not well-known enough. Suffice to say, our target listeners don't want to hear them. We put every single song through market research.' Diesel paced through the open entrance door into the hallway of the building.

An elderly woman was standing in front of the letter boxes in freshly polished patent leather shoes. With trembling fingers, she was struggling to retrieve her post from the rusty box reserved for her. One letter had already fallen onto the floor. Diesel picked it up and handed it to her, and she smiled at him gratefully. Then he continued on towards the rear courtyard.

'Nothing that's been played over the last half hour is on any of our regular playlists.' Diesel went over to the steps and started to climb. Locating Leoni's building hadn't been too much of a challenge. Hawk had left the radio on throughout the entire flight, and after Jan had named the street and then described the blue building, Diesel had known which one he was talking about. After all, he knew the area. He had grown up around the corner from here. Even finding the apartment itself didn't pose any problems. Leoni Gregor. Her name was still on the doorbell plate.

'And what's that supposed to mean, Sherlock?' Götz was sounding more and more irritated, but Diesel still hesitated before answering. He was distracted, a little taken aback by the fact that the door was only pushed to.

'Hello? I'm talking to you! What were you trying to tell me?'

Diesel pushed the door carefully inwards and stepped in hesitantly. He noticed the smell at once. But for now he focused his mind back on the conversation at hand.

'I think the songs are clues. Consider, for example, "We Are Family" by Sister Sledge or "We Belong Together" by Mariah Carey. All titles which, under normal circumstances, Markus Timber would never play on his show. Unless there was a reason for it. Assuming that Timber is being permitted to choose the music line-up, what does this tell us?'

'The lyrics are similar.'

'Very smart, comrade.'

Diesel looked around and walked slowly through each room in the small apartment.

'Loosely translated, they're all about how we're one big family, where everyone knows each other and belongs together. Do you get it? But there's more. After that came "Little Lies" by Fleetwood Mac and then Simply Red's "Fake". What's the master DJ trying to tell us with this?' Diesel went on to answer his own question. 'It's obvious that everything in the studio is a scam. They all know each other.'

'That's possible,' said Götz quietly, then the line crackled. 'Just a minute…'

The background noises became louder, and Götz could be heard giving some instructions. Presumably he was demanding the list of the recently played titles, but his subordinate didn't seem to catch on right away. The pause lasted a little longer, and Diesel used the time to look around some more. He couldn't remember ever having stood in such an empty apartment. There was nothing here. No furniture. No fixtures in the kitchen or bathroom. No sink or bathtub, no shower or toilet. Not even doors or wallpaper. *Nothing at all!*

In addition, it smelt as though a world disinfection championship had taken place here just moments ago. Even advertising phrases like 'clinically clean' or '100 per cent sterile' seemed like an understatement here.

'I'm back,' announced Götz. 'Was there anything else?'

'Yes. You can call me crazy if you want, but I think Timber is using the music to send us instructions. Like "Come On Over". Shania Twain sings that we should come over. Kate Bush wants us to run up a hill. We're supposed to...'

Götz interrupted and finished the sentence for him:

'... storm. Okay, that matches with some discoveries that our mission leader has made.'

'Steuer. The Big Mac?'

'Yes.'

'Huh. I didn't think he had it in him.'

Boom!

The door slammed shut, presumably because of a gust of wind, making Diesel jump with shock.

Dammit! He looked angrily at the exit.

'Fuck,' he cursed loudly, trying to release the stored-up adrenalin.

'What's wrong? Why is it echoing so much your end? Where are you?'

'In Friedbergstrasse, in Leoni's old apartment.'

'Why on earth?' Götz sounded as dumbfounded as though Diesel had just reached out and grabbed his hand.

'To have a look around.' In order to change his perspective, the chief editor lay down on the freshly stripped and varnished wooden floorboards and stared at the empty ceiling. Nothing. There wasn't even a single spider's web hanging in the corner.

That's so unfair, he thought. At his place, dust bunnies crept in even while the cleaning lady was still there. And this apartment was supposed to have been empty for eight months?

'Listen to me closely, Diesel.' Götz's tone had changed suddenly. He no longer sounded irritated, but concerned. A warning tone.

'Was the door open?'

'Yes. It was ajar when I arrived. It looks like someone literally just cleared away the evidence. It's spotless. Compared to this, an intensive care ward smells like a landfill.'

'So just to be sure,' Götz didn't even respond to Diesel's last comment, 'the door was open when you arrived?'

'Yes, but…'

'Is there anyone else there? Did you run into anyone?'

'Just an old dear down by the postboxes.'

'Okay, listen to me. You're in danger. Leave the apartment at once!'

'But why?'

'Just do it.'

'Okay, but...' Diesel took his mobile from his ear. *The bastard just hung up on me!*

He was just about to stand up when he heard music. Muffled bass, as if it was booming its way out into the open air through a closed nightclub door. Diesel turned onto his side and put his ear against the floor. The music became louder. He knew the record. One floor down, someone was blasting out hip-hop. And that made him very uneasy. The letter he had picked up downstairs had been addressed to Marta Domkowitz. The Marta who, according to the doorbell panel, lived on the first floor. In the apartment the music was coming from. Diesel pulled himself to his feet and left Leoni's apartment without a backward glance. One thing was for sure. Either he was just about to meet a seventy-three-year-old with a penchant for gangsta rap for the first time in his life, or the music was intended to drown something out.

31

She pushed the handle down. The heavy fire safety door to the climatised control room opened without any problems. Kitty pulled off her sneakers and laid them in the doorframe in such a way that the door couldn't close behind her.

She tiptoed into the room on her bare feet, pedicured only yesterday, and suddenly felt a lot more vulnerable.

'Wait for my sign,' she heard her mother say. Her voice was even more of a whisper than in the kitchen. Her words were swallowed by the loud hum of the ventilation unit in the technical room, which made her feel like she was in an aeroplane.

'I'm in already,' answered Kitty. And the body bag was directly before her. It was right by the entrance, before the first shelving unit.

'No! Wait... I... wan... distract.'

'Too late. It's now or never. The walkie-talkie is about to give up the ghost.'

Kitty leant down, unsure whether her mother had been able to make out her last few words.

She opened the zip, and the accompanying sound was as loud in her ears as a chainsaw at full speed. Kitty remembered this acoustic phenomenon from her childhood. The quieter you tried to be, the louder the noises around you seem. Once, when she had wanted to sneak out of the apartment to a party in the middle of the night, the floorboards had creaked with every one of her steps more loudly than they ever did at a normal hour. She opened the body bag until she had revealed the man's head, then looked at his face.

Is he dead? Or just sleeping? Unsure as to what she should do next, she let her gaze wander over his veiled body. The body bag looked like a coffin made from crumpled fabric. Stiff and immobile. Her gaze lingered briefly at the height of his ribcage. *There!*

A sharp cry escaped her. Just briefly. Not loud. But despite that, it echoed in her ears as though she was standing in a church.

Dammit! Hopefully Jan May hadn't heard it!

'Wha… wro… ou, Ki…?'

She ignored the scraps of her mother's words. First she needed to check her suspicion. Kitty wasn't sure. Had the body in the sack just moved? Her hand trembled as she touched his pale lips. No reaction. *Where's the best place to check someone's pulse?*

She tried his neck. The skin was leathery. Badly shaven. It felt unpleasant, like a frayed cleaning sponge. Kitty couldn't feel much more than that; her fingers were so cold and stiff with tension. As if she had just scraped a layer of snow from a car windscreen with her bare hand.

Is the coldness coming from me, or the dead body?

Suddenly, Kitty yelped again. Not loudly. Even quieter than the first time, in fact. But now her panicked reaction was definitely grounded. She had to tell her mother.

She activated the walkie-talkie. 'Mama, I think he's…'

'What?'

Kitty took the thumb from the speech button and summoned all her strength. Only after a couple of seconds did she manage to bring herself to turn around. She was right, she had known it.

She wasn't the only one who had made a discovery. Jan May had too.

He was no longer in the studio.

But directly behind her.

32

With every ring, the telephone receiver in her hand became a kilogram heavier.

Please no!

Her child had cried out. Then the connection had abruptly died. And now Jan wasn't answering the studio line any more either.

What was wrong? What had Kitty wanted to tell her? And why had she cried out?

Ira's left leg was shaking. But she didn't notice it any more than she did the sweat which was running from her forehead into her eyes, mixing with her tears. Half of her was begging for Jan to pick up at last. But the other half wanted to hang up, because she was too afraid of the terrible reality.

What happened to Kitty?

At last, the eighth ring tone was interrupted. She only heard crackling at first. Then came the first word.

'Hello?'

Never before had Ira felt two such contradictory emotions at the same time: Happiness and grief, joy and horror, relief and panic. She felt it all simultaneously. Unleashed by one single, hesitant word from her daughter. He had let Kitty answer. So she was still alive. But at the same time, closer to death than ever before.

'Are you okay, sweetheart?'

'This is all your fault, Mama,' sobbed Kitty. She was beside herself. 'I was so safe in my hiding place, but you had to…'

'… abuse my trust,' completed Jan, who had grabbed the phone away from Kitty. 'May I ask what is going on? Have you snuck in your own daughter as a spy?'

'Do we really have to talk about this right now on the radio?' asked Ira, suddenly realising that this conversation was live too.

'Why not? None of the rules have changed. Everything we discuss here is for everyone to hear. So, what's the meaning of this, Ira? And don't tell me it's a coincidence.'

'But it is. I had no idea until today that my daughter was working at the station as a temp. You overlooked her, and she got locked in the station kitchen.'

Without Jan saying even a single word, Ira sensed that he was slipping away from her. So she decided to launch a counter-attack while she still had time. Soon Steuer would come and pull her off the mission.

'And why would I sneak Kitty in with you anyway? And how could I have done that? No. She was just in the wrong place at the wrong time. Just like your UPS driver. Am I right?'

If she had made him nervous, he didn't let on. 'You talk too much,' he snarled.

'Put my daughter on again.'

'I don't think you're in the situation to be making demands, Ira.'

'Please.'

She could barely make out Jan's next words. His voice was coming from much further away. He must have pushed the microphone away from him.

'She doesn't want to talk to you,' he explained.

'Kitty, if you can hear me, then…'

'And she can't hear you any more, either.' Jan's voice was now clear and distinct again. 'I turned off the loudspeaker in the studio and I'm the only one wearing headphones. I'm sure one thing is clear to you, Ira. This will be our last telephone conversation. We both know that.'

Ira's hand clenched into the right trouser leg of her cargo pants. Out of sheer nerves, she ripped open the poppers of a large outer pocket on her upper thigh and shoved in her balled fist. If it were possible, she would have fixed every movable limb of her body with a strait jacket, in order to at least attain some outer calm. But nothing would help against the battle that was raging inside her.

'Only a few hours have passed, but you've achieved so much: No one wants you here any more. The mission leaders have to pull you off the case because you're personally involved. I feel like you went behind my back. No one wants to talk to you, and even your own daughter shakes her head violently when I ask her to come to the phone. Can you tell me how you managed that, Ira?'

Ira flinched. The door to the negotiation centre had flown open. Steuer thundered in with heavy steps, his hair clinging sweatily to his forehead. He had two uniformed officials in tow. He didn't say a word; he wasn't stupid enough to arrest her in front of a live microphone. But he was already getting in position. Whatever Ira could do to help her daughter, she only had this last telephone conversation to do it in.

'Listen to me, Jan, you're a psychologist. You have to let my daughter go.'

'How are those two things connected?'

'My daughter hasn't gotten over the trauma of Sara's suicide. She hasn't talked to me since then.'

'So I'm seeing. Does she blame you?'

'I think so, yes.'

'Why?'

Ira closed her eyes. Scraps of her last conversation with Sara rose into her mind.

You won't take any pills, will you?

No, Mama!

'I already told you that Sara called me. Shortly before her death.'

'Yes. You were on the train. The connection was bad. But I don't think I want to listen to all that again.'

'You do. Wait a moment. I mean, you can hang up right now if you want, but you should know what's going on in your hostages' minds. Kitty is unstable. She could cause difficulties for you.'

'Fine then. So what happened in this last telephone conversation?'

'I made the worst mistake that a negotiator can ever make.' Ira searched for the right words, but couldn't find them. There was nothing that could make what she was about to say sound less ugly: 'I asked the wrong questions. And I didn't listen properly.'

33

You're not going in there, thought Diesel, as he found himself standing before an unlocked door for the second time in a matter of minutes. Marta Domkowitz hadn't heard his repeated ringing on the doorbell, which didn't particularly surprise him considering the loud volume of the rap music. Right now in the song, a DJ from Brooklyn was invoking all the contagious diseases in the world on his ex-wife.

'You must be out of your mind,' said Diesel to himself as he eventually stepped into the apartment regardless. Later, he would deny having felt anything but curiosity driving him along the hallway step by step. But in fact, the fear inside him drowned out even the rap, which became louder with every metre as he approached the old lady's living room. In contrast to Leoni's completely empty apartment, the furnishings down here exuded a cosy feel. Thick, cream-coloured wall-to-wall carpeting swallowed every footstep. Two small Biedermeier commodes made of dark grained walnut wood caught his eye. Just like with her shoes, Marta Domkowitz seemed to place a lot of emphasis on quality her with furniture too. Diesel didn't know for sure, but guessed that the antiques, polished to a high shine, were genuine. And expensive.

He stopped abruptly.

And his fear intensified.

At the end of the long, high-ceilinged hallway, there was something lying on the floor which fit just as little into the picture as the deafening hip-hop music. As he got closer, he saw that he wasn't hallucinating. In front of him lay a set of dentures. And next to them, a bundle of freshly printed €500 notes.

Diesel squatted down and studied the find. *Don't touch it!* he cautioned himself. Whatever was going on here – he didn't want his handprints to be found in a stranger's apartment, and especially not on a bundle of notes.

And what's that?

He would never have seen it without the change of perspective. Diesel stayed down on his haunches, wrapped a tissue around his hand and pulled the shredded shoe box out of the cupboard. The cardboard box looked as though someone had set off a firework inside it. The lid was no longer in existence; the sides were torn open, and the contents spilled out all over the floor as he pulled the box towards him. The passports were jutting out from among the other documents. Diesel undid the elastic band which was holding the two documents together. At that moment, the music stopped. But unfortunately only for a few seconds. Then a new song began. Even more furious this time. The background chorus was more like a wailing sound than anything else.

Diesel opened the first passport, confirming the suspicion the incomprehensible lettering on the fragile binding had given him. Its owner was a Ukrainian citizen. And according to the photo, she was called Leoni Gregor.

What does this mean? So Leoni's accident was faked, the hostage situation in the studio is staged, and now it turns out that she's from the Eastern Bloc?

Or from Germany! He had now opened the second passport. It looked just as genuine as the other, except that this one had been issued in Berlin.

Diesel reached for two envelopes that were lying alongside his right boot. One of them was addressed to 'Papa'. The other, 'Jan'. He opened the latter and skimmed the first few lines:

My darling, if you're reading this then the whole world will have changed for you. You will think I've been lying to you the whole time. Maybe you've even already heard about the awful things, the crimes, which...

Hang on a minute! He stopped reading.
Was there something in the living room?

Diesel stood up and peered cautiously around the corner. Empty. Just a further collection of antiques, a leather sofa suite and a wingback chair with the back facing him. But no sign of Marta Domkowitz.

To the right of the door into the living room, Diesel discovered a multi-plug socket. He pressed his foot against the red power switch, and the din of music stopped instantaneously. Diesel turned around again and looked over towards the front door. His brain tried to put all the events of the last few minutes together into some logical order, holding an inner dialogue with himself as he slowly walked back over to the entrance.

Okay, so let's assume that Leoni was living a double life

with at least two identities. She didn't even say anything to her long-term partner. Why not?

No idea.

She had known that someone would search her apartment.

So she had skeletons in her closet?

Maybe! She had written about 'bad things'. Maybe she even cleared out her apartment herself, before she disappeared.

Where to?

No idea. After all, that's what Jan wants to find out too.

Or someone killed her, destroyed the evidence at the scene of the crime, and overlooked something? But what?

The old woman of course, you idiot. She was nice to strangers. She even smiled at a bum like you.

So had Leoni entrusted her valuables to Marta Domkowitz instead of keeping them with her? The money, the passports…?

Yes, but why shred the carton? Why was the money on the carpet?

Maybe the answer was in the letter?

Yes, exactly. The letter, you fool. Keep reading!

But then Diesel's thoughts were abruptly interrupted by a new noise. In fact, it had been there the whole time. It wasn't the background chorus that had made the wailing sound, but something else.

Diesel rushed back into the living room. Ran over to the wingback chair. Walked around it. And his face contorted with horror.

Marta Domkowitz was slumped in the chair, her mouth gaping open like a fish.

Even for a horror movie enthusiast like Diesel, the sight

of her blood-covered face was hard to bear, primarily because of the pen which had been plunged into her right eye.

Fuck, fuck. fuck… Diesel didn't know whether he should pull out the pen or whether that would just make it worse. He grabbed for his mobile in order to get help. But before he had even opened it, Marta Domkowitz slid down from the chair and lay there lifelessly on the Persian rug. He turned her onto her back and felt her pulse. Nothing. She was dead.

Fuck! What now?

He vaguely remembered the first aid course he had done at driving school. Heart massage! He laid his hands one over the other and pressed down on her ribcage. *One, two, three, four…*

Now for mouth-to-mouth. He held her nose, opened her mouth and laid his lips on hers. Something in him registered that the old woman must have made an effort for her outing today. She was wearing pale pink lipstick.

Five, six, seven, eight… then mouth-to-mouth again.

At seventeen, Marta began to twitch. At eighteen she coughed. At nineteen Diesel stopped the respiration. He had done it. Marta was alive!

If only for another three seconds.

'Not bad.'

Diesel spun around and saw a face he knew only too well.

'But, unfortunately, totally in vain.'

The almost silent bullet hit the old woman in the centre of the forehead. After that, Diesel too felt a searing pain. Followed by redemptive darkness.

34

Human beings are creatures of habit. Even where suicide is concerned. Ira had discovered that most people, when selecting the method, went for the tools they were most familiar with. Policemen and women knew their way around guns, while doctors and chemists were more familiar with medication. Suicidal individuals who lived near train stations were more likely to jump in front of trains than those who lived by the sea. In turn, seaside-dwellers' fear of drowning was less than the psychologically disturbed who had wasted away the last years of their life in anonymous high-rises. These individuals tended to choose a jump from the roof as their final journey.

At police school, Ira had also had to learn the gender-specific differences. While men preferred the so-called 'harder' methods like hanging or shooting themselves, women reached for the supposed 'softer' methods.

Sara had loved flowers. For this reason, she too had conformed to the statistical pattern when she took her life with yellow oleander.

Ira was describing to Jan the last minutes of her daughter's life: 'I heard the water running into the tub. Her voice was completely calm. And totally clear. So I asked her: "You won't do anything to yourself, will you, darling?" She answered: "No, Mama." "You aren't going to slit your wrists, are you?" She said no to this question too. Instead, she told me not to worry. That she loved me, that I hadn't done anything wrong. I promised her that I would come to her as quickly as possible. She lived in a flat-share with an old school friend, Marc, in a small but beautiful apartment in Spandau. The bathroom was upstairs, on the second floor. It was clear to me that, if she was going to do something to herself, I had no chance. The taxi ride from Lehrter train station to Spandau alone would take half an hour, and my train had only left Hannover fifty minutes before.'

'Where was her friend, this Marc guy?' asked Jan.

'At work. I spoke with him briefly at the funeral. He seemed to blame himself, and was just as paralysed by grief as I was. I'm still not sure, even today, what their relationship was. I mean, you know how Sara was. I always thought Marc was asexual. Otherwise I couldn't imagine how he could have spent a year sharing the apartment with her and, presumably, all the men too.'

'And Sara lied to you when she said she wouldn't hurt herself?'

'No. She told the truth. The mistake was mine. Don't you know the textbook case about the suicidal person on the window ledge?'

It had really happened. A policeman had negotiated with a 'jumper' for an hour, and built up a good relationship of trust with him. Then the policeman made a big mistake. He said: 'Okay, let's bring this to a close. Now I want you to come down here to me.' The jumper came. He crashed down onto the pavement right in front of the policeman's feet.

'I didn't pay attention to my words. I was so afraid of a terrible answer that I asked vague questions. "You aren't going to slit your wrists, are you?" "You aren't going to take any tablets, are you?" No, she wouldn't. Not any more. Because she had *already* done it. When I noticed that her voice was becoming heavier, that her breathing was suddenly fitful, I knew that it was too late. She had killed herself. And with completely ordinary seed capsules that you can get in any garden centre.'

'Digoxin,' completed Jan.

'Correct.' The yellow oleander seeds had achieved a sad fame among suicidal individuals ever since two girls in Sri Lanka had eaten the highly poisonous capsules by mistake. One grain of the seed contained a hundred times the dose of a high-potency medication for heart defects. Just one single capsule is fatal, with 100 per cent certainty, as it slows the heartbeat more and more until it comes to a complete stop. The fact that Sara had also slit her wrists was just additional proof of her firm resolve to bring her life to an end.

Ira was surprised by her composure. Her right leg was shaking, admittedly, as though someone had attached an electrode to her thigh muscle. But she wasn't crying or screaming. Whenever she thought about her last conversation with Sara, especially when she was alone in her apartment, the psychological pain usually led to complete physical paralysis. She would lie there on the bed, stand in front of the open fridge as though she were nailed to the spot, or lie for hours on end in the bath even once the water was long cold. She still found it soothing, somehow, because the cold inside her was even greater. Now, talking about it for the first time, she was even managing to simultaneously hold the telephone, rummage around in her trouser pocket and turn her head towards Steuer, who was looking at her with an expression of unexpected sympathy.

'Just a minute,' she heard Jan say. Then he was gone. Something was happening in the studio. Ira registered a sudden surge of voices. She wasn't sure, but it sounded like Timber, shouting something incomprehensible into the microphone from a distance, accompanied by concurring cries from the other hostages. Mid-sentence, the star DJ was suddenly cut off, and along with him all the other background noise. Jan must have switched to Mute. Ira was convinced that never before had a radio silence on 101 Point 5 been followed so attentively by so many listeners.

She tried to stand up, and was amazed once again at how easily she managed it. She pushed the hair from her forehead and held both hands out towards Steuer.

'I guess there's no point in asking whether you can give me one more minute with him?'

He shook his head vigorously. His bloated upper body wobbled in rhythm with the movement.

'You can have five,' he growled, to her surprise. 'Keep him on the line for at least another five minutes. He can't move from the spot. And under no circumstances towards the experience area.'

Ira's arms sank down. This could only mean one thing. It also explained why Götz wasn't up here too. He was briefing his men. They were going to storm.

'What if I don't do it?'

'Then your daughter's chances of survival will be much

lower, and you'll go with these two gentlemen here right now.' He gestured his head towards the officials.

'And what happens to me if I continue here?'

'That depends.'

'On what?'

'On how the mission goes. What we find in the studio. Maybe you'll get off with disciplinary action.'

'We have to stop now.'

Ira looked at the telephone receiver, from which Jan's voice had just echoed out once more. She picked it up and covered the mouthpiece.

'Okay, on one condition,' she whispered to Steuer.

'What?'

'I need something to drink.'

He looked her quickly up and down. His gaze rested on the fine beads of sweat on her forehead.

'I can see that.'

'No. I mean a cola. Preferably a Cola Light Lemon.'

Steuer looked at her as though she had just ordered a lap dancer.

'And I want two bottles,' she added.

One now. One for at home. For the remaining oleander capsules that I found in the bag next to Sara's bathtub. Which are now in my freezer compartment.

She took her hand from the mouthpiece and debated feverishly how she could keep Jan on the line for a further five minutes. Especially as he already wanted to hang up.

35

Götz clapped down the visor of his titanium alloy helmet. He always chose a different camouflage cover depending on the nature of the mission. The Crush-Proof was not just his life insurance, but his good luck charm too. The more dangerous the mission, the darker the cover. Today it was pitch black.

Götz climbed onto the concrete ledge that ran around the roof of the MCB building, held onto the crane winch for the window cleaning rig, then looked down into the depths. Somewhere far beneath him hovered the cleaning rig, which in fact was supposed to have two cleaners sitting in it today, scrubbing the northern glass front. And Potsdamer Strasse, usually so packed with people, was deserted. Apart from several mission vehicles and three press broadcasting vans, no one else was allowed through the expansive exclusion barrier into the 'hot zone'. Steuer had even had local residents' parked cars towed away.

Right then, said Götz to himself, clipping the carbine hook to his belt just beneath his bulletproof vest. Then he turned his back to the abyss and jumped.

After just a few metres, Götz pressed together the two levers of a small black metal device through which the green-and-yellow rope he was currently hanging onto was wound. The rope immediately tightened, and the SEK team leader braced himself with his feet against the outer wall between the twenty-second and twenty-first floor. He lowered himself down another few centimetres so that he was hanging almost parallel, with his back to the street. Then he loosened the grip around the Rollgliss pulley again and walked slowly down the outer wall. The Swiss device was smaller than a briefcase and cost just a few francs to produce, but Götz had no fear about entrusting his life to it. It had proven itself on thousands of missions. Even if he were to be shot at right now, or if he lost consciousness, this device would prevent complete catastrophe. Götz fully trusted the producer's guarantee that every abseil procedure would be immediately halted as soon as the device was released.

'We're in the starting position,' he heard Onassis say loud and clear over the built-in helmet headset.

'Good. What about the helicopter?'

'All set.'

Including Götz, there were eight elite police officers taking part in the operation.

Team A would be led by Onassis, who was currently pushing his way through a ventilator shaft for the second time today. Team B, equipped with a battering ram and stun grenades, was positioned right in front of the studio, and Team C was waiting for the go-ahead on the outer parking deck below. Götz's plan, and consequently his life too, was dependent on these three teams working hand in hand and not making a single mistake.

I'll get Kitty out of there, he had said in the instant

message he'd sent to Ira's screen. There hadn't been any time for a goodbye. Ira couldn't stop her negotiation for a single second. And he had to hurry. If Jan were to bring a premature end to their conversation, they would no longer have the element of surprise on their side.

Götz slackened the rope a little more. His pulse quickened a little, but was still far below that of an untrained civilian. And yet his life was literally hanging on several thin, interwoven threads.

His part of the mission hadn't actually been planned. That was why he was having to abseil down here now without a dry run. Alone, because the others were occupied with the official plan. Luckily he could depend upon Onassis and the other boys. They would cover him. In many ways.

'Put the radio programme in my left ear,' he demanded over his headset, climbing down another storey. He was now level with the twentieth floor. Just another few metres separated him from the studio terrace. It hung like a pointless appendix between the eighteenth and nineteenth floors, put there purely for aesthetic reasons. Diesel had told them that no one had ever sat out on it; it was forbidden for reasons of structural safety. But right now Götz didn't have time to waste pondering the architect's bad planning. He had to concentrate on his next steps. The technician in the mission control centre finally reacted and connected the programme to his helmet headset. Götz noted with relief that Jan and Ira were still talking to one another. But the hostage taker seemed more agitated than ever. There was an argument going on in the studio, chaos in the background which resembled an out-of-control classroom. At least three people were arguing with one another.

This isn't good, thought Götz. The hostage situation was escalating. This would make Jan increasingly unpredictable.

'Do you have his position?'

'Yep,' he heard Onassis answer in his right ear. After the first few run-throughs on the sixth floor, the mission leadership had decided against storming from below. In order to prevent the hostage taker from noticing persistent vibrations in the floor, they would have needed to chisel out the reinforced concrete ceiling with handheld devices, and that would have taken far too long. So they were trying to access through the ventilation shaft once more. Onassis was in position again, and had put a second endoscopy camera in place. The one from the first mission had been discovered by Jan and destroyed.

'All clear,' said Götz, setting both feet on the untended lawn of the station terrace. He slackened the carbine hook and walked in a ducked position over to the spiral staircase, which led half a floor upwards to the entrance. He ran through the plan in his mind one more time. When he gave the command, the helicopter would start up. He would then have thirty seconds at most to break open the door and get himself positioned for the attack. As soon as he had assessed the situation, Team B would break down the front door and throw a stun grenade into the studio.

Götz fastened a strip of plastic explosives to the lock of the metal door into the experience area, then checked his weapon. It had an added SureFire light, just in case for any reason the light in the studio should go out.

'Good,' he repeated again, even though he didn't feel it. He looked at his digital watch and checked the time.

Let's hope that Steuer's right about Jan faking all of this.

Then Götz banished all his doubts into the recesses of his mind, and gave his first order.

'Team C – go!'

'Okay,' came the response. This was followed moments later by the muffled hum of rotor blades. There was no going back now. The helicopter had started up.

36

Jan didn't want to talk to Ira any longer. Nor was he able to. The situation was spiralling completely out of control. During his time as a psychologist, he had led a number of group therapy discussions. Including many in which several people had ended up screaming at each other all at once. But never before had he been the centre of the attack, as he was right at this moment. And it didn't look as though the enraged mob were going to constrain themselves to verbal abuse for much longer.

'Jan, you idiot, accept it. The show's over. Give up!'

'Or at least let us out of here!'

'Your plan didn't work. You've lost control!'

He listened to the hysterical chaos without making any commentary. The earpiece was in his left ear, and the Glock in his right hand, still aimed at Kitty. She was standing directly before him, the only one on his side of the mixing desk. All the others were standing at the 'bar' opposite him.

'Dammit, Jan,' said Theodor Wildenau, trying a calmer tone. 'Listen. You said we would be out of here in two hours at most. Without any violence. That no one would get hurt, apart from perhaps that jerk Timber. And now look at you...'

Flummi, the show's producer, stared at Theodor in disbelief. Unlike Timber, it was only dawning on him now.

'Hello? Jan? Are you still there?' Now Ira was trying to get his attention again too.

'Yes. But there's nothing more to discuss.'

'What's that noise where you are?'

'Nothing.'

He hung up the phone. Composed himself for a moment. Then he began to shout: 'Shut your goddamn mouths!' His voice became louder with every word, and it had the desired effect. The 'hostages' fell silent.

'*I* say when it's over. *I* decide what happens next? Can you get that through your thick skulls?'

His voice cracked.

'If we give up now, we've lost everything. *Everything!* Is that clear to you? That's their tactic. They *want* to wear us down. They *want* this to be happening right now. Do you think you can just stroll out and say: 'April Fool! Don't be mad. It was just a joke!'? You have no idea! If we leave the studio now without any proof, they'll lock you all up. Your careers will be over. And your futures! To them, you'll be nothing but a bunch of nutjobs who hijacked a radio station with some maniac.' He shook his head. 'No, we can't give up now. We have to keep going. Only if we prove to the public that Leoni is still alive – if we uncover the conspiracy and the reasons behind it – only then do we all have a chance.'

'But what if there isn't any proof?' Sandra Marwinski asked. She leant against the studio wall and removed the rubber attachment from beneath her blouse. The show was over; her performance as a pregnant woman was no longer needed. Nor would she need to tell any more stories about Anton today. The picture of the disabled toddler in her handbag had been downloaded from the internet.

'You mean, what if I'm really crazy? If Leoni really is dead?'

Jan felt his strength dwindling. The psychological strain was exhausting him. And he hadn't eaten anything in hours. His stomach felt as though it had shrunken to the size of a two-euro coin, and the muscles in his right arm were burning like fire. After all, he wasn't accustomed to pointing a gun at someone for so long.

'Okay. I'll make a suggestion. I admit that things are not going the way we planned today. I misjudged things. But let's be honest for a moment; every one of us thought they would lay their cards on the table right after the first execution.'

'But they can't!' interjected Timber.

Jan didn't respond to his comment, but continued, 'I expected everything to go much more quickly. But why are they messing around out there? Why are they putting all your lives at risk? After all, they don't know we know each other. Despite that, they didn't think twice about sending a sniper through the shaft. They don't want to negotiate, and they don't even tell their own negotiator what their strategy is. Instead, they redirect the calls.' He tapped the gun on Kitty's shoulder. 'They're trying to hide something. Just like Kitty hid herself away, the truth isn't supposed to come out either. Do you see? They want to silence me. But why? That's the question: What happened to Leoni?'

'She's dead!' shouted Timber.

Jan just waved his hand dismissively and looked at each one of his accomplices in turn.

'Sandra, Maik, Cindy, Theodor! Listen to me: You know the facts. You've helped me get this far. Now I'm asking you for one last favour. Give me one more hour. One more Cash Call. If they still let me carry on – and if I can't give you any conclusive proof that Leoni is still alive by then – then you can all go.'

'This is completely insane!' Maik slammed the palm of his hand down on the bar. His 'girlfriend' Cindy, who in real life preferred women, nodded in silent agreement. 'Why would the cops change their tactic now? What difference will an hour make?'

'This girl here makes a difference!' Jan prodded Kitty again. 'Ira Samin is personally affected. If we play the next Cash Call with Kitty, she'll pull out all the stops to find Leoni. Nothing is stronger than a mother's love and nothing—'

What was that?

Jan turned around mid-sentence and looked over at the fire safety shutters in front of the windows. What was happening?

He felt the vibrations in his feet first. Then the CDs in the shelving unit next to the studio door began to clink. Before long, the entire room was filled with surging sound waves. He couldn't continue talking now anyway, even if he had wanted to. The drone of the helicopter outside was so loud that it was unpleasant. No, worse than that. It hurt! And the intensity was still increasing. Jan was sure he could feel wind pressing against his eardrums with brute force. He screamed, let the gun fall and pressed his hands to his ears. Turning around, he saw that all the others were doing the same thing. No one would grab for the pistol. No one would try to flee. They were all being tormented by the same pain. Jan felt certain that if he were to pull his fingers out of his ear canals, into which he was pressing them as hard as he could, they would certainly be smeared with blood. The pain was unbearable.

37

For the first twenty seconds, everything went like clockwork. Then began what the police report would later define as a 'tragedy'.

At the same moment as the helicopter directed its sonic canon at the studio, Götz used the explosive charge to open the door to the experience area. He stormed into the small studio kitchen. Despite the ear protectors activated in his helmet, he felt a pressure in his ear canals as intense as if he were standing right next to the speakers at a rock concert. The canon was unbelievable!

The ocean liner *Queen Mary 2* was equipped with a similar device, to chase away the modern-day pirates who were especially prevalent off the coast of Africa. The version installed in the helicopter was smaller, of course, but even this volume was only bearable *behind* the source of the noise. Götz flipped open a mini computer which was attached to his bulletproof vest. On the monitor, he was able to follow the progress of Team A on the first floor.

'Secure the CER,' he roared into the microphone. Acoustic comprehension was out of the question amid the din, but his voice would be sent from a speech computer as a text file to the other teams and into the mission control centre.

After two paces, he was in the technical room. Solely to make sure that there was no danger to be expected from there. In two seconds' time, Onassis would remove the ceiling panel and capture the entire studio with a bigger camera. One and a half seconds after that, as soon as Götz had obtained an overview from the monitor screen of the situation in the studio and Jan's position, he would put on his gas mask and give the go-ahead to Team B.

As soon as the stun grenade was ignited, his next step was to overpower Jan, while Onassis covered him from above in case any of the hostages posed a danger. Should it prove to be necessary, Götz would shatter Jan's neck with a knuckleduster between C2 and C3 vertebrae, making sure not to sever his spinal cord in the process. This would paralyse him, leaving him unable to activate the explosives, which no one still believed that he had strapped to his stomach anyway. No one, that is, except Götz.

He saw from the digital display of his helmet that only four seconds had passed. After ten seconds, at most, the first shock phase would be over. As soon as Jan realised what was going on, he would overcome his pain and initiate some kind of counter-attack.

But from one second to the next, the situation spiralled out of control. The first shock was the news about Manfred Stuck, the UPS driver. Götz briefly informed mission control, knowing the paralysing horror that the words would transmit: 'He's dead. Stuck is dead.'

And that could only mean...

... that Jan really is dangerous. And that he's prepared himself for this eventuality.

'Abort,' roared Götz into his microphone. 'The target is dangerous. I repeat...'

The noise in the CER suddenly became louder, even though the helicopter hadn't changed the direction of the sonic canon. And there could only be one reason for that, a suspicion which Götz confirmed with a single glance at his monitor: Jan was standing in the doorway to the experience area.

That's impossible! screamed Götz in his mind. *How can he stand the noise?*

But he could. It was crystal clear on the monitor. Jan May was coming towards him. Without headphones, completely vulnerable to the supersonic sound. He must be in agony. But he was being driven on by the courage of hopelessness.

Götz saw only one dwindling chance of leaving the CER alive. It didn't matter which direction he went in. If he wanted to get out of here, he would have to get past Jan, who at this moment was stretching his left fist upwards, holding in it a small blinking device. He said something, but of course Götz couldn't understand a single word.

'Turn it off. Turn the canon off!' he bellowed into his headset. A moment later, everything suddenly became calm. Götz deactivated the electronic ear protectors in his helmet and heard the blood rushing in his ears; an involuntary accompaniment to Jan's agitated threats.

'You asked for it. Now I'm sending us all to the other side,' yelled the hostage taker. Obviously he was trying to drown out the high-pitched buzzing sound in his own ears after the sonic attack. May had stopped level with the sink and was now standing just three paces from the entrance to the CER.

He's completely insane.

It was now or never. Götz lifted the corpse of the UPS driver, pulled it against himself like a shield and began to exit the room.

'Don't shoot!' he yelled in Jan's direction, who didn't seem at all surprised to see him there. He just stood there coolly and repeated his threat one more time:

'I warned you all. If I press this button, it will tear us to shreds. I hope you're ready!'

One quick glance at the monitor, and Götz saw that Onassis was trying to climb down into the studio. He had already removed one ceiling panel. It seemed he thought he could help Götz as long as Jan was in the studio kitchen and with his back to him.

'I only came to get this man out of here,' said Götz, just as coolly as Jan, moving backwards towards the door, behind which lay the spiral staircase down to the terrace. He had laid the arms and head of the UPS driver over his shoulder, which meant that Stuck's back offered him additional protection to his bulletproof vest. But neither would be of any use to him if the hostage taker stood by his word and ignited the explosive charge.

'He's staying here,' Jan demanded. 'Just like you. Because all of us are just about to witness a very special fireworks display...' The hostage taker lifted his fist. Only now did Götz notice the pistol in his other hand.

And then everything happened very quickly.

Götz saw the red laser beam on the monitor. Onassis seized Jan from behind. He wasn't wearing a helmet, because he had needed to fit his head and the hand holding the weapon through the narrow slit in the ceiling. Jan's hand gripped more tightly around the remote control with which he was about to unleash the explosion. Onassis now had half a second at most to deliver the paralysing shot.

But it won't work, thought Götz. *Onassis's weapon is too powerful.*

At this proximity, Jan would be sure to die. And then they would only have another ten seconds…

'Onassis, no!' roared Götz, his words preventing a death sentence for all the people who were on the eighteenth and nineteenth floors at this moment.

With one exception.

Jan May turned around, lifted his weapon and aimed at the policeman. A heartbeat later, the shot was fired, hitting the SEK man's unprotected temple. Onassis's expression was one of amazement. Disbelief.

Then his slackened body was pulled backwards into the ventilation shaft.

Jan May paused in shock in the middle of the kitchen and gaped in disbelief at the spot in the ceiling from which the SEK man had been staring out just a minute before. Then he looked down and stared at the weapon in his hand, as though he himself couldn't believe what he had done.

Götz made use of the moment to run as quickly as he could, with the UPS driver on his shoulders, towards the exit. Through the forced-open door, down the spiral staircase, towards the outer edge of the green terrace.

Then, in expectation of an explosion in the studio, he put everything at stake and jumped down into the depths.

38

The well-known radio station 101 Point 5 may well have reached the highest listener quota in its fifteen-year history today. And yet no one has any reason to celebrate. Since shortly after 7 a.m. this morning, a man who is obviously mentally disturbed has been holding six people hostage, one of whom he has already executed live on air. More shocking news from the studio has just reached us. A SWAT team's attempt to storm the studio has ended in a bloodbath. According to reports which have now been confirmed, there was an exchange of fire in Studio A, during which a SEK official was fatally wounded. A further police officer, the leader of the mission, escaped the danger zone with a death-defying jump from the nineteenth-floor terrace. Miraculously, his fall was broken two floors down by a window cleaning cart. Unfortunately, the hostage who he was carrying on his back was not as lucky; he was already dead. Shot through the hand by the Radio Killer, who has now taken two lives. All over Germany, everyone is wondering how long the insanity will last…

'Just look at that!' bellowed Steuer as he approached. He gesticulated furiously with one of his fat hands towards the television. Ira was standing in the lobby of the MCB building, staring at the large wall monitor directly above the reception desk. Usually it displayed short advertisement films of the various companies based here, running on a continuous loop. Due to today's events, the custodian had switched to a twenty-four-hour news channel. Now the solemn voice of an androgynous newsreader was echoing through the lobby, and her strict reporter's gaze was flickering simultaneously on sixteen screens.

'This is all your fault!' cried Steuer. He pushed his bulky body in front of Ira, cutting off her view of the television.

'Do you have any idea how deep in shit you are right now, Ira? Compared to what you've unleashed today, Chernobyl was just a minor hiccup!'

'I wasn't the one who wanted to storm in!' Ira didn't look at him as she spoke. Not because she was afraid of him, but because she was afraid of herself. Her fear for Kitty was numbing all her senses. And possibly her self-control too. She was afraid that, if she had to look Steuer in the eye for even a fraction of a second, she would slam her fist into his fleshy face.

'You were the one who said it was a bluff. That Jan was harmless.'

'And *you* had an eyewitness who was able to testify to the contrary,' bellowed Steuer in response. 'You didn't tell me, and you consciously let my men walk straight into a catastrophe.'

But I wasn't sure, thought Ira. The second-worst feeling right now was that he was right. She had pulled the wool over his eyes, and put the lives of the other hostages before that of her daughter. And the worst was the thought that it might all have been in vain.

'Stop,' roared Steuer, this time at a group of paramedics who were in the process of rolling two stretchers towards the exit. He strode over to them and pulled back the sheet.

'Here. Look! This is better than TV, Ira. This man here' – he pointed to the face of the dead Onassis – 'had a family, children. And this one here' – he hastened over to the other stretcher, – 'was planning to go bowling with his girlfriend tonight. I now have to call their next of kin and tell them that these men won't be coming home tonight. Nor tomorrow. Never again, in fact. And all because some washed-up alcoholic couldn't play by the rules.'

He spat on the floor and waved over two policemen who were guarding the entrance.

'Get her out of my sight. Take her to the precinct.'

The men nodded diligently. Ira wouldn't have been surprised if they had also said, 'At your command, sir,' and clicked their heels together. Instead, she heard a snapping sound, like a zipper. Then the plastic handcuffs were fastened around her wrists, and she was ready to be led away.

39

The black wide-base tyres squeaked like new sneakers on freshly polished linoleum as the heavy Mercedes estate car raced up around the tight bends of the multi-storey car park. Ira sat in the back, leaning her tired head against the tinted windows. She was leaving the crime scene in a similar state to how she had arrived. Exhausted, ravaged by alcohol withdrawal and handcuffed. Steuer had at least been considerate enough not to expose her to the press. Presumably he was afraid of the headlines. It would certainly throw a bad light on the SEK leader, too, if the negotiator were to be photographed being led from the MCB building like a criminal. In order to spare himself the troublesome explanations, he had arranged for her to be practically smuggled out through the back exit to the next precinct.

'Is there anything to drink in here?' she asked the young officer who was driving. Her seat belt tightened as she tried to lean forwards.

'This isn't a limo, you know,' he answered brusquely. 'There's no cocktail cabinet.'

She hadn't paid any attention to him as she had climbed into the vehicle, and could now see just his brown eyes and matching eyebrows in the rear-view mirror. It was too little to go on to hazard a guess at his character.

'Maybe we can make a quick stop?' she asked in jest. 'There's no Cola Light in the vending machine at the precinct.'

Ira leant back again as the officer made a sharp right turn. If her sense of orientation hadn't failed her, they were now driving eastwards down Leipziger Strasse.

Just make another right at the next light, then I'll be home in ten minutes, she thought. *Then I won't be anyone's problem any more. I can just take the capsules the regular way. With water.*

Ira was under no illusions. Even if she could take down the level of her headache a notch with half a bottle of vodka, she would still be powerless. She was no longer in the game. She had been sent to the penalty bench by Steuer himself. There was nothing more she could do to help Kitty.

Ira saw the imposing Federal Assembly building rush past on the right-hand side. The speedometer of the Mercedes was showing a consistent ninety. An unusual speed for the Leipziger Strasse at this hour. If it weren't for the exclusion zone, the car would be stuck in rush-hour traffic with all the other commuters.

As the car took a sharp left turn into Friedrichstrasse, a wave of nausea rose up in Ira. She retched, and was still choking as the detective suddenly stepped on the brakes and turned to the right down into an underground garage entrance.

'Where are we going?' she asked flatly. She heard the click of the automatic door lock. With the headlights turned off, the car made its way down the winding descent of the sparsely lit multi-storey car park. Three levels further down, the vehicle finally came to a halt.

'Where are we?' Again, Ira didn't receive an answer. She lifted her cuffed hands and wiped her damp forehead on her lower arm. She wasn't quite sure if the sweat was from fear or one of the withdrawal symptoms. The same applied to her trembling fingers as she fumbled to open the door. *Wherever we are, it's certainly not the next precinct*, she thought. She was strangely reassured when the car door opened without any problems. The officer, who had already gotten out, had clearly not locked the car when she heard the clicking sound, but unlocked it. A moment later, Ira saw why. He was standing two parking spaces further back, directly beneath a bright-green emergency exit sign. 'Thank you,' said the burly man to the officer, clapping him on the upper arm. 'You did a good job.'

Then he laid his arm around the officer's shoulder and turned around with him towards the dark-grey concrete wall of the car park. Ira couldn't hear what they were whispering to each other. She only saw that he handed the driver something the size of an envelope, then gave him another pat on the upper arm. The officer stood there waiting as the other man came towards her.

'I sorted it, Ira. Get out. We don't have much time.'

She raised her eyebrows, shook her head and looked at him in complete confusion.

'What are you doing, Götz?'

40

Pandemonium broke out shortly after the newsreader had finished reading her report. Jan was the only one still staring at the studio TV suspended beneath the ceiling. The others were screaming frantically at one another in panic. Timber had even left his seat, and there was no mistaking his intentions: He wanted to get as close possible to the door leading into the kitchen without being noticed.

'Don't move an inch!' roared Jan, aiming the Glock at his body. Timber flung his arms up instinctively.

'And the rest of you' – he looked each one of them in the eyes – '*listen to me!*'

His yelling quickly achieved the desired effect. Even Theodor Wildenau, who had now become the spokesman of the group, stopped his verbal torrent for a moment.

'All I did was shoot into the air,' called Jan. He sounded like a speaker at a rally filled with a hostile audience. 'I didn't kill anyone. Neither the UPS driver nor the policeman.'

'Do you think we're complete idiots, Jan?' screamed Theodor. His face was contorted with rage. Nothing about him was reminiscent of the good-tempered wisecracker from that morning.

'We all saw you lift the gun. Then there was a shot and

the policeman collapsed. And now they're showing two corpses on the news. Do you seriously think we can't put two and two together?'

'How many times do I have to tell you all? This whole thing is a staged performance. No one died. They want to turn us against one another, and by the looks of it they're doing a pretty good job!'

'You're out of your mind,' piped up Sandra Marwinski. 'I didn't actually care whether your girlfriend was alive or not. I just wanted to earn some extra cash and was happy to play the pregnant woman to do that. But I refuse to let you implicate me in a double homicide.' She climbed down from the bar stool and pulled her mobile out of the inside pocket of her denim jacket.

'I'm going now. If you don't want to open the door for me, that's fine. I'll take the same route as that guy who dragged out the UPS man. Through the kitchen and onto the terrace.' She waved her mobile phone. 'And then I'll call for help.'

'No, Sandra. No you won't.'

'Oh, yes, she will,' hissed Timber angrily. Theodor, Maik and Cindy nodded. Only Kitty just stood there, the picture of misery, directly next to the man-sized loudspeaker. She watched them all, her eyes wide in fear.

'We're all leaving together,' continued Timber. 'And if you don't like it, you can shoot us in the back.'

The mob set off. Even the shy Flummi didn't seem to be afraid any more. He pushed past Jan and hurried over towards the already-open door into the studio kitchen.

Jan lifted his arms helplessly, pressing the backs of his hands against his throbbing temples. He thought feverishly.

What should I do? How can I stop them? The thoughts were hammering in his mind like pistons.

Timber was already in the doorframe. None of the group were paying any attention to Jan. He had completely lost control.

And if I don't get it back again, everything will be lost. Jan made a decision. He had to act. He had to take extreme measures.

The gunshot stopped them all in their tracks. Theodor was the first who dared to look Jan directly in the face again.

'Next time, I'll send the bullet right through her head,' said Jan. He had Kitty in a headlock. Her whole body was shaking, but she didn't even whimper. 'Maybe you don't value your own lives any more. But can you live with yourselves if this little one snuffs it because of you?'

'You won't do it, you asshole!' Sandra was the first to find her voice again.

'Why not? You've seen for yourselves what I'm capable of.'

'So, you did...' All the colour drained from Theodor's wide face.

'Yes, you're right,' confirmed Jan. 'I admit it: I killed them. Both of them. The policeman and the courier. I'm evil. I was right from the start, and you all fell for it hook, line and sinker. And do you want to know something else?' He looked into their shocked eyes.

'I'm going to kill at least one more time today. Or did you really believe I'm doing all of this just because I love Leoni so much?' He spat his words. 'That slut deserves to die. And as soon as I get my hands on her, she will.'

41

Götz came slowly towards her with the serrated knife. Ira lifted her hands above her head in a pointless gesture.

'Hold still,' he growled. Then he cut through the binding around her hands.

She rubbed her wrists. The tear-proof plastic bands were certainly better than the usual heavy metal handcuffs. It was just that her hands weren't accustomed to being bound together twice in one day.

'Why are you doing this?' she asked, looking around.

Hardly anything had changed in the small apartment. It still looked like the window display of a furniture store. Functional, clean, but completely impersonal. Admittedly, Ira had never taken much interest in how Götz's living room was furnished. Back then, they had spent significantly more time on the upper level of the maisonette apartment. Up where the bedroom was. To her, Götz had been nothing more than an anchor in the sea of men she had drifted through aimlessly after her failed marriage. He had definitely seen more in their relationship, something which was becoming increasingly obvious to her now, given everything that he was doing for her today.

'The policeman who drove you...' Götz began, '... he fucked up. Big time. His blood alcohol level was one point eight when the officers stopped him. His big dream is to make it into the SEK some day. But with a penalty like that on his file he wouldn't even have been able to get a job as a taxi driver.'

'And you deleted the record from the database?'

'Yes. And in return he brought you here. To me.'

'But why?'

'Maybe because I can't stand Steuer? Because I don't want you to end up writhing in pain while you go cold turkey in some police cell? Or because I'm looking for a way for you to get back into the negotiation so that you can save Kitty.' He shrugged his broad shoulders. 'Take your pick.'

Ira pulled off her beaten leather jacket and let it fall down onto the cream-coloured carpet. If she could, she would have sunk down onto her knees, wrapped her arms around Götz's ankles and fallen asleep right there.

'I need something to drink,' she explained. 'Something strong.'

'Upstairs, next to the bed. Go up and take a bath. Or a shower. You know your way around,' he answered. He led her over to the gently curved wooden steps.

Ira was shaking, holding tightly onto the banister with one hand.

Götz was right behind her, propping her up. His chin resting on her neck. She could feel the warmth of his breath.

As she looked down at the first step, the memories washed over her like a heavy downpour.

The notes. At Sara's place. One on every step.

'What's wrong?' whispered Götz as she shivered. 'Are you thinking about how it was back then, too? About what it could have been?'

'Yes.' She freed herself from his embrace, and her eyes filled with tears. 'But I'm not thinking about us.'

'Who then?' He stroked the hair from her face and kissed her gently on the mouth. She let it happen.

'About Sara,' she said after a while. She sat down on the first step. 'Did I ever tell you how I found her?'

'Yes. In the bathtub.'

'No, I mean what happened before that.'

Götz shook his head and knelt down in front of her.

'She lived in Spandau. In a maisonette like this one. Only smaller.' Ira sniffed. 'When I finally got there, the front door was open, and I knew it was too late. I ran in, and the first thing I saw was the note.'

'Her suicide note?'

'No.' Ira shook her head vigorously. 'Or yes, something like that, maybe.'

'What did it say?'

'*Don't go any further, Mama!*' Ira looked up at Götz, who despite his kneeling position was still half a head taller than her.

'There was another note on every step of the stairs: *Don't go any further!*, *Call the ambulance!*, *Spare yourself the sight!* I collected all the notes as I went up, step by step. Slowly, as if I was in a trance. But I didn't obey Sara's last wish.' Fat tears were running down Ira's face.

'By the time I got to the second-last step, my legs were refusing to move. '*I love you, Mama,*' it said on the note. But then I saw the last step…'

'What was there?' Götz kissed her tears away, leaning forwards and pulling her shaking body against his.

'Nothing,' sobbed Ira. 'Nothing at all. I ran into the bathroom, but of course it was too late. There was nothing more I could do for Sara. But whenever I think about it now, that last step haunts me. No matter whether I'm asleep or whether the memories are going around in my mind during the day. I can't shake the feeling that there was a note missing. My daughter wanted to tell me something, but I never got to read the final note!'

42

Jan waved the distraught group back into the studio with his gun. They obeyed, albeit reluctantly.

He yanked Kitty's head upwards and pushed her away from him. Then he ordered Timber and Flummi to drag the metal unit containing the archive CDs across the entrance of the experience area, to block the escape route once more.

My God, what am I doing? Jan asked himself as he stepped back over to the mixing desk. By now he knew where the slider for the microphone was. He interrupted an early 80s hit by Billy Idol and went on air:

'This is 101 Point 5, and I need to announce a further rule change.'

He could barely hear his own words, so loud was the persistent ringing in his ears caused by the sonic canon. And he felt miserable and exhausted. Sweat was running in a steady trickle down the nape of his neck.

I can't keep this up much longer.

He coughed briefly before he spoke again.

'Based on recent developments, it seems that all of you out there are keen for a final round. So you wanted to kill me? You wanted to storm the studio? Fine. If you want to up the stakes, then consider it done.' He coughed again, this time into microphone.

'Next time, it's all or nothing. I'm going to call a phone number again. It doesn't matter whether it's a mobile or landline. Or a company or private line. We're playing with higher risk, but with higher stakes too. If someone answers with the correct slogan, then I'll set all of the hostages free.'

Jan looked around.

'But if not, I'll *kill them all*.'

He looked at the blood-red LED display of the studio clock.

'Next hour – next round!'

43

Ira was feeling guilty. Guilty because she had greedily knocked back the clear liquid in the heavy vodka glass on Götz's nightstand. Guilty because she was in the process of unbuttoning her white blouse to take a bath, while just a few hundred metres away her daughter was in mortal danger. But mostly she felt guilty for the intimacy she had just shared with Götz. Not physically, but in a far more intense way, through the conversation about Sara's last moments.

She held her hand in the steaming-hot stream of water that was pouring into the whirlpool bathtub from a wide-curved stainless steel tap. There was a knock on the door behind her.

'Just a minute.' She held her blouse together at the front as she padded barefoot over the cold tiles. 'Did you forget something? It's okay, I haven't undressed yet...'

As she opened the door, her face froze into a mask.

She reacted a split second too late. The door rebounded off the paratrooper's boots as she tried to close it again. A moment later, the masked man hit her with full force in the face with a wooden bat, violently pushing his way into the room. Dazed, she tried to break her fall on a handrail, tearing it and the towels draped over it to the floor.

The last thing she felt was the syringe in her neck, followed by numbness. It felt like the local anaesthetic you get at the dentist, except that it was spreading throughout her entire body. Then everything went black.

She was already unconscious as the killer, humming softly to himself, laid her out on the bathroom floor. With the melody of 'I Did It My Way' on his lips, he buttoned up her blouse, pushed her cold feet back into the sneakers she had discarded next to the toilet a few minutes ago, then wrapped her up in a thick white towelling dressing gown. Now he all he needed to do was dispose of her.

PART III

I don't want to start any blasphemous rumours
But I think that God's got a sick sense of humour
And when I die I expect to find Him laughing.

Depeche Mode

Strangely, I find that the best and most reliable disguise
is always the pure and naked truth. Because no one
believes it.

Max Frisch, *Biedermann und die Brandstifter*

1

The opened bottle cast its amber glow into the darkened room. Held by an invisible hand, it was defying gravity. By all rights it should have tipped and spilled its high-percentage contents over the filth-ridden carpet, but just like the heavy lead crystal glass alongside it, the bottle simply stayed attached to the wall.

Ira blinked again and again until her sense of balance improved a little. Initially, she thought she was leaning against a wall, but then she felt the pressure flattening her body down onto the hard wooden surface. She wasn't standing, she was lying down. But where?

Ira tried to shift position, hoping that this might help to reduce the migraine-like nausea, but she didn't succeed. Neither her upper body nor her legs would move.

'What's that you're trying to do?' she heard an amused voice say. 'Press-ups?'

Summoning all of her strength, Ira turned onto her back and saw a blurred face hovering above her. She lifted her head and slowly took in her surroundings. Bottles, glasses, a sink. She was in a bar, without a doubt. The wooden surface beneath her back was the bar itself.

'Who are you?' she mumbled. Her numbed tongue lay in

her dried-out mouth like a dead fish, producing the barely comprehensible speech sounds of a stroke patient.

'Please excuse the side effects of the anaesthetic,' said the voice in mock sympathy. 'I just wanted to make sure that you got to our meeting on time.'

Ira felt two hands grab her, wrench her upwards and sit her on the bar stool like a mannequin. The fragmented images of her surroundings were rolling around in her numbed brain. By the time they settled again, the man behind her had disappeared, and a familiar face pieced itself together before her eyes. It was on almost every front page at the moment: Marius Schuwalow, otherwise known as 'the Masseuse'. In two days time, the Ukrainian was supposed to face trial. But no one seriously expected him to be convicted. Due to the scant evidence, he would probably get off with a caution. The boss of organised crime had either manipulated, bribed or 'massaged away' all the witnesses.

His nickname was meant literally. For the massages in question, he used special gloves soaked in fluoric acid. It was his speciality. He strapped his victims naked to an autopsy table and massaged their skin with the deathly hydrogen fluoride until their tissues and muscles were so corroded that they bled to death. Mostly, though, their lungs would collapse long before that, from the poisonous gases they inhaled while screaming out their death cries.

'Can I offer you anything, Frau Samin?' asked Schuwalow now, pointing like a bartender at the collection of bottles around him. 'You look as though you could do with a sip or two.'

He spoke German perfectly, without any trace of an accent. Schuwalow had studied law and economics in

London and Tübingen, and thanks to his over-average IQ had graduated with honours. As always, he would be representing himself in the forthcoming trial. A further humiliation for his opponent, Johannes Faust, who was leading the hopeless prosecution.

'What's all this about?' Ira managed to get the words out at last. 'Where am I?'

'In hell.'

'I can see that.'

'Thank you for the compliment,' grinned Marius Schuwalow, 'but I don't mean it in the metaphorical sense. This establishment is called Hell. I take it you're not a frequenter of Drinkers' Alley?'

I haven't sunk that low just yet, thought Ira. Of all the options for getting drunk in Berlin, the Alley was one of the seediest. A good dozen bars lined up like shoeboxes in the furthest corner of a shopping complex between Lietzenburger Strasse and the Ku'damm, and there was only one difference between them all: they were either in the process of going bust, or already had.

'What do you want from me?' she asked again. This time, Schuwalow seemed ready to respond. He reached for a remote control and turned on a dusty television, which was hanging to the right behind Ira, directly over a sofa.

'Your young friend asked me that too.'

Ira turned around and saw who else was in the room with her. Directly beneath the TV screen sat the man who must have pulled her onto the stool, a steroid-fuelled baldhead with a V-shaped face. Next to him, she recognised the chief editor of the radio station, his head laid on the table in exhaustion. The V-face wrenched Diesel's head upwards by his hair. Blood dripped from a wound on his forehead down over his swollen eyes and onto the table.

'Great party, huh?' he said, giving a tortured smile as he recognised Ira. Then he fell unconscious again.

'I want to know where Leoni is and whether she's still alive,' demanded Schuwalow as Ira turned back to him.

'Then you're not the only one.'

'Your friend said that too, and his sarcasm brought him some unnecessary pain.' Schuwalow blew the smoke from his cigarette into Ira's face. 'I had you down as being more sensible, and was hoping we could talk business more quickly.'

'I don't know anything. And even if I did' – Ira gestured towards the brown-tinted window, through which passers-by could easily peer into the inside of the bar – 'I wouldn't tell you *here*. Unless you're planning on torturing me before an audience.'

'Yes, why not?' asked Schuwalow, looking genuinely surprised. 'What would happen? Look at that one for example.' He pointed at a stressed-looking housewife who was hurrying past the glass window with a rickety shopping trolley. For sure she was using the Alley as a shortcut to the Ku'damm. 'She doesn't want to waste her time looking at the poor excuses for human beings getting drunk here in the early afternoon. And even if she did' – he held a mirror, a promotional gift from a local brewery, in front of Ira's face – 'what do you think she would see if she risked a glance?'

'A washed-up alcoholic,' admitted Ira.

'Exactly. You don't stand out in the slightest around here. You can scream, bleed and kick the counter all you want. The crazier you act in here, the quicker the embarrassed busybodies out there will go on their way. That's why I like doing my business in public, my dear Frau Samin. Because – and you should take note of this: Nothing is more anonymous than public life.'

Ira had met many psychopaths in the course of her negotiations. She didn't need a lie detector to know that Schuwalow was completely insane and telling the truth. 'Let's make a start then. Are the vats of acid behind the counter ready?'

'No, what are you thinking? I've got something much more fitting planned for you. I'm a businessman, and you're a negotiator. That's why I'm going to make you an offer.'

Schuwalow looked at the delicate clockface on his watch. 'You're in luck; it's Happy Hour right now in Hell. That means I'll give you two pieces of information in exchange for one from you. How does that sound?'

Ira didn't even make the effort to respond.

'Information number one: Leoni Gregor is definitely not dead. Do you see that picture over there?'

Ira turned around again and stared at the TV monitor. A blurry digital photo was monopolising almost the entire screen. It looked like a paparazzi shot. The pregnant woman busy shopping in a Spanish supermarket didn't seem to have noticed that she was being photographed.

'That's Leoni, presumably eight months gone,' explained Marius. 'We got it from the hard drive of a high-ranking state prosecutor, Johannes Faust.'

'How did you get access to that?' asked Ira in amazement.

'Unfortunately that is *not* the second piece of information you will receive, Frau Samin. But don't worry, because it's not anywhere as interesting as what I'm about to tell you.'

Schuwalow grabbed her chin between his thumb and index finger and squeezed it painfully. He emphasised his next words as though he were the American president addressing the nation:

'Leoni Gregor is my daughter!'

2

For a moment, Ira was so stunned that she forgot her nausea. This last statement was almost more incomprehensible than the situation she was in.

'I haven't seen Leoni in almost two years,' Schuwalow continued. 'She disappeared shortly after my fifty-sixth birthday. At our last family get-together, by the way, she was still called Feodora.'

Feodora Schuwalow. Ira could remember well the young Ukrainian woman whose face had once filled the pages of fashion magazines. She was a model, and her proximity to the mafia had made her an object of great interest for the tabloid press. Then, two years ago, she had suddenly dropped off the radar. There had been talk of some rare disease keeping her bedbound. The speculations ranged from multiple sclerosis to Aids. From one day to the next, she was never seen in public again. And that still hadn't changed. Because, as far as Ira could remember, Feodora's face possessed only a distant similarity to Leoni Gregor's.

'She underwent quite a few facial surgeries,' continued Marius.

'Why?'

'Well, certainly not for aesthetic reasons. She was beautiful already.'

'What are you getting at?' Ira wanted to scream and shout at her future murderer, but every word she uttered caused her pain.

'My dear Frau Samin, it seems you too have had to go through difficult family problems, as I found out on the radio today. It won't surprise you to hear that it happens in even the best of homes. Including mine.'

'Feodora ran away from home?'

'You could put it like that. We had a fight. You know how it is. A small fissure grows into a deep chasm which seems impossible to bridge from either side. Our father–daughter relationship had always been strained. Let's just say that we had our differences regarding the way I run my family business.'

'What, she didn't want to stir the vats of acid any more?' asked Ira, rubbing her eyes.

'She wanted to testify against me.' Marius let the poignant words hang in the air for a while, before adding: 'Faust recruited her as the prosecution's main witness for the trial.'

'And so you made her disappear.' Ira's hands cramped up on the edge of the bar. 'You murdered your own daughter!'

'Wrong.' Marius made a disdainful hand gesture, as though he was shooing away a bothersome waiter. 'I wish that were true. But Leoni betrayed me: She went to the other side. At this moment, Leoni is in a witness protection programme.'

3

It was all slowly starting to make sense. The reason why Leoni had been so secretive, even with Jan. The reason why she had disappeared without a trace. And why Jan had never been able to find her. Marius paused for a long while. As if his last sentence had been a sip of wine which needed to be appropriately savoured before more was poured. Or maybe he was just feasting on Ira's shocked expression.

'Leoni was already in the witness protection programme when she met Jan,' he continued. 'Her face had already changed. Faust had given her a new name, a completely new identity. Over the last few years, our ambitious state prosecution lawyer has done everything in his power to save his trial,' continued Schuwalow, shedding more light on the mystery.

To Ira, the horror this man exuded was almost worse than the physical pain she was in. But if what Marius was revealing right now was true, then Jan's crazed love for his fiancée would be sure to condemn her to death. After all, the mafia was just lying in wait for Leoni to finally creep out of her safe hiding place!

'It wasn't a bad move on Faust's part to hide Leoni

right under my nose. After she disappeared two years ago, Berlin was the place where we searched for her the least. But then Leoni made a big mistake. She fell in love with a psychologist.'

'Jan May.'

Ira felt the loose threads weaving themselves together ever more tightly.

'Exactly. To this day, the poor guy has no idea what he let himself in for. He started a relationship with a woman whose past is one big lie. With *my* daughter! No wonder that when he pursued his own investigations he only ended up with more questions and no answers. He wanted to marry the chief witness in a witness protection programme. I would never even have noticed if he hadn't drawn so much attention to his undying love for her. It was just pure chance that we had Jan May under observation a year ago. We were looking for a reputable expert witness who could testify favourably for us in future trials. Jan was just one of many psychologists we had in our sights.'

'And when you were doing a background check on him you suddenly found your daughter again.'

'No. It wasn't like that. Faust had already betrayed her to me himself.'

'That can't be true,' protested Ira. 'There's a lot I wouldn't put past that bastard, but he's not a murderer.'

'People surprise you again and again, don't they? Whether it's your own daughter or a high-ranking state prosecutor. His price was €750,000, by the way.'

'For your daughter?'

'No. For her death!'

'Stop, stop…' Ira gaped at the screen in disbelief. 'You had your own daughter murdered by the *state prosecution service*?'

Schuwalow nodded briefly. 'That's what I believed for a long time, at least. Until yesterday, I went to sleep each night with the comforting conviction that my daughter had lost her life in a tragic car accident. A staged accident that cost me three quarters of a million euros. The fatal outcome of which, until now, I had never doubted. After all, Faust provided me with conclusive proof.'

'What was it?'

'Feodora's corpse.'

'You examined the body?'

'Faust arranged an appointment in the forensic pathology department. My own doctor took a dental impression and the necessary tissue samples. I even have a print of the middle finger on her right hand. The only one that wasn't burned. Two further specialists later confirmed the results, independently from one another.'

'So Faust really did have your daughter killed.'

'So I thought. Until I unsuspectingly turned on the radio this morning and heard Jan May asking some questions which, I have to admit, were well-founded in part. Why, for example, was there no reference to the pregnancy in the autopsy report? Why is the accident photograph faked, as Herr Wagner here confirmed after his own intensive investigations?' Marius's forehead wrinkled with concern, as if he had just found an irregularity in his annual accounts. 'Jan May's hijacking of the radio station sowed the seeds of doubt in my mind, and rightly so. I hate doubts. In my business, they are fatal. What if Leoni really is still alive?

What if Faust pulled a fast one and my daughter is going to testify against me the day after tomorrow?'

'How would Faust have managed that? So is Leoni dead or not?' asked Ira breathlessly.

'You tell me. First I found out for sure whether or not my daughter really was pregnant. For that, we had a little conversation with Leoni's contact person in the witness protection programme. An old woman who lived a floor below Leoni's old apartment in Friedbergstrasse. What was her name again, Herr Wagner?'

The V-face wrenched Diesel's head back up from the table, shocking the chief editor back to consciousness. Marius repeated his question.

'I can't remember her name right now. Or maybe. I think...' Diesel spat a drop of blood in Schuwalow's direction.

'You don't have to be quite so fluid in your responses, my friend. But I think you meant to say "Marta". She was quite old, but still on the state payroll. Not a bad idea, really. Who would suspect a seventy-three-year-old of being a witness protection contact person? She was Leoni's only confidante. It's amazing what people will tell you when you show them a pen in close-up.'

'Why are you telling us all this?' Ira asked.

'Firstly, because you will never be tempted to use it against me. I've made precautionary measures to make sure of that. And also because I now want to find out from you in return where my daughter is.'

'I have no idea,' said Ira. 'Why don't you ask Faust?'

'The good man fled his villa at a rate of knots. This meant we were able to secure the data on his computer without any interruptions. He doesn't seem to be very technologically adept. We found the images of Leoni in his computer's recycle bin. His email correspondence, by the way, gave us reason to suspect that our state prosecutor is planning to fly abroad in a chartered private jet. It's only a matter of time until we catch up with him. Until then, I'd like to know what he revealed to you during your discussion on the studio roof, Frau Samin.'

'Nothing at all. I'm not part of his team. In case you hadn't caught on: I was pulled off the negotiation and have been officially suspended! I'm the last one who would be told that kind of information.'

'Possibly. I believe you, even. But I like to make sure.' He pushed an empty glass towards her. 'You should probably have a quick refill.'

'Why?'

'Because in the place we're all going now, there won't be anything more to drink for a long time.'

Schuwalow grabbed an unlabelled bottle and poured so much into the whisky glass that the clear liquid almost flowed over the rim. 'I'd love to offer you some whisky from my homeland, but I'm pretty sure you'd prefer something stronger.'

He pushed the glass carefully towards her.

'Stroh rum, eighty per cent proof. You should drink up, otherwise you'll spill it on the way.'

As if this had been his wake-up call, the henchman behind Ira stood up, heaved Diesel onto his shoulder and set off.

4

Just one minute, thought Götz, drawing his gun. *They can only have been gone a minute*. He carefully kicked the door of his apartment fully open and crept in silently, even though he knew he was too late. No one was here. Ira had been kidnapped.

He recapped the minutes since he had left her, thinking about the moment when he had got back to the MCB building and tried to call Ira again. To apologise. He had taken advantage of her fraught state and let things go too far. By the third ring, he had been standing in the lobby of the high-rise already, waiting for the elevator. When she didn't answer and her mailbox clicked on, he had turned around at once and rushed back to Friedrichstrasse. But he was too late. By just a minute. His door was broken open, the rooms empty.

Götz sat down on the sofa, the payments of which he was defaulting on, just as he was for all the rest of the furnishings, and debated what he should do next. He had to inform mission control. But if he did that, Steuer would pull him off the case. And not just that; he would lose his entire professional existence. After all, he had taken it upon himself to disobey the very highest of orders, and had removed a suspect from police control.

The mobile phone vibrating in front of him on the glass table showed an incoming call. *The mission control centre.* Steuer.

They were already looking for him.

Götz made a decision. There was no other choice.

5

True hell was just a few steps away. The short journey, which Ira put behind her on trembling legs, ended after four metres through the unappetising kitchen and into a back room.

'Haven't you often wondered how all these little shops survive in the city?' asked Schuwalow, typing an eight-digit code into the keypad next to an aluminium door. Ira heard a hydraulic hiss, followed by the click of a lock being released.

'I mean, cheap junk shops in the most expensive areas? Boutiques that have more staff than customers, and abandoned bars like this one here?'

Marius's hatchet man pulled the door open and tipped Diesel, who was hanging over his shoulder like a roll of carpet, head first into the room. The chief editor began to cough as he crashed down onto the floor.

'I'll explain it to you,' said Schuwalow in a friendly tone, as though he were an estate agent guiding a new client around rooms for rent. 'Some of these localities belong to me. And like so often in life, the real business concept only becomes clear when you look more closely. In this case, it's this room here.'

After Ira got her first glimpse of the room, she swayed and felt the urgent need to grasp onto something, but she would rather have fallen over than taken Marius's proffered hand.

'What's that?' she croaked, even though she didn't really care, because there was no way she was stepping foot in this room. It was empty, like the skeleton of a building site. No table, no chairs, no radiators – there was nothing to distract the eyes from the horrific tapestry which stretched over the floor, ceiling and all the walls.

'I call it the Memory Room.'

Marius took the glass from Ira and pushed her into the room. She was too exhausted to put up a fight. After just the second step, she stumbled over her own feet and had to lean on the wall to prevent herself from losing her balance. Now, in physical contact with the tapestry, its effect was even more sickening. The entire chamber was one big optical illusion, making the viewer believe that he was trapped in a downwards vortex.

White torture shot into Ira's mind. Among experts, this method of torture was also referred to as sensory deprivation. Normally the victims' eyes, ears, mouth and nose would be covered, while they were forced to kneel on the floor for hours on end with their hands bound. White torture was particularly popular with foreign intelligence agencies, because it didn't leave behind any physical traces, and Schuwalow seemed to have refined the method even more. On the one hand he intended to put her in solitary confinement, but on the other he was exposing her to an optical sensory overload with the unbearable wall covering.

'I'm sure you don't need me to tell you that no one will be able to hear you once I shut the door. And apart from the slightly too bright halogen spotlight on the ceiling, there is neither electricity nor gas nor water. Your mobile phones have, of course, been robbed of their functionality. The only thing I'm leaving you with is air to breathe.'

Marius looked up at the ceiling. 'Don't go to the bother of breaking your fingernails. The small grill to the ventilation shaft is sealed, and you wouldn't even be able to fit your little finger through there anyway.'

'How long?'

'I see you've grasped the purpose of all this, Frau Samin. Whenever my conversation partners don't respond to the usual methods, I bring them here, into my memory room. The change of scene often works wonders. After a short time, most of them remember the topics that lie so close to my heart.' Marius grinned. 'So far I haven't yet found out whether this is down to the extravagant interior furnishings or the lack of water supply. Do you now understand why I wanted to give you one more drink for the road?'

Marius put the glass, from which Ira had only drunk a sip, carefully down on the floor.

'Okay, one last thing: normally I come by once a week and bring a little picnic. In your case, however, time is a bit more pressing, so I've thought up something which might speed up your memory processes.'

The next thing Ira heard was like the result of some sound engineer of horror succeeding in concentrating the essence of physical pain into acoustic form. The oscillating sine wave, at a frequency barely above the human threshold of perception, burrowed down into Ira's pain centre as if her ears were one great big inflamed root canal, the sound waves jarring against it like a rusty dentist's drill.

'I'll be back tomorrow morning,' said Schuwalow, and these five words in themselves were a reassuring distraction. After just a few seconds of the acoustic torment, Ira already had the horrifying sensation that she was chewing on aluminium foil. Diesel had woken up again, and his blood-encrusted face was contorted into a grimace.

'If you aren't ready to tell me where I can find Leoni by then, then I'll forget you here in the memory room.' The door cut off Marius's laughter at his inane joke as it locked behind him.

6

Ira stood beneath the ventilation grill and searched in vain for a way to fasten her trouser belt to it. The iron bars were lined up alongside each other as closely as on a fine-toothed comb. Besides that, the ceiling was too high, and Diesel was hardly going to give her a leg up so that she could hang herself. She closed her eyes for a moment to escape the sight of the wall covering, which provoked a state similar to an LSD high. This intensified the acoustic sensory overload even more. Her gaze fell on the glass of Stroh rum on the floor next to the door.

Why did I leave the capsules at home? In fact, why did I even leave my apartment this morning? she thought despairingly. She pulled her T-shirt up and stuffed the twisted shirt tails into her ears for the umpteenth time. Pointless. She could hear the sounds inside here even in her bones. The harrowing vibrations were using her ribcage and skull as a soundbox.

Ira slid down the wall and reached for the glass of liquor. Unfortunately, her tolerance level was now so high that the high-percentage content would barely even make her sleepy, let alone knock her unconscious. But she planned to down it in one go regardless. She was just about to do so when

Diesel grunted something incomprehensible to her from the other side of the room.

'What?'

'Don't drink!' he wheezed.

'Do you think it's poisoned?' she asked, hoping that maybe she could bring this whole thing to a quicker end after all.

'No, it's our only way out.'

Diesel crawled over to her on all fours and took the glass carefully from her hand. He looked at it as though it were some venerable relic, placing it back down on the floor with trembling fingers.

'So what now?' asked Ira.

'Now you have to take your clothes off.'

7

Despite all the psychological pain, the white torture had brought with it at least one positive side effect: Diesel's survival instinct was now fully awake.

'My underwear too?' she asked him. Ira was standing there naked apart from her pants and bra. Diesel, too, was just wearing his crumpled boxer shorts, and the fact that he had taken off his T-shirt was worth it just for the sight of his tattooed torso. Now Ira was able to stare at the iridescent sea of flames around the chief editor's belly button, and for a few seconds it even distracted her from her surroundings.

'You can keep your frillies on for now; we don't know each other that well yet,' grinned Diesel, exposing a number of missing teeth. Schuwalow certainly hadn't held back.

'I still don't understand what this is supposed to achieve,' said Ira, while Diesel poured the high-percentage Stroh rum over the bundle of washing at their feet.

'I'm sorry about the drink, but I promise I'll treat you to a whole bottle if we manage to get out of here.' Diesel reached into his trouser pocket and pulled out a box of matches.

'I never leave the house without my work tools,' he commented, smiling again.

'Tell me you're not serious.'

'About making a campfire? Of course.'

Diesel drew the first match over the igniting strip. Without success. He fished out a second.

'What if your plan doesn't work?'

'Trust me. There are offices, shops and even apartments above us. I worked in this complex for four years before the radio station moved to Potsdamer Platz. They have an extremely sensitive smoke detector. The fire brigade had to come twice because of me, just because I smoked in the office.'

Ira crossed her thin arms in front of her torso.

'But how do you know whether this room is connected with the building smoke detector?'

'I don't.'

The flames were licking at Ira's cargo pants and already eating a hole in Diesel's T-shirt. As with most fires in enclosed spaces, the fumes were the quickest to develop.

'And how long will it take for the headquarters to react to the alarm?' coughed Ira, realising now that it would probably have been more intelligent to keep a scrap of material as a breathing mask.

'Well, that's a bit of a sticking point,' wheezed Diesel. The smoke was making Ira's eyes water so much that she could barely see him any more. In addition, the room was getting darker by the second, because more and more ash particles were settling on the plastic screen of the halogen spotlight.

'What do you mean by that?'

'As I said. The smoke detector unit is very sensitive. There are a lot of fire alarms.'

And as a result they're often ignored, thought Ira. A

darting flame shot upwards out of the bundle of clothes; presumably because there had been some other flammable materials stored in Diesel's jeans. The heat was now almost as unbearable as the cough-inducing smoke, and Ira wasn't sure if she would rather suffocate or burn to death.

8

At the same time, three hours' drive away from Berlin, Theresa Schuhmann was hanging up her freshly washed coloured garments in the cellar, which meant she could neither hear nor see the danger her young son was currently teetering towards.

She thought he was in the back garden, near the run-down wooden hut which had originally been reserved for garden tools but now housed the rabbits, until the temperatures dropped back below zero and Theresa had to tolerate them in her farmhouse kitchen again whether she liked it or not. But in fact, little Max was currently kneeling at the edge of the swimming pool, studying the tarpaulin cover as though he had just discovered a new species of animal.

Max was at the 'caffeine age'. That's what Theresa called the current phase of her five-year-old when describing to her friends how he couldn't sit still for even three minutes, unless the seat in question was whirling around in a circle at breathtaking speed and also attached to a rollercoaster. Her husband, Konstantin, was an over-cautious father, and had eliminated any danger sources in their comfortable and well-looked-after family property before his only son had even been born. To this day, there were still no plug sockets without safety guards, no sharp corners or edges at head height, and the contents of their first aid box would have enabled a doctor in the Congo to supply a whole village with medication. Nonetheless, Konstantin was unable to reduce the overall risk level to zero. For that reason, Max was not allowed to go anywhere near the pool unsupervised until after he had passed his swimming proficiency. Konstantin had told Theresa this very clearly. But unfortunately he had forgotten to explain how she could simultaneously do the washing and keep an eye on her highly stimulated son without having him on a leash.

Theresa fastened the last item of clothing from the load to the line with a plastic peg, leant down one more time to check that there was nothing still hiding in the drum of the machine, then paused and wondered.

Why was it so peaceful all of a sudden?

Not that it had been loud before. But a certain noise she had registered only with her subconscious now seemed to be missing.

She looked at the grey cellar ceiling as though she were able to look up through it into the living room. And it actually seemed to work.

Oh, my God!

Even though she could neither see nor hear nor smell anything, she could sense the danger.

Max!

She ran up the stone steps and kicked open the ajar cellar door which led into the hallway.

Where are you?

She didn't want to call out, because that would mean admitting to herself that something was different to a few minutes ago. She glanced quickly into the kitchen. *Nothing*. Turning around, she looked through the window to the veranda into the garden. No sign of Max. All she could see was the indented tarpaulin of the swimming pool.

And then she realised. She heard the alarm bell ringing and immediately understood her mistake. Because the bell wasn't ringing inside her. And it wasn't Max who was in danger, but a complete stranger.

The ringing died away abruptly. She hurried into the living room. And saw him. Max. She had no idea how he had managed it. How he had managed to stretch far enough to reach the telephone receiver.

He was holding it in his chubby little hands, and to Theresa it seemed as though his pouty lips were moving in slow motion.

'Hello?' she heard him say before she managed to tear the phone away from him.

'I listen to 101 Point 5, now set a hostage free!' she screamed.

Because now it was okay to be loud. Now she had to shout if everything was still going to be okay.

The peeps after the person at the other end hung up sounded like mocking laughter to Theresa, the blood in her ears pulsing in rhythm with it. She felt dizzy.

Had that been him?

She stared at the display. Noted in her mind the short, memorable number with the Berlin prefix. Had that been the psychopath? The man Konstantin had called from work earlier today to tell her about? About the drama that was taking place in Berlin right now, sending even the people here in Jena into a panic. Her gaze wandered over to the television, the silent images of which had been illuminating the living room all day.

She pressed the green button on the telephone, heard the dial tone and began to tap in the number.

Was that the psychopath from the radio? And was it her imagination, or had he really said the following words before hanging up?: 'Too late!'

She held her breath and prayed for salvation. But it would not be granted. In its place came an automatically generated computer voice, delivering the merciless certainty.

'This is your favourite radio station, 101 Point 5. Unfortunately all the lines in the studio are busy right now. Please try again later.'

Letting the receiver fall, Theresa wondered whom she had just killed.

9

Ira's rib snapped like a dry branch. She almost wished it would bore into her fume-filled lung. Then the day would finally be over, and she wouldn't even survive being carried on the SEK man's back.

When she regained consciousness, an oxygen mask was covering her reddened face, and the paramedic was injecting her with an infusion. She looked around and recognised Götz, who was holding her hand. The doors of the ambulance, which she had been wheeled into on the emergency stretcher, were still open. A cacophony of traffic noises, walkie-talkie orders and fragments of heated discussion forced their way inside the vehicle.

'Where's Diesel?' asked Ira. Then she asked again once she had torn the mask from her face. Fear was suddenly unfolding inside her that the eccentric chief editor might not have survived. In her lifetime, she had liked men for a damn sight less than what Diesel had done for her today.

'He's already en route to the hospital,' answered Götz softly. He stank of smoke; it was he who had broken down the door and dragged her from the inferno.

Breaking at least one of my ribs in the process.

'He has severe burns and, like you, presumably smoke poisoning too, but he'll make it.'

The team leader's last words were drowned out by Ira's fit of coughing. The paramedic put the mask back on her face, but it only stayed there for another two breaths.

'How did you find us?' she asked stertorously. She tried to sit up, but the pain stopped her.

All she could remember was the din of the buzz saw cutting a hole in the aluminium door. Then the pain as Götz had put her across his back and carried her from the 'memory room'.

Götz explained to her how he had realised she had been kidnapped. About how he had gone back to his apartment. The open front door. The call to the mission control centre.

'I had to tell Steuer something,' he whispered. He leant over so close that, to anyone else, it must have looked as though he was kissing her. For Ira, the warm touch of his breath was the most pleasant moment of the day so far.

'I lied, I said you had escaped. That gave me the grounds to locate you by your mobile bearings. I had the signal from your phone sent directly to my squad car.'

'But it wasn't working any more in that dungeon,' she said.

'Correct. The signal suddenly cut out. But before that we were able to narrow down the area to the size of half a square kilometre. When a fire alert was recorded in that very area, it helped us to locate you.'

Then Diesel really did save our lives with his crazy idea, thought Ira, not knowing whether she should laugh or cry.

'What about Kitty?' she asked. The most important question.

'We'll talk about that once you've recovered a little,' said Götz, trying to placate her, but this time even the broken rib couldn't keep Ira on the stretcher.

'Stop that – we have to get you to the hospital!' ordered the paramedic.

'For what?' asked Ira, shaking off Götz's helping hand.

'To treat you, to examine how severe the internal damage to your organs is, to—'

'You can save yourselves the bother,' Ira interrupted the stunned medic as she ripped the canula from her arm. 'I have my own test for that.'

'Excuse me?' asked the doctor, completely bewildered. Ira turned around.

'Look at me. Am I bleeding from the eyes?'

He shook his head.

'Then I can keep going,' said Ira, gripping onto a shoulder strap at the rear exit of the ambulance and stumbling down the metal steps.

10

'You look absolutely awful.' Götz was the first to break the silence. The fire brigade's large-scale operation had now brought the Ku'damm to a standstill too, so they were winding their way through the side streets towards Mitte in his squad car.

'I can't help that. You guys were the ones who gave me these cheap threads,' she answered laconically. She was wearing one of the frog-green police training uniforms that the SEK usually only put on criminals who had either been arrested naked, startled out of their sleep, or in a brothel.

Ira stared at the autobahn from the passenger seat. Then she slowly unscrewed the little bottle of Novalgin which the dazed paramedic had given her through gritted teeth. There was no way she was going to waste valuable time having pointless examinations in the hospital; they would prove nothing other than what she could already feel for herself. That she was at the end.

'So what now?' Götz asked.

She looked over at him, feeling woozy. *Great.* The side effects of the Novalgin were kicking in already, it seemed.

'Now we have to rescue Kitty. And for that we need to go through Faust,' she answered. 'He's the key!'

Götz raised his right eyebrow, but other than that didn't look particularly surprised. He overtook a slow-moving lorry and stayed in the left-hand lane.

'First tell me what just happened. Who was trying to kill you?'

'Marius Schuwalow.' As quickly as she was able, Ira gave him a summary of the information which the boss of organised Ukrainian crime in Berlin had given her. 'Leoni is alive, and Schuwalow wants to have Faust murdered for that. That's why he's chartered an aeroplane and wants to leave the country. So we can't waste any time,' she concluded.

'I have to take you to the precinct, Ira.' Götz looked at her out of the corner of his eye. A worry line was etched across his forehead. 'Or to the hospital. But under no circumstances anywhere else.'

'I know.' She sighed. He had already put enough on the line for her.

'Why don't we just call the studio and tell Jan what we know?' suggested Götz.

Ira answered without looking at him. 'Because we don't have any proof. No photo, no telephone number. He has no reason to believe us.' She shook her head carefully. 'He wants Leoni to be brought to the studio. If I've judged his personality correctly, he wouldn't even be satisfied if we get her on the phone.'

She grimaced. Her ribcage hurt more with every breath she took, and she felt as though an invisible weight was pressing her body down into the car seat. Then she realised that the weight had a name. It was called *fear*.

'You still haven't told me how Kitty is,' she said, not even trying to make her tone sound casual. She moved to turn on the car radio, but Götz stopped her.

'She's good,' he said, gripping her hand tightly.

'But?'

'But there was a development while you were being kidnapped.'

'What happened?' Ira's throat was so dry that she had to struggle to articulate her words.

'Jan set six of the hostages free!'

Six? Why so many? Why not all of them?

'Who's still in there?'

She read the terrible answer in his eyes.

Oh God…

'We suspect that he was unable to keep them all under control in the studio,' he explained. 'The hostages didn't want to play along any more once the killing started. Presumably he wanted to pre-empt a revolt, and played the last round for all or nothing. He said he would either let all the hostages go – or kill them all.'

'Then why is Kitty still under his power?'

Ira scratched nervously at the label of the pain medication bottle in her hands.

'Well, the last Cash Call only half worked.'

'What's that supposed to mean?'

'A little boy picked up before his mother was able to grab the phone away from him and say the right slogan.'

'Oh God.'

'Herzberg wanted to speak with the maniac, but he couldn't even get through to the studio at first. When Jan finally took the call, they went from pillar to post, then Jan suddenly let the hostages go after all. But because the little boy messed it up, he ended up keeping Kitty as collateral for another round.' Götz scratched his neck in embarrassment, as though he were the bad guy and not the sad messenger. 'I'm really sorry.'

Ira swallowed. The tiredness had suddenly been swept away. 'And what is he planning to do with her?'

'What do you want me to say?' Götz turned his gaze briefly towards her, and the sadness in his gaze pained Ira even more than her broken rib.

'He's made another ultimatum?' she asked tonelessly.

'Yes,' he answered hoarsely. 'We have another fifty minutes. Then he wants to do the very last round. If we don't have any sign of life from Leoni until then, he'll make another call.' He paused, then added: 'But not in Berlin. Somewhere else in Germany.'

Oh no, he's raising the difficulty level.

'It could work, Ira,' Götz reassured her. 'If someone answers correctly, he'll let Kitty go and then shoot himself,' he murmured softly. He himself had to admit how slim the chances were of that happening, and didn't tell Ira that the psychopath had already called a number outside Berlin, in Thüringen, for that last, nearly disastrous Cash Call. With almost 40 million landline numbers in Germany, Kitty's chances of survival were practically zero. Ira reached back towards the radio. This time he let her turn it on without protest. Music was currently playing on 101 Point 5. A rock ballad by Silbermond. She ignored Götz's frown.

'So Steuer was right after all? It was staged?' she asked him.

'Presumably. The hostages are still being questioned, but it certainly looks that way. All the studio guests, with the exception of the UPS man, know each other. The mock hostages are still denying they were in on it, but the statements of the DJ, Timber, and his producer, both say they were.'

The Mercedes was approaching the maze-like intersection behind the Kaufhaus des Westens shopping complex on the Urania.

'But unfortunately, as we now know, this isn't some harmless Punch and Judy show he's playing out. He killed Stuck and Onassis.'

Götz's rage as he thought back to the mission increased in line with Ira's intensifying worry for Kitty.

'There's only one chance of saving my daughter,' she said, interrupting her brief silence. 'We have to go to the airport and stop Faust.'

'How are we supposed to do that? And at which airport? Private jets aren't allowed to take off from Tempelhof, Tegel or Schönefeld.' He pointed his finger at a large sign at the side of the road, which showed the route to all three airports. 'Aside from the fact that my head is on the chopping block already, how do you see this whole thing playing out? And in such a short time? Even with the blue lights we'll barely make it across the city in that time.'

'Can't you send out a missing person announcement?'

'Sure. Why I don't I just close down all three airports while I'm at it? And what would the reasoning be? Ira Samin, who is actually supposed to be in custody right now, has received some controversial information from Marius Schuwalow himself. And that's why, instead of taking her to the station, I'm completely shafting the state's leading prosecutor instead. Is that it?'

He slammed his strong hand down on the leather steering wheel and accelerated jerkily.

'And besides – how would we go about it? With private jets there aren't any public passenger lists that we could check. And we now know that Faust is a hustler. A master of disguise. He gave Leoni a new face and hid her in Berlin right before the mafia's eyes. He won't check in under his own name. Someone who outsmarts the witness protection programme...'

'What did you just say?' Ira interrupted him frantically.

'What? That he'll use another name.'

'No, the thing about him being a hustler.'

'Yes. He leads everyone around by the nose.'

'That's it. Drive back.'

'What's *it*?'

'Our last chance. How long will it take to get to Reinickendorf?'

'In this traffic? On the autobahn? At least half an hour.'

'Then drive as quickly as you can.'

Ira was jerked forwards in her seat belt as Götz slammed his foot on the brake. Behind them, two cars began to beep simultaneously.

Götz looked at her and held his thick index finger up in front of her face threateningly. 'Do you realise what you're asking of me? You expect me to give up everything I worked years for? My position as SEK team leader, my future financial security, and last but not least my dignity? I'm close to being fired right now, you know.'

Ira was silent. She didn't know what she could say in response. Götz was right. He had already sacrificed far too much for her.

'My apartment isn't paid off, I had bad luck playing poker last year. I'm up to my ears in debt, and I can't afford to botch up my career.'

'I know.'

'Fine, but you also know how I feel about you. So if I'm really going to do this for you' – he was almost yelling now – 'then I sure as hell want to be included in your goddamn plan for the future. So what's it going to be?'

Ira closed her eyes. Then her trembling lower lip gave him his answer.

Twelve seconds later, the Mercedes was racing along the bus lane, its blue lights flashing. Towards the autobahn.

11

The period villa on Heiligensee, built in 1890, was under the special protection of the Department for the Maintenance of Monuments. The classical fifteen-bedroom property, with its blossom-white facade and high lead-glass windows, had been completely restored just recently. The voluminous loft space, complete with little towers and alcoves, was like a crown set atop the floors beneath.

But Ira and Götz had no time to note the loving devotion with which the owner had tended to his property. Almost as soon as they stepped foot on the gravel approach to the villa, the first bullet hit, shattering a reddish terracotta vase right next to them.

'So he's home,' murmured Ira, following Götz in a ducked position. The SEK pro had already pulled and cocked his gun. They left the gravel path and ran in snaking lines through the landscaped gardens. Two pines and a mighty maple tree offered only scant protection on their way to the winding stone steps, which led up to the front terrace.

But whoever was shooting at them from the bay-windowed room beneath the roof, they weren't a very good shot. Ira heard the characteristic bang of a Beretta two more times. But both bullets plunged into the grass metres away from them.

Götz didn't hesitate for long, and was already firing at the glass windows of the veranda doors as he ran.

'Stay down here,' he called to Ira, without turning around.

No chance, she thought, jumping behind him through the shattered glass shards into the living room. Götz was already storming into the entrance hall and from there up the sweeping wooden staircase. The laser beam of his gun grazed the expensive artworks and sculptures, which were either hung on the walls or positioned in the softly lit niches set into the masonry.

Ira was surprised that he wasn't exercising any caution. He sprinted the three floors up to the roof without checking the rooms one by one first. Only just before the door to the room the shots were coming from did he go into position: With his shoulder directly next to the doorframe, he stood parallel to the wall, his gun held at head height in one hand, its mouth pointed to the ceiling. With the other hand, he made a dismissive gesture to Ira, who was approaching from behind.

'Wait,' she called to him, but her plea came too late. Götz kicked out forcefully with his GSG9 boots, and the dark-brown lacquered walnut door flew open with a crash.

'Drop your weapon!' bellowed Götz. His laser was resting on the state prosecutor's forehead. Faust stared at his uninvited guests with an empty expression.

'Oh, it's you,' he said, and it almost sounded like an apology. As if someone else had been the intended recipient of the bullet reception. Ira could only make out the torso and right arm of his tall figure, including the pistol he was holding in his hand. He was covered from the belly downwards by the old Biedermeier desk he was sitting behind. The room was presumably a kind of study, or library. The warm light of the afternoon sun fell through the open window from which Faust had fired the shots, illuminating the room enough for Ira to be able to make out the tasteful furnishings. Dark wooden shelving stretched from the parquet floor until just under the ceiling, accommodating countless books. Their numbered and text-filled leather-bound spines revealed their law-focused contents. Ira felt a little out of place here in her worn-out trainers and oversized tracksuit.

'I said: Drop your weapon!'

'No,' replied Faust firmly, shaking his white-haired head. He propped his elbows on the writing desk and aimed his gun at Ira.

'If you want me to do that, you'll have to go ahead and shoot me.'

'He won't be doing that,' said Ira, trying to ignore the gun which was being aimed at her stomach. 'Not until you've told us where Leoni is.'

'She's dead.'

'She's not. I saw pictures of her. Eight months pregnant. They came from this house. From your hard drive.'

'Oh, Ira,' sighed Faust sadly. His right eyelid was twitching. 'Do you realise how much destruction you've caused today?'

'No, what? Did I mess up your planned flight to South America, perhaps? To whatever destination in which you were planning to blow the €750,000 you pocketed for Leoni?'

Faust stared at Ira as though she were speaking in a foreign language.

'I have liver cancer,' he told her.

'And that gives you the right to sell your chief witness to the mafia?'

'You don't understand. You don't understand a damn thing about this,' Faust raised his voice. A thread of spit freed itself from his mouth and clung to his chin. 'How can you be so clever as to look for me here, and yet so stupid that you can't grasp the connections, Ira?'

'You're easy to see through, Johannes,' she retorted contemptuously. 'A card player never changes his tricks. You kept Leoni hidden right beneath her own father's nose, and you thought it would work with you too. Given that the mafia had already searched your home once today, you thought you'd be safe for now. The chartered private jet was only to give the bloodhounds the wrong scent.'

'Well figured out. Chapeau,' said Faust in admiration. 'I even outsmarted my chauffeur and gave him the slip at Ostbahnhof. If he gets interrogated later, anyone would assume that I took a train out of the country or to one of the airports from there.'

'But what would be the point? I mean, you can't hide here forever. Everything will be out in the open by tomorrow at the latest.'

'That would be enough time.'

'For what? For your plans with Leoni?'

Ira jumped as Götz spoke. She was so concentrated on Faust that she had almost forgotten he was there.

'We have less than twenty minutes until the next round. So hurry up and tell us where she is.'

'She's in a safe place,' answered Faust. Then he emphasised this again: 'Or she was, at least. Do you realise that you've destroyed this today, Ira? If Leoni dies, then you'll be the only one to blame.'

12

'You money-grabbing piece of shit.' Ira couldn't contain herself any longer. She brushed the hair from her forehead and balled her fists. What she really wanted to do was jump over the desk to Faust and beat the living daylights out of him. But now she had no other choice but to hit him with her words.

'You betrayed and sold out Leoni. Don't talk to me about guilt. I know she was a state witness. That she was in a witness protection programme. But then you saw the chance to make a lot of money. How did you do it? Did you call Schuwalow in person to suggest the deal?'

'Ira, think of Kitty,' cautioned Götz. 'Another seventeen minutes.'

'He's right.' A weak smile was playing on Faust's ageing lips. 'You're wasting valuable time with incorrect speculations. I may be career-driven, but I'm not evil.'

'Oh no? Great. Then you can prove it to us right now by telling us where Leoni is.'

'I could only do that if we were alone, Ira.'

'What's that supposed to mean?'

Ira looked back and forth between Faust and Götz. The

latter took a step forward and positioned himself in the firing line in front of Ira.

'How stupid do you think we are? You expect me to leave the room so that you can shoot me? Come on, old man. Stop playing games. Where is she?'

'Ira, listen carefully to what I'm saying.' Faust spoke as though Götz wasn't there. It seemed to her as though he was suddenly having difficulty articulating his S's as he spoke. Much like she did after consuming a strong red wine.

'I didn't sell Leoni out. At least not how you think. She was my most important witness, and as you know, the trial is supposed to be in two days' time. A year ago, when we found out that Marius Schuwalow was looking for a psychologist and doing checks on Jan May, we knew that it was only a matter of time before he would uncover Leoni's identity. So we came up with a daring plan. I offered Marius a trade: the death of his daughter in exchange for three quarters of a million euros. So far, so good. But of course we never intended to actually kill her. It had to happen quickly, before Schuwalow took care of it himself. So it became a cloak-and-dagger operation, which Leoni only found out about once it was already underway. I staged a car accident and had her moved into a secret witness protection programme abroad. A place where she could bring her child into the world in safety. The accident was perfectly staged, with a photo montage of archive pictures for the file and the body of an unknown homeless woman from the pathology department. Even the autopsy was a pretence. One of the pathologists in the forensics department is a hobby magician. Marius's henchmen took the samples from the homeless woman themselves. The pathologist then discreetly switched the bags containing a tooth, tissue samples and a middle finger impression from the real Leoni. A card-playing trick, as you would say, Ira. Simple, but it worked. In order to protect Leoni – or Feodora, as she is actually called – from her father, everything had to be watertight. Only then would Marius believe that his daughter was dead, and that he had nothing to fear in the trial.'

'Why did Leoni never get in touch with Jan?' Ira wanted to know. The whole story seemed logical, but still didn't quite sit right with her.

'She did, remember. Leoni called him on the day of the supposed accident. Around thirty minutes after it. She wanted to tell him that she would come back after the birth of their daughter and that he didn't need to worry. But that was exactly what he was supposed to do. His grief had to be genuine so that Marius would be reassured. Jan May was the only security risk. That's why I interrupted the connection on Leoni's call to him, and made sure that she wouldn't try and make contact with him again. To do that, I had to make her believe that Jan was the real reason why we had to take her abroad.' With every word he spoke, Faust was looking more and more tired. Almost as though he were some toy whose battery was slowly dying. But she could see from his tensed posture how important it was for him to tell someone this story.

'I simply claimed that Jan had betrayed her to Marius. That way we could be sure that she would never call him again. I would have told her the truth after the trial, of course.'

'But until that point you did everything you could to destroy Jan May's life! You even took away his licence to practice as a psychologist.'

'Because he was asking too many questions. As I said: He was the only security risk.'

A trace of his familiar arrogance flashed in his eyes.

'This isn't just about Jan May and Leoni Gregor, remember. Winning this trial against Marius Schuwalow would break up a crime ring and save thousands of lives.'

'I don't believe a word of that. You're doing this for yourself, not for your love of the common man. After all, you took the money and fled.'

'I didn't flee. And I haven't spent a cent of the money.' She followed his gaze, only now noticing the yellow canvas bag to the left of the desk.

'Of course I took Marius's payment. Don't you think he would have smelt a rat if I'd killed his daughter for free? That was all part of the plan. Just to remind you: I have liver cancer. What would I want with €750,000? I have another five months to live at most. I want to spend that near German doctors, not in some village hospital on the Bolivian coast, especially given I don't speak a word of Spanish.'

'Just a minute.' Ira tilted her head to the side, as if she could hear him better this way. 'Then you mean Leoni was supposed to come back to Berlin?'

'Yes, of course. In two days' time. It was all arranged. I was planning to lull her father and the mafia, the entire holy family, into a false sense of security, and then...' He opened the fist of his left hand like a blossoming flower. 'In three days' time, Leoni would have testified, Schuwalow's organisation would have been destroyed, and Jan would have been happily reunited with his fiancée. Now do you see what you've done? You and your lovesick maniac on the radio station? In your desperate attempts to search for Leoni, you've brought the mafia onto her trail. The case is ruined. My life over.'

'So why don't you tell us where you're keeping Leoni hidden?'

'If I do that, she'll die. A very painful death!'

'People have already died,' replied Ira. 'How many more do you want to sacrifice? My daughter is in that goddamn studio of death right now, and Jan's going to kill her in just a few minutes if you don't tell me where you took Leoni. Do you know what I think? To you, none of this is about Leoni. You're only afraid for yourself. Otherwise you wouldn't have done everything you could to silence the hostage taker. You wanted to storm into the studio before Jan May said too much or before I found out too much about Leoni. Before Marius's doubts were confirmed. And yet all you needed to do this whole time to end the hostage drama was pick up the phone. Leoni could be sitting in an aeroplane to Berlin right now, and no one would have died. But you didn't do it. Out of fear. Fear that the Masseuse would vent his fury on you with his acid gloves, because you took his money.'

The state prosecutor's eyelids twitched, and he suddenly looked utterly exhausted.

'Yes, that's right. I am afraid. Of course I am. But this was precisely why fleeing was never an option.' He swallowed. 'As you can see, I still have all my hair. I rejected chemotherapy. And do you know why? Because I'm afraid of pain. But the way things look right now, all the paths left to me lead to a painful end. Either I wait for my morphine pump to lose its effect. Or for Marius.'

He turned back to Götz.

'So now you know everything, have you perhaps changed your mind?'

'What do you mean?'

'Are you going to shoot me?'

'No.'

'Then I'll do it instead,' said the lawyer. And fired a bullet through his own head.

13

Just ten minutes left.

Ira ran to the desk and checked Faust's pulse. Dead.

This can't be happening. Please, God, don't let it be true.

Like a mantra, she repeated this silent plea again and again until she ended up hitting herself on the head to interrupt the endless loop. She tore open the drawers of the desk. Nothing. Only the usual office paraphernalia, plus some papers and utensils used for pipe smoking.

As though through a veil, she weakly registered that Götz had established a walkie-talkie connection with mission control. He was probably fetching an ambulance.

Think! Why didn't he tell you where Leoni is? It doesn't make any sense.

Why would he protect her even after his own death? Her thoughts stuck, revolving around this aspect alone.

Why didn't he reveal Leoni's hiding place? Doesn't he know? He must do, otherwise he would have just said that he didn't. So again: Why did he keep his silence? Perhaps because...

She grabbed her temples with both hands.

Just a minute. Maybe he DID say it!

Ira looked around. In the lower compartment of the glass cabinet, there was a stereo unit. She ran over, tore open the door and turned the radio up to full volume.

101 Point 5 was saved in the memory as the first station. A Motown classic was currently halfway through.

'What are you doing?' Götz lowered the walkie-talkie and looked at her questioningly.

She went over to him and laid a finger on his lips. Then she grabbed him by the sleeve and pulled him down towards her.

'Bolivia is a landlocked country,' she whispered.

'What?' He looked at her as though she had lost her mind.

'It doesn't have a coast. Do you see? Faust said just then that he didn't want to end up in a hospital on the Bolivian coast, because he couldn't speak a word of Spanish.'

'Then he made a mistake.'

'No. Think. He said he couldn't tell us because we weren't alone. I think he's afraid that the room is bugged by Marius. He didn't want to speak openly. But he gave us a clue.'

'Bolivia?'

'No. Don't you remember the strange way he spoke about the mafia? He called them the "Holy Family" In Spanish, that's "Sagrada Familia". That's a...'

'... a church. In Barcelona. I know.'

'And Barcelona is on the coast!'

Götz put away his walkie-talkie and laid both hands on her shoulders.

'How the hell are we supposed to find Leoni there? It's one of the biggest cities in Spain! And we only have' – he looked at the clock – 'another seven minutes.'

Like a threatening confirmation, the song on the radio was slowly fading out.

'Think, Götz!' pleaded Ira. 'What else did you notice? What other sign did Faust give us?'

She wasn't whispering any more now.

'Did he say something, make some gesture, point at something? Did he…'

Götz and Ira looked at each other. Then they both looked over at the corner of the room.

Over at the yellow canvas bag.

14

The border control official passed her new American passport through his scanning device for the second time. It hadn't taken this long with all the people who had gone through in front of her. Susan switched little Maja onto her other arm and smiled at the young man. He actually looked quite sweet, if you ignored the big pimple between his eyebrows and the red patches on his neck which indicated an inexperienced handling of a cheap disposable razor.

But instead of returning her smile, the officer just stared grimly at the faked document as if it were his miserly pay cheque. Then he reached for the telephone.

What was wrong? She had never had any problems with her documents so far. They were perfect. Besides, she was only trying to get into Switzerland, not Baghdad.

While the man called some office in Barcelona's El Prat airport, he continued to compare Susan's passport photo with her face. She could almost see the thoughts floating around in his mind. There was something about her that had caught his attention, and he didn't seem to be able to make sense of it. He shrugged. Clearly no one was answering the phone.

With a brief sigh, he pushed the documents towards her

beneath the glass panel and sullenly called the next person in the queue to come forward.

What was all that about? Susan wondered as she walked on. A sign ahead of her alerted the passengers to intensified security measures. Anyone who was carrying a laptop with them had to take it out of its case. Women and men with heeled shoes were advised to put them onto the conveyer belt to be scanned along with their hand luggage. Susan didn't need to do either of those things. She was wearing light strappy sandals, which emphasised her slim ankles. And her hand luggage consisted of Maja on her arm, a bag of baby things, her mobile phone and a little key in her right trouser pocket. It was supposed to fit the locker at the Zurich train station. That was where she would find out the directions to the hideout and the name of her new contact man. The apartment at Plaça de Catalunya and her previous confidant in Barcelona had served their time.

The woman in front of her in the queue was also travelling with a child. The little boy was wearing a dinosaur T-shirt and was about five years old. His mother was holding him tightly by the wrist, as if they were standing at the supermarket checkout and she needed to stop him from putting a chocolate bar on the conveyer belt without permission. The little one turned around and smiled at Maja. Susan kissed her baby and stroked the soft fuzz on her head. Then the little boy in front of her saw her face, and his expression changed in an instant. His smile died away and was replaced by a look of pure amazement. Susan turned around abruptly and looked back towards passport control. Then back to the boy with the dinosaur shirt, who was already being pulled forwards by his mother.

What's going on here? she asked herself for the second time in a matter of minutes. The little boy had looked at her with the same expression as the officer at the counter. Was there something wrong with her face? Something to do with the scars?

She needed to get to a mirror urgently.

It was Susan's turn. She lay her bag on the belt and the key into a green plastic bowl.

'No,' she replied briefly in response to the question from the fat Spaniard behind the X-ray machine. 'I don't have any more luggage.'

She was waved through. When there was a beeping sound, she suddenly knew why. Why the man had looked at her passport for so long. Why the boy in the dinosaur T-shirt was still pointing at her now, as he was pulled away towards the departure gate by his oblivious mother.

Susan saw her own face, and yet she wasn't looking in the mirror, but at the television. It was hanging over the checkout of the duty free shop, right opposite security. '¿Dónde está Leoni Gregor?' was the caption.

Susan let the procedure at security wash over her as though she were in a trance. She followed the instructions from the bored blonde with the red strands in her hair, put each foot in turn on a small grey stool and kept the silent screen in her sights the whole time.

Where is Leoni Gregor? Who knows this woman?

A phone number was displayed. And then it was joined in the right-hand corner of the screen by something that Susan had never wanted to see again in her life. A picture of the person she had dreamed of while she was still Feodora Schuwalow. The person whom she had loved more than herself while she had needed to call herself Leoni Gregor. And the person whose betrayal meant she now had to hide away under the American alias of 'Susan Henderson' if she didn't want to die. Simultaneously, she was seeing the photo of the love of her life, and her worst enemy. The father of the child on her arm. Jan May.

'I think someone wants to speak to you, baby,' said a rowdy teenager whose beltless jeans were flapping around his hips. He grinned at her as he passed by with his laughing friends.

Only now did she register that she had already passed security and walked over to the duty free shop. The mobile in her hand was ringing.

Don't answer, was her first impulse.

There were only two people who knew this number. Three, if you included the new contact man in Zurich. But none of those names was on the display right now.

She looked back up at the television, which was still displaying a large picture of her. Only the text beneath had changed. Now it said something about a hostage situation in a Berlin radio station. She put away her mobile, which had stopped ringing some moments ago, and continued to read the breaking news on the ticker band. It said there had been several fatalities. That Jan May was a perverse killer. That he was calling up people at random and killing hostages. And that he was looking for her.

Me? How does he know I'm still alive?

All Faust had told her this morning was that she had to be relocated again for her own security. A routine measure. That apart from that everything was fine.

And now Jan May is looking for me via international

television? And killing innocent people until he finds me? No one told me anything about that.

Maybe it's a good thing I don't know the number that was calling me, she thought to herself. *It seems that Faust and his people aren't telling me the whole truth anyway.*

She hurried to the toilets, locked herself into a cubicle and dialled the only number in her phone under the category of 'Missed Call'.

15

Kitty gripped the water glass with her clammy fingers. She looked for a sign in Jan's eyes. Some indication that the good side in him would take the upper hand. He wasn't a bad person. At least not entirely. The man pointing a gun at her while he searched the internet for a telephone number to continue his game was just a victim of circumstances himself. He was in despair, and exhausted. This morning, dressed as a psychopath, he had forced his way into the studio. Little by little, he had shed his masquerade, and a pitiful, helpless human being had emerged. She wasn't the real victim here; he was.

Am I right in thinking that? Or am I already suffering from Stockholm syndrome? Kitty wondered. According to this psychological paradox, many hostages developed friendly thoughts towards their tormentors in the course of their imprisonment.

'You don't have to do this,' she spoke up hesitantly. She placed the glass carefully down on the studio bar. As though it were made of valuable porcelain.

'Unfortunately I do.' He looked at her.

'Why? What will it achieve? My death won't bring Leoni back.'

'I know. And actually I really don't want to...'

He didn't finish his sentence.

'So why don't we stop?'

'Because life is about just two things, Kitty. Hope and decisions.'

'I don't understand.'

'Some people say life is about having a dream. Or goals. But in my opinion, it's hope that drives people on. The hope of getting a better job than your father, of being able to afford a convertible some day, perhaps of snatching a few minutes of fame. And without a doubt, the hope of meeting the love of your life. But hope alone isn't enough, Kitty. In order to make those things a reality, you have to make decisions. That's the other side of the equation. But very few people do that. Most people on this planet are happy to lean back in their cinema seats and watch the heroes on the screen making decisions that they themselves wouldn't dare to make. Hardly anyone sets off on a journey into the unknown. We shout inwardly at the main character of a film to finally quit his well-paid job and search for hidden treasure in the wilderness. But in real life we would never do that, not unless our employers were to give us a year of paid holiday. There's only a miniscule difference between the masses and the few at the top. Some of them just hope, and the others also make a decision. They put everything they have at stake. And they are prepared to lose it if they have to.'

'So you're *still* hoping that Leoni will come back to you?'

'Yes. I made the decision to go this far.'

'And to kill people, too?'

'Honestly? I don't know. No. That wasn't part of my

plan. Even though no one out there will believe me: I didn't shoot the policeman or the UPS driver. You yourself noticed that the man in the body bag was still moving, right?'

'Yes,' lied Kitty. In truth, she was no longer sure. It had all happened so quickly.

'And during my preparations, I never addressed the question of how far I would go if my plan failed.'

'And now you have?'

'I think so.'

He put the headphones on, pushed a control on the mixing desk upwards and pulled the microphone closer to his lips. The music which had been playing until now was fading away.

'I like you, Kitty,' he said, and his words were transmitted on the radio for all to hear. 'I'm going to pick a number in Berlin for this round. One that will give you a good chance.'

'Who are you calling?'

'You're going to find out right now.'

16

'Hello, are you still there?'

Götz was speeding the Mercedes off the autobahn into Beusselstrasse at 120 kilometres per hour while Ira spoke on the phone with Leoni. Every sixty seconds, the navigation system was calculating a new arrival time at the MCB building. Now it was just another four minutes.

'Yes, yes. I am. But I can't believe all this. Who are you again?'

'Ira Samin. I spoke at length with your fiancé as a psychological negotiator today. What I'm telling you is the truth: Jan May never betrayed you to your father. And right now you are in extreme danger.'

Ira explained to Leoni how she had gotten hold of her secret number. Just minutes ago, in Faust's villa, she had been close to a breakdown. They had found a notebook in the canvas bag with a Spanish mobile number written in it. But on the first attempt, no one had answered.

'Faust is dead?' asked Leoni in horror. 'My father knows that I'm still alive? And Jan is going to shoot hostages until I come back to him in Berlin?'

'That's correct,' confirmed Ira, cursing Faust in the very same breath. How could he put Leoni on a public passenger

349

plane in this situation, without any protection or disguise? In the mortal fear of his last hours, he had clearly no longer been able to think clearly. Either that or he was counting on Steuer storming the studio before Leoni's photo was disseminated in the Spanish media. And now Leoni was stuck at the airport in Barcelona like a sitting duck. Or to be more precise, hiding in the cubicle of a public toilet, from where – thank God – she had called Ira back.

'Is there someone who can confirm all of this for me?' she asked breathlessly.

'Yes. Oliver Götz, the SEK team boss dealing with the case. He's sitting next to me.'

'I… I'm not sure. I think I'm going to hang up.'

A door creaked in the background, and Ira heard the clack of high heels. There was no longer an echo when Leoni spoke. She must have left the bathroom.

'No, don't do that. This isn't a trap. Where are you going?'

'To my gate. My plane takes off in just a few minutes. I'm already late.'

'Okay, okay. I know how much I'm asking of you. But I'm not one of your father's accomplices. I can prove it to you. Do you remember the foam?'

'What foam?'

'That you put in Jan's bedroom so it would feel like making love on the clouds.'

'How do you know about that?'

'Jan told me. See, I'm not lying to you. Here…' Ira turned the radio up. 'Listen for yourself, that's his voice. He's talking to a hostage on the radio right now.'

Ira decided not to mention the fact that the hostage was

her own daughter. Leoni was already scared and confused enough. Right now, Jan was talking to Kitty about heroes and watching films at the cinema or something. He seemed a little dazed. The next round was running late.

'Okay, so it's Jan's voice. But it could be a recording.'

'It's not.'

They were on Altonauer Strasse and speeding towards the roundabout that led around the towering golden Victory Column. All the lights were green, but that didn't help much, because the traffic was backed up along the entire Strasse des 17 Juni because of the blockades today. Götz continued to drive at high speed and relied upon the other cars moving aside for the flashing blue lights.

'Fine, so what do you want from me?' asked Leoni.

'Please turn off your mobile phone before you board,' said a friendly female voice in the background.

Ira kicked the glove compartment in front of her with such force that it fell open.

'No, don't do that, Leoni. Under no circumstances get on that plane. I'm begging you! Talk to Jan first!'

'I can't do that.'

'Please turn off your phone, Mrs Henderson,' demanded the woman from the ground staff. Her tone was a little less friendly now.

'It's just one conversation. You just have to prove to Jan that you're still alive.'

'So that he finds me and my daughter?' whispered Leoni angrily. 'And kills us? No, thank you. I'm getting on the plane now. I'll think it over, then I'll speak to my contact man. If he gives me the green light, I may be in touch with you again.'

'Leoni, please…'

She had hung up.

'No, no, no!' screamed Ira, hitting her hand against the airbag cladding. In order to get around the traffic, Götz had veered off along an unsurfaced forest path that led straight through the park. But now two empty vehicles from the Nature Protection Authority were blocking the route. They were stuck. Just a few hundred metres from the MCB building as the crow flies. But without any contact to Leoni.

'Where are you going?' called Götz, but Ira didn't answer. She left the car door open and ran through the park towards Potsdamer Platz. She bit down hard on her lips to stop herself from screaming with every step. The combination of a broken rib, smoke poisoning and alcohol withdrawal weren't the best conditions for a run through the Tiergarten. After just 200 metres she had to pause, panting for breath. Suddenly, hope was triggered inside her, numbing all of her pain instantaneously. Her mobile phone was ringing. *Leoni had changed her mind.*

She looked at the time before she answered. It might not be too late. Jan hadn't played the next round yet.

'Thank you for calling me back,' Ira panted into her wireless phone.

A few moments later, the unbearable pain was back. And much worse than ever before.

17

'That was the wrong slogan, Ira.'

Jan May went to the cabinet and swept a whole row of CDs onto the studio floor with his hand. Then he turned around and kicked the cladding of the bar. The curved metal buckled, but it didn't help him to vent his despair and rage. He was beside himself.

'What have you done? I wanted to give your daughter a fair chance, for God's sake. So I dialled your number. Do you know what this means? Do you?'

His eyes filled with tears as he looked at Kitty, but there was nothing he could do to hold them back. She would just have to see his weakness.

He was so damn tired. As though someone had struck a match deep inside him and burned away his very last reserve of strength.

'Now you've killed your second daughter too,' he said softly, wiping a tear from his cheek with his elbow.

Please, begged Kitty's silent lips. He couldn't bear the sight of her face any more. The shock had glazed her eyes, but taken nothing away from her beauty. When he saw her standing there in the half-destroyed studio, in front of the bullet holes in the wall, it reminded him of photographs of children in the third world playing in war zones or on landfills. They were all young, innocent and lost. Just like Katharina Samin.

'I have to hang up now, Ira,' he said.

'No, Jan. Please. Don't do it. Let her live,' pleaded Kitty's mother at the other end. She was wheezing heavily, as though she were in the middle of running a marathon.

'Give me one reason why I should listen to you.'

'I have the best one there is: Leoni.'

'What about her?'

'I found her.'

Her last words were like a stab to the base of his spine. Afraid of losing his balance in front of Kitty, he leant against his chair at the mixing desk.

'Where is she?'

'I can't tell you that.'

'You're bluffing again, Ira. You just want to save your daughter's life.'

'Yes, I do. But I swear I'm not lying to you. I've found Leoni Gregor.'

'Then prove it.'

'I can't. Not over the radio.'

'Why not?'

'Because if I do, it will put Leoni in danger. If I tell you I know what happened to your fiancée and where she is at this moment, then that would be a death sentence for her. Please. There are several million people listening to us. Including some who...'

Jan waited until Ira's fit of coughing passed. He looked at the studio clock above Kitty's head. After six seconds, Ira had regained her composure again. But she still sounded like an asthmatic on the brink of an attack.

'There's someone listening to us who under no circumstances can be allowed to find out where Leoni is and what I've found out. You have to trust me. What I have to tell you is strictly confidential. Take our conversation off the air. Then we can talk.'

'This is a trap, Ira. First you redirect the calls. Then you keep it a secret from me that your daughter is in the next room. Then you distract me while your boyfriend tries to storm the studio. And now you expect me to believe that you've found Leoni? Now, of all moments? Just like that? Without any proof? How stupid do you think I am?'

'I consider you to be a very intelligent human being. That's why you will understand how important it is that we speak one-to-one. Without anyone listening.'

'You just want to take me off the air so that no one out there catches on to whatever scam you're going to pull next.'

'That's nonsense, Jan. What would I achieve from that? Maybe a delay of ten minutes. And if I was trying to deceive you somehow, there's no way that would save Kitty. I swear to you: I know where Leoni is. I can bring her to you. But right now I can't tell you more than that.'

'You're a good negotiator, Ira, but I fear you've gone too far this time. You have to give me more than that.'

'Like what?'

'Okay. I know I said I would stop only when Leoni was standing alive in front of me. But fine, if you don't want to tell me where she is, then at least get her on the phone for me.'

Ira coughed again, and could be heard spitting several times after another.

'Unfortunately I can't do that either.'

'Right. I'm intrigued to know what excuse you have for that one.'

'Has it not occurred to you that perhaps Leoni might not want to speak to you? After all, your face is there for all to see on TV right now. They're calling you the Radio Killer.'

'She loves me. She knows who I really am.'

'I wouldn't be so sure about that.'

'Why? What did she say to you?'

'That's precisely what I can't talk about right now. Please! Our telephone conversation has already lasted too long. Turn off the transmission.'

Even if I wanted to, I have no idea how, thought Jan. Before he let the producers go free, he had told Flummi to programme the incoming calls so that they all went directly on air. Now Jan didn't know how to reverse it.

I could ask Kitty, of course, but...

'No, I won't,' he decided. 'And if one of you out there cuts the power, then Kitty will die. Do you hear me? I won't let you stop me any longer. So, I'm asking you one more time: Where is Leoni? Either I get an answer right now, or I'm hanging up and putting an end to the final round.'

When he only heard a loud crackle, he asked one more time.

'Ira?'

The combined sound of breathing and the wind became louder. Jan shivered. It had sounded like that eight months ago. During his last conversation with Leoni.

Don't believe what they tell you...

'Fine...' Ira's hoarse voice dragged him back into the present.

'I can tell you only this: Right at this moment Leoni is on an aeroplane. Taking off. I won't be able to get her on the phone for another ten minutes at least. And even then I don't know if she'll want to talk to you.'

'Ten minutes is too long. I want Leoni *now*!'

'What's wrong with you? Aren't you listening to me?' Now Ira sounded as furious as he had been before when she answered her phone with the wrong words. 'Do you want to see your fiancée again?'

'Yes.'

'Alive or in a coffin?'

'What do you think?'

'Good, then I'll suggest a deal. I'll be with you very shortly. Take me in exchange for Kitty.'

Jan frowned. *What was she planning?*

'What would be the point of that?'

'It's proof that I'm serious. This isn't about my daughter for you, Jan. It's about Leoni. I'll come in now, turn off the microphone and tell you everything I know. After that, if you don't like what you've heard, you can play a round of Cash Call with me.'

'The round is already over. Kitty lost.'

'Jan, you are so close to what you wanted to achieve. You've gone through hell for months on end. You've put your entire life at stake. Innocent people had to die. Do you really want to sacrifice your last hostage now, and live the rest of your life with one single question?'

'What would that be?'

'Whether I would have led you to Leoni if you had accepted my proposal.'

'You in exchange for your daughter?' Jan couldn't help but laugh. 'Every textbook around forbids that.'

'They also forbid someone who is personally affected by the case from leading the negotiations. Jan, listen to me. Do you still remember the question you asked me just a few hours ago? About what I would do if I was on the open seas with a little raft and had to decide who I would rescue: Sara or Katharina?'

'Yes.'

'I still haven't answered you,' he heard her wheeze. 'This very morning, I was about to blow my brains out in my kitchen. I probably still will. But this way my death would have some point to it. Let Kitty go, and take me as collateral.'

'You want to redeem your guilt, Ira. You want to rescue both Sara and Kitty at once, am I right?'

'Yes.'

'But you can't. The raft is too small for three people.'

'That's precisely why I would jump into the water. That's why I'm coming to you in the studio.'

Jan slowly climbed down from the leather stool, where he had been sitting during the conversation. He took three paces backwards until he was standing with his back to the external wall.

As far as possible away from Kitty. He looked at the weapon in his hand. For a while now, it had no longer been pointing at his final hostage. His right arm reflected the entire state of his being. It was hanging limply downwards. And Ira didn't seem to be doing much better. In the last minute alone, she had needed to interrupt her words three times because of a fit of coughing.

'Okay,' he said finally, looking Kitty directly in the eyes again for the first time since the beginning of the telephone call. Hope had been ignited. He had made a decision.

'We'll see each other in five minutes, Ira. No tricks.'

18

Leoni's white blouse turned blood red. She looked down at herself in disbelief. Even Maja, on her lap, was completely saturated.

Why does the turbulence always start just when the stewardess is handing out the drinks?

She mopped first her daughter's face and then her own upper body with the little paper serviette that was wrapped around the plastic cutlery. But in vain. She didn't have any appetite for the microwave-heated chicken in any case. First she was given a new identity and had to leave Barcelona without warning. Then she saw her own image on all the TV channels and knew she would be taken into custody by the time she reached the Swiss authorities, if not before. And now the waves of the past were crashing over her head like a tsunami.

Jan May.

Either he really wanted to kill her, or there was something she didn't know. One way or another she was in danger, and she had no intention of trusting this Ira Samin woman, of whom all she knew was her voice on the telephone. Nothing on this earth could drag her back to that hellish terror. Back to Berlin. Where her father was waiting to murder her.

Her stomach rumbled as though she had eaten something bad, and the bitter taste in her mouth intensified the feeling. The seat belt sign went off, and she decided to get up and quickly go to the toilet to wash off the tomato juice. Leoni placed her daughter gently on the seat next to her. Luckily they had the whole row to themselves; the flight to Zurich was only sparsely populated. She pushed up the left-hand armrest of her window seat, crept past Maja and was just about to straighten up fully when a heavy hand pushed her back down into the aisle seat.

'Miss Henderson?'

'What do you think you're doing?' she answered in English. After the events of the last few years, role-playing had become instinctive to her.

'I'm afraid you can't leave your seat.'

'On what grounds?' She shook the co-pilot's suntanned hand from her shoulder.

'I'm afraid you pose a flight security risk, and I have to request that you don't move from the spot, otherwise unfortunately I will have to sedate you.'

Stunned, she registered the electro shocker in his hand. The burly pilot was holding it in such a way that no one in the rows behind would be able to see.

'Please don't cause any trouble.'

'But what's the meaning of this? I haven't done anything.'

'I can't be the judge of that. I received instructions from ground control.'

'What instructions?'

The aeroplane dropped a couple of metres, but Leoni was too distracted to be affected by her usual fear of flying. *What was going on here? Whose team was this man playing for? Had her father planted one of his henchmen here too?*

The answer came in the passenger announcement, which interrupted her thoughts while the co-pilot stepped aside for a stewardess, who positioned herself in the aisle next to her seat. She too was holding an electro shocker in her hand.

'Ladies and gentlemen, please can we have your attention. For reasons of national security which we are unfortunately not at liberty to disclose, we have just been instructed to alter our flight plan. We will not be flying to Zurich, as scheduled. Our flight is being redirected to Berlin-Tegel.'

The sincere apologies offered by the pilot for the inconvenience caused were drowned out by the tumultuous outcry of about fifty agitated passengers.

Leoni looked outside at the seemingly endless blanket of cloud, and wondered whether she would survive the day.

19

Ira slowly pulled the tracksuit bottoms down over her cramped legs. Every touch of the fabric against her dried-out skin felt like coarse sandpaper on an open wound.

'I can't allow this.' Steuer made no move to leave the negotiation centre on the nineteenth floor while Ira undressed before his eyes.

'Try and stop me,' she retorted, turning her back to him. She knew that his impotent rage was tearing him apart inside. On the one hand, he could have her arrested. But on the other, he would then have to justify himself to all the media and public as to why he had prevented the announced exchange of the final hostage.

Götz had already told the mission leader about the newest developments over the phone. From Ira's torture at the hands of Marius Schuwalow to Faust's confession and suicide. Steuer also knew that Leoni was still alive and leaving Spanish air space at this very moment.

Suddenly, she felt his damp breath on the back of her neck. She jumped.

'You think I'm an asshole, and that you're the hero in this drama, right? But you're wrong.'

Ira freed her other leg from her trousers and threw them

onto an office chair half a metre away. Just this movement alone was as painful as a kick in the ribs. She groped her fingers over the fist-size swelling beneath her ribcage, and jumped as though Steuer had just electrocuted her.

'It's your choice whether you believe me or not. But I'm on your side.'

Ira snorted with laughter. 'I haven't seen much evidence of that today.'

'Oh really? The fact that you're still able to notice anything is already proof enough. Why do you think I pulled you off the case? So that *this* wouldn't happen. So that you wouldn't do anything foolish. Your emotions have taken over.'

Ira felt his aggressive gaze on her back.

'When it comes down to it, I don't really care about you, Ira. But this isn't just about you or your daughter. Have you considered the possibility that Jan might be in cahoots with Schuwalow?'

No. In fact, it hadn't occurred to her.

'There isn't any reason to trust him. How do we know what's driving him? Is it really love? Or is he being paid by Schuwalow to find Leoni and get rid of her before the trial?'

After a brief pause, Steuer continued.

'That's what some of the hostages we've questioned have been saying, at least. Apparently Jan stated openly that he was planning to kill Leoni as soon as we bring her to him. Just like he did Stuck and Onassis.'

Ira wondered which arguments she could use to dismiss Steuer's hypothesis. But she couldn't think of any conclusive ones. Maybe Jan had been bluffing again? Maybe he had wanted to shock the hostages in order to re-establish peace in the studio? On the other hand, Jan was an actor with an academic background in psychology. He had already pulled the wool over their eyes several times today. He was certainly capable of this deception too.

Just as she was about to respond, the warm breath on her neck was suddenly gone. She could no longer feel Steuer's physical presence. Ira didn't want to turn around, but she was pretty sure that he must have taken a step back.

Or several. As proof of this, his voice now sounded further away.

'Leoni is on the passenger list of Swissair flight 714 from Barcelona to Zurich, as Susan Henderson. I've set the appropriate measures in motion. The plane is being diverted.'

Now she could no longer keep quiet. She turned around to him, but could only see his broad back. He paused in the doorframe a moment longer.

'Keep going at least another two hours, Ira. We'll bring Leoni to the roof of the building.'

With those words, he was gone.

20

'*Enjoy the Silence*'. Jan May must be a Depeche Mode fan. Now that he was alone in the studio, he was selecting the music himself. The song currently echoing out of the loud speaker on the ceiling of the large editorial room was the second he had played by the British synth pop legends.

Ira approached the studio area like a tormented wife edging towards an irate husband who was about to beat her. Her entire body burned with pain as she slowly shuffled her way past the empty desks. When she saw her reflection in the glass wall of the studio complex, she couldn't help but think of her mother. Salina Samin had always been fastidious about dressing appropriately. Not in order to please men, but through fear of an accident. 'Emergencies always take you by surprise,' she used to say. 'And if you end up being taken to hospital, you don't want the doctors to see you in unsightly underwear.' As the irony of fate would have it, she had died stark naked after slipping in the shower and breaking her neck.

I should have listened to Mama, thought Ira in resignation. For the second time in just a few hours, she was now wearing only her underwear, as Jan had demanded. Her bare feet tapped over the cool parquet floor as she walked towards the studio complex with her hands held high. Studio A was still sealed off by the fire safety shutters. There was no visual contact. Nonetheless, her wretched form was being captured at this moment by multiple security cameras. She could just imagine the comments from the officers who were studying the flesh-coloured slip and black lacy bra she was wearing.

'That's what you get for getting dressed in the dark,' said Ira to herself. 'All I wanted to do this morning was run out and buy a Cola Light from Hakan.'

And then poison myself, she added in her thoughts.

Ira was now just two metres away from the thick glass panels which separated the news studios from the editing zone.

'Open the door and come into the entrance.' The order suddenly droned out of a loudspeaker above her. Depeche Mode had gone silent. Jan was back on air. He was talking to her over the radio.

Ira did as she was told. She pushed the heavy soundproofed glass door inwards and took a step inside. She looked around. To her left, there was a slightly raised platform with a row of broadcasting booths, each with a microphone, computer and stool for the news and weather presenters. The narrow corridor, which ran alongside them and in which Ira was now standing, led directly to the closed door of the A studio.

'Now put your hands up.' This time, the voice came from a small computer loudspeaker at the news desk.

Ira lifted both arms in the air. A vertebra clicked unhealthily as she raised her upper arms past shoulder height. She felt like one of the drug-addicted prostitutes from the 'baby strip' of the nearby Kurfürstenstrasse. Half naked, her body covered with blue bruises, utterly vulnerable to the perverse whoremaster who was awaiting her in the studio. The only difference being that her reward wouldn't be a measly twenty euros, but her daughter's life. Hopefully.

At least I shaved under my arms yesterday, she was thinking to herself just as the door to Studio A was yanked open from the inside.

'Kitty!' called Ira loudly. The first thing she saw of her daughter, standing there in the doorframe at the other end of the corridor, was the blonde hair she had inherited from her father. She had let it grow it long. At first it looked as though it was combed over her face, but then she saw that Kitty had her back turned to her.

'Turn around,' ordered Jan. She obeyed.

'And now walk backwards. To me. Nice and slowly.'

Even as a little child, Ira had never wanted to play the game of falling backwards into her friends' arms. She had never had enough trust. Once she had brought herself to do it, and had been utterly convinced she would crack open the back of her head on the sandy floor of the playground. Even though it hadn't happened, the fear had stayed with her to this day. Ira preferred to look danger right in the eye, not turn her back to it. But Jan wasn't giving her a choice.

'Hurry up.'

Her heart swelled painfully against her broken rib as she placed one leg in front of the other. She looked down at the skirting board. If she walked parallel alongside it, sooner or later she would reach the door. And Jan.

She had only covered two agonisingly slow metres in this

manner when she screamed. Something had brushed against her. Something soft. Fleetingly, on her right wrist. One step further on, she found herself looking into her daughter's startled face.

He ordered her to do the same thing, thought Ira with admiration. He had ordered Kitty to walk backwards too. By that simple trick they were distracted, defenceless and unable to communicate. It also enabled Jan to see whether Ira was carrying a weapon on her body.

'Now turn around again. Both of you, right now.'

That, too, was an excellent move. Ira was only able to throw Kitty a brief smile, which presumably looked even more frightening than if she had been crying. Kitty's face, too, was frozen into a mask, like the work of an incompetent plastic surgeon.

Ira turned as slowly as she could away from her daughter and towards Jan. Too brief. The time hadn't been enough to make sure Kitty was doing okay, let alone to give her some kind of sign.

'Very nice,' said Jan, as Ira looked him in the eyes.

'Now just keep going. Kitty towards the exit,' he said, aiming his gun at Ira's forehead, 'and you're coming to me.'

21

The satellite telephone rang just as Marius Schuwalow was putting the toilet paper on the checkout conveyer belt. He didn't find it embarrassing, going shopping at Aldi. On the contrary: He enjoyed the disbelieving looks from the other customers as he parked his limousine on the parking lot. Some of them recognised him. After all, with the trial imminent, his picture was all over the papers right now. This meant he never had to wait long at the checkout. Someone always let him skip ahead in the queue.

Marius enjoyed these brief forays into real life. At least once a week, he drove to the Schmargendorf branch of Aldi to watch the commoners. He conversed with the pimply employees and alerted intimidated housewives to special offers, basking in the knowledge that he spent more on his dinner each day than many Aldi customers earned in a week. The bail payment alone that he had needed to cough up would have enabled most of them to live out the rest of their lives without working.

'Situation report!' he barked, answering the phone curtly. He had been waiting for this call for half an hour already.

'Kitty is free. Ira is now in the studio in her place.'

'Good. Then everything's going to plan again.'

Marius took a small jar of caffeine-free instant coffee out of his shopping trolley. In front of him, a little girl still had to pay for her purchase. It seemed that the money her mother had given her wasn't enough.

'Yes. The daughter is being interrogated right now.'

'Did she see anything?'

'We don't know yet. It's unlikely. None of the other hostages noticed anything.'

'Good. But we'll still have to take care of her.'

Marius wasn't particularly careful with his choice of words. The satellite line was bug-proof.

'Just a minute.' He pushed down the antenna and put the grey telephone on the conveyer belt with his shopping. Then he leant down towards the little girl. She was about seven years old, with her mid-length brunette hair tied into a ponytail, and was shaking all over.

'What's wrong, little one?' asked Schuwalow in a friendly tone. He tousled her hair with his manicured hand.

'She's a euro short,' answered the checkout woman.

'That's no problem, princess,' smiled Marius, lifting the little girl's dainty chin towards him. 'Take your things and tell Mama to do her sums better next time, okay?'

The little girl nodded.

'I'll take care of that,' he said to the checkout woman, taking a Kinder egg from the selection alongside the conveyer belt.

'This is for you, sweetie.' He put it in the girl's hand. She brightened up instantly.

Marius pulled the antenna of his satellite phone back up and continued his conversation. 'Where is Kitty being taken now?'

'The same place the chief editor, Diesel, is waiting for his operation. The Charité.'

'Do we have one of our men there?'

'Not yet.'

'Then see to it. Right now!' Marius waved at the little girl, who was making her way to the exit with her bulging bag of shopping. She had turned around to him once more, and was smiling.

'That'll be twelve euros and forty-nine cents please,' said the cashier. Schuwalow handed her a €500 note without a word.

'What about Leoni?' he asked, as the clearly vexed cashier counted out the enormous amount of change.

'She's landing in Tegel in two hours, and then she'll be flown to the roof of the MCB building by helicopter.'

'Good, I want to see her again as soon as possible. I've reserved a table for the two of us at Gudrun. We'll sit outside.'

'Understood,' confirmed the nameless voice at the other end. Berlin's Gudrunstrasse was the home of the Friedrichsfelde cemetery.

'The same goes for Kitty.'

'Yes.'

'I don't want there to be any more glitches. Extend the invitation as soon as she gets to the hospital.'

'Of course.'

The man on the other end sounded matter-of-fact and practiced, as though he often received these kinds of orders.

Marius said goodbye to the mole and looked down at his purchases with a smile. He wouldn't go to the effort of loading them into the boot. Everything would go in the big rubbish container by the exit. Just like always. He never degraded himself by actually using the things he bought here. He would rather go without his change. Or let Leoni and Kitty live.

22

For the first few seconds of the encounter, Ira was overcome with disbelief and denial. *This* man was supposed to be responsible for the terror inflicted today? Jan seemed more like a victim than a psychopathic mass murderer.

Too nice, was her first thought as she stood before him.

Ira had firmly resolved to hate her daughter's potential murderer, but at this moment it was proving to be very difficult. They were both standing in the small station kitchen, where Kitty had hidden herself away beneath the sink. Jan had heaved back the CD cabinet blocking the escape route, because Ira had asked to have a glass of water before explaining the situation to him in full detail.

And he clearly believed her.

That Leoni would be coming to him soon.

That she was already on her way to Berlin.

Ira should really have felt relieved. Jan hadn't tied her up, nor threatened her in any way. He didn't seem dangerous at all, in fact, just exhausted. But Ira knew she couldn't let herself be lulled into a false sense of security by the intelligent face and profound gaze. Even the most basic textbook of criminal psychology warned against drawing any conclusions about someone's personality based upon physical appearance. In that sense, Jan was like a stray dog. He could look perfectly harmless one moment, then launch into a violent attack the next. She knew nothing at all about what was going on inside his mind. Was he really madly in love? Or did he actually want to kill Leoni, as Steuer suspected and some of the hostages had asserted in their statements?

Inconceivable, thought Ira the whole time as she informed Jan about everything that had happened to his girlfriend. But at the same time, everything he had done so far today was just as inconceivable.

'So now you know,' said Ira, bringing her breathless explanation to an end.

Jan stood in front of her as though he were rooted to the spot, not moving a millimetre.

'But...' he stammered, '... that means everything I've done for Leoni today...'

'... has put her in mortal danger, yes.'

Ira shivered. She pulled the hostage taker's discarded sweatshirt over her in an attempt to cover at least some of her nakedness. The grubby material smelt inappropriately pleasant, of some fresh aftershave, and hung loosely down around Ira's hips like a skirt.

'Is there anything to drink other than water here?' She opened the fridge. The weak halogen lamp hesitated a second before illuminating the interior with light. Nothing. Just an open jar of Nutella and an uncovered block of rancid butter. No cola. And definitely no Cola Light Lemon. Ira closed the fridge, the door falling shut with a smacking sound. She grabbed a glass from the sink and turned the tap on. In truth, she needed something strong again already. The tiny sip in Hell, the Novalgin and the raised adrenaline output of the last few hours had delayed her tremors somewhat. But now she would have to start making up for lost time, or her bloodstream would quickly make her aware of it.

'Now we need to talk about what's going to happen on the roof,' she continued.

'On the roof?' Jan, who was sitting on a stool next to the small folding kitchen table, lifted his head in her direction. He was holding his weapon tightly in his left hand, but pointing it at the floor.

'Leoni is being flown in by helicopter, and we're going up there. You'll see your girlfriend, then you'll be arrested, and I can go. That's the deal.'

'I want to be able to embrace her!' he demanded.

'You should count yourself lucky you won't be embraced by a rocket-propelled grenade,' answered Ira. 'A dozen armed elite policemen will be waiting up there for you: two mobile task forces on this building and a sniper team on the one opposite. Once we step foot onto the roof, you can't make any quick movements. Drop all your weapons, then raise your hands nice and slow. Every one of those boys will be just waiting for you to make a mistake. After all, you murdered one of their own.'

'I didn't kill anyone,' he protested.

'Apart from Manfred Stuck and Onassis.'

'You mean the UPS driver and the sniper?'

'Yes. That officer was one of our best men. It's his little boy's ninth birthday tomorrow.'

'Stop the play-acting, Ira. We both know the truth. Stuck and Onassis are alive.'

'No.' Ira shook her head sadly and downed the last of the water in one go. 'I saw the bodies myself.'

'You're lying!' Jan looked as though a coiled spring inside him, keeping him energised until now, had just snapped. 'That can't be true.'

'Just to remind you: You killed Stuck yourself. Millions heard it. And my daughter saw it.'

Jan blinked tensely. All the colour had drained from his lips. Ira could sense him thinking. Searching for explanations.

'She *thought* she saw it,' he replied after a long pause. Then he pointed at the floor, two metres away from the sink. 'It happened right here. I sedated Stuck by giving him a fast-acting tranquiliser. Highly concentrated flunitrazepam. It knocks the body out for up to seventy-two hours, and the victim can't remember a thing afterwards. Then I fired a blank gun so that everyone listening on the radio could hear. And that's why' – Jan went over to the sink and flung open the panelled door – 'your daughter was able to see it from here. But it was only a bluff.'

That could be possible, but… Ira tried to think, staring at the glass she was still holding in her hand.

'But what about Onassis?'

'He… well… I, I…'

Jan's eyes wandered nervously around the kitchen and found no point to fixate on. The question seemed to unsettle him even more than the one about the UPS driver.

'I don't have any explanation for that,' he began. Then he added quietly, as though he was talking to himself: 'Maybe he was on the wrong side.'

'On Schuwalow's side?'

Was it possible that Onassis had been the mole?

'Of course.' A jolt went through Jan's body. 'Come with me!' He pointed the way with his gun, gesturing for Ira to go back into the studio. Once in there, he looked up at the ceiling, at the ventilation shaft.

'He was working for the mafia. I was *supposed* to discover Onassis. He made all that racket up there on purpose.' Jan rushed around the studio in agitation, clapping his hands as he went. 'Yes, that's it! There was a war going on behind the scenes. A much greater one than could be heard on the radio.'

'How do you mean?'

'To the mafia, the hostage-taking was a gift from the gods. At first they thought I was some lunatic, just like the rest of the world. But the longer I continued in the negotiation with you, Ira, the more doubts arose in Schuwalow's mind. He asked himself: "What if the lawyer double-crossed me? What if I paid €750,000 only to find that my daughter is still alive and ready to testify against me in two days' time?"'

'So far, so good,' Ira nodded. 'You and Marius have a common interest on this point. You both want Leoni. But there's one small difference. *He* wants to kill her.'

'And that's why Schuwalow had to stop the studio from being stormed.' Jan's energy was rejuvenated now. 'At any cost. I couldn't be dealt with until it became clear what had really happened to Leoni. Do you see the utter lunacy of it? The mafia sabotaged the storming. Marius Schuwalow was your ally, Ira. The longer you negotiated with me, the greater the danger for Leoni became.'

'And for Faust.'

'Correct. If the trial had been the only thing that mattered to him, he could have gotten Leoni on the phone for me. But he had pocketed dirty money. Under no circumstances could Schuwalow be allowed to find out that his daughter was still alive. Faust had to silence me, and as quickly as possible. That's why he put Steuer under pressure, sabotaged the investigation and pulled you off the negotiation. He wanted to storm at any cost.'

Ira shook her head.

'But something about the story still doesn't make sense. Why aren't Stuck and Onassis still alive? I mean, Onassis would hardly have shot himself as a cover-up,'

'Counter-question: How long did you inspect the body for?'

Ira hesitated.

'Steuer opened the body bag, and I just glanced at it.'

'That's what I thought. My bet is that they're still alive.'

Then Steuer must be in on it too. Ira cocked her head to the side. *But that doesn't make any sense.*

23

'You're making a huge mistake!'

'And you should be happy that I haven't yet withdrawn your command over your team.'

The two brawling men were separated only by Steuer's desk in the mission control centre on the ninth floor. Götz had closed the door behind him after storming into the SEK boss's office two minutes ago. Ira had now been under the hostage taker's control for over an hour. Since she went in, they had heard nothing more from her.

The radio was playing an automatic line-up of 80s hits. Even though no time had yet been announced for a further Cash Call, the programme was still being broadcast by almost all of Germany's 250 radio stations. The last time so many people had gathered in front of their radio sets was in 1954, the year of the Miracle of Bern and West Germany's World Cup victory.

'Have you completely lost your mind, Götz?' They were alone in the room, but both were tempering their enraged voices so that no one outside could overhear their confidential discussion. 'What were you thinking? That I would just stand back and watch you take off with a suspect? Who do you think you are? You go AWOL from your team, evacuate some burning back-alley bar and break into a state prosecutor's property with a suspended suspect, all instead of taking care of the rescue of hostages here. And now you want to take off *again*?'

'I'm a trained helicopter pilot, as you know. Leoni is landing at Tegel in just fifty minutes. I can get her to the top of the MCB building safely and securely.'

'No.' Steuer propped himself up against the desk with the tips of his fingers. He looked like a sprinter just before the starting shot.

'But why? We can't trust anyone here. Faust must have been working with someone. Marius Schuwalow most definitely planted a mole here among us. If you give me the mission, I can personally guarantee Leoni's life and wellbeing.'

'I don't like having to repeat myself. I should be pulling you off the case, just like I did Ira. But unfortunately you're still needed here.' Steuer sat down and leant back in his leather chair. 'And I mean *here*, not somewhere in the air.'

Something's not right here, thought Götz. *Why is he being so stubborn?*

'That's nonsense, and you know it. As soon as Leoni lands, it's the snipers' job to cover her. They're already positioned on the roofs. My team is superfluous now. If I'm really going to protect Leoni, then I need to be close to her from the word go. At least let me go in the helicopter with them.'

Steuer's eyes narrowed suddenly as he frowned. Then he pulled the clunky device of the intercom system towards him.

'What are you doing?' asked Götz.

'I'm instructing all the officials guarding the exits to inform me if you try to leave the building without permission again.'

Götz waved his hand and sighed heavily. 'That won't be necessary. Message received loud and clear.'

The old man must have lost it.

He turned around to go, but stopped suddenly.

'Do we at least know who's picking Leoni up?'

'Yes.' Steuer wasn't even looking at him any more, and answered him with his gaze trained on the computer as he typed in some order. Presumably he was informing all his men not to let Götz leave the building.

'Leoni is safe. The GSG 9 are sending their best man.'

He lifted his head again, in such a way that implied it took a great deal of effort for him to do so, and shot Götz a contemptuous look.

'Trust me.'

24

'Have you given any thought to what will happen to you when all this is over?'

Ira studied every one of Jan's facial muscles. If this question had unsettled him, he was hiding it well. When he didn't show any reaction, she answered the question for him: 'Prison is waiting for you. Leoni isn't some fairy godmother, flying in with three wishes in her hand luggage. It won't make everything okay again just because you get to hold her hand. Nothing will be okay again. You're going to prison, Jan. You'll be separated from her for years. When all is said and done, you have achieved nothing.'

'I disagree. Just a few hours ago she was considered officially dead. I have proved the opposite and uncovered a conspiracy. Leoni is alive. And she's coming back.'

'She would have been anyway. The day after tomorrow, for the trial.'

'That's nonsense. Faust lied until the very end. He manipulated the witness protection system and made it into his own private cash machine. He wanted to take the quarter of a million and blow it.'

'He had liver cancer,' interjected Ira.

'And that's precisely why he didn't care about the trial.

Think for a minute: How long did the doctors give him? Six months? I bet he wanted to live out his final days in luxury and leave Leoni to rot abroad.'

'That's ridiculous. You can't keep that kind of thing a secret forever. At some point it would have all come out.'

'Why? Leoni would never have voluntarily gotten in touch with me. She would have stayed hidden her whole life for fear of her father. And even if she didn't, why would Faust have cared whether his lies would eventually come out? He was terminally ill. By the time everything blew open, he would have been six feet under for sure.'

'Maybe. But that still doesn't give you any right to do what you've done today.'

She raised her hand to silence Jan's objections before he could even utter a sound.

'Yeah, yeah, I know what's coming. You're just a victim of the circumstances, right? You got messed around. A power-hungry prosecutor manipulated the state apparatus in order to win the trial of his life, or to get money. Either way. And to do that he lied to everyone. His colleagues, Leoni, even the mafia. And you lost everything that was important to you: your career, your savings, and your honour.'

'You're forgetting my fiancée and baby,' interjected Jan. He laid his head to one side. A second later, Ira heard a thudding sound above them. She continued undeterred.

'Of course. And that's all very serious, Jan. But still, nothing gave you the right to launch a terror attack on innocent people. Stuck, Timber, Flummi and my daughter had nothing to do with it. The station's chief editor had his teeth knocked out, then he was tortured along with me and almost burned...'

Ira stopped for a moment, remembering Diesel's promise. The invitation of sharing a drink, if they should survive all of this.

'Besides all that, you've caused a mission costing multi-millions of euros and put the whole of Germany in a state of emergency,' she concluded.

'I know. I'm sorry. But I didn't have any other choice.'

'That's probably the most ridiculous sentence that a man like you could come out with. You always had a choice. You just weren't brave enough to pay the price for your decisions.'

'Oh no? So what alternatives did I have? I tried everything. I went to the police, to the politicians, and to the media. I was laughed at, ignored and sabotaged. I exhausted every legal path open to me, but there was nothing I could do against a conspiracy of this scale. Even this hijack only worked thanks to your help. So, Frau Samin, I'm listening: What other choice did I have?'

'Very simple: You could have forgotten about Leoni.'

'Never.' The answer came quicker than a lightning bolt.

'You see,' triumphed Ira, 'that's how it is for all of us in life. We always have a choice, but we're afraid of the consequences. We could give up the job we hate. But then we would be unemployed. We could leave the man who betrays us. But then we would be alone. And you could have chosen to never see Leoni again. But this price would have been too high for you. That's why innocent people had to pick up the tab today.'

'Are you just preaching, or are you going to apply the same rule to yourself?'

For a moment, Ira thought that her headache was

intensifying. But then she realised that the humming was coming from outside. A helicopter. It was getting louder.

'You want to talk about me? Great, be my guest. This morning I was going to kill myself. I could have carried on staring at the four walls of my apartment and drowning my misery in cheap liquor. So I had the choice. And I made an independent decision. I wanted to die.'

'And isn't Sara's suicide to blame for that? Or Kitty, because she hasn't wanted to talk to you since?'

'No. That would be too easy. There isn't some natural law of the psyche that states: "If the daughter poisons herself, the mother must follow." We always blame others. Or we blame the circumstances. But in reality there is only one person who can finish us off. Only one person has the power to completely destroy us, if we let them. And that is ourselves.'

At first she thought he would mock her. But then she saw genuine admiration spread across his face.

'Bravo.' Jan clapped his hands softly. 'I should really be charging you for this session today.'

'Why?'

'Because you've just found the answer!'

'To what question?'

'The one driving you, Ira. The question of who caused your daughter so much pain that she could no longer see a way out.'

What is he talking about, Ira asked herself, before suddenly remembering the last step. The missing note.

'Repeat Sara's last words one more time,' prompted Jan softly. She answered him in a throaty voice, almost as though she were in a trance: 'Soon you will know who did this to me. And then everything will be okay.'

'Do you see? Sara was right. You experienced it for yourself, Ira. Within yourself. When you were making preparations for your suicide this morning, you were standing on the same precipice as your daughter was that day. No one led her towards it. No one abused her. Your daughter went through hell alone. You are not responsible for that.'

The muffled sounds were now increasing in volume. The helicopter was either in the process of landing or had already done so.

'There's no one we can blame for what happened. Apart from Sara herself.'

Ira shook her head. Her hair was so stiff with dirt, sweat and specks of blood that it barely moved. 'How can you be so sure about that?'

'Because you and Sara are so similar. Not just physically, but in the way you go about things. Willing to go to extremes. Willing to sacrifice yourselves.'

'But you didn't even know her.'

Jan opened his mouth, but his words took a little longer to come out. 'Maybe I knew her better than you think, Ira,' he said eventually.

Before Ira had the chance to ask him what he meant by that, the computer monitor of the telephone unit made two brief peeping sounds.

A text box opened, alerting them to an incoming call.

She recognised the number. Götz. It was time.

25

'Leoni is here,' said the team boss briefly when Jan answered the phone.

The hostage taker nodded, his facial expression impenetrable, and ended the call without saying a word.

When he turned back to Ira, he seemed to have regained some of the self-confidence with which he had unleashed these disastrous events this morning. Clearly adrenaline was mobilising the last of his reserves.

'Turn around and put your hands together as though you're praying, Ira,' he ordered her. His voice, too, was slowly winning back its steadiness. Ira obeyed and listened as he ripped something open behind her back. Then he came close to her and fastened grey, rigid tape around her wrists.

Why is he standing behind me? Ira wondered. *What is he planning?*

'Don't turn around,' said Jan, as though his proximity was enabling him to read her thoughts. The next thing she felt was him grasping her around the hips with his left arm. She shuddered inwardly at his touch. Just a few seconds ago she had thought she had the situation under control. But now she couldn't control even her own thoughts any more.

What if Steuer was right? What if Jan is double-crossing us and really does want to harm Leoni?

'Please excuse the physical proximity, but unfortunately it's the only way,' explained Jan. Then he pressed his stomach even closer to her back.

Some of the hostages said it themselves. That he had threatened to kill Leoni. But then who is the mole who helped him from the outside? And what would Jan's motive be, anyway?

While Ira's thoughts circled around these unanswered questions, Jan switched the grey roll of industrial tape from his right hand to his left.

He's tying us together! Ira realised. He really was. *Like a package.* An intense pain jolted through her as Jan rolled the tape close to her broken rib.

Jan had used almost the entire roll. Around her front at belly-button height, over her hips and then behind his back.

'It's simple, but very effective.'

Ira had to agree with him. She couldn't rip the four-layered tape with her bare hands, especially given that they were tied together. She felt like a little girl stuck in a tiny hula hoop. There was no chance of escaping. It also meant that Ira would be in the line of fire the whole time. The snipers wouldn't fire a single shot. Even a well-aimed bullet into Jan's back would be too dangerous because of its penetrative power. Plus the fact that he was possibly still wired up.

'Listen…' said Ira, as Jan pushed her forwards with his body, gently but firmly. She had to start walking, otherwise she would have fallen over and taken him down with her.

'Neither of us knows how all this is going to play out, right?'

'Right.'

'So can you do me one last favour?'

He manoeuvred her towards the studio exit by shifting his weight from one foot to the next. Their progress was clumsy and slow.

'What?'

'I'd like to speak to my daughter again. I didn't have the opportunity before. Please.'

He hesitated only briefly.

'Okay,' he said softly. A second later, there was a peeping sound right next to Ira's head, and she felt his mobile phone by her ear.

'But I don't want to lose any time. You'll have to have your conversation on the way up.'

'Okay.' Ira began to cough, which caused her even more pain than every step she took, with the tape cutting into her injured torso.

'The telephone has automated speech recognition. Just say the number, and it will dial.'

They laboriously reached the door, which Ira opened. The key was still there, and she was able to grasp hold of the handle despite her hands being bound. A far greater obstacle was posed by the little step that led out of the studio area into the open-plan editing space. As expected, there were already two snipers here, positioned by the rear exit near the reception stairway. Ira had told Jan about them already. Along with the fact that they were only there to secure the route. No one would shoot while they made their way up to the roof. And they still had a long way to go.

She had to repeat Kitty's number three times until the connection was finally made. By which time they had already made their way across half the editing space. She nervously counted the dial tones as it rang. Another fifteen metres to the elevator. Once they were inside it, there would no longer be any reception. Ira knew that whatever it was she wanted to say to her daughter before she climbed up onto the roof as the hostage taker's living shield, it would have to be said in the next three minutes.

26

'Has he let you go? Are you safe?'

Kitty hadn't recognised the number on the display, and was stunned to hear her mother's voice. She stepped over to the window of her hospital room on the top floor of the Charité, and stared over towards Potsdamer Platz. The Sony Center was obstructing her view of the MCB building at the height of the radio station studio, but she was able to orientate herself by the brick building alongside it, which towered above everything.

'Yes, everything's fine, sweetheart.'

Kitty felt a cramp-like strain ebb out of her body. Only now did she register the tension headache pounding against her temples.

'So what's happening? Whose phone are you calling from?'

'That doesn't matter right now. I just wanted to make sure that you're okay.'

'Yes, I'm fine.'

Kitty noticed that she was slipping back into her curt, harsh tone. She had resolved to stop talking to her mother in that way, especially after everything that had happened today. But on the other hand, she wasn't yet ready for a reconciliatory conversation. For what needed to be said, she definitely needed much more time. Time to compose herself.

'I'm glad to hear you're okay, Mother, but…'

She frowned. *Mother*. She had never called Ira that. It sounded so cool and dismissive.

'I know, sweetheart, you're angry with me,' said Ira.

'No, it's not that,' protested Kitty, going back over to her freshly made bed. The sheet was so starched that it made a crackling sound as she sat down on it in her denim skirt.

'It's just that I need to freshen up. There's a psychologist coming in a few minutes who wants to speak to me about the hostage situation, and I haven't even showered yet.'

'Do I know him?'

'No idea.' Kitty stood up again and went over to the bathroom door, which was standing ajar. The luxurious bathroom was just like one in a hotel, except that there was a bidet and a corner bath.

'His name is Pasternak, or something. He called me on the room telephone and will be here in a moment.'

'Pasternak?' shouted Ira, her voice booming out of the receiver so loudly that Kitty had to switch ears.

'Yes, something like that. Pasternak. That was it. Why?'

'You… to… ge… help… tty!' Only brief fragments of Ira's words were comprehensible.

'I can't hear you any more, Mama, you must be losing reception.'

'… leav… oom… immed…!'

'What are you saying?'

Kitty pressed the mobile closer to her ear, but was unable to hear her mother begging her to leave the room at once and get help.

The connection was interrupted, and along with it the message that Dr Pasternak would definitely not be coming to see her. Ira's colleague and friend had been practicing in South America for the last six months, and wasn't expected back until after Christmas.

Kitty re-dialled the number from which her mother had called her, but only got through to an automated message telling her what she already knew. That her mother was currently beyond the reach of the mobile network.

She'll call again as soon as she has reception, was Kitty's last thought before she got undressed, slipping under the warm water of the shower a few moments later.

27

There was no way she was getting out. The din here inside the shaking tin box was already bad enough. And out there? The masked men were scaring her. The ones over at the back, to the left of the huge satellite dish. And the ones a little further to the side, by the grey box with smoke pouring out. No, she didn't want to get out. She whimpered softly. Then she started to cry, and in no time at all was screaming her head off.

'Shhhh.'

Leoni whispered reassuringly into her baby's ear.

'I'm here with you, Maja, shhhhh.'

She looked out of the Perspex window of the helicopter, which had set down gently thirty seconds ago on the roof of the high-rise. Two SEK teams armed with machine guns were getting into position. They were ducking behind a number of light metal blocks, which presumably played some important role in the climatisation system of the MCB building. They looked like oversized extractor hoods. Now and then, a little water vapour escaped from them.

'Please stay seated until I tell you otherwise,' requested Leoni's escort. The uniformed policeman had collected her at Tegel Airport and led her to the awaiting helicopter of the

Federal Border Guard. He looked as though he'd done his buzz cut himself at home. Patches of reddish skin gleamed through his blond hair.

'Okay,' said Leoni, so quietly that her voice was swallowed by the din of the still-spinning rotor blades. When she glanced back out of the window, the scene on the flat roof had changed dramatically. The policemen were no longer to be seen. There was now an indefinable mass blocking the steel door at the other end, the only access to the roof.

Leoni pressed the flat of her hand against the window, as though she wanted to check whether it provided a sufficient barrier between her and the outside world.

The mass billowed out of the door and onto the roof. At the same moment, Leoni felt a strange pressure in her ears. The sounds around her took on a muffled character, similar to the sound of the music when you go to the toilet in a nightclub. Omnipresent, but distant.

The body mass began to take on contours. Two heads, four arms, four legs and two torsos. A woman, and directly behind her a man. It was Jan! Unmistakably.

With every step the unearthly looking pair took towards the helicopter, the pressure in Leoni's ears increased. This was joined by a tingling sensation in her thighs, where Maja was sitting, but she barely noticed it. Her full attention was focused on the man who, just a few months ago, she had wanted to spend the rest of her life with. And who was now attached to a stranger like some grotesque version of a Siamese twin. The woman must be Ira Samin. Steuer had sent a photo of the negotiator to her phone, so that she recognised the woman with the black, smooth hair and high cheekbones when she found herself standing before her. Admittedly, in the photo Ira had been wearing clothes much more flattering to her slim form. Now she had exchanged the jeans and close-fitting T-shirt for an oversized pullover, and if Leoni wasn't mistaken, Jan was pushing her along in front of him barefoot. Leoni blinked. Once. Then again. *Was he really holding a gun to her head?*

All of a sudden, a shadow darted past in the background. A member of the swat team, dressed in camouflage gear, ran away from the entrance with a loaded gun and a megaphone in his hand, concealing himself again moments later behind a satellite dish.

What was going on?

Leoni looked back at Jan. There were just a few metres now between the helicopter and the teetering duo. By now she could make out the contours of his face. His arched eyebrows, the full lips she had kissed so often as he fell asleep. Right now, his lips were moving. He was talking on the phone, holding a mobile to his left ear.

They had told her she didn't need to be afraid. That he wasn't inherently evil, just in despair. That he had done it all out of love, with one goal: of seeing her again.

For Leoni, one glance into his green-blue eyes was enough. The way they lit up when he saw her. She didn't need the proof of the tears running down his cheeks, which he wasn't even attempting to blink away. They were right. He wasn't a threat. He never had been. Not even now, even though he was exposing her and the other woman to unimaginable danger.

Even though she wasn't cold, her entire body was covered with goosebumps. But her soul felt lighter. Only now did she realise the weight of the burden she had been dragging around these last months. She had put it down to the betrayal, and the humiliation. When Faust had told her that Jan had denounced her to her father, those words had hurt her more than anything else. She had thought it was her hate for Jan that had been smothering her. But in reality it was her grief at him having allegedly betrayed her.

'Do you know who that is out there?' whispered Leoni, caressing her baby tenderly. Maja was trembling on her lap.

Leoni began to cry. She cried because Faust had used her. Because of all the time she had lost. And because Maja would be meeting her father for the first time in a moment of mortal danger.

28

His whole life, Götz had lived by one simple motto: If you believed something to be wrong, then it usually was. He couldn't quite say what was making him nervous as he stared at the notebook-sized display in his hand. But *something* was definitely not right. He squinted his eyes and looked straight ahead. The afternoon sun was at an unfavourable angle, but he didn't want to close the visor on his helmet.

Ira and Jan were stumbling towards Leoni like two drunkards attempting a polonaise. She was still sitting in the helicopter, and he could just make out her blurred profile behind the angular plastic window. From this distance, it was impossible to gauge her emotional state. Götz guessed it was a mix of fear and nervous agitation. There was no way that the scene before her eyes could be provoking any great joy at their reunion. Götz had positioned his entire team behind two large, grey metal-clad extractor blocks for the air conditioning system. They had their laser pointers aimed at the wavering duo, but due to the jerky movements were unable to make out a uniform target. One moment the back of Ira's head was in target, and the next Jan's. And his left arm, with which he was pressing the gun to her temple, was shaking far too much as well.

Götz himself was standing behind the small roof exit from which the hostage taker had emerged into the open air with his victim. The Team A duo to his left were equipped with bulletproof shields, with which they would advance on command towards the target while the Team B troop to the right of them gave covering fire.

But something was not going to plan.

Götz touched the display and called up the individual helmet cameras of each of his men. All were focused on Ira and Jan. All of them except...

What's going on?

'Everything okay, Speedy?'

'Yes.'

'So why aren't you at twelve o clock?'

'I am.'

Götz activated camera four again, to be certain. Nothing. Like the others, Speedy should have been aiming at the perpetrator and his hostage. Instead, the screen was showing the grey-black roof surface across which Ira and Jan were slowly trudging their way. Directly towards the helicopter. They were still several metres away from the oscillating rotor blades.

'Check your helmet, Speedy,' radioed Götz, searching the surroundings with his eyes. From where he was positioned, he couldn't see his men. But he could see the snipers on the roof of the Deutsche Bahn building opposite. The glass high-rise towered over the MCB building roof by two floors. The three snipers were awaiting his order, just like the other five SEK men. There should really have been six, but Onassis couldn't be with them any more. And Götz had always depended on him most. *More, in any case, than on...*

'Speedy, I still can't see anything.'

Ira and Jan were now just six metres away from the helicopter.

'Just a minute.'

There was a crackling sound from his headset, but Götz couldn't make out any change on the monitor. The problem would have to wait for now, though, as Jan had just come to a halt before the helicopter at the pre-planned chalk marking. Götz reached for his megaphone and yelled against the wind on the roof.

'This is Oliver Götz, the leader of a SWAT and sniper team. At this moment, eight fully automatic weapons are aimed at you. If you keep to what has been agreed, then everything will end well here today. Now let your final hostage go.'

During his announcement, the image from Speedy's helmet camera still hadn't become any clearer. So Götz decided to leave his shelter behind the exit. He ran in a crouched position towards Team B, the megaphone in one hand and semi-automatic rifle in the other.

He paused behind an oversized satellite device. From here he could at least make out his men's backs.

Dammit! Where is he? Why are there only two?

'Speedy?'

No answer. And nothing was happening in front of him, either. Jan was making no move to untie Ira.

'You don't have a choice, Jan,' bellowed Götz through the megaphone. 'Leoni is sitting in the helicopter. She's only coming out once Ira is set free.'

Jan formed an imaginary telephone receiver with the thumb and little finger of his hand, and held it to his ear.

Götz looked back and forth between Jan and Ira in front of him and Team B to his side. He had to make a decision immediately. Should he establish a mobile connection with the hostage taker, or abort the mission until he knew whether or not danger was imminent?

'I need May's mobile. Left and only!' he instructed mission control. Left and only was the internal code to indicate that the conversation should be put into his left headset and not listened to by anyone else. Especially not by Speedy.

'She has to get out!' Götz heard the hostage taker demand over the phone just thirty seconds later.

'She will, as soon as you let Ira go.'

'No. That's not how this is going to go. First I need to be sure that the woman in the helicopter isn't a double.'

Dammit! Götz got down on the floor and slowly crawled over to Team B's position.

Despite the strong wind whistling in his headset, he could hear that Ira was saying something to Jan. Then, a few minutes later, he heard his voice in his left ear again.

'Ira has suggested that I lay my weapon down. Then Leoni can come out. And then I'll cut Ira free with the knife.'

From the corner of his eye, Götz saw Jan hold something up in the air which glinted in the late-afternoon sun.

Either that or you're going to stab her with it, thought Götz, crawling further forwards.

The distance between him and the SEK men behind the ventilation boxes was now just six metres.

Götz switched channels. 'Speedy. Show yourself!'

'Just a second!' came the answer. In his right ear this time.

'Now!'

'Sorry! The camera got twisted. I had to take off my helmet and I'm undercover.'

That sounded plausible. *But then shouldn't I be able to see him again by now?*

'Okay then, Jan,' Götz switched back to the hostage taker. 'Drop your weapon.'

'Then Leoni will come out?'

'Then she will come out,' he confirmed. He ordered his men not to shoot under any circumstances.

'Leoni needs to get in position and climb out on my signal,' he instructed mission control, who were in contact with the helicopter via the pilot.

A few moments later, in tortuously slow motion, Jan pulled his gun away from Ira's temple. He stretched his gun out away from him at a right angle and threw the pistol on the floor.

'Go!' Götz radioed to mission control. A moment later, Leoni's face disappeared from the bullseye window of the helicopter.

'She's coming, Jan.' Götz was still lying on the floor, now just two metres away from Team B. He saw in shock that there really were only two men before him. And an outstretched leg. *Was Speedy ducked around the corner, behind the ventilation device?* That would certainly back up what Speedy had said in their last radio contact. There were currently multiple blurred images on the screen, as though someone was shaking the camera violently.

By now, Leoni had appeared in the open sliding door of the helicopter and was climbing out. Götz looked at her.

In her fashionable business outfit, with her hair blowing

in the wind, she looked like an actress in a commercial for some expensive perfume or new brand of cigarettes. With the minor difference that it was being directed by a maniac, and that Götz didn't know how this film was going to end. Right now, only Jan knew the script. He was clearly convinced of Leoni's identity. With three deft hand movements, he cut Ira free from him and unfastened her hand ties. But for some unknown reason, Ira stayed right by him, watching as he and Leoni slowly moved closer to one another.

'I'm going to greet my fiancée now,' said May in a voice which was trembling with emotion. 'After that you can have me.'

'No hasty movements. Keep to what was agreed!' warned Götz. Ira was still in the firing line, too close to Jan for an attack. During the mission planning, everyone had agreed to wait out any potential embrace between Leoni and Jan, because the distraction would be too great then. Unless, that is, Jan's intentions were not sincere after all.

Suddenly, the screen of the portable monitor flickered. And now Götz saw the mistake he had made. Speedy's camera was working faultlessly again – and the image it transmitted sent his heart rate sky-high. His brain dissected the scene into individual images: Jan, taking Leoni's hand, which she was hesitantly extending to him. Ira, who was watching the events unfold as she freed herself from the rest of her duct tape shackles. The two faces, slowly moving closer to one another. And the helicopter in the background, its rotor blades finally coming to a standstill.

The policeman! The policeman who had accompanied Leoni here! His head was slumped lifelessly against the

Perspex window of the helicopter, while blood dripped down from an exit wound on his neck.

The cockpit! screamed Götz in his thoughts. The danger wasn't coming from Speedy. It wasn't from his team. It wasn't from behind. It was from *in front*! From the pilot who had left his seat, killed Leoni's escort, and who was no longer to be seen.

From one second to the next, Götz switched to his instinct, no longer thinking through the individual steps. First he activated both speech channels. Then he stood up and began to run.

'The pilot!' he roared. As he ran, he turned around and gave both teams a brief signal. They were to shoot as soon as he raised his hand.

As soon as he turned back around, the pilot appeared in the door of the helicopter. With a gun in his hand.

Nooooo!

Götz raced forwards diagonally across the roof, to get into position from the side. As he ran, he kept his gun trained on the killer.

Oh, my God. From this distance he'll hit them all. Jan, Leoni. And Ira.

'Get down,' he screamed, so loudly that they would hear him even without the radio. The pilot lifted his head and looked over at him.

Götz kept running regardless. Directly into the line of fire.

29

For Jan, only one thing mattered at this moment: embracing Leoni. His nervous fingers trembled as though he was a teenager trying to get close to his crush for the first time in a darkened cinema. Filled with excited anticipation and the simultaneous fear of a humiliating rejection. As Leoni's petite hand grasped his and squeezed it softly, the joy of their reunion was so intense it almost hurt. He closed his eyes and shut off all his senses to what was happening around him.

He had waited so long for this moment.

This was what he had lived for these last weeks, what he had sacrificed his entire life for. Now there was only him and Leoni. He pulled her closer to him, and she put up no resistance. On the contrary. It almost seemed like their first time. When they had made love without saying a single word. Neither before, nor during. Any words would have devalued the moment. No language of this world was capable of describing its significance. And yet Jan still opened his mouth as he felt her breath on his cheek, something he had missed for so long. Their faces were so close that the tiny hairs on their face had already touched imperceptibly. Their lips followed. Leoni moaned as Jan embraced her, pulling her close to him and kissing her. With an intensity as though he wanted to make up for the eight months of separation.

He would never let her go again. He wouldn't let her out of his second for a single second. He wouldn't allow someone to tear her away from him again. Everything was like before. Her immaculate skin, exuding the scent of freshly baked cake. Her silken hair, which caressed his skin as he touched it. The tangible jolt that coursed through their bodies as she raised herself on tiptoes to kiss him more deeply. Even her tears tasted like before. Although perhaps with just one difference.

Jan tried to suppress the thoughts disturbing him, but the sounds around them were forcing their way into his consciousness.

The only thing that had changed was the taste of the kiss. *Hadn't it?*

It was slightly metallic. Slightly ferrous.

Another jolt coursed through Leoni, but this time it was not because she was trying to make herself taller. Jan was still kissing her. But the bitter taste was becoming more intense. And the noises louder. There was nothing else for it: He opened his eyes.

Looked at her. And wanted to scream.

Her gaze was empty. From one second to the next, the warmth had drained from her gaze, and her pupils had gone rigid.

Jan heard a metallic shunt. The deadly sound of a pump-action shotgun being reloaded. He pulled his head backwards and saw the tiny red pearls freeing themselves from the corner of Leoni's mouth, then dripping down to her chin. A further shot rang out. Then she coughed and spat out even more blood.

30

The first bullet didn't hit anyone. Götz wasn't yet in position and fired into the air. The diversion won him half a second before the pilot depressed the trigger of his slide gun.

While Jan and Leoni offered the perfect target in their closely intertwined pose, Ira immediately threw herself on the ground. A wave of pain coursed through her body, and for a moment she thought she had been hit. But the pain was emanating from her broken rib, which she had fallen on roughly.

The second bullet was a slug from the pilot's pump-action gun. It grazed Götz on the left shoulder. But unlike in some cheap action movie, he didn't fly several metres backwards. His upper body was swept to the side as though a football player had barged into him at full pelt. He teetered. But he stayed on his feet. And fired his semi-automatic rifle directly at the pilot's unprotected head.

The pilot was already reloading. His pump-gun spat its first used shells in a wide arc across the roof. At the same time, he jumped down from the helicopter, escaping Götz's bullet in the process. But the killer had given up his cover. And now he found himself opposite another danger: Ira.

She was aiming the weapon which Jan had let drop onto the roof shortly before. She closed her eyes and pulled the trigger.

The coroner would later establish that a total of three shots reached their target: the first glanced Götz. The second, the killer's neck. He died. Just a nanosecond before his shot went sideways into Leoni's back.

There was nothing Ira could do except watch. Jan had loaded blanks.

31

'I'm going to kill you!' roared Götz as he stumbled toward Steuer in fury. His leather jacket was torn open above his left shoulder blade, where the shot had grazed him. Ira couldn't tell how badly injured he was, but it seemed he still had enough strength to almost knock down the mission leader with just one arm.

'You're in shock,' panted Steuer, edging backwards nervously. Götz was beside himself with rage. It must have released a litre of pain-suppressing adrenaline into his bloodstream.

'It was *you*!' he roared, shoving the mission leader once more. '*You* chose the pilot...' Götz stopped mid-sentence, making way for several paramedics who were trying to roll two stretchers past. One held the murdered policeman from the helicopter. A medic was squatting on the other stretcher, performing cardiac massage on Leoni.

'Where are you having them taken?' asked Götz in confusion, staring after the medical team. Jan and the baby had been the first to be removed from the danger zone. On the stretcher, Leoni's legs began to shake uncontrollably.

'Where they need to go,' answered Steuer. 'There's an

ambulance waiting downstairs to take them to Benjamin Franklin.'

'Oh sure, the hospital that's the furthest from here. Why don't you go the whole hog and take them to Moscow?'

Götz spat on the ground in disgust.

'It would be very convenient for you if Leoni snuffs it on the way, right? And yet the Charité's so close we can see it from here!'

Ira looked over at the Sony Center, behind which the brick-red hospital with its iconic signature on the roof rose up into the Berlin sky.

The Charité. Just the name alone intensified a horrific thought which had caught in the walls of Ira's nerve pathway like rusty barbed wire. *Kitty!*

She had to get to her. As quickly as possible.

'There's another reason why he doesn't want to take Leoni there,' she whispered into Götz's ear.

'What?'

'Kitty! She's in the Charité. And Schuwalow has sent a killer there after her.'

'Have you completely lost your mind, Ira?' protested Steuer, who had clearly overheard her last words despite her efforts to talk quietly. He flung both arms up in the air.

'There's no other option. The traffic is at a standstill all around Potsdamer Platz. We'll get the ambulance to Steglitz quicker than it would take to go a hundred metres towards Mitte!'

Götz wasn't even listening any more. His eyes flitted restlessly between Ira, Steuer and the metal door behind which Leoni's stretcher had just disappeared. As their eyes met, Ira saw that Götz was slowly coming out of the first phase of shock. In its place, pain was mercilessly burrowing its path into his consciousness.

Ira cleared her throat and opened her dry lips.

'Please help me,' she wanted to say. 'Help Kitty.' But it was as though the fear was weighing down on her vocal cords. She no longer had the strength to make them vibrate. But it wasn't necessary. Götz had understood.

'I won't allow that,' he said to Steuer.

'What are you talking about?'

'I won't allow Leoni to be given an overdose of atropine in the ambulance.'

'You're in shock, Götz. You're talking nonsense.'

'Fine...' Götz spat again, and Ira hoped she was wrong. That she was just imagining the blood-red shade of his saliva. '... then I want to go too. With Leoni in the ambulance. And I'll decide where it goes.'

Götz signalled to Ira to follow him into the stairwell.

'No, you can't...' Steuer boorishly positioned himself in his path.

'Why?'

'We'll lose too much time. And there's not enough room in the ambulance.'

'Of course,' Götz smiled sarcastically. Another wave of pain coursed through his body and tears shot into his eyes. 'That's exactly what I thought you'd say, you piece of shit!'

He looked into the darkening sky, as though the slowly approaching rainclouds might be bringing a solution along with them.

'Then there's only Plan B.'

'Plan B?' repeated Steuer, dumbfounded.

Götz stepped closer to the mission leader.

'Take out your walkie-talkie. I'll explain it to you.'

His words hit the mission leader's face in a spray of fury. But all Steuer felt was the barrel of the gun which Götz had placed right against his temple.

32

'This is absolutely insane…' shouted Ira. She was standing directly behind Götz, who was in the process of lifting the lever next to his seat in order to change the stall angle of the rotor blades. The helicopter was already at full rotational speed, and they were communicating with one another via the headphones which they had hastily put on.

'I know how to fly this thing, remember,' he yelled.

'But you've been shot. You're losing too much blood.'

'No more than Leoni!'

You're probably right about that.

Ira threw her headset onto the co-pilot seat and climbed into the back. Leoni's stretcher had been provisionally fastened to the back row of seats with luggage restraints, her body covered with blankets. The paramedics who Steuer – under duress – had ordered back onto the roof seemed to have stabilised her condition somewhat.

Ira felt the helicopter gaining speed and whipping up a strong wind outside. The machine veered right up Leipziger Strasse in a steep curve. The famous high-rise hospital was just two minutes away by air, so they had left the sliding doors open for the flight. She held tightly onto the backrest of the passenger seat and leant over towards the invalid.

Leoni's entire body seemed peaceful. Still.

Too still. Ira carefully stroked the blood-soaked hair from Leoni's face – then flinched back as if she had been electrocuted.

'Götz!' she called pleadingly. He hadn't heard her. The drone of the helicopter swallowed her brittle voice.

More than a minute passed in which she just stared helplessly at the floor. Only when some slight turbulence seized the helicopter did she free herself from her paralysed state. She stood up, reached for the headset that hung from the ceiling above her, and put it on to communicate with Götz over the radio. Then she looked down, and what she saw convinced her that she must be losing her mind.

Her gaze had fallen through the angular window right next to where Leoni had been sitting earlier. It had been hit by Götz's bullet when he tried to distract the pilot, and now the shattered plastic window provided an appropriately gruesome frame for what Ira could see beyond it in the distance.

'What's going on?' Ira found her voice again. What she really wanted to do was rip the headset off. She didn't want to hear the horrific answer.

'We're landing,' replied Götz, stating the obvious. The Brandenburg Gate, the glass dome of the Reichstag, the Holocaust memorial – none of these landmarks were in sight any more. They had turned around and weren't anywhere near the Charité. Instead, they were coming down to land on an abandoned Kreuzberg railway site.

33

'I don't understand,' said Ira as the spine-chilling realisation opened up in her belly like a pair of shears, slashing at her guts from the inside.

'Oh come on!' shouted Götz, turning around to her. His face was expressionless. 'You understand everything.'

She balled her fist and bit into her knuckles so as not to scream out loud. Of course she knew. Now. Much too late. *He* was the mole. Götz was Schuwalow's henchman.

How could I have been so blind?

He had only had one goal the whole time: to find out whether Leoni was still alive. For that, he had needed to do everything he could to delay the storming for as long as possible. That was the only reason he had brought Ira to the crime scene and convinced Steuer to let her take over the negotiations. He had sent Diesel away from the station when he was too hot on the trail of the identities of the fake hostages. Protested loudly against the mission in the conference. And only went into the studio himself once he could no longer prevent an attack.

'Manfred Stuck was still alive when you found him!' It wasn't a question, but a despairing statement of fact. Götz nodded.

Ira continued: 'He was only sedated. It was you who shot him, not Jan. Just like you did Onassis. You didn't want anyone else to dare go into the studio after that mission. You did everything you could to make the hostage situation continue until Leoni was found.'

Götz swerved the helicopter back and forth and laughed cynically. They were just a few metres above the floor now. 'And you knew that Schuwalow had kidnapped me, didn't you? That was staged too. From the abduction to the rescue.' Ira's thoughts were whirring faster than the rotor blades above her head.

Of course. After Steuer had banned her from the crime scene, Götz had needed to ensure that Ira was brought back into the negotiations. That was also why Marius had been so forthcoming with information. She was *meant* to find out the necessary information about the connections between Faust, the witness protection programme and Leoni, and then persevere. Götz had used and manipulated her. Without knowing it, she had become a puppet of the mafia. And she had almost climbed back into bed with him in the process. Even Faust must have sensed that Götz was playing dirty. 'I could only tell you that if we were alone,' had been one of his last comments. Now it had taken on a completely new meaning.

'I guess I don't need to ask you why you're doing all this, right?'

My apartment still isn't paid off, I had bad luck playing poker last year. I'm up to my neck in debt. Götz had admitted it to her himself. *I can't afford to mess up my job.* Now she realised who he was in debt to and which job he had meant.

Ira pulled off her headset and leant unsteadily forwards

into the cockpit. 'How much money are we talking about here? Would Marius not have let you off the hook if someone else had finished off Leoni? Is that why you had to shoot the pilot?'

'Why are you asking if you already know?'

The floor of the helicopter was made of transparent plexiglass, and Ira saw the weed-choked ground moving closer towards them. Götz had found a spot to land, directly between a dilapidated brick hut and a pile of abandoned railway tracks.

The bleak surroundings reminded Ira of this morning. Of the capsules in her freezer. Her daughter, who was probably already dead. She remembered Sara and the conversation with Jan. Leoni. All of a sudden she felt completely calm. Her pulse slowed, and an almost cathartic peace spread out within her as the skids of the helicopter touched down on the stony ground.

Ira turned around again and looked into the passenger area, past Leoni, to the shattered window. The gun which only minutes ago had been keeping Steuer in check was now aimed at her back.

34

Everything was a lie. Every single line on the grey-toned A4 sheet she was signing right now. The trauma of the day had not broken her. She did not want to follow her sister. She was not going to take her life of her own free will. Nonetheless, Kitty put the date and signature next to her name. Purely because the elegant man in the snow-white doctor's coat wanted her to, the man who had claimed to be Dr Pasternak and then shoved a gun in her face.

'Excellent,' he said, holding the silenced pistol slightly at an angle so that he could take a look at his expensive watch. 'Now take the tablets.'

In a daze, Kitty registered that her murderer was married. There was a platinum ring on the hand with which he was pointing at the pills in front of her on the swivelling bedside table. There were four. They lay there harmlessly next to the bottle of still water, as though they were just sweets.

'You won't get away with this,' protested Kitty.

'I can take care of myself,' replied the man, with a hint of a smile. He handed her a half-full plastic beaker.

Kitty thought feverishly about how she could buy herself

some more time. *I struggled, almost got away from him in the bathroom, wrote the letter as slowly as possible. What else?*

'But I didn't even see anything in the studio,' she tried one last time. 'There's nothing I could reveal.'

'Hurry up!' he said, ignoring her pleas. 'Your grace period is over.'

Kitty sat on the edge of the bed, her legs shaking. Outside the window, she saw a dark cloud drawing over. *So now I'm going to die with a double lie*, she thought with a heavy hearted. While she was taking the first two pills, she couldn't help but think of Sara's last letter. The one her mother had never read. The two notes on the last step. Kitty had arrived at her older sister's apartment just a few minutes before her mother, and had taken it with her before creeping out again. So that Ira would never find out what Sara's true motivations had been. As irony of fate would have it, Kitty had changed her mind today, of all days. She wanted to confess. She wanted to see her mother and talk openly with her about everything. But now she wouldn't be able to. Now she would take what she knew with her to the grave, and this extorted suicide note would put another lie into the world.

'Quicker.' The killer hurried her on, and for a brief moment Kitty wondered why she didn't just give him a reason to shoot. Then at least her mother would know her true fate. Eventually, her survival instinct prevailed, and with it came the hope that perhaps she could get out of this alive after all.

The third tablet disappeared into her mouth. She leant her head backwards as she swallowed. Her gaze fell on the cut emergency cord. That had been explained in her letter too. She had done it so there was no way back.

The respectable face of her murderer blurred as the fourth pill clung to her swollen tongue. It took an incredible amount of willpower to stop herself from grimacing at the bitter taste.

Kitty lost balance and toppled sideways onto the bed. Her eyelids no longer possessed the strength to close, not even granting her that small mercy. So she wasn't spared the sight of the man tying a rubber strap around her arm. It didn't take him long before he had found the right spot for the injection.

35

'This is the final stop.' Götz stayed seated in his pilot's chair. 'You have to get out here.'

Given that he hadn't turned the rotors off, Ira presumed he was planning to fly on without her. Certainly he would have already broken the transponder so that the helicopter couldn't be located.

'No, I'm not going to.'

She was too disgusted to look him in the face as she spoke. Ira reached her bare hand towards the shattered window and pulled out a large shard.

'What are you trying to do? The game is over.'

'No it's not.' Ira overcame her revulsion and looked Götz directly in the eyes. For the desperate act she was planning, she needed direct eye contact.

'I'm the negotiator, or have you forgotten that? So I'm not giving up. Instead, I'm offering you a trade.'

Götz laughed in disbelief. 'You're unbelievable, Ira. What is there left for us to negotiate? You're completely powerless. You don't have any trump cards left.'

'Yes I do. This one!'

Ira raised the sharp-edged plexiglass shard, but Götz only laughed harder.

'What are you planning to do with that? Half my shoulder is torn open. Do you really think I'm afraid of a shard of glass?'

'It depends where I use it,' said Ira, before slitting her own wrist.

36

'Fuck! What are you doing?' screamed Götz in horror.

Blood was streaming from Ira's left arm. She had sliced lengthways along the vein. Not across, like ninety per cent of suicidal individuals did, their attempts promptly failing because they were only severing the flexor tendons.

'Have you already forgotten?' she answered him, while watching the trickle of red make its way across the floor. 'I have nothing left to lose.'

Götz shifted anxiously on his seat. The weather was getting worse, and a wind had started up. He couldn't leave his seat if he wanted to keep the helicopter on the ground.

'You're completely insane, Ira.' She could hear his shouting even without the headset now. 'If you don't get out at once, I'll have to take you with me. Either you'll die here on the flight or Schuwalow will finish you off as soon as we land.'

Ira shook her head weakly. 'We both know you won't let that happen, Götz. You don't want me to die.'

'I shot the UPS courier and one of my colleagues today. Do you really think I'll stop at that?'

'Yes, if it's me we're talking about. I'm your weak point, Götz. Your sore spot.'

Ira was starting to feel dizzy. Her bare feet were now in a small puddle of blood, which was slowly spreading out towards Leoni's stretcher.

She had to sit down, otherwise she would faint.

'You couldn't bear to see me bleed to death before your eyes.'

'Then you're wrong about me.'

'Not on this. So listen up. Both of us are close to the end. We don't have any time to lose. So let's make a deal: I'll give you Leoni if...'

'I *already* have Leoni,' he interrupted her angrily. 'I just need to fly her to Schuwalow.'

'No, no, no.' Ira leant her head back and closed her eyes. She suppressed the thought of what was happening in her body right now. Of a slow, torturous death.

'You're not listening to me. I'll give you Leoni in exchange for my daughter!'

Götz looked genuinely shocked. He didn't seem to be understanding a word.

'Make sure that nothing happens to Kitty, and I'll climb out at once and let you fly on with Leoni.'

'You're completely insane,' he answered, turning back to the front. 'I'm going now.'

'No!'

'Yes!' He flipped two switches above his head. 'I can't help you, Ira. Even if I wanted to. As soon as I've delivered Leoni, Schuwalow will strike my name from his hit list. I'm just small fry to him. I don't have the power to whistle back some killer who's already with your daughter.'

The entire helicopter was shaking like a malfunctioning washing machine.

'Then your last memory of me will be of how you tried helplessly to stop the flood,' said Ira, playing her very last card.

Götz looked back towards her again.

'What flood?'

She stood up, so that he could see her better, and lifted the loose sweatshirt up over her pale hips. All the colour had drained from her face.

'This artery thing takes too long. You could tie a ligature on my arm as soon as I lose consciousness.' She was staring him directly in the eyes again. 'But just one little cut here, and there's no way I can be saved without a professional tourniquet.' She placed the shard against her groin artery. 'Save my daughter, or I die right here before your eyes!'

37

The twittering of birds from the nightstand was getting louder with every second that passed. It began shortly after the last drop had left the disposable syringe and entered Kitty's vein. Now the ringtone was taking on an unpleasant piercing volume. The bogus doctor pulled the syringe from Kitty's arm, reached for her mobile and was about to turn it off when he recognised the obtrusive caller by his number.

'What is it?' he asked curtly. Then he listened silently to the explanations at the other end.

'And this is really an instruction from Schuwalow?' He dropped the used syringe into the pocket of his white coat. He kept on for now the cream-coloured surgical gloves which he had been wearing the whole time he was in the room.

'No,' he answered after a short while. Then he repeated himself, this time more insistently. 'No! That's no longer possible. It's too late. I've already given her the injection.'

His knowledgeable gaze checked to see whether he had forgotten anything. But everything was perfect. No witnesses, no proof. The suicide note lay on the bed, folded once, on the blanket that covered half of Kitty's lifeless body.

'But that doesn't make any sense,' he protested. 'Okay, fine,' he relented eventually, once the caller's torrent of words had died off once more. 'If that's what Marius wants.'

The killer stepped closer to the bed and opened Kitty's left eyelid.

He did what he had been instructed. He didn't care anyway. He would get his money either way. And it was a lot of money. So much that he was happy to do something this pointless for it.

After he had completed the actions he had been told to carry out, he took the battery from the mobile phone and put both parts in his trouser pocket. Then he walked briskly from the room without looking back once. His work for the day was done.

38

Can you trust a person who is planning to send someone to their death?

Ira watched as the helicopter moved away from her at an increasing speed with its motionless cargo, and tried to tell herself that she hadn't had a choice.

'She can't speak with you,' Götz had explained to her. 'But she's still alive.' As proof, he had laid his mobile phone in her cramped hands. The keypad was already covered with blood, just like the scraps of the sweatshirt which he had bound around her wrist into a makeshift tourniquet.

Was he telling the truth? she wondered. Probably not, was the first answer that entered her mind. It was over. Finished. Except that, now everything was lost, the resigned indifference was no longer spreading out within her. Not like this morning. But it didn't matter. She would never see Kitty again either way. At least she had seen one final picture of her, even if it had been taken by her murderer. She wiped a drop of rain from the green-toned shimmering display and looked at her daughter's open eyes on the digital photo. A second drop fell, and then another. This horrific day's beautiful weather had come to an end. Just like her.

Out here in no man's land. And just like Kitty. Because this picture didn't prove a thing.

'Do you see how her pupils are reacting to the flash?' Götz had said, pleading with her to get out of the helicopter. The killer had taken two photos and sent them to Götz's mobile one after the other. 'Two images, two differently sized pupils, do you see?' It was laughable really. At that moment, just like now, she had already been close to falling unconscious. She was no longer able to make out a thing.

But at least she had achieved certainty on one thing before leaving this world: Götz hadn't wanted to kill her. Hadn't been *able* to. She was his Achilles' heel. It was just a shame that she hadn't been his downfall. After all, Götz had been just as stunned as her when she had kept her word and climbed out of the helicopter. But she had wanted to at least make this final decision in her miserable life autonomously. Neither Götz nor Schuwalow should be permitted to determine the time of her death. For that, she wanted to be alone, like she had planned this morning.

The drizzling rain was getting stronger now, and the helicopter had shrunk to the size of a tennis ball in the darkening sky. Ira stared after it and wondered how much longer it would take for Götz to deliver the lifeless body to Leoni's father. When she had seen Leoni's face in the helicopter before, the shock of the realisation had paralysed her. At first she had wanted to tell him. But then everything had taken an unexpected turn, and now it would remain her final comfort that, at the very end of the game, she had denied Götz the simple truth. 'Right then,' she said to herself. She took a deep breath and captured for the last time the scent of wet grass, blending in with the dusty air of the big city.

I'll miss that, thought Ira. *It's not much, but I'll miss these smells.*

Her right arm was shaking, and it took her a few seconds to realise that the vibration setting of her mobile phone was the cause. The blurred photo of her daughter had disappeared and made way for an incoming call.

> *Unknown number*

She shrugged.

I would have preferred a Cola Light to finish things off, was her last thought. *A Cola Light Lemon...*

Then she positioned the shard, ignored the final call. The call that would have explained everything.

39

Two Weeks Later

Seen from above, the five-pointed star-shaped wings of the Moabit correctional facility had always reminded him of an oversized windmill. Down on the ground, however, the sight of the red guard towers behind the barbed-wire fences surrounding the prison's main building was a lot less romantic. Even after so many years, Steuer always felt a little uneasy when he had to go to the high-security sector.

He looked at his watch; he was early. They had arranged to meet just before eleven after the security control. Just like at the airport, everyone who wanted to access the high-security zone had to remove all metal and dangerous objects at the entrance and then pass through a metal detector. He had already gone though, and was now sitting on a wobbly chair with no armrests, his large frame subjecting it to a severe endurance test.

'I'm sorry,' were the first words she greeted him with a few moments later. Her face had a little more colour now, but she still looked as though she was in the slow process of recovering from a very long illness, which in a certain sense was true.

'Why are you apologising? You're early.'

'No, not because of that.' Ira's lips hinted at a smile.

He was familiar with this reaction. Steuer knew that he was the kind of person who most people respected but would never like, and it was clear to him that Ira's shy smile was the highest measure of sympathy she would ever extend.

'I'm apologising for my error of judgement,' she admitted. 'I was convinced that Faust had greased your palm.'

He laughed drily. In truth, he had unwittingly let the state prosecutor manipulate him completely for free. Shortly after the first Cash Call, when Jan had made his demand on the radio for the first time, Faust had informed him by telephone that Leoni was an important witness whose existence could under no circumstances be revealed. That it would be better to storm immediately, no matter what the price was.

'I was wrong about you...' said Ira, 'and I'm really sorry about that.'

'Well, then we have at least one thing in common.' He turned away from her, and they walked together along the long corridor, at the end of which the real reason for their meeting today was awaiting them.

'I made a big mistake too. I thought you were in cahoots with Götz. That's the only reason why I ever let you get into the helicopter with him.' Steuer was making a genuine effort not to sound too brusque. But at the same time, he didn't really care whether she took his apology seriously. He had saved her life by having Götz's mobile located shortly after the helicopter's transponder signal had disappeared from the monitor. If Ira had answered the phone, she could have saved herself the ugly scar on her groin. It may not have been the very last second when the paramedics had reached her, but it was most probably the last minute.

'Now don't get me wrong. I still consider you unfit to lead a negotiation. You're ill. An unstable alcoholic. I wasn't wrong about *that*...' He articulated his next words with particular emphasis: 'That's the reason, and the *only* reason, why I didn't want you involved from the start.'

'When did you know?' she asked him. 'When did you realise that it was him?'

'I first got suspicious when Götz was so insistent about picking Leoni up at the airport. But I wasn't sure by any means. All I knew was this: If the mole was going to reveal himself, then it would be on the roof of the MCB building.'

He stopped and looked at her.

'How are you dealing with the whole thing, anyway? Psychologically, I mean?'

Ira's high-pitched laugh echoed off the bare concrete walls. 'So you're saying that from a physical point of view it's obvious I'm a wreck, right?'

Steuer twisted his mouth in irritation. 'I'm asking because of your daughter.'

Ira ran her hands nervously through her freshly washed hair before answering. 'Well, at least Götz was telling the truth about her.'

They walked on, unconsciously falling into step with one another.

'How is she doing?' asked Steuer, just out of politeness. He already knew the most important details from the file. The killer had given Kitty a sedative first, and then injected her with a narcotic. The poison, the second injection, hadn't been used once Götz had called the killer on Kitty's mobile.

'By the way, if you had confided in me then that contract killer wouldn't have gotten away.'

They had reached the door to the lobby leading to the interrogation room. A tall policewoman, who had been flicking through a magazine, stood up, greeted the SEK boss sheepishly and opened the door for them.

Steuer let Ira go into the room first. Once inside, they positioned themselves silently alongside one another in front of the one-way mirrored glass window, through which they could see into the room beyond.

Jan May looked good. And not just considering the circumstances. If Steuer hadn't have known better, he would easily have mistaken him for a lawyer, waiting in a dark suit for his mandate. Steuer looked over at Ira, but she couldn't take her eyes off the beautiful woman at Jan's side, running her hand through her fiancé's hair. With her other hand, she was holding tightly onto her baby so that she didn't slip off the square metal table.

40

The ageing air conditioning system in the newly built wing of the correctional facility wasn't even capable of cooling down the small interrogation room. At best, it was just whisking around the bacteria. Almost as proof of this, Jan May put a starched linen handkerchief in front of his mouth and coughed. Then he blew his nose.

'Are you happy now?' asked Ira, breaking the silence which had filled the room since she had stepped in. She propped herself up with both elbows on the table, where they were sitting opposite one another.

'I'm happy that Leoni and my child are still alive, yes,' he answered with a smile. 'I'm very grateful to you for that.'

'Oh no,' Ira waved her hand dismissively and jerked her thumb towards the mirrored glass behind her. 'Your praise is being directed at the wrong recipient. Steuer is responsible for that.'

The SEK boss's coup had been the focus of the media over the last days. Steuer had initially planned to replace Leoni with a double. But no one could predict how dangerous Jan really was and whether he would end up unleashing chaos if he discovered the deception manoeuvre on the roof. And so Leoni had been equipped with a top-notch, police-issue bulletproof vest, which ended up saving her life. What had looked like cardiac massage on the roof had actually been the futile attempts of the paramedic to find the source of her internal bleeding. In reality, Leoni had only bitten off a piece of her tongue in shock. When Steuer was coerced by Götz into bringing the barely injured woman back to the helicopter, his men had known what to do. Leoni was switched in the stairwell with one of the two plastic dummies which had been prepared in order to cause confusion. Downstairs in the MCB building, three ambulances had been waiting to drive in different directions with the dummies, so that the killers didn't know which vehicle the real Leoni was in.

And not only had Götz ended up arriving to meet Schuwalow with a display-window mannequin, the dummy had also contained a GPS transmitter which had ultimately led the police to the mafia.

'What were you talking to your fiancée about just then?' asked Ira. Shortly after she had walked in, Leoni had gently shaken Ira's hand, then left the room silently with her baby in her arms.

'I was telling her the wonderful news I got from my lawyer. That with a bit of luck I'll be able to celebrate my daughter's third birthday in freedom,' answered Jan. 'And with a lot of luck I'll get an electronic ankle bracelet and be able to serve my sentence under house arrest.'

'In witness protection?'

'With my family, yes.'

'Great. And now you want to hear some more good news from me in order to round off the whole thing perfectly, right?'

He looked at her, motionless.

'I mean, surely you want to hear some words of praise for the fact that you uncovered a major conspiracy?'

In the end, Jan had indeed turned out to be right. Faust had single-handedly smuggled Leoni into a secret witness protection programme over the heads of the official channels. The seized files from his trial preparations had conclusively proven that he had never intended to bring Leoni back to Germany.

'Leoni is alive, Marius has been arrested, and his daughter's testimony will presumably crush the biggest organised crime ring in Berlin. And now you're being let off relatively lightly, Jan. The ballistic investigations have clearly identified Götz as the murderer of Stuck and Onassis.'

Jan nodded in agreement.

'I never wanted to hurt anyone. Apart from Timber, perhaps.'

Ira laughed briefly. She knew the history between him and the star DJ. Jan had sent Markus Timber an email with the request that he address Leoni's unsolved fate on his radio show.

'Tell the nutcase no,' had been the one-line answer which Timber had intended to send Diesel back then. Accidentally, he had also copied it to Jan. Ira would probably have punched in his nose for that too. Nonetheless, she found herself unable to feel much sympathy for the psychiatrist. She had spent the whole of the previous night lying awake, trying to, but the anger she felt towards him simply refused to dissipate. 'I guess you think I owe my life to you, Jan. Don't you?' she continued, posing her next rhetorical question. 'You're really proud of yourself, right? Because I didn't kill myself, and instead I'm sitting here before you.'

He stopped smiling.

'No. I'm happy about that. And grateful. But not proud.

'Bullshit. You feel great. You think you saved my daughter and kept me from committing suicide. But I'm afraid I'll have to disappoint you on that one. You're smart, I'll give you that. The fact that your mock hostages' statements all match perfectly is proof of your excellent planning, and it will be difficult to raise any charges against that amateur dramatics troop. On that, I have to congratulate you. But our analytical discussions during the hostage taking... well, you can forget it. I still haven't overcome my trauma. My world does not now consist of rose-tinted Sundays spent with my daughter, who by the way is still ignoring me.'

Jan just stared at her silently. The friendly warmth of his green-blue eyes had not cooled, despite her harsh words. This only incited Ira's rage more. She stood up so abruptly that her wooden chair tipped backwards and came to a crashing halt on the stone floor.

'You're an excellent actor, but a goddamn awful psychologist.' She circled around the table. 'Everything you said ten days ago was basically hot air; you didn't bring me to any realisations. And what was that nonsense when you said in the studio that you knew Sara better than I realised?'

Without a word, Jan opened the middle button of his blazer and pulled a folded letter, consisting of several pages, from the inside pocket of his lapel. He laid the pages carefully on the table as though it were some valuable painting.

'What's that?'

'The answer to your question.'

Ira stopped her pacing and picked up the pages with the tips of her fingers. As she did so, she made a face as though she were opening a can of maggots. She unfolded the well-thumbed paper and glanced quickly at the first, handwritten lines. Then she looked more closely. A curved, elegant, girlish handwriting.

'The last step,' he said.

This can't be possible.

Ira felt as though the temperature in the room had suddenly plunged by at least ten degrees. She wanted to throw the letter in Jan's face, but all the strength had gone from her limbs.

'I treated her,' she heard him say as she leant over to pick up her chair.

'Sara?' Ira had to sit down before the attack of dizziness beat her to it.

'Sara first came to my practice around eighteen months ago. We had a number of sessions, in which she told me about her feelings, compulsions and complexes. And about how much she loved you.'

'You were Sara's therapist!' repeated Ira as though in a trance, leafing through the pages of the letter as she spoke.

'Why do you think I refused to speak to Herzberg and from the very beginning only wanted to negotiate with the famous Ira Samin?' asked Jan. 'After Sara's death I followed her fate in the media, Ira. You went through the same thing I did with Leoni. You also lost a loved one without knowing why. I knew you would understand me. That you would talk with me. They said you were the best. That you only let them storm when there's no other option left. That's exactly what I needed. An ally on the other side. Someone who could give me time. I needed you.'

'But...' She raised her head, ignoring the thick strand of

hair that had fallen across her forehead. '… then did you know Katharina too?'

Jan nodded again.

'Sara spoke a lot about her little sister Kitty. And to be honest, that was what gave me the idea of doing the hostage taking in the studio. At first I was planning to hijack a local TV station, but then I realised it wasn't at all suitable for what I needed. Too many people. No sealed rooms. Then I remembered Sara talking about Kitty. She had mentioned in one of our sessions how much her sister wanted an internship with 101 Point 5, and that gave me an idea. A radio station barely has any security. No one would expect it to be subjected to a terror attack.'

'So you knew the whole time that my daughter was under the sink?' Ira was back on her feet again.

Jan shook his head fervently.

'No, that wasn't intentional, just an unfortunate coincidence. But unfortunately she went into the kitchen while I was in the bathroom shortly before entering the studio. Although when I hijacked the station and Kitty wasn't there with the hostages, admittedly I assumed she was in the room next door.'

'You lied to everyone!'

'No. Not everyone. What you asked me that day was whether I wanted to hurt Kitty. The answer was no. I just used her as an eyewitness so that everything looked genuine. I even intentionally left Stuck's walkie-talkie there for Kitty so that she could make contact with you, Ira. She confirmed a murder that had never taken place. It was only when she was close to discovering that Stuck was still alive that I had to step in.'

'You used me,' declared Ira, standing up. In just two paces, she was over by the door, and she smacked the palm of her hand against it. 'You're no better than Götz.'

The olive-drab steel door was unlocked from the outside.

'Think what you want about me. But read the letter,' said Jan, while Ira was already halfway out of the door. She didn't look back.

'Read it.'

That was the last thing she heard him say. The policewoman had already closed the steel door behind her.

Epilogue

She did, of course. She read the letter that very same evening.

There were two pages. Grey, recycled paper. Written on both sides. After just the first two words, Ira needed to stop for half an hour while she threw up in the bathroom. After that, she managed to compose herself, at least slightly. She sat back down at the old dining table and ordered her eyes to obey her. Another quarter of an hour later, she was finally able to read on.

My testament

Dearest Mama, dearest Kitty, dear Dr May,

If you are holding these pages in your hands, it means I am no longer with you. I'm writing a collective letter because presumably you will all have something in common after my death: feelings of guilt. Each of you will think you have failed, whether it be as a mother, as a sister, or as a therapist.

Mama, I'm sure you are blaming yourself the most, on account of being both my mother and a psychologist. That's why you will be the first to find this letter on the top step. I'm sure you ignored all my other notes. You continued on despite my warnings and found me in the bathtub. Well, I guess stubbornness runs in the family.

The rest of you will hopefully have received my testament a day later in the post. But don't hold out any false hopes. I don't have any valuable assets to leave to you. Take whatever you want from my material possessions. I'm sure you'll quickly come to an agreement on how to divide up my clothes, the TV and my rusty old Golf.

The only really valuable thing which I can leave you are my feelings and thoughts.

Ira stared at the last lines of the first page. A thick teardrop fell on the paper, blurring the royal-blue ink in which the sad words were composed.

'Is everything okay?' asked an anxious voice from the other end of the room. She wiped the tears from her face and looked over to him. Diesel had chosen the most inconvenient of moments to make good on his promise. He had limped into her apartment half an hour ago with the words, 'Well, I did say I'd shout you a drink if we got out alive.' He had been holding a bunch of flowers from the petrol station in one hand, and in the other a bottle of 'Mr Bubble' non-alcoholic champagne.

Now he was leaning in the doorframe between the kitchen and living room, propping himself up additionally with a crutch. He had a flesh-toned bandage around his neck, on which 'I Hate Radio' was written. The burns had scarred his entire torso; in a fit of panic that they would suffocate in the 'memory room', he had thrown himself onto the burning bundle of clothes.

'What are you reading?' asked Diesel, as softly as his voice would allow. He seemed a little helpless. Ira contemplated briefly whether she should ask him to go again. Before, he hadn't let her shake him off, presumably because she hadn't tried that hard. In all honesty she was happy to have someone nearby, in case what she was afraid of proved to be true. In case she was really about to read what she suspected to be written on the next page.

'I'm almost ready,' she reassured him, turning the page.

Mama: You've spent half your life searching for a 'why'. Why am I so different with regards to men? Why was I always so sad when you visited me? Why couldn't you help me to get my problems under control and find some joy in life again?

All of you want to question everything. Is there any more pointless way of wasting away your life than searching for answers that will bring you nothing?

Mama: You're the expert when it comes to the psyche. You will agree with me when I say that some problems are so complex it's not possible to find the root cause, even after years of trying. In the end, all that remains is the cause. We occupy ourselves with the symptoms and know nothing about their roots.

My polyamory (did I spell it right, Dr May?), my alternative sexual behaviour, wasn't the problem, as I was able to learn in your therapy sessions. It was the symptom of a deep underlying inferiority complex. You did a good job in recognising it, but unfortunately it didn't help me. So now I know that I enjoy having power over a multitude of men through the very fact that I am surrendering myself to them. You wanted to dig deeper, Dr May. To find out why my complex has become stronger recently. But that seemed even more useless to me than the way I already felt. Don't get me wrong, but I think we could delve deeper and deeper into my mind and still not stumble upon the 'big bang' of my psyche. At some point there will be questions to which no one knows the answer. And we can already rule out the usual clichés: No, I wasn't abused. No, there was no family friend who climbed into my bed when I was young.

I love you, Mama. You never neglected me. You didn't overlook anything. You don't carry any blame.

Kitty, I'm not mad with you either. Sure, I was horrified when I found out that you had slept with Marc, of all people. Initially I wanted to convince myself that he was perhaps the first man who I could have built a normal relationship with. But the truth is: My feelings for him had already died away. I was trying to convince myself that, with him, I might have been able to leave the whole scene. But in reality I was just making myself smaller with this thought, feeding my inferiority complex. So don't blame yourself, Kitty. What you did, by letting yourself get involved with my housemate, was neither the cause nor a reason for what I'm about to do.

At this moment, Ira's concentration was disturbed by the unnerving ring of the telephone. At the moment when she had finally found out why this letter hadn't been on the top step. Kitty must have been in Sara's apartment before her and taken it with her. Ira swallowed, feeling the emptiness inside her fill with an almost burning sadness. *That explains her sudden rage towards me*, she thought. Kitty hadn't wanted to accept Sara's absolution. She still felt guilty for having betrayed her sister. She hid the letter out of shame. And ended up projecting her guilt onto another person. Onto her own mother.

How right you were, Sara, thought Ira. *We do all have something in common.*

'I'm coming!'

The telephone was still ringing insistently. Diesel breathed heavily as he limped into the kitchen to take the call. Ira's old-fashioned, cream-coloured phone was a relic from the German Bundespost and even had a rotary dial. It hung directly next to the sink.

'I listen to 101 Point 5, now jump out the window if it's not something important,' she heard Diesel bark into the receiver. Then it went quiet. When he remained silent, Ira shrugged.

Wrong number.

She pulled her legs up towards her, sitting cross-legged on the chair before her old dining table. Her hands wet with sweat, she reached for the next page.

> *You're a good psychologist, Dr May, even though I'm sure my actions won't exactly do your reputation any favours. You were 100 per cent correct with your suspicion. I followed your urgent advice. Thank you again for suggesting the referral. The MRI scan confirmed that my growing depression had an organic cause, and also taught me a new word: gliobastoma. Kitty, if you type it into a search engine on the internet, you'll increase the*

hit ratio if you also include the keywords 'brain tumour', 'inoperable' and 'fatal'. The rest of you know that most sufferers die within a year at most. Chemotherapy would only prolong the suffering, and an operation is impossible in my case, because the tumour cells seem to be penetrating all the cerebral tissue.

So what now? Now you all know the reason why my already frail personality has been changing more and more recently. I'm even giving you a comprehensible justification for my suicide. I don't want to wait until I fall unconscious at the kitchen table and can no longer move the right side of my body. I don't want to live to see myself helplessly reliant on complete strangers while I die a slow death in a shared ward of some public hospital.

When I read the patient information leaflet from the medication the neurologist prescribed for me, I found myself unable to make any other decision. I'm sure, Mama, that this will be hardest for you. It's always terrible when children go before their parents, that's what people say. But how awful would it be for you if you had to watch me dying in the months to come? And how horrible for me? Call me selfish, but I don't have the strength to cope with my pain and yours at once. I'm sorry. I have to act now while I still have my symptoms under control.

The warm hand on her shoulder radiated through her T-shirt to her skin like a branding iron.

Nonetheless, Ira was glad to feel Diesel's touch. She had no idea how he had made it across the living room without her hearing the creak of the floorboards.

'Who was that just then?' she sobbed, not understanding a single word that was coming from her mouth. A shudder coursed through her entire body.

Instead of answering, he began to massage her neck gently.

'Maybe it's better if I leave you alone,' he whispered after a while.

'Yes,' she said, but then she reached back and pressed his hand down onto her shoulder. He stopped. And they read the last lines together.

So, enough of the long preamble. Here it is: My last will and testament:

Dr Jan May, to you I leave the confirmation that you did everything in your power to help me. Because of you, I leave this world with the comforting realisation that I wasn't a completely useless subject after all.

To you, Kitty, I leave the consolation that I was never really angry with you. One should never go to sleep angry, and I won't do it either. I love you, my darling sister.

And to you, Mama, I leave the certainty that you carry no blame for my death whatsoever. You loved me, and did everything you could for me. Even though I rejected your offer of therapy, it did eventually prompt me to go to Dr May's practice. Maybe I'll call you one more time before I embark upon my last journey, so that you can hear how much I already miss you.

My bequest to you has one last condition: Please don't spend any more time brooding over the 'why'.

Why did I become the way I am? Why do I have a

glioblastoma? Why does it have to be my brain that these bastards are destroying? Why couldn't I see another way out?

You could keep asking questions forever, Mama. But don't. Eventually it will destroy you. If you don't stop, it will tear you apart from the inside. Just like it did me.

I'll love you forever. See you soon.

Sara Samin,
in full possession of her mental capabilities

For thirty minutes, neither of them said a word. Maybe even longer. Neither of them looked at the clock. Neither wanted to break the silence with some empty cliché. In Ira's opinion, the most frequently used yet utterly pointless phrase in existence was: *If there's anything I can do for you...* It's what people usually say after someone dies, at funerals or after the diagnosis of some fatal illness. In other words, whenever there is no longer anything that anyone can do for you. To Ira, those empty words ranked just before: 'I'll always be there for you.' She was happy that Diesel didn't make use of this compassionate lie. Instead, eventually, he just changed the subject:

'I saw all the bottles, Ira.'

She blew her nose noisily, then twisted the corners of her pretty mouth into an intentionally artificial smile.

'You know I'm an alcoholic.'

'But do you really have to have a whole fridge full of them?'

'Get me one.'

'Sure, it's not like I have anything else to do.'

'You invited yourself, remember. I didn't ask you to come by. But now that you're here, you can at least make yourself useful.'

Diesel waved his hand dismissively, already limping his way towards the kitchen.

'Pour that kiddie champagne down the drain and bring me a real drink,' she called after him. 'Then we'll drink together.'

'You're on your own destroying yourself with that witches' brew,' came his snide response from the kitchen. The fridge door opened, and she heard the clink of bottles.

'This poison will send you to your grave,' he said, coming back to the dining table with a litre bottle.

'What's *this*, by the way?' He put a freezer bag down next to the bottle on the table. Ira opened the screw cap and took her first sip.

'It was in the freezer compartment. Do you still need them?' he persisted. She didn't look at the little bag with the capsules.

'Maybe.'

Ira didn't want to argue with him, so was happy to be distracted by a knock at the door. It was hesitant at first. Then again, a little louder.

'Who was that on the telephone before, by the way?' she asked as she stood up.

'The same person who I assume is outside your door right now. I told her to come by.'

'Who are you talking about?'

'I'm sure you can guess.'

She turned around to him and pointed her index finger at his torso.

'Watch it, Diesel. If we're going to see each other again, then you need to keep to certain rules with me, okay?'

'I can see why Götz was so fond of you,' he replied with a grin.

'Rule number one: never invite someone to my apartment without my knowledge.'

'And number two?'

'Don't lie to me. I thought you couldn't stand Cola Light Lemon.'

'I can't.'

'Then stop drinking my bottle behind my back. There are plenty of other things in the fridge for you.'

She couldn't help but smile as she turned her back to him again and opened the door.

Then she pulled her daughter into her arms.

Acknowledgements

First of all I would like to express my gratitude once again to the person without whom this book would be meaningless: You. As a reader, you have put your trust in me by buying *Amok* without knowing whether you would like the contents. So once again I am eager to hear your opinions, criticisms, thought-provoking comments or any other feedback. You can find me online at www.sebastianfitzek.de, or email me directly at fitzek@sebastianfitzek.de.

Unfortunately there isn't enough space to list all the colleagues at Knaur, my wonderful publishing house. Representing the entire team there, I would like to thank Dr. Andreas Müller – for having discovered me on behalf of the publishing house, for championing me there and for shaping my writing by coaxing the very best out of my sentences with her excellent editing.

My thanks also go to Beate Kuckertz, the publishing director (my favourite person to fare-dodge with, even in Rome!) and the marketing manager Klaus Kluge, whose incredible efforts ensured that my megalomaniacal dream of writing a bestseller didn't become a pathological one. Of the four domino bricks that had to fall to ensure my books found readers, the two of you pushed over one of the biggest.

I thank Andreas Thiele for his enormous dedication, and

also in representation of everyone else in the sales department I unfortunately wasn't able to meet in person.

A special thanks in this context is reserved for Andrea Kammann, on whose website www.buechereule.de my first book was discussed back when no one yet knew about it. And also to all the booksellers who read and recommend my books.

Sabrina Rabow – thank you for your unbelievable PR work (someone who manages to get my photo in the paper really is good at their job!), and to David Groenewold and Iris Kiefer – thank you for wanting to film my books. Thank you to Thomas Koschwitz and Manuela Raschke for their friendship and support, and to Stephan Wuschansky for his genial efforts as a sparring partner.

Amok is entirely a work of my imagination. But in order that the facts in the fiction measured up, a number of experts regaled me with their knowledge. And they will now have to take the rap for my 'artistic license':

Above all, thanks to my brother Clemens and his wife Sabine – as experienced doctors, the errors you weeded out weren't just medicine-related.

Frank Hellberg – thank you for the fact that we were able to set your entire fleet of aircraft on fire in the Treptow docks, and for showing me the best way of crashing a helicopter, even though I didn't really need it in the end. (But what a perfect topic for someone like me, with my fear of flying).

I also owe my thanks to a police insider who prefers to remain anonymous after revealing a vast amount of insider information (over long dinners at the local Persian) regarding the process of an SEK mission of this scale.

Christian Meyer – thank you for your valuable tips. I'll be

sure to contract you and your security company should the bad guys ever come after me.

Arno Müller – thank you for everything you taught me about the world of radio. Luckily you have nothing in common with Timber in real life, just like none of the characters in the novels are based upon real-life individuals. Okay, with one exception: Fruti. But you are even sicker in the head than Diesel.

I'm happy to have one of the best literary agents, Roman Hocke, on my side. Through him, I was also able to meet Peter Prange, who was on hand to help once more – as an author and, even more importantly, as a friend.

Gerlinde – even though I'm not too fond of rollercoasters, I promise you ten free rides for always being my first reader.

Last but not least, I thank my father Freimut for his valuable support during such a difficult time. We both know that Christa knew the ending, even though she was only able to read the first one hundred pages. Just like she always knew everything long before I even dared to dream of it.

I would also like to apologise to everyone who thinks these acknowledgements are too long, even though I have left out hosts of helpers who I will now have to invite for dinner. I could, of course, have been much more succinct: Thank you to everyone who has helped me. I am deeply indebted to you all. But don't get any ideas about me helping when you next move house...

Sebastian Fitzek
Berlin, December 2006

About the author

SEBASTIAN FITZEK is one of Europe's most
successful authors of psychological thrillers. His books
have sold twelve million copies, been translated into
more than thirty-six languages and are the basis for
international cinema and theatre adaptations. Sebastian
Fitzek was the first German author to be awarded the
European Prize for Criminal Literature. He lives with his
family in Berlin.

sebastianfitzek.de

About the translator

JAMIE LEE SEARLE is a translator from Germany
and one of the co-founders of the Emerging
Translators Network.

NEWPORT COMMUNITY
LEARNING & LIBRARIES